THE DOGS OF WAR
&
OTHER STORIES

A Prestwich Boyhood

Best wishes
Bob Wild.

Many thanks for making Cuba so memorable.

THE DOGS OF WAR
&
OTHER STORIES

A PRESTWICH BOYHOOD

Bob Wild

Published November 2008

Laughing at the Blackshirts *was first published in the Penniless Press issue 13 2001*

Making Sense of War *was first published in The Penniless Press issue 14 2001*

© Bob Wild

The author asserts his moral right to be identified as the author of the work. All rights reserved. No part of this publication may be reproduced, stored in a retrieval system or transmitted in any form or by any means, electronic, mechanical, photocopying, recording or otherwise, without the prior permission of the publishers

ISBN 978-1-4092-8890-9

CONTENTS

Acknowledgement & Disclaimer	6
Laughing At The Blackshirts	7
First Day At School	12
Making Sense Of War	18
Nothing To Write Home About	21
The Andersen Shelter	31
School Dinners	35
Mr. Askew's War Work	38
The Day The Tramp Came	41
Those Poor Boys	51
The Dogs Of War	52
Four Pies And A Bottle Of Sauce	62
Friday Night Callers	80
Digging For Gold	94
Feeding The Guinea Pigs	109
Getting My Own Back	120
Looking Forward To Friday	127
Moving On	133
The Year Of The Butterflies	144
Selective Education	158
Heys' Road School	166
A Tale In The Sting	173
A Musical Interlude	180
Radcliffe Tec.	183
A Miscarriage Of Justice	219

Acknowledgement

I would like to express my warm thanks to Ken Clay for his many helpful comments, suggestions and encouragement and for his tireless efforts with the production of this book

Disclaimer

These stories are for the most part based on autobiographical incidents; they are the product of memory and imagination, and in some cases gossip and scandal overheard in childhood, but they are fiction not fact. I have in some of the stories used the names of people who at one time or another lived in Polefield estate as a trigger for memory. If by chance readers know or knew people of that name they should not make moral inferences about them on the basis of these stories.

LAUGHING AT THE BLACKSHIRTS

My dad was always talking politics. It was politics that lost him his job in the Police force. You don't take out a writ against the Chief Constable and get away with it, now do you?

My dad, a big six-footer, was twenty-two years of age in 1926, the year of the General Strike, and I suppose he had been in the Bobbies about a year. He'd been doing well, so my mam said: commended for going up a ladder to rescue a woman from a blazing house; broken up Friday-night fights; arrested drunks and even caught a couple of burglars but then came the General Strike. In the General Strike you had to take sides.

In Rochdale where my dad was stationed the mill-hands and the engineering workers were solid for the strike and the unemployed were with them too. The employers and the Government were worried because they feared revolution was a possibility. "Look what happened in Russia!", they said to each other. "It's got to be stopped". In Rochdale, birthplace of the Co-op movement, the marches and demonstrations had too much public support for the Chief Constable's liking and were too orderly for him to ban them. None-the-less he ordered the police to "go in and make some arrests". My dad was detailed to the dole queue and instructed to "heave some of those bloody work-shy scroungers through a shop window and arrest them". Being a Socialist---though what a Socialist was doing in the police force you might well ask---my dad refused. He naively believed the police were there to uphold the law impartially, not break it, and besides his sympathies were with the strikers.

As if refusal to obey an unlawful order were not reason enough for them to get rid of him he also urged the other Bobbies to disobey the order and was put on a disciplinary charge for incitement. My dad was not one to be intimidated though, and a bit of a barrack-room lawyer. He took out a writ demanding the Chief Constable withdraw his unlawful command. After much interviewing and arguing, many threats and the intervention of

THE DOGS OF WAR

lawyers, the order was rescinded and the charge dropped: my dad's writ withdrawn. It was a Pyrrhic victory: from that moment on they were out to get him. To avoid being "fitted up for a long spell inside" my dad had no choice but to resign from the force. He was also black-listed, though he couldn't prove it, and was not able to get a regular full-time job, anywhere, after he left the police.

For the remainder of the 1920's and most of the 1930's my dad was unemployed. He was active with the *Communist Party*---though I'm not sure that he actually carried a card---and *The Unemployed Workers' Movement*. He got quite a name for himself in and around Prestwich for organising demonstrations and heckling at political meetings. Him and his mate Jimmy Crudeson even went on one of the hunger marches to London and he would have gone to fight in Spain had he not had two young children and a pregnant wife to support. As 'the thirties' progressed and the recession deepened towards war the poverty became chronic. My dad's only suit, the one he had got married in, went in and out of pawn each week for a couple of bob. My mother stole my grandma's rings and pawned them to buy food, then told my grandma, who had a small widow's war pension but was tight-fisted, from where she could get them back. Times were bad, bad, bad, very bad indeed. Three-and-a-half million unemployed and the only policy on offer, wage cuts. The Government said the economic recession was caused by workers asking for too high wages: it was a "load of rubbish". I heard my dad telling every-one: "Always believe the opposite of what they tell you: you'll be a lot nearer the truth".

The local Tories called the unemployed "work-shy" but my dad was not "work-shy", he was a good worker, given the chance. He had cleared rubble, humped soil, laid turf and made a show-piece garden to our house out of nothing and he kept it immaculate. It was laid out formally like a French Chateau garden and full of flowers: mainly Stocks, Antirrhinums, Asters, Alyssum and Blue Lobelia in the formal parts and a riot of Roses elsewhere and with dozens and dozens of Dahlias in the centre-beds in the Autumn. But if you are poor even being a good worker can be a disadvantage.

LAUGHING AT THE BLACKSHIRTS

A group of Councillors and Assessors came to our house to apply the Means-Test. They refused us relief even though we had hardly a stick of furniture and no proper bedding, except a few old sheets and a pile of old coats, and no food except for a meat and potato pie my mam had made and hidden under an old sewing-machine-lid upstairs in a bedroom. At least they couldn't order us to sell anything: there was nothing to sell, but they said my dad must be earning money somewhere to be able to have such a wonderful garden. The plants were, in fact, mainly "throw-outs" from McAlpine's Nursery where my dad occasionally did odd jobs, though I suspect some of the bedding and rockery plants "fell off a lorry".

After the Board refused us money and my dad's dole was cut things got desperate. My mam was six weeks behind with the rent and hadn't told my dad. There were debts at the butchers and the grocers and the coalman was refusing to deliver. We had to tell the doctor's man my mam was out when he called on Friday. The clothing club lady and Michaelson from the shoe shop had to be content with sixpence instead of their weekly half-crowns. It was a good job our Ernie and me were on free school-dinners.

One afternoon my mam came and collected us from school. She was carrying our Arthur in her arms. She took us round to the house of Councillor Mrs. Keitch who had been to our house for the Means-Test and begged her to give us some money for food. I remember the glass porch and the red geraniums and the warmth coming out through the door from the carpeted hallway. Mrs Keitch handed my mam a shilling. My mam looked at it in the palm of her hand saying: "I've three children to feed. Is that all you can give me!" On the way home my mam bought a loaf with the shilling from a horse-drawn Co-op van and a pot of jam from Bellhouse's grocery shop. She bought an *Evening Chronicle* and five Woodbines for my dad from Whittaker's newsagent's. My dad was furious with her for going begging to Mrs. Keitch but he smoked the fags. I remember him saying he would rather steal than beg for food from "that bloody lot".

My dad worked hard on the garden. I used to help him, emptying the grass-box from the mower or picking up privet clippings. When he'd done he would say to me: "By God I'm whacked out".

THE DOGS OF WAR

But that didn't stop him talking politics. He used to stand, leaning with his back against the front garden gate, looking admiringly at his work, fishing for the always fulsome compliments of passing neighbours. Once engaged he would discuss the political situation with them, or rather, use the opportunity to air his knowledge of current affairs and his left-wing views. My mam would say to us: "He's on his soap box again", but he was always interesting, and he knew a lot about Russia.

Once the war started people from Prestwich Labour Party came to our house for advice and to discuss the war and the Russians with my dad. I used to think he knew Stalin personally the way he used to talk about him. It was all Joe will do this and Joe will do that and don't let them kid you. When finally Germany attacked Russia he said to Cecil Davis, the Labour Party Secretary: "Don't worry. Old Joe'll soon sort Gerry out". He said it with such conviction you'd have thought he'd been on the 'phone to Moscow the night before.

One thing puzzled me though. My dad knew and got on with practically everyone on Polefield estate, if you discounted my mam; I couldn't understand why he wanted to put somebody called the Bourgeoisie up against the wall, or hang them from the ladder cross-bars on the lamp-posts on Bury Old Road. And Moseley's Blackshirts were destined for a similar fate. I remember once being very frightened when I was about four years of age. A small, black van with a loud speaker on the top and a white circle on the side, with a zig-zag flash like lightning inside it, stopped outside our house and some men got out. My dad was doing the garden. He walked down the path to the gate with his spade in his hand and started shouting something about Spain at them. Two of the men came running over, shouting and swearing, and one of them punched my dad in the chest. My dad shouted: "Don't you bloody try that on with me!" and swung his spade at him but the man jumped out of the way and the two of them ran back to the van. My mother ran down the path shouting "Harry! Harry! Come in! You'll get yourself killed!" I was very frightened and started crying and I put my arms around my dad's leg and held it tight. "Bloody fascist cowards!" my dad shouted. The men shouted something back and got into the van.

LAUGHING AT THE BLACKSHIRTS

But the van wouldn't start. The engine whirred and wheezed a bit but didn't fire. Another whirrrrer, whirrrrerh, a couple of loud bangs, then another, and then, nothing. They had to get out again and push it. My dad just stood at the gate laughing, ha ha ha ha! And laughing, ha ha ha ha ha! And though I was still shedding tears, I started laughing too. They were still pushing when they reached the main road.

FIRST DAY AT SCHOOL

Apart from a sense of excitement, and apprehension, and the feel of the cold, wet, chrome of the pram handle I was clutching, as I trotted along beside my mam, I don't recollect much about the start of the journey to school on my first day. We had to cross Bury Old Road to get to *the British School* I remember. My mam wagged her finger at me, saying: "Now don't forget! Always use the Hoare-Belisha beacon!" She had wanted me to go to St. Margaret's because it was on our side of the road, and safer, but my dad said we were not to go there. "I don't want bloody priests pumping all that religious nonsense into their heads. They must go to *The British*".

The pictures become clearer as we get nearer the school. There are children, boys like me, and girls, all holding their mother's hands or, like me, gripping the handle of a pram. Most of the children are dressed in small, belted, blue, gabardine raincoats, some with sleeves so long they have only their fingers sticking out; others with the sleeves turned under showing half their hand. The boys all have grey, black or navy-blue caps on, with assorted cloth badges. Those without garters keep hopping on one foot as they reach down with one hand to try to pull up their long, grey socks. Some of the girls have coloured coats on: not bright like today but dull-red, -blue or -green and one or two have small, black, brown or silver-grey umbrellas. Most of the clothes are hand-me-downs from older brothers and sisters but one or two children have conspicuously new shoes on, or obviously new coats, which are worn with self-conscious pride or embarrassment. It is raining quite hard and a puddle has formed on the pram cover. As the pram tilts up the curb at Orange Hill Road the water sloshes over the edge and spills down onto my feet. I try to jump out of the way. I slip and fall. I still keep hold of the pram handle but twist round and have to let go. "Now look what you've made me do!" I shout. "I'm all wet". I begin to cry. My mam says: "Well it was your own fault, you should look

FIRST DAY AT SCHOOL

where your walking. We haven't time to go back: you'll just have to put up with it."

The nearer we get to the school gate the tighter the children hold on to their mothers. As we pass Heaton Park Cinema some are blubbering and saying they don't want to go to school. One or two are having tantrums. I've stopped crying. The excitement has returned. I can't wait to go in to school!

The playground was quite small, concreted, and sloped steeply down to the sooty, brick, school building. There was a steep ramp with railings leading up from "the yard" to the cloakroom door. A door on the right inside the cloakroom led into a big, open room. There were large, high, mullioned windows, pointed like you see in churches, all along the opposite side-wall. The mums with their children and prams and dripping umbrellas stood in a crowd in the large, empty space at the back of the room chattering energetically. It was hot and the windows misted up with condensation. Most of the children were still clinging tight to their mums and some were still crying and protesting. I remember staring at them, puzzled as to why they didn't want to come to school. My feet were still wet. I said to my mam: "I'll be alright, why don't you go home".

In the hearth, which was set diagonally in the right-hand front-corner of the room, there was a blazing red fire with tall, yellow flames leaping up the black back of the chimney. A large, mesh-fireguard stood on one side of the hearth and a huge, conical coal scuttle, a bit like a milk churn, stood on the other side. A raffia mat covered the floor in front of the hearth. The room itself was quite drab. The lower-half of the walls were painted dark, glossy green, the upper-half cream. The paint was so thick it was flaking off in parts. There were large, framed-pictures with words in big, square print below them. One showed a boy sitting on a box by a pond fishing. The pond was grey and gloomy and there were dark, lowering clouds in the low sky. Another showed a girl dressed in a shiny, black mackintosh, wearing wellingtons and carrying a raised umbrella. Rain was sloping down and there were puddles in the road. Other pictures had snowy or sunny days. There were cupboards round the side- and back-walls of the room. One with a double, glass-front had a trumpet, a drum and a

THE DOGS OF WAR

tambourine and a tin whistle in it. The other-half housed a kite and a bird's nest with real eggs.

The desks were honey-coloured, quite solid, and made a lot of noise when moved as there was no carpet covering the grey, dusty-looking floorboards. The desks were close together and arranged on three sides of a square the open end of which faced the wall at the front of the classroom where Miss Hulme's table stood against the wall. There was a second, inner-square, with gaps occasionally so that the teacher could get through to the outer-square. Tiny chairs were arranged in pairs behind each desk. Four desks, with eight chairs, were arranged in pairs within the square between the inner-row of desks and the teacher's table. There were about fifty places altogether.

Miss Hulme, a tall, straight-backed, thin woman in her late fifties, with a severe look and a lined, grey, powdered-face, clipped a half-lens pince-nez, attached to a black string, onto her nose and read out the names. Each mother guided her child to the place pointed to by Miss Hulme. Some children went quite willingly; some diffidently; some snivelled and went reluctantly. Some hid behind their mother's twisting, turning back; some had to be dragged; some bawled and screamed and stamped their feet. Some threw such a tantrum they had to be taken outside, or even, perhaps, back home. When my name was called I walked quickly forward on my own. I didn't want my mam to come with me. I was put on the back row next to the fire. Clive Coburn sat next to me and Jane Hutchinson and Elsie Bain sat in front.

Everything I remember about my first year in the infant's seems packed into the remainder of that exciting first day. A group of us are standing in a horseshoe in front of Miss Hulme's desk. Margaret Whitney is in the middle looking up into an imaginary sky. The sun is shining despite the billowing white clouds and the wind. Both her hands are raised as if holding the string of a kite. We can all see quite clearly the kite she is struggling to hold on to as it swoops and snakes and then resumes its static flight. It's exactly like the kite in the glass-fronted cupboard at the back of the room. The same painted cat's face on it and the same long tail with twists of paper tied to it. We are all singing the song Miss Hulme has just taught us:

FIRST DAY AT SCHOOL

"I looked in a toyshop window
To see what I could see
And there I saw a paper kite
Which mother bought for me"

After each verse is completed the child in the middle steps back and another takes his or her place, boys and girls alternating. The paper kite is replaced by a trumpet, pram, a drum, a doll.
After play-time we are standing in the group again. Margaret Whitney---why is it always Margaret Whitney---is singing: *"This old man, he played two, he played nick nack on my shoe"*. She has just got to: *"Nick nack paddy whack give a dog a bone"*. When for some reason I look down at the floor opposite, where Jane Hutchinson is standing. A pool of water is spreading outwards from around her feet. I put my hand up and say: "Please Miss, Jane Hutchinson has made a puddle on the floor.
Just before ten-thirty Mr. Askew, the caretaker, comes in carrying a metal crate containing twenty-four tiny milk bottles. He comes a second time with a similar crate but with four or five extra bottles on top, wedged at angles between the necks of the bottles in the crate. Clive Coburn and me are the milk monitors. We have to put a bottle on the desk-top in front of each child.
Miss Hulme takes the small packs of biscuits, toast and dripping, or jam and bread, that my classmates have brought for their lunch, off the piled-high tray on her desk and reads out the names she has written on them. Some of us don't bring lunch for some reason or have forgotten it. Miss Hulme says: "Those without lunch: put your hands up". We walk out one by one and she gives us each a silver-paper wrapped chocolate teacake from a large, round tin.
The silver-paper rolls into a nice, tight, light, metallic ball which I will later flick at someone, with the aid of my pencil, when Miss Hulme is not looking. The teacake has a blob of bright, red jam on the biscuit below the dome of chocolate-covered marshmallow. It's delicious. I hear the click as my teeth crack through the chocolate and sink into the soft breast-like texture of the marsh-mallow. The jam is sweet and the biscuit makes a soft, crunchy noise. Sometimes I eat all the marsh-mallow and

chocolate first and then lick the biscuit clean before I eat it. It goes mushy in your mouth if you suck milk into it through your straw. Miss Hulme says: "Don't be disgusting!" when I make a noise trying to get the dregs up my straw from the bottom of the bottle. Sometimes she gives me and Clive Coburn an extra bottle of milk if there are some over.

In the afternoon we learn to count. Miss Hulme has a large, wooden bead-frame on a tall stand. The beads are red and blue-green and make a sharp, clicking sound as they whiz along the bars and knock against each other. We have to go to the front of the class in turn to flick the beads across and count them. In our desks, under the lids, we each have a box of Cowrie shells. They are small, hard, and very shiny. They bounce a long way if you drop them on the floor and always end up under the radiator where you can't easily get them.

I have a slate for writing on with chalk. Ann Porter gives out the damp cloths to clean our slates with. After writing we take out our sheets of coloured gummed-paper and small pairs of round-ended scissors. We cut out shapes like the big ones Miss Hulme cuts out and holds up. There are squares, pyramids and circles for us to copy. We stick them on our blue sugar-paper in patterns to make people.

I liked clay modelling best. I made a long worm of clay and coiled it round and round to make a bird's nest. I rolled four eggs like those in the nest in the cupboard. The clay is kept in a large box. The new sticks look like closely packed tram lines and have bright colours but the balls of clay are all mixed up, dirty, brown in colour. The clay is hard when it's given out but once you have rolled it on your board and squeezed it in your fingers it goes soft. Sometimes when it's a hot day the clay is so soft you can't get your horse or the elephant you have made to stand up.

After playtime in the afternoon Miss Hulme teaches us reading and writing with flash-cards. I can still see the pictures and the words on the cards. The figure of Old Lob, the farmer, with his battered hat and fringe beard and "I am Old Lob" printed underneath. One by one, chanting in chorus, we read out the flash-cards: "I am Mrs. Cuddy the cow. We are the Chicks. I am Percy the bad chick. I am Rover, the dog. This is Mr. Dobbin, the

FIRST DAY AT SCHOOL

horse". I soon knew the flash cards and before long I had read all the books in the cupboard and most of those Miss Hulme borrowed for me from Miss Mather who taught the next class up. When I'd finished my book I got into trouble for talking. Once, when Miss Hulme was out of the room, Clive Coburn gave me some chewing gum and I stuck it in Jane Hutchinson's hair. She started crying and when Miss Hulme came back she had to have some of her her hair cut off. Miss Hulme told the headmaster. He put his face very close to mine and said: "You and me are going to fall out young man. How would you like it if I did something nasty to you!" and he pushed me in the chest with his fist. I was made to stand in a corner for the remainder of the day and when our Ernie came to collect me after school Miss Hulme told him to tell my mam what a naughty boy I had been.

MAKING SENSE OF WAR

My earliest memory of the war was listening to Mr. Chamberlain announcing that as Germany had refused to give an undertaking to withdraw from Poland the country was at war. I remember because I wanted to tell everyone I had found my rabbit. The day before it had dug a hole under the fence, made havoc in next doors garden and disappeared; but I was told: "Be quiet Mr. Chamberlain is speaking". The slow, sad, deliberate voice echoed as it droned interminably out of the beehive wireless set that sat on top of the sideboard in our cramped little living room. It was 11.0 a.m. on the 3rd of September, 1939 and my father, an unemployed labourer and a member of the Communist Party, had been talking of war for weeks: "If Gerry ever comes here", he said, "I'll be one of the first to go up against the wall". I was five years old and my father's words made me very frightened. I thought the Germans would kill my rabbit. Apart from that though, war didn't make sense to me.

The 3rd of September was a Sunday so the news was old by the time we got to school on the Monday. Mr. Hume, the Head Master of *The British* school we went to, gathered us into the big classroom where Standard 3 and 4 were taught and told us, very solemnly, what Mr. Chamberlain had said. We sat still, subdued. But as soon as we got into the playground everybody exploded into noise and fighting. Kids flying Spitfires and Messerschmit were zooming around the schoolyard with their arms stretched sideways stuttering out machine gun sounds or jumping on each others backs to strangle one another. "You're a Gerry". "No I'm not". "Yes you are". "This is what we do to Germans". "Oh you swinehunt, you've shot me in the groin!"

For weeks afterwards my dad spent days and nights with his ear tuned to the wireless set. Knobs were twiddled this way and that so often you thought they would come off in his hand. Valves were taken out, dusted, changed, swopped around and changed again. The set was cursed (bloody hopeless set!), praised (it's a good little set this!), and at times all but shaken to pieces. And all to the accompaniment of the most astonishing warbling, gurgles and shrill pitched whistles. Blasts of national anthems blurted out from countries I had never heard of interspersed with rapid bursts of foreign words gabbling away like machine gun fire. When my dad was out our Ernie would imitate the voices. He would start up with *The Marseillaise*. "D der der der der der der derrr d der . . ." . ". . .Ici Londre, Ici Londre. . . ." Later he would impersonate Lord Haw Haw: "Germany calling. Germany calling. How are you down there in Polefield, Prestwich?". Our Ernie had learnt from somewhere that William Joyce had lived for a time in Failsworth on the east side of Manchester and that his mother still lived there: he never tired of telling us that Lord Haw Haw knew exactly where we lived!

Frank Phillips and Alvar Liddel continued to read the news but nothing much happened. Nothing much, that is, if you call the sinking of *The Royal Oak* and the death of 810 sailors nothing much. It was the period known as the phoney war but it became real soon enough. By June we had lost Dunkirk and one or two neighbours. Mr Hitchen, from round The Circle, had come home deaf, shell shocked and wounded "in the groin!" "It's a terrible cross for his wife to bear!" my mam said, but it didn't make sense to me.

Despite the war, life went on much as normal for us kids. Later there were Flannagan and Allen songs to sing. As we marched home we were: *"going to hang Adolph Hitler on the Seigfried Line, have you any dirty washing mother dear . . .".* And there were propaganda chants to chorus: *". . . if you want to get your gas mask free, go and join the ARP"* but *"Run rabbit, run rabbit, run run run. . ."* was our favourite. We sang it repeatedly for weeks. Soon, there were gas mask drills and siren alarms. We trooped out of school and across Bury Old Road, squeezed through a small gateway newly made in Heaton park wall and into the air raid shelters which smelt of pine wood, urine, damp earth and rabbit droppings.

Airmen were based in Heaton park and though the shelters were out of bounds to them, and fenced in with palings, some palings had been removed and the airmen could easily get into the shelters. I heard an officer, with two rings on his cuff, whisper to Miss Fish that he would bring her some parachute silk after school. One of the girls, up against the wall, said: "Please Miss there are a lot of little barrage balloons on the floor here Miss". Miss Mather said the rabbits must have dropped them but that didn't make sense to me.

To pass the time the teachers organised games of *I Spy*. It was dark in the shelters, though, and if you were not sitting next to one of the storm lamps you couldn't see anything to guess at so we sang *Cherry ripe* and *Sweet lass of Richmond hill* instead. Mrs Mitchell used a battery torch to read us a story about Mr. Todd Fox and Mr. Brock the badger. The one I liked best, though, was about Mr. McGreggor with his gun and Peter Rabbit hiding in the cabbage patch. Miss Jackson had a painted clay model of Peter Rabbit dressed in a jacket and trousers. She always took it to the shelter with her. She said it would keep us safe if there was a real air raid but it didn't make sense to me.

The rough unplaned, pinewood planks we sat on were full of splinters which pierced the backs of our legs. Some of the girls without knickers squealed with pain. We had to sit there until the "all clear" went. Later on the raids were real. I remember looking up along the sleeve of someone's arm. At the end of his finger, high in the sky, way up above the silver barrage balloons I saw a small black speck - a German reconnaissance plane. It moved imperceptibly. A tiny iron cross hanging in the bright blue sky. We wondered why the airmen in the park didn't fly after it and why the anti-aircraft guns didn't fire. It just didn't make sense to me.

When we came out of the air raid shelter airmen in tin helmets were scampering about the park. The barrage balloons were high in the sky. Rabbits were running around the banking. Nothing had dropped. The German plane had gone.

When I got home Mr. Hitchen was dead. My dad had a job. Our Ernie had broken the wireless set.

NOTHING TO WRITE HOME ABOUT

In 1939 with war in the offing employment picked up. My dad got a labouring job with Prestwich Council. It was the first regular job he'd had since the General Strike of 1926 when he'd been blacklisted out of the Bobbies for refusing to attack a dole queue. The job didn't last long. When war came and conscription started the younger men were drafted into the army leaving the older men to empty the bins, shift snow and mend the roads. My dad and his mates in the middle age-group were drafted into the Rescue Service, though one or two chose the Auxiliary Fire Service.

They kitted my dad out with an army type uniform. It was dark blue instead of khaki, with a beret rather than a forage cap. The shoulder flashes below the epaulettes said Rescue Service in yellow. The Greatcoat was the best overcoat my dad ever had.

My dad had to learn First Aid and how to tie knots. They gave him a St. John's Ambulance Book and a sheaf of papers with diagrams on. There were arrows all over the sheets showing how to tie the different knots. In the evening when he wasn't on nights and there was nothing much on the wireless my dad would sit for hours reading the First Aid book or practising knots on a broom handle wedged between the sideboard and the table.

To impress his mates my dad learnt the First Aid book off by heart. When he'd learnt a page I had to hold the book whilst he recited it and tell him if he missed a word out. He used to shout at me sometimes for not looking at the book. He was more than a bit put out when he discovered that I'd learnt the page before he had. He always missed out "obliquely" when he recited the circulation of the blood. "The organs concerned in the circulation of the blood are the heart, arteries, capillaries and veins. The heart is a muscular organ which acts like a pump. Situated in the chest cavity, immediately above the diaphragm, it lies (obliquely) with one quarter of its bulk to the left and the remaining three quarters to the right of the middle line of the body". He didn't like it when I told him he'd got it wrong, again.

THE DOGS OF WAR

I used to hate having to stay in whilst he practised bandaging my foot, my leg or my head or carefully put my arm in a sling. I wanted to be out playing hide-and-seek or black rabbit. I was glad when Bert Richards, one of his pals from the Rescue Service, asked my dad to teach him knots and bandaging. He brought young Bertie, his son, with him to practice on.

Bert was in trouble. Mr. Rogerson, the boss of the Rescue Service had said: "If you can't learn First Aid and how to tie knots you'll have to go back on the bins". Bert said to my dad: "That's the last thing I want Harry: they'll have me in the army in no time. Annie would never manage on her own".

Like many of the folk on Polefield Estate Bert and his family had been moved from Salford to Prestwich in a slum clearance. He lived with his wife, Annie and his two kids, Bertie and Irene, in Polefield Hall Road. My dad told me that as a boy Bert had attended *"The Ragged School"* in Salford. To keep out of mischief he'd joined Salford Boy's Cub and had taken up boxing. I'm not sure whether my dad said he was a fly weight or a bantam weight but he was one or the other. He definitely had a boxer's nose: no bone at all and a dark blue scar which matched the colour of his chin. Despite his small size he looked rock solid, total bone from the head down and a lean as a whippet. He kept himself fit and in pocket by walking everywhere. He told my dad he hadn't been on a bus or a tram for ten years. He used a skipping rope to exercise, night and morning. When not in uniform he wore an old, threadbare, pin stripe, dark blue suit, neatly pressed with an off-white, blue striped, flannel shirt without collar but with a front stud showing. When it was cold the flat cloth cap he wore had an off-white silk muffler to keep it company. My dad liked him. He said to my mam: "He's a good sort Bert: not bright but a good worker. Wouldn't let his mates down. He's a good union man".

Bert came to our house two evenings a week for about a month. My dad tried to teach him knots and how to do First Aid. He was no scholar, Bert. He couldn't remember the bones of the body. My dad bored us to death repeating them to him. "One parietal, one occipital, two temporal, one sphenoid, one ethmoid, two superior and one inferior maxilla . . . and at the root of the tongue is a "U" shaped bone called the oslingar or hyoid bone". Bert couldn't get his tongue round that one. "I don't think they gave me one of those buggers", he said. And he couldn't get the hang of making a Large sling or a St. John's sling either. The best he could manage was a Small Arm sling for a broken humerus. And when it came to knots he was hopeless: he didn't seem to know his left from his right. "All you've got to remember for a Reef knot Bert is left over right and under and right over left and under. Two lefts or two rights and you've got a Granny", my dad said. Young Bertie tried to keep his face straight. Come the next week Bert would have forgotten how to do it and as for a Clove Hitch or a Bowline and Bite my dad tried everything: "round the back of the tree", "mouse down the hole": he might just as well have tried to teach an elephant to play the piano with its toes. When it came to the proficiency test I think his mates must have done Bert's knots for him. I heard Annie Richards telling my mam he'd passed and that Mr. Rogerson had let him stay on in the Rescue.

As war intensified men were killed and new fronts opened in the Middle East and elsewhere. There was a shortage of manpower. Women went into munitions factories. The age of conscription was raised. More and more of my dad's mates were culled for the army from the Rescue Service and other reserved occupations. My dad, being thirty-six and quite valued, was kept on in the Rescue. Bert Richards was one of the first to go. Because he couldn't read or write, except his name, he was put in the Pioneer Corps—the pick and shovel brigade.

Annie Richards was more than a little upset when Bert went into the army. Despite not being bright Bert was a good husband. He put his wages on the table, didn't drink or gamble and kept the kids in line. He helped out when she was ill, which she frequently was. She would find it difficult to cope without him. Like Bert, Annie was a good sort but she was a poor specimen: more the size of a twelve year old girl than a woman. Round shouldered, hollow chested and asthmatic, she had a curvature of the spine which thrust her pale, sharp-featured, bespectacled face forward in an aggressively inquiring manner. Her dyed black hair was ginger and grey at the roots. She looked as old as my grandma but she told my mam she was only two years older than Bert.

Annie was in the habit of calling at our house for a gossip on a

Wednesday after collecting Irene from school. Each week my mam asked had she heard anything from Bert and each week Annie said "no". At first she made excuses for him. "Give him a chance, he's only been gone a week" but after the fourth week and still no letter she said: "Just wait till the bugger comes home: he needn't think he's coming near me!". It was my mam's turn to make excuses for Bert. "Perhaps they don't let them write till they're out of training"; "Maybe the letter's been censored"; "Perhaps they've sent him abroad. They won't want Jerry to know where they are you know!"
Annie was not consoled. "I bet he's got another woman", she said. "Don't talk so daft Annie. They don't let them out till they've finished their six weeks training", my mam told her. Annie wouldn't have it. "There's all those A.T.S. girls". "Well Bert's not exactly an oil painting is he now!" my mam countered. Annie said nothing. She finished her tea abruptly and said: "I'll have to be going".
As it happened it was Bert and not a letter, that arrived home. Bert's father died, suddenly, of a heart attack. Annie asked the Post Office to send a telegram and got the doctor to write to his C.O. Bert was given three days compassionate leave. He came round to see my dad before going to the funeral.
"How's it going then?" my dad asked him.
Oh not so bad but it was bloody awful at first. Head shaved, drill, bull, kit inspections, square bashing, weapons training, digging latrines, fatigues. Running around like a blue arsed fly. Everyone taking the piss because of my nose and the skipping. It's alright now though. P.T.I's put on a boxing contest. I knocked bloody hell out of the lot of 'em. That shut the buggers up. We've got the assault course and the five mile bash when I get back and then posting. God knows where we'll end up. I would't be surprised if it's somewhere in the Middle East.
Bert finished his cup of tea, then went quiet and started fiddling with his cup, running his finger slowly round the rim and staring into it. He seemed reluctant to get up to go to his father's funeral. When eventually he did stand up he said to my dad: "I've been getting some stick off Annie, Harry. I wonder if you could help me out?"

NOTHING TO WRITE HOME ABOUT

"Of course I will Bert. What is it you want?"
"I wondered if you could write a few letters for me Harry, so I can post one home now and again. It's so long since I did any writing I've forgotten how. I wasn't much good in the first place. I missed a lot of schooling as a kid and it's no use asking the blokes in our outfit. Most of 'em are worse than me. It would help me out a lot Harry if you would. Even just a couple".
"You mean to Annie?"
"Aye, I'll call back after the funeral".
Bert's metal-studded army boots sounded weary as he walked up the path after the funeral. He knocked on the back door and came in without waiting to be asked. He was wearing a diamond shaped black patch on the left arm of his tunic mid way between the shoulder and the elbow. His eyes looked red and sore. My mam was out so my dad brewed him a cup of tea. He told my dad the funeral had been at a church in Salford not far from his mother's house. His mother had been in a club for years saving up for it. "She did my dad proud" Bert said. They'd had a shiny black coach-hearse pulled by a pair of black horses decked out with black harness and plumes and a coffin with silver handles: that was the tradition in Salford. There'd been cold ham sandwiches in his mother's parlour afterwards. She'd managed to get a big tin of boiled ham, off the ration, through a neighbour whose husband worked on the docks. "It cost her an arm and a leg but she had to have it".
Bert said that despite it being wet there were a lot of people there, neighbours as well as family. He'd overheard a friend of his mother's saying his mam should have had his dad cremated and done something useful with the ashes. She'd said: "I had a big hour-glass egg-timer made for my husband's dust. He never did any work when he was alive: the bugger can do a bit now he's dead!" When I told our Ernie this, later, he said she'd made it up. He'd heard a comic tell that story on the wireless.
When Bert had finished telling my dad about the funeral and they'd swapped a tale or two about the Army and the Rescue Service my dad produced a writing pad and took his pen off the mantelpiece.
"Now then Bert, what do you want me to say?"

"Oh, I'll leave it to you Harry. I'm no good at that kind of thing".
My dad thought for a moment and then started to write. Bert looked on.
My dad wasn't used to writing letters but his hand-writing was good. He had found a fountain pen in the street which he kept on the mantelpiece out of our reach. At night, when he'd finished reading the *Evening Chronicle*, he used to write his name repeatedly in the page margins and fill in the blank spaces of the advertisements with his name: Harry Wild, Harry Wild, Harry Wild, Harry Wild ... I used to think he did it out of boredom but it was more likely egotistical obsession. He would put curly finials on the ends of the capital straight strokes and a curly loop on the tail of his Ts'. He'd been taught copper-plate writing at school so his letters were all joined up and sloped to the right. It looked very neat.
When my dad had finished the first letter, which took up almost one side of the paper, he said to Bert: "Do you want to sign it yourself Bert or shall I sign your name?"
"You'd better sign it Harry or she'll know I've not written it".
"Why? Doesn't she know you can't write?"
"No. I've never had to write anything. I can sign my name. That's all I've ever had to do. She won't remember what it looks like. She can hardly see, anyway, with those glasses of hers".
"Do you want me to read it to you?" my dad said, starting off: "My dearest. ..."
"Nah, It'll be alright. Just do us a couple more".
My dad shook his head and wrote another two brief letters. He asked Bert the number of his house and addressed three envelopes.
"There you are Bert. Those should keep you going for a while".
Bert thanked my dad and said: "You won't tell Hetty about writing the letters, will you Harry. She'll only tell Annie, and then the fat will be in the fire".
"No, you can trust me Bert, tell'em nowt".
When Annie came to see my mam the following Wednesday she was much more cheerful. She'd told Bert that he must write and he'd promised he would. He was going to ask to come off the overseas draft and be given a home posting on the grounds that

his mother was ill and had just buried her husband. If he got one, and it wasn't too far away, he would be home occasionally on a 48 hour pass.

Three weeks passed. Annie started to look glum. No word from Bert, despite promises.

On the following Saturday afternoon Annie came round to our house, unexpectedly. She was carrying a letter with a stamp on it saying "Passed by Censor". She took the letter from the envelope and said: "Can you read this to me Hetty. I can't see a thing in these glasses and I've never been much good at reading. I missed out on a lot of schooling what with my asthma and having to nurse my mother.

My mam took the letter and unfolded it. Oh!, she said, "this writing is exactly like Harry's: they must have taught all the boys to do copperplate handwriting".

My mam started to read the letter. "My dearest darling Annie. ..."

"Eee it never says that does it! He's never called me that ever in my life!"

"Well it's what it says here", my mam said, before continuing. "I've missed you so much it's like a light going out in my life being away from you. . . ."

"He's never written that has he?" Annie giggled.

"Well it's got his signature at the bottom so he must have done. He's a dark horse is your Bert. I'd have never guessed he was so romantic. Just listen to this Annie!".

"At night I think of you with longing and shed a tear. It's so unfair that we two lovers should be torn asunder by this cruel war. ..."

The letter went on in similar vein terminating in: "Your everlasting, loving, Bert".

"I don't believe it!", Annie said. "They must have got the letters mixed up when they censored them!"

"Count your blessings Annie. I wish Harry had some bloody romance in him. I don't think he's said one tender word to me since the day we got married".

I was very much surprised by the content of my dad's letter. My dad was a great talker and quite knowledgeable. I'd expected something different. He could do the *Evening Chronicle* crossword. He knew a lot about politics too. He was full of

THE DOGS OF WAR

opinions about Germany and Russia and how "Old Joe" would sort out "Jerry". Where he got his knowledge from was a bit of a mystery. He listened to the wireless but said he didn't believe half of it and he thought the newspapers were "nothing but a pile of propaganda". He never read books either. Apart from the *Evening Chronicle, The Football Pink* and *The News of the World* I never saw him read anything except the St. John's Ambulance book and a dogeared, second hand, "Teach Yourself Russian" text he'd picked up from a junk shop and struggled with for a few weeks. My mam said he fancied himself as People's Commissar for Prestwich. He'd must have read a lot at some time in his life though, or perhaps he picked it up at political meetings. What surprised me was that none of my dad's knowledge or opinions appeared in Bert's letters. But come to think about it, perhaps my dad was a lot more clever than I thought.

A month later another letter arrived. It was packed with similar phrases and sentiments to the first one. Annie was over the moon.

After passing out, Bert was posted to an army training camp "somewhere in Yorkshire". He came home on a 48 hour pass. Annie was all over him.

"I hadn't realised till I got your letter Bert how much you cared for me" she said.

Bert called round at our house when my mam was out. "What the hell did you put in that letter Harry?" he said to my dad. "She's gone bloody daft: I can't put a foot wrong".

"Well make the most of it", my dad said.

When Annie next came round for her Wednesday afternoon gossip she said: "I feel quite different about Bert since I got those letters. I had a lovely weekend".

Annie usually made do with two cups of tea but when my mam offered a third she didn't refuse. My mam was watching the sugar. As Annie distractedly took a second spoonful she said: "I'm in a bit of trouble Hetty. Bert asked me why I never write to him. You don't think you could do a letter for me do you Hetty?"

"'Course I will Annie love. What do you want me to say?" "Oh I'll leave it to you. I'm not much good with words".

"Well neither am I", my mam said. "I suppose I could say something like: My dearest darling Bert, my fondest love, I've missed you so much. . . . . . Always and for ever, your loving wife, Annie."

Two weeks later it was Bert who was round at our house. My dad said: "Bloody hell Bert, you're always home. We'll never beat Jerry like this. How did you wangle this one?". Bert told my dad he was home on a week's embarkation leave. He'd been posted overseas. His mother would have to get over his father's death on her own. He asked my dad would he do a few more letters for him.

"I could do with about a dozen Harry, If I send one about every couple of months or so that should see me through. I can't see the war lasting three years now the Yanks have joined in".

My dad reluctantly agreed to write the letters. "I'll do them tomorrow at the Yard", he said, I'm on nights. I don't think there'll be much doing".

So the war continued with my mam and dad's letters going back and forth to the Middle East. Each time Annie received one of my dad's letters from Bert she brought it round for my mam to read and reply to. It used to make me laugh my socks off: my dad writing letters to my mam and my mam writing letters to my dad without either of them knowing it! And it was all so arse about face. A total waste of stamps! My mam should have given her letters to Bert, before he was posted, with instructions to open one every three months, and my dad should have handed his direct to Annie.

A funny thing happened though. My mam and dad never wrote to each other. My dad was sent with the rescue team on various courses to places such as Little Budworth in Cheshire and Holker Hall at Grange over Sands in the Lake District. I remember she once took our Arthur and me to a Families' Open Day at Little Budworth to watch my dad demolish a mock building. Each time he went away my mam said: 'You will write won't you Harry", but he never did. She didn't hear from him for months on end.

As Jerry targeted different cities: Manchester, Coventry, Liverpool, the Prestwich Rescue team was sent, like a flying squad, in a special Rescue Bus equipped with tunnelling and demolition gear. Towards the end of the war when Hitler concentrated his VI and V2 rocket attacks on London and the

South East my dad's outfit was posted to Croydon. He'd been there nearly two months, stationed in a building adjoining a mortuary. A V2 hit the canteen killing nineteen people and destroying the Rescue Bus. My dad's team were sleeping in a dormitory at the time and woke up with part of the building on top of them and the twenty-three bodies that were in the mortuary mixed up amongst them. My dad said: "It was bloody awful. You didn't know who was supposed to be dead and who was supposed to be alive". As they were in shock and had no equipment the Prestwich team were sent back home.

My dad was in trouble the moment he stepped through the door. "Why didn't you write? You could at least have let me know you were coming home. Even Annie Richards gets letters from Bert and he's in the bloody Middle East!"

When she'd heard what my dad had been through she quietened down and said she was sorry. She was even more contrite when my dad said that he had written and that she should have had the letter.

The letter, with a Croydon post mark, arrived in the afternoon post the following day, Wednesday. My mam was gossiping with Annie. My dad had gone to the Town's Yard. As she opened the envelope she said to Annie: "Wonders never cease, he did actually write after all". She started to read the letter.

"My dearest darling Hetty, I've missed you so much it's like a light going out in my life being away from you. . ."

"Well I'll be buggered!" she exclaimed." He must have got your Bert to write it for him before he went abroad. Just wait till he get's home!"

THE ANDERSEN SHELTER

Soon after war was declared, in 1939, my dad got a job as a labourer working for the Council. Shortly afterwards, along with his mates, he was drafted into the Rescue Service. One of the first tasks he had to do was help distribute air-raid shelters to the residents of Prestwich. You could have a Morrison shelter--an iron mesh structure to go under your table, or, if you had space and money, a brick and concrete one, or an Andersen shelter. Like most people we opted for an Andersen. The council wagon which stopped outside our house to deliver it was piled high with glittering shelter parts. My dad carried the shiny sheets of curved, corrugated, galvanised metal over his head like a sack of coal. Burdakie and Midgeley, two much smaller men, carried the straight pieces for the front and back of the shelter, and the base-frame girders, and a hessian sack containing the washers, nuts and bolts. There was a sheet of paper inside the sack with a diagram and instructions as to how deep to dig the hole and how to put the pieces together.
The shelter had to be erected in a hole at least three feet deep. Some people dug them deeper but in some parts of Prestwich they filled up with water if you dug down deeper than two feet. You had to heap the earth from the hole on to the top and sides for extra protection. The shelter was six feet in height, eight feet wide and nine feet long. With its rounded roof it looked a bit like an igloo. My dad marked out an area in the back garden and dug the hole. It seemed enormous to me. After a foot or so down the rich, black soil turned to gravel and then to pure, golden sand like on Blackpool beach. I let my rabbit dig in it. I had only looked away for a second and it had disappeared down a hole. Our Ernie put his foot on the sand and the hole caved in. I screamed. My dad came to the rescue and quickly dug out the rabbit.
My dad made duck-boards for the inside of the shelter and built two wooden bunks and a slim, wooden bed for my grandma. There was no room to move when we all got inside. Our Archie and me used to fight with our Ernie for who would sleep on the

top bunk. My grandma made sleeping bags for each of us out of some old eiderdowns she had got from a jumble sale. The sleeping bags only came level with your armpits but they had crossed straps sewn on to slip over your shoulders so that the bags wouldn't slide down and leave you uncovered in the night. Once you were strapped in, you couldn't get your arms free to get out. We kept candles in the shelter but nothing much else. Some people, my dad said, had everything in their shelters bar the kitchen sink. We had a hedgehog.

The hedgehog was not in the shelter from choice. We had come across Mr. Prickles, as we christened him, while we were scuffing through a pile of leaves in the park, looking for conkers. I had noticed a gleam of polished-brown-light through the split shell of a spike-studded green husk the size of a small fist. I felt an elation of luck when I spotted it. I split the shell with my thumbs and a beautiful, dark, brown-stained, gleaming-new chestnut with a matt-white horseshoe scar on its side popped out. I held it, cold and waxy in the palm of my hand. Our Ernie nudged me and it dropped back down into the pile of leaves and was lost. I delved my hands deep into the leaves to search for it and shrieked with pain. I had pricked my fingers on the thorns of a hedgehog that was buried, deep down below the crispy leaves. It was wrapped in a ball of dry grass and bracken. We prodded it with a stick but it remained tightly clenched, its prickles menacingly proud. I took off my jacket and rolled the hedgehog onto it with my foot. I wrapped the bundle up and took it home with me. The hedgehog was full of fleas. When I next put my jacket on I got badly bitten. "Serves you right for messing about with such mucky creatures", my mam said.

At first we kept Mr. Prickles in a rabbit hutch: a small, square, wooden box with a hole in its side and a hinged lid that lifted up. A flimsy-framed wire-netting pen was fixed to the side with the hole in it so the hedgehog could stroll about, which it obligingly did. We fed it worms from the garden and black-beetles which we collected from inside the shelter each morning. I couldn't bear the crunching sound the hedgehog made as it geedily gobbled them up so it seemed a good idea to let it catch the beetles for itself. When the hedgehog next made a ball I scooped it on to the coal-

THE ANDERSEN SHELTER

shovel and wobbled it down the wooden shelter steps and left it to hunt the beetles on its own. I moved the steps so it couldn't climb out. When I came back it had gone. We took up the duck boards and moved the bunk beds but there was no hedgehog to be found.

A few nights later there was a heavy raid on Manchester. Bombs were dropping the moment the siren wailed out its warning from the roof of the Co-op at Kirkhams. A mobile Ack Ack gun was cracking off shells from in front of the shops on Bury Old Road. Incendiary bombs were falling all over Polefield estate. I could hear shrapnel from the shells clattering over the roof slates and clinking against the cast iron gutter. I remember lying in bed, thinking I must ask Mr. Hunter, the window cleaner, to get some fragments for me.

My dad was out with the Rescue Service. My mam and my grandma were on their own with us. My mam rushed into the bedroom shouting: "Get up! Be quick! Get up! She grabbed our Arthur in one arm and a blanket to wrap around him in the other and bundled our Ernie and me down the stairs in our pyjamas. The dull boom of distant bombs filled the spaces between the bursts of pom pom guns from Heaton Park. There was a small wedge-shaped space under the stairs into which she crammed the three of us whilst she helped my grandma out to the shelter. We had caught my mother's panic and were whimpering with fright. Our Arthur was crying. Our Ernie had his hands on his ears.

In a brief lull in the raid my mam dragged us out from under the stairs and herded us towards the shelter. It was no more than four yards from the back door but the grass was wet and it seemed a long way. Whilst my mam and our Ernie were clambering down the steps I looked up into the sky. I could see long straight lines of silver tracer-bullets chasing each other deep into the darkness. Searchlights crossed like wigwams as they sought out German planes, or probed in jerks and jumps about the sky. There was a smell of smoke like bonfire night and a flickering orange glow in the sky behind the houses down Polefield Grange.

I pulled the shelter door to behind me and fixed the catch. The candle light cast big black shadows on the walls of the shelter. Our Ernie was in the top bunk. My grandma was sitting on a chair, her lame leg stretched out in front of her. Both hands

THE DOGS OF WAR

gripped the curved handle of her walking stick. "We'll be alright if we don't get a direct hit", she said. "Oh don't say that Annie!" my mam shouted.

The candle wick was too long and there were no scissors to trim it with. The smoke tainted the air and made a black stain on the silver, crystalline coating of the corrugated metal roof. As the wax spluttered and dribbled down the candle the flame flickered and the shadows danced menacingly around about us. Our Ernie was making silhouettes of animals on the walls with his hands. Suddenly my mam shouted: "My god! What was that! Be quiet will you!" We held our breath and listened. There was a loud rasping sound like a wire brush being scraped across metal, then silence.

My grandma's head slumped forward, jerked back up a couple of times, then settled down, chin on chest, and she quietly snored herself to sleep. One by one, my mam, our Archie, then our Ernie, trailed off after her. I couldn't get to sleep. I lay in the dark listening to the muffled thuds of distant bombs and the occasional crump of anti-aircraft guns. Each time I closed my eyes a picture of Mr. Prickles appeared. Magnified in my mind I could see his two, black, opaque, shiny eyes set in a small, tapering, hairy face with a dry, black snout and wet nostrils. A huge ball of spikey criss-cross spines encircled me as I curled up to try to get to sleep. Four years later, when the war ended, the Council asked everyone to dig up their shelters and have them ready for collection. Alternatively you could buy your shelter for a pound and use it as a shed above ground. I helped my dad dig ours up. We cleared the earth from the top and sides and dug a trench round the outside of the metal. There was a hollow run round the back. In a corner, crumpled up, was what looked like a large leather glove. My dad picked it up on the tip of his spade. It was the dried-out body of the missing Mr. Prickles.

SCHOOL DINNERS

Dinner time always seemed ages away on a Friday so I went up to the front and said, like we had been told to do: "Please Miss may I leave the room?" "You must wait until Carol Bell comes back" Mrs Mitchell said, in an irritated voice.

When the bell finally went for dinner-time we wiped our pens on our cloths and the ink monitors collected them. They counted them carefully and put the inkwells on a tray whilst we put our sum-books on the shelves under our desk-tops. Because there was too much noise, and Michael Hamberger had banged his desk-lid down, the pens had to be handed back and we had the collection again. "Quietly this time!" By the time we had filed out and lined up in the yard for dismissal we had lost nearly ten minutes of dinner-time.

I wanted to be first in the queue for dinner so I'd have time for a game of marbles afterwards. I didn't wait for our Archie but ran down Whitaker lane with a swarm of other kids. It had been raining and the wet Chestnut tree leaves were stuck to the earth, glowing like orange star-fish. There were Chestnut husks floating like sea-mines in the pot-holes and puddles. You couldn't help splashing and getting your feet wet despite leaps that would have pleased an Olympic long-jumper.

My boots had gone in for sole-and-heeling so I had my pumps on: we were not supposed to wear plimsolls for school. With my pumps on I was able to run faster than most of the other kids. By the time I reached the allotments on the left at the end of the lane I was well ahead of them. There were gaps in the hedge which over time had filled with tangled brambles and spears of pink Rosebay Willow Herb. Last year we found Elephant Hawk moth caterpillars on them. The caterpillars had long black velvety trunks with tiny legs at the tip, two frightening, round, yellow eye-markings and a spike for a tail.

The railings fencing in the allotments were hanging on rusty broken wires. As I ran I could see rickety sheds with cracked and missing windows and brimming water butts beside them spilling out the drainings caught off the corrugated-iron roofs. I could hear pigeons cooing in the loft of the big pigeon cote that took up a good half of the end allotment. Broken wicker bird-carrying-baskets were stacked in front of the coop. I wondered if I could pinch a basket after school. I was going to Tib Street in Manchester on Saturday with my friend, Twissy, to buy a guinea pig: a basket would be useful.

When I got to the Congregational Hall the door was locked. The dinner delivery must have been late. By the time the doors were opened all the others had arrived, jostling one another and pushing in in front of me.

The dining hall, which had a makeshift stage at one end, had a wooden floor and a high vaulted ceiling. It made the clatter of plates and cutlery and the scraping of chairs and the din of gabbling children echo unbearably. And it wasn't helped by the constant shouts of: "Keep the noise down will you!", from the dinner ladies.

The small, square tables were set out, each with four tubular-steel chairs. Most of the chairs had torn, sagging, brown canvass bottoms and were so low your chin rested on the table top. All you could see if you looked around were heads with mouth-holes down which food was disappearing. And far too often reappearing. This usually occurred when someone had repeated one of the many disgusting rhymes we knew such as:

"A slab of matter custard, green snot pie.
Dead dogs giblets, green cats eye.
All mixed together, nice and thick.
Then washed down with a cup of cold sick".

Chairs would be pushed back, hands would be held over eyes and all to the accompaniment of loud, mocking urrghs!

I was not one of the "free dinners" any more because my dad now had a job in the Rescue Service: I could sit at a table. "Free dinners" weren't allowed to sit on chairs at individual tables. They had to sit at a long trestle-table to one side of the room on forms which were always toppling over backwards. When I had sat there I used to feel that everyone was staring at me because we

SCHOOL DINNERS

were poor. My dad said it was all wrong. It was two years ago but I could still remember it. I was nine now. I could even remember Mrs Crompton, the dinner lady, showing me how to use a knife and fork when I started school at the age of four.

The school dinners came from Woodthorpe in a large grey van with Prestwich Borough Council in curved letters on the side. It was the Rescue workers who delivered the dinners to the schools around the district. They didn't, at that time, have enough work to do: raids on Manchester had eased off. Quite often I saw my dad and his pal Cliff Nicholson carrying in a dixie of potatoes between them. They wore blue battledress with Rescue in yellow on the sleeve below the shoulders and they had blue berets on. Later my dad and his mates were posted to Liverpool, Coventry, and Croydon near London, and older council workmen brought the dinners.

Mrs Crompton always served on a first-come-first-served basis but when she wasn't there the "free dinners" were made to wait until last. By the time they were served their dinners were cold.

It was smelly fish and white cabbage on a Friday. I didn't eat it, and the rhubarb pie was sour. Spud Ellis, Brian Naylor and me pretended to go to the lavatory. When we got outside we pooled our money to get three- pennyworth of chips from Newtown Street chip-shop. We played "follows up" on the way there. I lost two of my best marbles to Spud Ellis. The chips were really good though!

MR. ASKEW'S WAR WORK

On a Friday afternoon Mr. Hume often sent me to the storeroom to help Mr. Askew, the caretaker, pack into sacks the waste paper we had brought to school for the war effort.

Most of the kids in our class didn't like Mr. Askew. He had a knack of appearing from nowhere whenever you were up to some mischief. I quite liked him though. He gave me marbles from down the cellar grid and a threepenny-bit for shovelling the coke through the manhole into the cellar on Tuesdays after school.

Mr. Askew spent his days in the small, cramped cellar which housed the big boiler which burnt the contents of our rubbish bins and heated the water pipes and the large, finned, cast-iron radiators which stood under each classroom window. There was hardly space down there in the boiler-room to swing a shovel and it was hard work heaving coke into the boiler. He let me have a go once. The fumes got up your nose: they made your eyes smart and choked your throat. I could taste the fumes in my mouth for days afterwards.

When he wasn't in the cellar Mr. Askew did odd jobs about the school and kept an eye on the playground but you couldn't easily see him in the school yard amongst the throng of mixed infants and junior girls, running, jumping, skipping, or playing hopscotch. He was a dwarf! He was about the same size as the six year-olds in Miss Mather's class: about four feet tall. A congenital malformation had left him with a pigeon-chest, a camel's hump and no neck. His trouser belt was about where his collar would have been had he worn one. To me, as a child, he looked like a head on legs: like a miniature one of those sad-looking clowns on stilts you see at the circus. Often he would be turning the loose end of a long skipping rope attached to the guard-railing of the cellar steps whilst two girls, in the middle, did "a pepper" so fast you could hardly tell the blur was a rope, spitting up the dust or whirring over their heads.

When the Government, unable to import paper for newsprint and packaging, launched a book-drive to help the war effort I helped

Mr. Askew stack the books into boxes and took the badges round the classrooms for the teachers to give out. The more unwanted books you brought to school the higher the rank you became. You could become a corporal, a sergeant, a captain, and even a Field Marshall but you would have needed to have brought half Prestwich library to be that high a rank. We used to pinch books off the library shelves and tear out the date-stamp page but the lady at the library saw us nicking them and chased us out. She wouldn't let us in again after that. Keith Pakefield got into trouble because he'd taken books from home without asking his mother. His mother came down the steps into the cellar one day and rummaged through the boxes looking for a bible with the family's names in the front. There would have been many other parents there too had they known that their valuable encyclopaedia or half a set of Dickens novels had been donated for pulp to make their kid a corporal.

Mr. Askew sometimes collected books on his bike when they were too many for a child to carry: he tied a box on the carrier above his back wheel and put the books into it. The bike was usually propped against the school wall. It was an old, full-size, racing bike with dropped handlebars set so low down that the headstock-stem seemed to have disappeared into the forks. A saddle from a lady's bike had been fixed half-way along the crossbar, almost directly over the front chain-sprocket, but even so to ride the bike Mr Askew had to lie stretched forward, flat like a jockey, with his arms bent like wings. We all used to laugh at him. His chin seemed to hang just above the front wheel like a friction brake. There were blocks of wood screwed onto the pedals so that his feet could reach them. He must have had something like horse-mounting-steps at home because at school he had to stop against the low stone wall, which used to support the school railings before they took them away for munitions, and use the lip as a step to dismount. He often fell off and spilt the books out of the box on to the playground.

Mr. Askew helped me make a bogey from a plank and the wheels off an old pram I found on some spare ground near the tumbled-down houses on Cuckoo Lane. He screwed the axles across either end of the plank and fitted the wheels on for me. When I got home I burnt two holes in the end of the plank, with a red-hot poker I had heated in the fire, and threaded a loop of rope through them. Mr. Askew thought I was going to collect books with it but I had other things in mind. I had plans not to carry loads of books for nothing but to make loads of money with it. There were many women on our estate who would give you threepence to get them a sack of coal or coke from the Co-op siding at Prestwich railway station. They were always running out before the coalman came. I could get in on the kit-bag trade too.

On Saturday afternoon, after I had finished taking out orders for Roberts's, I earned six-pence carrying two loads of coke. Afterwards I went to the gates of Heaton Park, near the railway station, and waited for airmen to come out with their kit bags.

Heaton Park was used as an RAF training camp during the war and airmen were billeted all over Prestwich. Many householders with spare rooms had no option but to take one or two airmen as lodgers, though most took them willingly. My mam said some of the women took them just to get a feller into the house. There was a scandal about a young woman in Polefield gardens, whose husband was away, fighting in North Africa, who had produced a baby "that couldn't possibly have been his!" She moved house and the vicar of St. Margaret's church, and his wife, adopted the baby before her husband came back.

There was a constant trickle of airmen with kit bags coming and going through the park gates but four o'clock on a Saturday afternoon was the best time to catch them. A crowd of young kids with trucks and bogeys would be clustered round the gate waiting to carry kit bags. Sometimes the airmen would give you as much as two-shillings if you carried their kit bags, packs and gas-masks. They would pile the bogey high and holding on to the kit bags, help push it the two miles to Polefield. One of them gave me an RAF cap badge once and when they changed their headgear for berets another gave me his forage-cap. Joe Gooch, the lucky devil, got given a Black Mamba snake in a bottle by big, black, Jamaican airman. I swapped him a commando dagger for it.

When I told Mr. Askew how much I had earned carrying kit bags he said: "I'll be down there with you next Saturday!"

THE DAY THE TRAMP CAME

The day the tramp appeared in our street our Ernie and me had been to the Saturday morning pictures to see a Laurel and Hardy film and Tom Mix in the cowboy serial. We'd nearly stamped our feet off when the posse galloped out of town to catch the baddies. We shouted ourselves hoarse with warnings when a half-breed Indian from behind a rock crept up on Tom Mix to try to scalp him. At the end of the episode he had his arm round Tom's neck. Tom's head was back and the knife already making a cut when the screen went blank. There was a loud chorus of Orrh no's! We would have to wait till next week to see what happened. "Another fine mess you've gotten me into Stanley!", our Ernie shouted.

We played at cowboys and Indians all the way home, dodging behind trees and into doorways, firing at each other and rolling on the ground. I was wearing my new cowboy outfit. I'd saved up for it for months. A couple of pennies or so a week marked on a club card by Miss Weatherby who owned the Toy shop on the corner of Bury old road and Polefield Approach. I'd run errands and knocked on doors asking for jam jars and lemonade bottles to take back to the shops for the halfpenny returns. I'd even been round to the neighbours to show them my new shoes and I'd pestered the life out of my mam. I was desperate to get that outfit. My mam said I'd wear the window out I spent so much time staring at it to make sure it still had my name on it.

The outfit comprised a pair of strap-on floppy leggings, a belt with a buckle, a holster and gun, a neckerchief and a broad brimmed Stetson hat with a leather chin strap and toggle. I galloped up and down the street, shooting Indians hiding behind the privet hedges, pretending I was Tom Mix. Our Ernie was a baddie. I ran up the path and into our back garden and sat astride the mangle pretending it was a horse. My dad had dug a hole in the back garden and planted the mangle next to my rabbit hutch so that my mam could wring out the washing in the garden rather than having the mangle clutter up the kitchen. Our Ernie dashed round the corner of the house and before I could shoot him threw a log of firewood which hit me on the forehead. I fell off the mangle clutching my head, blood streaming down my face between my fingers. Our Ernie shouted "It was an accident! An accident!" I screamed: "My dad'll kill you". I knew he had done it deliberately.

A few weeks earlier our Ernie had been sitting on the low brick wall in front of the privet hedge which enclosed our front garden. I'd been sitting on his knees. Suddenly he opened his legs and let me drop through. I caught the back of my head on the sharp edge of the brickwork. He said that was an accident! My mam had gone hysterical when she saw the blood. "Oh my god! What have you done to him?" she'd screamed. When we got back from Dr. Jameson's surgery with three stitches in my head our Ernie still said it was an accident. My grandma had stuck up for him: he was her favourite, so he didn't get hit. She was always sticking up for our Ernie, she doted on him and secretly gave him sweets and money when she came to stay. She never gave any to me or our Arthur. "I've only come for a day or two. I want Ernest to come with me to Bacup to see uncle Sam". That was six weeks ago. Even though there wasn't enough room at our house my mam put up with my grandma staying. She could get the occasional shilling off her or get her to pay for the fish and chips but she didn't really get on with her and there were more rows with my dad when my grandma came to stay.

When my mam came out to see why I was yelling our Ernie ran off but he didn't run far. I could see him craning his neck round the corner of the house, trying to see how bad my cut was. When my mam had stopped the bleeding with her handkerchief she turned round and shouted at Ernie: "How the bloody hell do you think I am I going to pay another doctor's bill. Just you wait till your father comes home!"

My forehead only needed two stitches this time but we'd had to wait and it was mid afternoon before we got back from the surgery. My dad had come home and was doing the garden. He looked up and said: "Where the hell have you been?" and seeing the bandage round my head: "What's he done now!". When my mam told him what had happened they went in the house and had a blazing row about how they were going to pay the bill and what

THE DAY THE TRAMP CAME

they should do about our Ernie. My dad was for thrashing him but despite her earlier threat my mam intervened shouting "For god's sake leave him alone Harry". Again my grandma settled the matter: she gave my mam the money for the doctor's bill, so Ernie escaped a good hiding a second time. By the time the tramp appeared my dad had calmed down and gone back to doing the garden. Our Ernie and me were friends again. We were playing out.

My dad straightened up, dug his spade into the border to leave his hands free and cupped them to light a cigarette. Our Ernie and me were in the street swinging on the lamp-post from a rope someone had attached to the cross-bar. The tramp must have hobbled down Polefield Approach without our noticing him. He just suddenly seemed to be there at our gate, as though he had dropped down from the sky or popped up through the pavement. We left off swinging to stare at this bulky, pear shaped old man in his sixties. A grubby, misshapen trilby was perched on his head. His grimy, lined face was grey with whiskers. He was wearing a dirty, grease-stained raincoat, the pockets bulging. The Mac had a jagged tear down the back and was tied tightly round the middle with a piece of frayed rope. He carried a big bundle of clothes under one arm, bound up with hairy string. A dixie dangled from his fist. His other hand gripped a large, knobbly, walking staff. His baggy looking trouser legs dragged on the ground, partly covering his old, split boots. If our teacher had asked us to draw a tramp he would have looked just like this one. My dad abandoned his spade and walked towards the gate his eyes on the tramp. The tramp looked at the garden and then at my dad. "That's a fine looking garden you've got there Mister", he said, in a strange-sounding voice. "Aye it's not bad", my dad said, holding out his hand to the tramp.

It was no surprise to us when my dad invited the tramp in. My dad was an upside downer. He detested power and privilege and revered the poor and someone called the proletariat. When Stan Gee, "the union man" and a moderate Labour Party member called at our house for the union subs my dad would immediately get on his soap box and harangue him: "If I had my way I'd do away with the bloody lot of them". By the lot of them he meant

THE DOGS OF WAR

the rich, the judges, royalty, the lords and landlords, big business, the Tories, the fascists, Moseley's gang and the bourgeoisie. The whole "bloody capitalist class" was going to go "up against the wall". An inveterate supporter of the underdog my dad sided with Paul Robeson, the blacks, the Jews, the Irish, the Spanish republicans, the Poles, the Russians, the oppressed, the dispossessed, the miners, the strikers, the hunger marchers, the unemployed and anyone down on their luck (if you discount my mam). "When the working class get power you'll see some bloody changes" he would shout at Stan's back as he escaped through the front door.

"Come on in and get warm. I'll make you some tea" my dad said to the tramp, putting his arm round his shoulder. Our Ernie and me could hardly contain ourselves. We were laughing and giggling into our hands as my dad and the tramp walked up the garden path. Our Ernie said in a loud whisper "It's Desperate Dan, the cow pie man". I said to him: "Shurrup Ernie, my dad'll kill yer". "He's escaped from a comic", Ernie persisted. "Shurrup will yer!", I said. But he wouldn't. "It is him. It's definitely him! You can tell by the hat". It was true the tramp did have a hat like Desperate Dan's. "He's got the same chin with those whiskers". Fortunately my dad was too engrossed with the tramp to notice what Ernie was saying.

My dad steered the tramp round the corner of the house towards the back door. 'You can leave your bundle and your dixie in here for the time being, granddad", my dad said, opening the coal-house door. "Put your stick in as well". My dad went into our little kitchen-living-room and the tramp followed. There was a bamboo rack for washing over the fireplace; all the houses on our council estate had them. The shirts and sheets my mam had washed earlier in the day in the dolly tub, still standing beside the sink, hung low, almost obscuring the fireplace. My dad eased himself round the big, square dining-table which almost filled the room and reaching up to the rack shunted all my mam's washing to one end. He turned a chair, the only one we had with a bit of upholstery on the seat, towards the fire and having done so gave the fire a good poke to make it flare. "Sit yourself down. You'll soon be nice and warm. I'll just put the kettle on for a brew".

THE DAY THE TRAMP CAME

Our Ernie and me stood on the coconut matting near the door, our eyes stretched and our mouths open, wondering what my mam would say when she came down from upstairs. The tramp squeezed past my dad and the gas stove. His sleeve caught the handle of the frying pan, knocking it to the floor. He just ignored it and flopped himself down on the chair like a sack of flour. After warming his hands by the fire for a minute or so he began rummaging in his pockets, jettisoning wadges of paper, damp socks, boxes of matches, old handkerchiefs, bits of dried crust and assorted other things onto the peg rug my grandma made. At last he found what he was looking for: a clay pipe and a worn leather tobacco pouch. He tamped the baccy down into the bowl of the pipe with his forefinger, struck a match and held the flame above the pipe. I watched with amazement as the flame, which had been flaring upwards, did a somersault and disappeared into the bowl of the pipe. The tramp began puffing and coughing. The pipe belched out clouds of dense bluish smoke. It rose at once to the low ceiling, curling, hanging, then dipping like a big, blue-grey whale to hover a couple of feet above his head. It was amazing that such a tiny white pipe could make so much smoke. And the smell was lethal. Our Ernie whispered in my ear that it was horse manure not tobacco he was smoking.

The hall door opened and my mam came in. My mam was quite a small woman but she could stand up to my dad, big as he was. She had a temper too. She once told me that as a child she'd had bright, red hair, down to her waist. It was her pride and joy and it had darkened in colour as she got older to a beautiful chestnut shade. She said that about the time she met my dad it was fashionable for women to have an Eton crop and she'd had most of her hair cut off. When she grew it long again it was hardly red at all, just a brown colour. You could still tell she had been a red head though, by her freckled arms. My mam was good looking in her way, no irregular features, and she had a sufficient fat layer for her face to remain unwrinkled all her life. Her nose was normal in size and length, though it did have a slight, roundish dent in the tip from a minor accidental injury in childhood. Her dominant feature though, was her bright, highly polished, beady brown eyes.

THE DOGS OF WAR

My mam stood staring at the back of the tramp, her arms akimbo, her eyes flashing and her face rapidly reddening. "What in the devil's name is going on!", she shouted, not looking at anyone in particular. I knew immediately from the tone of my mam's voice she was furious. My dad had been reckless to invite the tramp in. You could smell the damp, musty smell of his dirty raincoat and you could not ignore the whiff of pee as soon as you got near him. My dad must have noticed it but it didn't seem to worry him. Fortunately the smell was masked to some extent by the overpowering pipe smoke. "We've got a visitor", my dad said. "A gentleman of the road". "Well he can bloody well get back on the road. He's not staying in here with that mucky stuff', my mam said, wafting the smoke with her arms. "And what's all this mess on the rug? And just look what you've done to my washing!", she shouted. The tramp didn't turn round. He just sat there, puffing on his pipe; staring at the fire, pretending not to hear. "He can sit outside" my mam said, scowling at my dad and jerking her thumb towards the door.

"He's all right where he is", my dad said in a near normal voice. My mam moved round the table towards the tramp. "Oh for god's sake Harry, you've not gone and sat him on the best chair have you!?" My dad poured some water into the teapot and began stirring it vigorously. "Now don't start. Be quiet and get him some grub". "It's soap he needs and a bloody good scrubbing", my mam said.

My dad put an older, more rickety, plain wooden chair near the door and said to the tramp: 'You're probably warm enough now. Here's your cup of tea. Come over here by the door and talk to me while your drinking it".

"See if you can get him a bit of something to eat", he said, turning to my mam.

"I don't think we've got anthin", my mam said, tutting and shakin her head as she went into the pantry.

My mam never had any food in the house. Even when my dad occasionally managed to get a casual job at the docks in Salford or did a garden for a bob or two we still lived "hand to mouth". Anything we needed someone had to run down to the shops to get, usually me, and usually on tick until the end of the week, or

THE DAY THE TRAMP CAME

put on the ongoing bill at Roberts's if it was grocery. I could hear my mam cursing my dad from in the pantry. "There's no food for us, never mind blessed tramps!" When she emerged she said, "There's this cake of your mother's. He'll have to have some of that". She knew my grandma would be upset and my dad would have to deal with her. With any luck there would be a row and my grandma would take herself off to her own place or go on another round of visits to her sisters at Tottington, Flixton, Crumpsall or her brother at Bacup.

My dad cut the tramp a big wedge of cake and put it on the edge of the table next to the mug of tea. Our Ernie and me said, almost in unison, "Can I have a piece of cake mam?". "No you can't it's your grandma's!", my mam said, snatching the knife out of our Ernie's hand.

"Where are you heading for then?", my dad asked the tramp. "Salvation Army place in Salford. Strangeways I think it is. Near the prison. I'm down on my uppers. I thought perhaps I'd get some boots off them".

My dad laughed at the tramp's joke and slapped his hand on the table.

My dad knew what it was like to be "down on yer uppers". He never had any money and what he had he spent on fags and Littlewoods pools. He'd not had a regular job since he'd been forced to leave the Bobbies for sympathising with the strikers in 1926. He was sure he had been blacklisted. He'd been out of work for most of the '30's and he too had tramped himself shoeless in search of a job. "Three million unemployed. What chance have I got?", he would say. He had given up going to Salford Docks. He'd been lucky now and again. Being a big, fit, six feet one and a half inches helped but you had to know a ganger or just be there when a boat came in. Living five miles away in Prestwich: "No chance!"

While they were talking my mam sat down where she could get a good look at the tramp. He really did need some boots; the soles were gaping open and the toe cap of one was missing. He had no socks on and his big toe was all black and the nail broken. There was blood caked round the quick. I could see by my mam's face she was shocked at the sight.

THE DOGS OF WAR

The tramp had taken his hat off to reveal a thinning head of grey hair, dusty as rubble. It matched the two weeks of stubble on his cheeks and chin. His eyes looked sore round the rims as though they had been hemmed with red cotton. He had sunken cheeks and no teeth. He was chomping vigorously at the cake with his gums. My mam was concentrating on the tramps face and frowning. He was scattering crumbs and spilling his tea and coughing and choking from eating and drinking at the same time. If it had been me I'd have got a telling off.

"Would you like another cup of tea?", my mam said. She was clearly starting to feel sorry for the tramp and was probably a bit ashamed for having tried to get rid of him.

The tramp and my dad swapped a few stories, but as usual, it was mainly my dad who did the talking. He hardly let the tramp get a word in. He told the tramp how he'd been on a hunger march to London with the *"Unemployed Workers Association"*, the *"Wobblies"*. I'd heard it dozens of times but I still liked to hear my dad telling it. How they had been accommodated in peoples' houses and church halls. How he had worked with his mate Jimmy Crudeson for the Communist Party, selling The Daily Worker. How he had heckled Stanley Baldwin and Chamberlain and fought Mosely's blackshirts. "We were fobbed off with nothing. The Tories called us loafers, corner street loungers, no goods. There's only one way to deal with those buggers: you've got to fight 'em. When they start cutting yer dole or yer pay rates you've got to get out on the streets and fight'em!".

The tramp was nodding his head in agreement. He said he had been a Welsh coal miner all his working life until he got too old for pit work. His son had been killed in a pit accident and after his wife died he had set off to walk to Newcastle; sleeping under railway arches, in sheds and shop doorways, anywhere to keep warm. He'd heard there were jobs in the steel works and the ship yards but when he got there the unemployment was worse than in Wales. "That was a good ten years ago. I've been on the road ever since", he said.

While the tramp was busy talking he was busy scratching and scattering more cake crumbs from the corners of his mouth. Our Ernie whispered to me that the tramp had got fleas.

THE DAY THE TRAMP CAME

My dad asked the tramp could he sing, being that he was Welsh. The tramp said, "Nooo man", but it didn't stop him. He promptly started to sing, in a totally tuneless, gravelly voice, a tramp's song that he said later he'd learnt from another tramp who'd been on the road in America:

Hallelujah I'm a bum
Hallelujah bum again
Hallelujah give us a handout
To revive us again.

Oh I went to a house
And I knocked on the door
And the lady said bum bum
You've been here before.

Hallelujah I'm a bum
Hallelujah bum again
Hallelujah give us a handout
To revive us again.

By the time he got to the third verse my dad was singing the chorus with him. They only stopped when my mam interrupted.
"Here, have this last piece of cake and another cuppa", my mam said.
All her antagonism towards the tramp had gone even though she quite clearly still had some left for my dad by the looks she kept giving him.
The tramp took the cake and wolfed it down as though it was his first piece. When he had drained the last dregs of the sugar from the bottom of his cup he thanked my mam and said he'd better be making a move before it got dark.
My dad carried the dixie and escorted the tramp down the path to the gate. He shook the tramp's hand and said, "Look after yourself and try to get those boots". When he let go of the tramp's hand the tramp looked down at his palm. My dad had given him a two bob piece. "Don't walk. Catch a 73 bus on Bury Old Road; in front of the shops", my dad shouted after him.

THE DOGS OF WAR

Our Ernie and me followed the tramp to the end of Polefield Approach. We watched him walk down the main road. When he got to Lawson's fish and chip shop he stopped, looked at his hand and disappeared inside the chippie.

When we got back home a row was going on. My grandma had her coat on and was stuffing things in her bag. My dad had locked himself in the front room. My mam was shouting from upstairs: "It's big hearted Harry outside but you won't lift a bloody finger to help me in here will you".

My grandma slammed the front door.

When my mam came down I said to her, "When I grow up I'm going to be a tramp".

'You'll end up like your father you will!", she snapped at me.

Our Ernie dragged me outside saying, "Come on, it's still light, let's have another game of cowboys and indians".

"THOSE POOR BOYS!"

A thin band of pale moonlight entered the bedroom from the landing window and the faint silhouette of a woman moved across the blackout curtain, darkened, grew, and spread across the faded, blue-patterned wallpaper and rested by the fireplace for an instant. There was no noise, but when the door closed the room was blacker and quieter than before. I wondered, had there been time for my mother to have slipped into the room. A few minutes later, almost imperceptibly, I heard the slow rhythm of her breathing and sensed her shape, standing by the fireplace, in the darkness, near the bed.

Faintly, through the cold, clear, winter air, from high above the house where the birds flew in summer, came the slow, pulsating drone of heavy, American bombers, bound for the marshalling yards at Bremen; a slower, deeper noise than the straining, angry, hum of the German planes we were used to hearing overhead, as they came in low to make their bombing run on the Exide works at Agecroft, or the docks in Salford.

Arthur was sleeping soundly against the wall, under the window. Ernie sighed deeply and mumbled something in his dream. Between the two I lay very still, my eyelids closed, breathing quietly, feigning sleep but straining at the silence in the room and wondering why my mother was there and why she didn't say something.

After a while I relaxed and was beginning to doze off when I heard a sudden in-drawn breath through parted lips as though my mother had suffered a sudden sharp pain in her side. As she breathed out, very quietly she said: "Oh those poor boys!" and I could tell that she was weeping.

Shortly afterwards the door opened again and again the band of moonlight moved across the blackout curtain. Once again the silhouette stole across the wall, paused and went out but this time when the door closed the room seemed not only blacker and quieter than before, it seemed to me a sadder and more lonely place.

THE DOGS OF WAR

Did I ever tell you why Toby Jones has a phobia about dogs? Admittedly his name didn't help and neither did that muzzle-blunt nose of his or that curly Airedale hair, but it wasn't any of those things. Nor was it living in Kenilworth Avenue. We kids used to bark and growl at him and say: "There's a good boy Toby", even when he lived near us in Polefield Grange. There were some who believed it was because he got the lead in the school play. But I'm joking of course, and it isn't a joking matter. No, Toby Jones does have a phobia about dogs. True, he doesn't piss himself any more when he sees one, or go rigid and stretch his quivering body against a tree or a wall like he used to, or span his fingers wide like fishes fins, or screw his eyes tight shut and hold his breath till his freckled white face turns from red to blue and he faints from constriction of the throat: but Toby Jones does still have a phobia about dogs. I know, I saw it again, yesterday

He didn't know I was watching from the bedroom window. Funny though, it wasn't a big dog like Leo; just a small mongrel bitch the size of a pet rabbit; but it had him going all right. The side of his sinewy neck twitched the moment he saw it and his mouth wrenched round to where his ear should have been, just like it used to do. There was the same terrified, eye-widening leer and the same deafeningly silent scream, rattling the street lamps, just like happened that day we had him tied to that tree all those years ago during the war. That's what brought it on, there's no doubt about it. It wasn't my idea but he blamed me for it.

It all happened the day after the oil bomb fell on a house in Bury Old Road, a few doors down from ours. We'd lain in bed that night, the three of us, sweating under those smelly great coats that served as blankets. Our Archie, two years younger than me, near the door; me in the middle because I didn't wet the bed any more and our Ernie near the window where I wanted to be.
As usual our Ernie had been playing at air-raids: us two under the

coats in our air-raid shelter and him doing the bombing with his fists and feet. I remember thinking that Mr. Andersen himself ought to have been in there instead of us two and felt what it was like to get a direct hit. He was a sadistic sod, our Ernie, as Toby Jones will tell you, but we were saved from a permanently maiming war wound by our mam screaming: "That's the last time I'm telling you three up there!" We could hear her getting the carpet beater from the pantry.
We'd done the carpet beating run once that day and we didn't want a repeat performance. "We'll come out if you don't hit us", we'd said. Little Archie had been pushed in front like a hostage. While my mam's plaited cane carpet beater was ferreting him out from under the kitchen table we dashed through the hall and galloped upstairs to lock ourselves in the bathroom. "Promise you won't hit us if we come out. Promise!".

We emerged, one by one, from under the sheltering coats not daring to breathe. Later, my mam came into the room where we'd been whispering and stood listening in the dark to the slow, pulsating drone of the Lancasters on their way towards the marshalling yards at Bremen; or back from some raid the B.B.C. man was always telling us two of our bombers were missing from. I remember her saying: "Those poor boys". I thought she meant us lying quiet in the darkness pretending to be asleep.
I woke up with the banging; shouting from under the blanket "Don't hit me . . . I'll come out if you don't hit me". I was wet with sweat and my heart was beating louder than the pom pom guns outside. Our Ernie was already up and looking out of the window from behind the blackout. We could see the sky all red and smoky behind the houses at the bottom of the Grange. "That's Manchester on fire", our Ernie said.
The siren had already long wailingly gone and we should have been in the shelter. Anti-aircraft guns were firing flak from their posts in the park and there were flashes of light in the sky. You could see big-bellied barrage balloons and hear them burst into flames. They were like fat, silver fish dying in pools of red and yellow blood. Occasionally a low plane struck one of the wires and spun screaming to the ground. Tracer bullets made curved

THE DOGS OF WAR

dotted lines across the sky and searchlights did their geometry on the inclined planes. The speed with which those lines switched position, straight as sticks, to make wigwams in the sky, amazed us.

A sudden loud thwack on the roof made me duck. I heard the shrapnel clattering down the slates to fizz in the gutter where the rain water was trapped. Later, Ernie used to remind me of it by chucking cups of water on the fire to make it hiss, sizzle and fizz when our mam was out getting fish and chips. "Oh!. Fancy letting the fire go out", she would say.

We could hear more shrapnel hitting the pavement and bouncing on to the road.

"We'll get lots of shrapnel in the morning", Ernie said. "Better be up and out before that beggar Toby Jones gets his thieving fingers on it". Just as he said this there was a terrible, earjamming bang that shook the house and rattled the windows even though we had left them open like it said in the leaflet. I don't know whether we were blown across the bed or jumped out with fright but we ended up in a heap on the floor. "Oh my god! We'll all be killed!", our mam screamed as she bundled us out of the room.

I stopped to look wide-eyed through the landing window. No need for a torch: the night was as light as day. A raging fire flamed across the street where the Baxendale's house had been. You could feel the heat through the pane. My stomach felt wobbly like frogspawn.

"Oh my god, those poor boys!", my mother shouted as she wrenched my arm and dragged the three of us tumbling down the stairs. "Get in there, quickly!", she screamed, as she ran us into the cubby hole under our wooden hill.

We cowered, shaking and sobbing, for what seemed hours until I heard my dad's long, urgent stride and the ring of his iron-heeled boots on the path.

"Hetty! Hetty!", he shouted, "Where are you?".

"We're under the stairs!"

Her voice sounded strange and muffled as it echoed in the confined space. It was like speaking into our milk jug. The night was full of strange noises.

THE DOGS OF WAR

Looking in there again the other day when I was round at our mam's house I didn't know how we could possibly all have squeezed in: there seemed hardly room for one small boy never mind three leggy lads and our mam. I shouted: "Under the Stairs", again, under the stairs, and again it was just like our mam speaking into the milk jug.
"What's happening out there?", my mam said.
"It's an oil bomb. It's hit a house on the front of the road. I thought it was here: we've got the Rescue Bus outside. They say there's still three in there. I think they've had it".
"Come on I've got to go. Get those three into the shelter".
"Is it safe out there Harry?"
"Yes, there's a bit of a lull at the moment".
"It's murder in here with these three".
"There's one on Alan Richardson's house. I'll have to go!"

When I woke up I was again shouting: "Don't hit me!" The candle had gone out and I was all by myself on the top bunk in the Andersen.
"Why do you always leave me in here when the all clear's gone!", I screamed. But there was no one to hear.
I struggled with the straps of the sleeping bag Grandma Wild had made for me out of an old eiderdown and tumbled off the bunk with a thump. I climbed the short, wooden steps and pushed open the difficult door.
The pale dawn was quiet like a normal morning but the air smelt smoky. In the distance a brown cloud, with orange tints here and there, hung over Manchester. Columns of smoke sloped westward in the light wind. My feet, wet from the dew on the grass, made patterns on the path. I cut my foot on the rockery but what did it matter: I'd beaten Toby Jones to the best bits of shrapnel. One jagged lump, a good foot long, had milled markings on the planed, smooth side and you could see crystals on the other. I'd be king of the collectors!
"Hello, hello, hello! What are you doing out in your pyjamas this early in the morning?" I turned and saw a squat, fat figure in blue battledress with a gas mask bag slung diagonally across his front and A.R.P. on his flat tin hat. It was the street warden, Toby's

father, Mr. Bloody Jones!
"Here give me that", he said prizing the piece of shrapnel from my fist. "It might be important: the War Office will want to see that. Now you run along home before you catch your death a cold".
"You bloody bugger". I said, not quite under my breath.
"'Ere, what was that? You'll get a clip round the ear if I get hold of you my lad!.
I ran round the back of our house thinking: I'll get your bloody Toby for that. I beat the door with my fists and kicked it repeatedly with my bare feet. "Let me in! Let me in! Let me in! It was like the cry of the wolf in "The Three Little Pigs".

Our mam made school meals at Woodthorpe Dinner Centre and had to be out by six o'clock. Later, Mrs France, from next door, knocked us up. We used to bang on the floor to make her think we were getting dressed. Sometimes we lay in, telling stories, pillow fighting and missing school and sometimes we'd still be there when our mam came home at three-thirty in the afternoon. But we were up and dressed when Mrs. France came the day the oil bomb fell. We'd done the keep fit exercises our Ernie made us do in time with that piano woman on the wireless. Plink plonk plink plonk one two three, arms together, follow me!; listened to the radio doctor, Dr. Charles Hill, say: "Good morning and how's yer liver bile today?" Our Ernie mimicked his deep, fruity voice: "Now don't go giving young Johnny the cat's milk: it won't do him the slightest bit of good". We'd been made to suffer Freddie Grisewood on "The Kitchen Front".
Our Ernie made the recipes up using substitute ingredients. He would boil half a bottle of ink for three minutes, add one egg, a spoonful of soap powder, two heaped handfuls of soil and a dead fly and chant:

> *A slab of matter custard,*
> *Green snot pie,*
> *Dead dogs giblets,*
> *Green cats eye.*
> *Mix it all together,*

THE DOGS OF WAR

Nice and thick.
Then wash it down
With a cup of cold sick.

He would chase us around the house with it cackling: "Stir the pot brothers", and make us eat at least a tablespoonful each before dashing the remainder on to the fire, a cup at a time, where it hissed and fizzed and smelt the place out. But he didn't make breakfast the day the oil bomb fell. We wanted to be out of the house before Toby Jones but the best bits had gone by the time we started combing the gutters.
"If only we had a ladder we could get loads off the roof".
Toby Jones had a shoe-box full and was still snouting about in the street: he'd have been wagging his tail if he'd had one. He wouldn't show us his shrapnel at first but we knew we'd only to wait.
"Aye! that's mine!, I said, grabbing the piece his thieving father had filched from me this morning.
"It's bloody not you know!", he said, snatching it back. "It's my best bit. My dad found this last night: it was red hot so he left it till this morning to cool".
"Yer lying sod!", I said, "He pinched that off me!", but he ran in.
"We'll get you for that Bonesy", our Ernie bellowed to his backside as he disappeared down the entry.
"We'll sell you to a Punch and Judy man yer bloody mongrel.
"Yeah, we'll get you later Bonesy", I added.

Later in the day we went to see where the other two oil bombs had dropped. One had demolished a house at the bottom of Phillip's Park Road killing four people and the other dropped a mile further on, about a hundred yards past Overdale Hall where my granny had a flat. They'd been aimed at the Exide Works at Clifton Junction, a quarter of a mile further on. Had the bomb aimer released them a split second sooner the first bomb would have killed us at Polefield and the third would have got my grandma.

We got shot of our Archie by doubling back through Prestwich

THE DOGS OF WAR

Clough and went to Twissy's house to look at his bird's eggs and butterflies. Toby Jones saw us and told our Archie.

Our Ernie dreamed up a scheme to get Bonesy. We showed ourselves at Twissy's bedroom window and our Archie spotted us just as we'd expected. He shouted that I had to look after him or he would tell my mam. I opened the sash window an inch and told him to go round the back and we'd let him in. We knew Toby would try to get in with him.

Our Ernie had the back bathroom window open and a bowl of washing up water perched on the sill. "Don't wet our kid you fool!", I tried to tell him. Too late, he'd tipped it over. Toby Jones leapt out of the way. Our Archie got the lot. He was gasping and gulping like a drowned water rat. "You've done it now, yer Charlie. My mam'll kill us!", I said to our Ernie as we raced down the stairs to the front door to catch Bonesy. Twissy was already after him with the bucket: we could see him stalking Toby behind the hedge. Twissy's body swung forward like a reaper as he swished the lot, bucket and all, over the top of the privets.

Mrs. Dickenson, the local gossip, was telling Mrs. Johnson about the bombing and how Eddie Tickle had gone in to try to get the people out. "If there'd been more water they'd have still been alive".

"More what?"

"More water". she shouted down old mother Johnson's right ear as a bucketful of the stuff poured down her left one. Old mother Johnson leapt more lively than she'd done for years. As we scattered across Twissy's dad's vegetable patch our Ernie, always ready to turn adversity into victory, shouted: "That'll flush the cobwebs out of your drawers you gassy old windbags". It was a big mistake.

But I was going to tell you why Toby Jones has a phobia about dogs. Toby split on us, of course. A people's court was called by our gang and we passed a unanimous sentence. Toby Jones should be bound by the hands and taken to the punishment tree to be whipped". After all he had the sign of the triangle on his thigh. Like the rest of us he'd been branded a gang member by Twissy with a penknife blade heated over the sacred candle stolen from

St. Margaret's church. He'd drunk from the communal jam jar filled with Gaymer's Woodpecker cider. There was nothing else for it but a whipping.

I was in the posse sent to bring him in; so was our Ernie. It was my bolas that made him bite the brick dust on Halfacre Croft. I got his legs just as our Ernie's lasso pinioned his arms. We brought Toby back with more rejoicing than Jesus got entering Jerusalem and tied him to the sacred whipping tree.

Toby's bite was a lot worse than his bark and between his squeals and grunts he'd taken several mouthfuls of my hair and a bit of lobe off Frank Kenyon's ear before we had him secure. Suddenly he stopped struggling and became quiet. His face whitened, even his freckles paled and he began for the first time what was to become his characteristic quiver. It was quite unexpected but how were we to know that Leo was loose. We'd been so engrossed in trussing Toby to the tree we hadn't noticed what he'd noticed---the silence settling on the chilly street. It was like "Bad Day at Blackrock". I expected two cowboys to appear.

"Christ!", someone shouted, Leo's loose!"

We were off like a cattle stampede leaving poor old Toby tethered tight to the tree. I glanced back and for the first time saw his neck twitching and his mouth wrench round to his ear. His eyes were screwed tight shut and his face was turning from red to blue. He opened his mouth and produced his silent scream. I could hear the street lamps rattling like teeth chattering when you get cold at the baths.

We scrambled up Twissy's stairs and looked out of the window. Leo was only a few yards from Toby! His nose was going and he was walking tall.

The Marshall's had two Great Danes. They terrorised the neighbourhood more than Hitler's bombers. They didn't often escape but when they did there was trouble, real trouble. Leonie was bad enough but Leo was something else. We were terrified, even though we were safe inside!

Leo stopped a yard or so from the whipping tree to sniff the scent of friend or foe on the side of the small brick wall which kept the gardens off the path. He was taller than a lion but leaner and his

THE DOGS OF WAR

fawn coat evoked the same associations. His name overlaid the savagery of dangerous dogs with all the scary ferocity of the big cats we'd seen fighting Tarzan on the cinema screen on Saturday morning. His jowls hung fleshy and black and his fangs dripped saliva. He put the fear of God into us: what he put into Toby was . . . but I'm jumping ahead.

Leo turned his attention to Toby by plonking paws like pancakes on the poor lad's shoulders and sniffing noisily at his averted face. Toby seemed to have grown a foot up the tree as he stretched to keep away from the slobbering brute. Leo seemed satisfied. He dropped to the ground and cocked his hind leg but there was already a large puddle soaking Toby's feet, making a river down the path to the kerb. Leo padded over to sniff at the wall once more.

Toby the while had gone limp and slumped down the tree. His head lolled forward on his chest. He looked like a soldier stricken with shot. Us kids all thought he was dead. Suddenly, without warning, Leo turned, paused, then sprang, snarling at Toby, tearing his clothes with his claws and savaging the side of his face with his fangs. We turned away from the window in terror, sobbing and whimpering with fright. But Ernie didn't. Our Ernie kept his eye quite calmly on the scene. After a second or so he raised his right arm and slowly turned down his thumb. It meant nothing to us: our Ernie was a nutter.

Toby would have probably been killed but for Sergeant Nipper Hewitt. Old mother Dickenson wanted the police on to us and she'd been earlier to Nipper's house to report the sousing we'd given her and her dumb friend, mother Johnson.

"I want something done about them this time! They nearly killed poor Nellie Johnson with that bucket!", she'd told him.

Nipper, on his way to see our mams and dads, was just in time to see Leo leap, but too late to stop him. You had to hand it to Nipper though, he showed no fear of Leo. He kicked the dog in the side, winding him. Then, grabbing him by the scruff, clipped one cuff through the dog's collar and the other round a railing. Leo leapt at him, rattling the fence like a tambourine as Nipper turned his attention to Toby. By the time he'd untied him Toby

THE DOGS OF WAR

was coming round. He took one look at Leo, screamed, grabbed Nipper Hewitt like a long lost lover and buried his bleeding head inside his coat. He was shaking like a duster at a spring cleaning. The whole street was out. He was still squawking like a demented parakeet when the ambulance came.

"He's a soft sod", said our Ernie.

Leo went missing, presumed dead. We never saw him again, in the flesh that is. There were, of course, almost nightly reports of a spectral form having been seen beside the whipping tree and it only needed someone to say: "Hey!, there's Leo!", to put the mockers on our game of Hide and Seek or to take the run out of Black Rabbit. But jam jars were found behind the wall where puddles of Leo's pee were supposed to be and by the time Toby came out of hospital three months had passed and unlike Toby, Leo was not even the ghost of his former self.

Toby moved out of Polefield Grange soon after he came home and went to live down Broughton. He used to tell the kids down there it was a piece of shrapnel that took off his ear, and in a way that was true. But he couldn't find words to explain his stutter.

He came came back occasionally, at first, to visit his auntie May. Our Ernie used to sneak up behind him and bark deep woofs like Leo used to bark. That's how we knew he'd never fully recovered. But all that was years ago and we'd lost touch with Toby. Lost touch that is until last week when he moved into Nipper Hewitt's old house.

You could have run me in with a rolling pin. True, he'd had a fetish for uniforms, ever since finding comfort in Nipper Hewitt's coat. And joining the Coppers, with a dad like that, I could understand. But dog handling! I'd have lost money if you'd told me he'd become a dog handler. But seeing him yesterday, stretching his fingers and quivering, and hearing the street lamps rattle, I'm not so sure.

And coming back to to live in Polefield? What's that all about!

FOUR PIES AND A BOTTLE OF SAUCE

On Thursday evenings at about nine o'clock in the weeks between the eighth of April 1940, my sixth birthday, and the eighth of April 1949, my fifteenth, I ate no more nor no less a quantity than four-hundred and eighty-three Ellis's meat pies. At ten pies a bottle I suppose I swilled down with them no less than forty-eight and three-tenths bottles of H.P. sauce. The quality of meat varied a little with the fortunes of war but the crusts were consistently crisp. If the jelly varied in glutinous consistency it was merely because the delivery man delayed a little longer than usual at some stop on the way. End to end, with a bottle of sauce between every ten pies, and thirteen pies between the seventh and eighth bottles they would reach a distance of forty-three yards: from the front step of Eddie Roberts's grocer's and confectioner's shop to our little back kitchen table because that's where they came from and that's where they went to.

I got the pies for services rendered and you might think the extra three pies in week seventy-five must have been especially well-earned and you'd be right. Pies don't come for nothing: I worked damned hard for old Eddie Roberts and pies were all part of the pay. Looking back on it I think I was being done from the start but at six years of age you haven't the same sense of commercial injustice. I suppose by the time I was eight I knew all there was to know about being exploited and at ten I was the retail trade's equivalent of an industrial saboteur: a few mouse droppings in the cake mix, a thumb-plaster in the bread and some nice fat maggots from my fishing tin on the bacon hanging in those fine gauze bags in the back room. By the age of twelve I was into the redistribution of wealth. I didn't pinch money though, that was stealing, I stuck to consumables, eaten on the premises. I drew a strict line after cakes and the odd bottle of dandelion and burdock but not so Eddie Roberts, he was always slipping the odd two bob out of the till into his pocket when his missus wasn't watching. He was shit scared of "Lu-Lu" Roberts but he liked his pint did Old Eddie and she kept him short.

I got the job on my sixth birthday---the day our Ernie got the

FOUR PIES AND A BOTTLE OF SAUCE

sack. I was unlucky really. If Ernie hadn't broken his glasses I'd have probably had a childhood but someone had trodden on his face through his specs in a fight at school and he had to have a patch put on to hold the left lens together till our mam had paid enough off the doctor's bill to let him get a new pair. It made him see funny and what with the glide in his other eye and the way that he held his mouth when doing anything more complicated than breathing he looked like a cross between Ben Turpin and Lord Nelson. And seeing "The Mummies Hand" at the pictures the night before ("Will you take me in please, Mister?") played no inconsiderable part in his downfall. He was making pyramids out of pots of jam on the top shelf at the shop. Five, four, three, two, one, crash!, Over!, the whole flipping lot came juggling down through our astonished Ernie's outstretched arms and smashed, one by one, like strawberry bombs on the lino. Old Eddie Roberts was livid. He just pointed a quivering finger to the door and then recovering himself a little shouted: *"You've been here too long for any good you have been doing. In the name of God go!"* It was like Mr. Amery dismissing Chamberlain.

Our Ernie walked out as I unfortunately walked into the shop to pay half-a-crown off my mother's bill. "How would you like to see if you can do any worse than that gormless brother of yours?" he said.

"How much?" I said.

"Sixpence a week but there might be a cake or even a pie if you're a good lad. Come in after school and see if I've anything I want doing. But not Wednesday. We're closed half-day on a Wednesday. Ask your mother when you get home. You can start by helping me clean up this mess".

I held the shovel for him whilst he scooped up the oozing heap of jam and broken jars with a piece of cardboard. As soon as the job was done I was off as fast as my seven league boots could carry me. Actually they were our Ernie's Wellies with a sock stuffed into the toe to make them fit but they were a lot quicker than pumps. I could even beat the bus to school in them. Sixpence! I couldn't believe my luck. I'd buy that Commando dagger off Joe Gooch and that Black Mamba in a bottle of rum their Denny had got off that Jamaican airman billeted with his auntie May. (He'd carried his kitbag from Heaton Park gates to the station on his bogey for it).

"Mam! Mam! Can I go to work for Old Roberts?" I shouted as I went through the back door, but there was no one in the kitchen.

"Mam! Mam!", I shouted up the stairs. "Can I go and work at Roberts's?" "Oh bloomin' heck, she's gone out!".

Later that evening my mam was only too ready to agree to me working for Roberts. For one thing it would save her from being pestered for money for toffees and she might be able to borrow a shilling or two off me occasionally, or get me to "save" the odd penny in the gas meter. Our mam, my grandmother said, was a bad manager: she never had a brass farthing to her name, though on the bit of money she managed to keep from going to the Dogs with my father she'd have had to have been a financial genius to make ends meet. She was pleased to have retained an agent in a grocer's shop. It gave her the possibility of levering Old Roberts into giving her extras, off the ration, like a ham shank or a tin of fruit or, occasionally, some spare bacon ribs.

Each day, after school, I called in at the shop on my way home to see if there was anything Mr. Roberts wanted doing. A dismal bell would tinkle over the door as I entered and echo distantly in the back room. Seconds later Eddie would appear in his freshly laundered, starched, white shop-coat and natty, striped tie. Though not very tall he was easily detectable because he whistled perpetually through a small hole at one side of his pouting lips, like a woman whistles. He wore such baggy, wide-bottomed, grey-flannel trousers you couldn't see his feet at all. When he moved you thought he was on wheels he took such tiny, quick steps. I suppose you could say he only just missed being a dapper man though his missus would have said he only just missed being a devious one. I could have put her right about that. His ruddy complexion, he claimed, owed something to a Cornish mother but I knew how he got it. Where his bent Roman nose came from was anybody's guess. He had wiry black hair, remarkably black for a man in his early fifties, brushed back from a bulging forehead in a fanned wedge of corrugated waves. Women would have paid pounds for a perm like that. When in trouble he would drag the fingers of both hands slowly down the length of his face in a

FOUR PIES AND A BOTTLE OF SAUCE

gesture of despair.

I would stand in front of the counter until he wanted an order for cakes delivering, a letter posting, a newspaper fetching, or the accumulator for his wireless set taking to the Electrical Shop for recharging. I used to fit the loose handle of the accumulator round the square glass jar with great care and carry it gingerly, as is if full of tiddlers I didn't want to slop on to the pavement, so that the acid wouldn't spill down my leg. I walked so far over to one side that the jar almost touched the ground.

Gradually he began to trust me behind the counter and let me sit on top of a set of small, wooden, folding step-ladders with Rinso stencilled on the side, out of sight in a corner. I felt very important perched there all alone guarding the shop. I had to look out for kids nicking things---a not too difficult task because most of the meagre stock was "under the counter" in those days. Even the non-rationed goods were reserved for regular customers. No one could see, except me, the thin, ragged ranks of Brasso, Silvo, Acdo, Zambuk and Zeebo. The tins of Wintergreen ointment, packets of Ex-lax, Syrup of Figs, Senna pods, packets of Lively Polly that made me sneeze and chunks of jade-green Fairy soap with lines across for cutting. There were boxes of Robin starch with rows of red-breasted, round-shouldered birds standing on splayed stiff legs all glaring at me malevolently with their beady brown eyes. Little frilly tubs of Dolly Blue with wooden pegs sticking up. They looked like crinolined Victorian ladies taking an afternoon stroll. Beecham's pills in tight little twists of paper crammed into small, circular, cardboard pill boxes. Bottles of Indian Brandy with a mysterious black-man on the label. Snowfire ointment for the winter-chapped knees of short-trousered boys. Monkey Brand, cream and white donkey stones for doing the front step. Some women used to do half the pavement outside their terraced houses, but they were fanatics. It was Mrs. Garner though, a woman who worked on munitions, with a headscarf done up in a knot at the front with the ends tucked in and a fag drooling from the corner of her mouth who was always pinching things: slipping a tin of peas or a small brown loaf into her shopping bag whilst she was lolling across the counter. I was too scared to tell Mr. Roberts though.

THE DOGS OF WAR

When our Ernie came into the shop I kept a look out for Old Roberts whilst he helped himself to a fistful of dried sultanas from a box near the scales. He could swipe things with the speed of a snake our Ernie could, but the mean sod never saved me any. Anyway, he picked his nose, our Ernie, didn't he, so I probably wouldn't have eaten them anyway. Most of the time I would just sit quiet in the gloom of the late afternoon aching to go out and play. To relieve the boredom I would guess the number of tins of assorted vegetables and count to check my self-laid bets. I was probably the only one at our school who knew the number of repeats of Lea and Perrin's name on the border of a bottle of Worcester sauce. I would occasionally scoop bits of yeast out of a packet on the shelf near the steps with my fingernail. It felt short between my fingers, like drying putty. I used to roll it into little balls and eat it, savouring the bitter taste, despite the slimy texture. I must have established a tactile sensuality that has never left me (I still roll damp beermats into little balls and make intricate designs with them). But most of the time I just sat there desperately longing to play out.

Sometimes, sickly looking grey mice would run hesitatingly along the base of the counter and into a box of prunes, or pause by a bag of sugar, or sit on their haunches nibbling a raisin. Once I'd established where the run was I would bait the metal prongs of a wood and metal spring-hoop-mousetrap with cheese or a bit of bread and place it in the path. Occasionally I'd set the trap so fine it would snap off as soon as I put it on the floor and frighten me to death.

Mr. Roberts was not too keen on me setting traps for the mice because one that he didn't know about had nearly taken the end of his finger off. I remember him leaping into the air cursing from behind the bread stand with the trap dangling from the second finger of his right hand. It got him just at the base of the nail and it turned black and blue. I was scared he was going to give me a belt round the earhole but he was in too much pain to think about me at the time. Old Roberts preferred to put down Dak. It reminded me of the codliver oil and malt that I had to have on a spoon after my weekly bath in the dolly tub on a Friday night. Like it or not though I had to scoop the treacly brown goo out of a

FOUR PIES AND A BOTTLE OF SAUCE

tin with a stick and smear it on to squares I'd made from the flaps of cardboard boxes. The following morning there would be contorted bodies fixed in weird poses in the glue. There would be one with a raised foreleg standing clear of the gunge with strands of sticky thread attached to the Dak from each claw. A beleaguered body half off the board in a desperate angle of defeat. Another, that nearly made it back to his own lines, would be a couple of feet down the end of a trail of brown slime. It was like a scene from the Flanders mud with the stricken bodies of soldiers caught on the barbed wire that I'd seen in those books Eddie kept in the lounge. It only needed Mr. Roberts to start whistling "Smile a while I bid you sad adieu" or some other nostalgic first world war song that he was for ever whistling, with low melancholic slowness, to complete the scene and make me feel really miserable about those dead mice.

Though not suffering as much as the mice, Eddie Roberts also had been having a bad war. He looked on me as a reinforcement but I'm not sure I was a turn-up for the better. He'd got married in 1910 and apart from four years respite in the trenches, in the fields of Flanders, he'd been engaged in total war with his missus ever since. "This business with Hitler", he used to say, "is a little local difficulty by comparison". The problem for Eddie, as I see it, was not so much that Mrs. Roberts kept him short of money, though she did that. But that like many a strong minded woman she saw her husband not for what he was but for what she believed, with a zealot's conviction, she could make him into. Her maiden name had been Dillon and she had spent the best years of her life, and his too, trying to change Eddie Roberts into Eddie Dillon. The funny thing was she believed she had succeeded. But she didn't see what I saw from the vantage point of my seat on the steps.

Mrs. Roberts was madly in love. Not with her husband or some other bloke or with possessions like a normal woman, but with money. She loved money. Not for what money could buy but solely for itself. She loved money the way I loved those Ellis's meat pies. She loved the look of it, the taste of it and the feel of it. No wonder she kept Eddie immensely short of it. Eddie was fond of a pint but she didn't approve of him drinking. I don't think it was the boozing "Lu-Lu" Roberts objected to so much as the money he would have spent had she allowed him a couple of drinks now and again. She said she didn't like people drinking because of what drink had done to her father but I think she was motivated more by what money had done for her mother when she married a rich teetotaller after her first husband drowned in his final pint.

"Lu-Lu" used to come into the shop from the bakehouse two or three times a day just to count the one pound notes. She would pull out the till drawer so that it hung down from the counter on the safety catch like a dog's tongue and run her fingers through the coppers and silver with the same delighted anticipation of ecstasy you might get from running yours through a lover's hair. Her one indulgence was a trip to town to the pictures in her late mother's fur coat on a Wednesday afternoon.

And as if being mean wasn't enough Mrs. Roberts was also suspicious of everything and everyone. She suspected the Travellers who called at the shop, desperately touting for orders, of giving short measure and of overcharging. The customers were suspected of thieving. Even I was suspected of helping myself to all manner of things. But most of all she suspected Eddie. She constantly asked him, when the takings were down, was he sure he hadn't borrowed anything from the till and forgotten to put a slip of paper in. Eddie would feign astonishment, widen his eyes, and send a ripple of wrinkles up his bulging forehead in amazed innocence. She knew damned well he had but she couldn't prove it, just as she knew he was secretly boozing but couldn't catch him at it. Worse still she was convinced that for extra rations he was getting favours of one sort or another from some of the younger women customers whose husbands were away in the army. Why else would those tins of fruit she had carefully stashed away in the air-raid shelter be diminishing at such a rapid rate? And what were all those quiet conversations or those "Oh geroff with yer!" or "Oh Mr. Roberts!" about which came to an abrupt end when she entered the shop? No wonder she was on a very short fuse. She would go off like a rip rap on bonfire night as soon as Eddie sparked the blue touch paper with some innocent remark about Mrs. Riley not having seen her husband for two-and-a-half years.

"It's not my bowels that are giving me stomach pains", she would say to Jean, her apprentice, "it's him!".
On his more rebellious days though, when less obliquely accused of lechery or of having had a drink, Eddie would argue her feminine lack-logic into a corner but he could never win. Before he could get her to admit defeat she would vanish as if through a hole in the skirting board or be away up the chimney or into another room.

Now I've always been good at being exploited, it's a working class talent I inherited, and within weeks of starting at Roberts's I was general dogsbody to the establishment. Besides working in the bakehouse on Saturdays and all day, everyday, during the school holidays, I only had four other jobs to do, besides taking the orders out, that is. One was putting up rations on a Thursday; another was cleaning Eddie's Home Guard kit and a third was de-icing the fridge. But the fourth and most important of all was fetching the booze. It was secretly fetching the booze that earned me my weekly pie. Mrs. Roberts thought he gave it me for putting up the rations.
On Thursdays, on my way home from school, I had to pick up a wicker basket from the back door of the Off licence. You know the kind, square with an arched cane handle, the kind that blind men make for butchers but about half that size. In it would be six pint bottles of Tetley's bitter with a fox-huntsman in red and black on the label or failing that four giant bottles of Gaymers Dry Woodpecker Cider. I used to take the basket back with the empties on Friday morning on my way to school. By the seventy-fifth week I had been working for Eddie Roberts I was a grandmaster of the routine. What I used to do was carry the arm-aching basket as far as the side passage between the shop and the garage and put it behind the gate. As soon as the shop was empty of customers I would go and spy out where his missus was and what she was doing. Whilst I nipped out to get the booze Eddie would ease the large bread stand at the far end of the shop out from the counter so as to leave a gap behind, big enough to take the basket. I would streak into the shop like a whippet and be behind the bread stand before you could blink. If the bottles accidentally

THE DOGS OF WAR

clanked together as I stowed then out of sight Eddie would wince contortedly. Then, starting at his forehead, drag the fingers of both hands simultaneously down his face.

The next part of the operation was easy. I would go round the counter to the far end of the shop and, concealed by the bread stand, I would secrete the beer bottles under the shelf behind some Lanry bottles in readiness for Thursday evening's illicit session.

The day before the Thursday of my great "Pie Bonanza" on week seventy-five "Lu-Lu" Roberts was going to see "Gone with the Wind" at The Gaiety in town. It was during the school holidays and I didn't normally work on Wednesday afternoon but Eddie had especially asked me to come in and not to mention it to his missus. I was sent to follow Mrs. Roberts to the bus stop and to keep a discreet lookout from a doorway to make sure she got on the bus. As soon as the bus was out of sight I went back and told Old Eddie "the coast is clear" and then I went home for my dinner. I was to come back to clean out the window display cake stands, do the windows and mop the shop floor, all jobs usually done by Eddie himself. Eddie had saved a bottle of Gaymer's from the previous Thursday and when I left he was in the back lounge unscrewing the top.

I went home and cut myself a big thick jam butty. I remember because Alex France, who lived next door was home on leave from the R.A.F., shouted to me: "Hey! What's the matter with your hand". "Nowt", I said, "Why?".

I gripped the butty between my teeth while I put my roller skates on but the key kept slipping and I couldn't tighten the toe clips properly and the left one kept coming off. Anyway, I went down the Grange on one skate and had a quick game of football with a couple of kids. By the time I got back to the shop an hour had gone by.

As usual, Old Eddie had left the side door open for me. I went into the back room without knocking. As soon as I entered I could smell something burning. I went into the back room and saw Eddie on a chair in front of the fire with his feet on the little ledge over the grate. He was snoring like a bloody owl. He was wearing his usual wide-bottomed grey flannel trousers and they were hanging almost into the dying fire, the turn-ups slowly charring away. I shook him awake.

"Christ!", he shouted, "What's happening!".

He was up and dancing around the room beating sparks off the bottom of his trouser legs and trying to get his braces undone. I just stood watching, gawping in amazement at the spectacle. When he eventually struggled out of the smouldering trousers he stood disconsolately in his long white comms. surveying the ruined trouser bottoms.

"Oh my God! She'll go stark raving mad if she sees these!"

Just then the doorbell rang.

"Quick! Quick! That will be Mrs. Riley. Go and let her in and take her into the other room. Don't let her come in here whatever you do. Tell her I'll be with her in a minute".

Mrs. Riley was a teacher at our school and though I didn't realise it at the time, looking back on it, Old Eddie was undoubtedly having an affair with her. She was a rather severe looking woman nearing forty, with an Eton crop, but with a nicely rounded figure. She wore pleated skirts and tight fitting blouses that thrust her bosom into rounded relief and her backside swung provocatively when she walked, I now realise. My mother kept asking me about Mrs. Riley. One time she asked me did she wear a gold chain round her ankle. "How the heck do I know", I said, but when I looked closely next day at school there it was, a fine, shining gold chain just showing faintly beneath her nylon stocking. It was probably an identity chain in case she got killed in an air-raid but our Ernie said she was a prostitute because that was how prostitutes advertised. I didn't know what a prostitute was. Anyway, when I got back from showing Mrs. Riley into the best room, Old Eddie was putting on another pair of trousers and still fuming for having dosed off".

"I think Mrs. Bishop at the Dry Cleaners mends trousers", I said.

"Son. You're a genius! If you can get these mended and back here before Mrs. Roberts comes home from the pictures there'll be an extra pie for you tomorrow night".

He knew all there was to know about incentives did Old Eddie. So off I ran to the Dry Cleaning shop up the road with Eddie's trousers neatly folded and concealed in a brown paper parcel.

THE DOGS OF WAR

The shop was closed: Wednesday, half-day. "Oh heck!", I said as I peered through the gloomy window. I could see the bare counter and the huge press with its toothless mouth open. It seemed to be grinning at me. Over the counter was a printed notice which I could read but not understand. It said: "Do not ask for credit, or favours, as a refusal often offends". I went back to the shop to ask what I should do.

I looked into the back room but there was nobody there. There was no one in the lounge either so I went upstairs. I could hear voices coming from the bedroom so I knocked on the door. There was silence, then whispering. Eddie came to the door, opened it a fraction and poked his head round.

"What is it you want. I'm trying to have forty-winks", he said, grumpily.

I told him the bad news. He thought for a moment and said: "Do you know where Mrs. Bishop lives?". I told him I did.

"Well, get a large tin of fruit from the air-raid shelter and take it round to her and ask can she do me a favour. Tell her I'll see her alright when she comes in for her order on Friday. Now run along and when you get back start on the shop window".

As luck would have it Mrs. Bishop was in and when she saw the large tin of "Golden Plums in Syrup" she nearly bit my hand off, as they say. She said she could do the trousers by taking some material off the inside at the waist and that I could collect them in about an hour-and-a-half.

I didn't hear Mrs. Riley leave. She must have gone before I got back, or perhaps Eddie had quietly let her out through the side door. I had almost finished the cleaning by the time he came into the shop. He'd put on a clean white coat and was whistling *"Goodbye Dolly Grey"*, and screwing the index finger of his right hand into his right ear.

He said: "If Mrs. Roberts asks you whether Mrs. Riley called this afternoon with her order say you don't know. Mrs. Roberts doesn't like me serving people when the shop's shut and she'll be cross if she finds out. There'll be an another extra pie for you tomorrow night if you can keep it a secret. Now run and see if Mrs. Bishop's got those trousers ready.

I was back at the shop with the trousers with a good ten minutes

FOUR PIES AND A BOTTLE OF SAUCE

to spare before "Lu-Lu" was due home from the pictures. Eddie examined the invisible mending with a rueful expression on his face but having convinced himself she wouldn't notice it he made to go up stairs to change. As he did so he said: "You'd better be off now "Jimmy". You can help Mrs. Roberts in the bakehouse in the morning. Don't be late now.

I had mixed feelings about working in the bakehouse. It was hot and cramped and I seemed always to be scraping the same tin hour after hour and day in day out. But it was mainly because I didn't like Mrs. Roberts that I preferred the shop to the bakehouse. She was always irritable and short tempered with me. She suffered from what she thought was constipation but it turned out later to be cancer. I had to keep nipping to Bursk's, the Chemist, for a bottle of liquid paraffin to ease her bowels. It didn't do her much good though and, come to think of it, it might have been the paraffin that gave her the cancer in the first place. I hated scraping the cake tins though, especially those dimpled sets of six. She was too mean to grease the tins properly and it was almost impossible to get the encrusted cake off with the kind of knife she made me use. Jean, the girl that worked for her, was almost as mean but she did occasionally give me trimmings off the iced jam slices.

By four o'clock the dry mixes for the early morning bake were rubbed in and I had taken the bowls of wet mix to stand in the cool of the concrete air-raid shelter which was attached to the back of the bakehouse. The shelter was full of black beetles and tins of fruit. I was just about ready to go home for my tea when the coalmen arrived. Just my rotten luck!.

Mrs. Roberts was, of course, as suspicious of the coalmen as she was of everybody else. She gave me a pencil and paper and told me to stand in the back lounge behind the curtains. I had to make a mark on the piece of paper each time I heard the crash of coal on the pile in the yard. I could see the hunched figures of two dwarf-looking, bent, coalmen through the lace-curtained window. Their white eyes seemed to roll about in their black faces and their teeth flashed white against their wet red gums. They were like two little black mice scuttling about the yard. One tottered from side to side slowly down the path bent almost horizontal by the load of coal whilst the other, at the coal cart, bent back his

THE DOGS OF WAR

arms like a footballer at a throw-in. He grabbed the sack by the ears and lunged forward spilling a few nuts over the shiny peak of his Co-op cap and scurried down the path on his heels at a breakneck pace. He ducked away from the sack and let it fly over his head on to the mounting heap of coal. Then he folded the sack in two and flopped it on to the growing pile near the door. The fiddle was to put an extra, empty sack over the brass studded, leather back-harness and conceal it under the full sack. In this way it was possible to get two empty sacks on to the pile of empty sacks for one bag of coal. If it was spotted it could be argued, quite plausibly, "an extra cushion for my bad back". They could hope to make two bags on a twenty-four bag delivery and that was what I was there to prevent. At the end of a delivery Mrs. Roberts would take the paper from me and count the marks I had made. She would then ask the men to re-pile the sacks counting them as they did so. One, two, three . . . . twenty-four. She demanded a recount. Again, twenty-four. An argument would ensue and Mrs. Roberts would produce the paper with my marks on it. Hot denials. Threats to make them re-bag the lot. Huddled discussion, then a grudging admission that one of them might, just accidentally, have put a back-sack on the pile in error. "But only one mind you, definitely only one! The lad must have made a mistake: easily done!" Mrs Roberts threatened to report them to their Head Office but when this had no effect she reluctantly paid up, saying: "Well, there'll be no tip this time". The two black mice shuffled off saying to each other, loudly, so that she could hear them: "This time! No tip this time! We've never had a bloody tip off the bitch all the years we've been delivering!".

I was about to go home for the second time for my tea when Mrs. Roberts took me by the arm and led me into the bakehouse in a confidential way. "Oh heck", I thought.

"When you put the rations up tonight", she said, "will you let me know whether or not Mr. Roberts cuts the points out of Mrs. Riley's ration book? Don't tell him I've asked you to tell me. If you do that for me I'll see you get a pie: there's a good boy. Will you do that for me?"

She knew I would give my shirt and inform on my own grandmother for an Ellis's meat pie. What she didn't know though

FOUR PIES AND A BOTTLE OF SAUCE

was that Eddie had already promised me two extra pies. However, my appetite for pies was insatiable and by my way of reckoning three pies were twice as good as two so "Yes" I said, eagerly.

When I got back to the shop at six-thirty Eddie was already well ahead with cutting the points from the ration books. He had emptied the big cardboard box in which they were stored on to the counter and was sorting the "A's", "B's" and "C's" into piles ready for counting and binding into bundles of one-hundred. He used to tie them with little strands of wool before putting them into envelopes addressed to The Ministry of Food.
"We've not got enough tea for all the regulars, again", he said. "Take these tea coupons and this ten-shilling note and see if you can get some in the morning from the Co-op or from Burgon's. Say they were cut out of your mother's ration book by mistake".
Eddie was working "the big tea fiddle". Tea could be bought anywhere with coupons. You didn't have to buy it where you were a registered rationed customer, though most people did. By sending me to various shops with loose tea coupons he was able to keep his regular rationed customers fully supplied despite having "lost" about ten pounds of their tea through using it for "favours" of one kind or another. He was "borrowing off Peter to pay Paul", so to speak, by turning over some of the tea coupons twice each month. It meant that his monthly supply from the wholesaler was down but so long as he could keep juggling the coupons and replenishing his stock in this way the authorities would never know and he could keep everyone, he hoped, happy. "Lu-Lu" would have had a "set of white jugs" had she discovered what he was up to.
I put the money and the coupons safely into my trouser pocket and went into the alcove in the hallway at the back of the shop where the fridge was located and began to mop it out. When I had finished the de-icing and cleaning I went upstairs to start my next job which was cleaning Eddie's Home Guard kit. He hated cleaning it himself.
The big wardrobe in the corner of the main bedroom contained Eddie's kit----boots, gaiters, haversack, water-bottle, forage cap, battledress with first world war campaign ribbons glowing

colourfully in the gloom, trousers, greatcoat, rifle, large and small pack and a tangle of webbing. I used to climb inside the wardrobe and stand among the coats sniffing the smell of mothballs and armies. I had to hump the lot downstairs and put the gear over the chairs in the hallway ready for cleaning. I could hardly manage to carry the greatcoat it was so big and heavy. Eddie had already blancoed his belt and webbing and it was my job to clean the brasses without smudging Brasso on to the dull, sage green blanco. Eddie had shown me how to polish the greatcoat buttons all at once with a brass button-stick. I had to take the hat badge out to clean it with an old toothbrush. Best of all I liked cleaning his rifle. I used to imagine I was a Russian shooting German's in the snow on the Eastern front but I couldn't hold the rifle out horizontal: it was too heavy for me. Eddie would come into the hall and fold a bit of four-by-two for me and pull it through the barrel with a string pull-through. Once, he showed me a clip of live bullets that he wasn't supposed to have. They were amazingly long, like shiny brass torpedoes. After the kit had been cleaned I had to hump it all back upstairs making sure not to put my thumb on the belt buckle. The Brasso used to make my hands black and smelly so I had to give them a good scrubbing in the bakehouse sink before putting up the rations.

Eddie had made out a list of the orders for the rationed customers registered at the shop. Three "rations for one"; eight rations for two; seven rations for three; five rations for four and two rations for five. He had cut the bacon, lifted the large slab of butter on to the counter, sniffed it, and put a half-round of soapy looking cheese on to the cheese-cutter. I got a box from the corner and put it on the floor in front of the Avery scales to stand on. Eddie cleared his throat a couple of times to summon up a little courage and shouted through to "Lu-Lu" not to come into the shop as he was working at the shelf over the door. He then quietly locked the door and put the ladders in front of it and went to the far end of the counter behind the bread stand and confidently settled himself down on an upturned crate of Cheshire Sterilised milk. Whilst I started to weigh out rations for one Eddie started on the first of the Tetly bitters.

I knew the rations by heart: rations for one was one-and-a-half

FOUR PIES AND A BOTTLE OF SAUCE

ounces of lard; two ounces of butter; a quarter of a pound of margarine; half-a-pound of sugar; one egg; a quarter of a pound of bacon; three ounces of cheese and two ounces of tea. As I weighed I reflected on what my dad, home on leave from a Rescue Service posting to bomb blitzed London, had been telling my mam this morning whilst he was having a shave in front of the cracked mirror on the wall in the kitchen. He said that rations for one had been put on a plate and shown to Winston Churchill. Churchill had said: "Well, that's not too bad. I think I could make quite a decent meal out of that". My dad said he was so out of touch he didn't realise it was rations for one for a week!

By the time I had weighed out all the rations Eddie had shifted all the booze except for one bottle and put the empties in to the basket ready to slip through the front door. As usual after his Thursday evening session his eyes were gleaming and he seemed a much more friendly person. I could hear him crunching peppermints whilst he marked the crosses in the ration books and cut the points out of the books of those customers whose turn it was for dried egg or spam. When he came to Mrs. Riley's order he put into her bag two tins of spam and a packet of dried egg and a large tin of South African peaches but he didn't cut any points out of her book. He must have noticed me watching him and seen my face go red.

"Did Mrs. Roberts say anything to you?, he said obscurely.

I shifted my weight from one foot to the other uneasily. "Er no, I mean yes. She said she would give me a pie".

Eddie looked startled and paled a little. "Oh she did, did she!", he said. "What for?"

"She said I was to tell her if Mrs. Riley's points were cut out of her ration book".

"Did she now!", he said, wiping his hands down his face and leaving his upper lip stretched glumly over his teeth so that his mouth turned down like a Mexican's moustache. "Well you'd better say they were hadn't you. I said I'd give you an extra pie on Wednesday didn't I? Well, you can have two but you mustn't say anything to Mrs. Roberts".

"No, I won't, I said.

Eddie went to the counter and tore a paper bag off the string. He

THE DOGS OF WAR

deftly flicked it open, punched his fist into it and went to the tray of pies in the window bottom and put my usual pie into the bag, the one I got for keeping quiet about the booze, and two extra ones, for the trousers and Mrs. Riley. He didn't notice me nick a bottle of H.P. sauce off the shelf whilst his back was turned and tuck it in to my trousers under my coat.

"There's half a dozen fancies there as well for your mother", he said in a somewhat slurry voice.

As he handed them to me the door from the hallway started to rattle.

"Just a minute, just a minute!" he shouted, straightening his tie and smoothing his coat down. "Let me move these steps". Quickly, he slipped round the counter, opened the front door and put the basket outside. Then, with a great deal of clattering he moved the steps away from the door to the hall and unlocked it.

"What on earth are you doing in here all this time?", Mrs. Roberts said, glancing round the shop, her nose twitching suspiciously.

Eddie steadied himself against the counter, kept his head averted and pronouncing his words very carefully said: "Putting the orders up. What did you think we were doing?!"

"Well, its time **he** went home", said Mrs. Roberts, testily. "His mother will be wondering where he's got to".

As I went out of the side door Mrs. Roberts followed me. "Well?", she said, holding her head to one side inquiringly. "**Did** Mr. Roberts cut the points out of Mrs. Riley's ration book?".

I caught a whiff of jellied meat and crispy crust and I hesitated. I started to say: "Er y . . . " but before I got it out I saw her face drop and I realised that Mrs. Roberts wasn't after a "Yes" even if it had been the truth. What she wanted was a "No". There would be no pie for a "Yes".

"Er, well, er, no he didn't, I don't think", I said.

"I thought as much!", she said with a gleam of triumph in her eye. She handed me a bag with a pie in it which she'd had in her apron pocket. "Off you go then".

I hurried round to the front of the shop to collect the empties to take to the Off Licence in the morning. As I picked up the basket and steadied it in the crook of my arm I heard her shouting from the hallway. "Eddie! Eddie!, I want a word with you!.

FOUR PIES AND A BOTTLE OF SAUCE

I turned into the street, my eyes alight with greedy anticipation. Old Eddie would be furious with me tomorrow but why should I worry. "Four pies!", I said out loud. "Four bloody pies and a bottle of sauce!.

FRIDAY NIGHT CALLERS

If our mam got to the Town's Yard on a Friday afternoon before my dad got to the bus for White City dog track then Friday night was a good night for me: if she didn't it was murder. But sometimes, even if she got there before he was paid she came home crying because he'd only given her thirty-bob instead of the usual two quid.
"Just look what he's given me! How can anyone manage on that?".
My dad was a council labourer, a big six-foot-oner in a blue bib-and brace and a cloth cap Lenin would have been proud of. He was a hard worker and he earned more than most but he never complained that he only got paid the same. And it wasn't his mates' fault, he said, if "From each according to his ability" never got translated into "To each according to his needs".
My dad spent most of his working life knocking hell out of Bury Old Road and the rest of his time knocking hell out of the Capitalist System. When he wasn't raising up sets with a crowbar or pick, or digging down to rain-damaged drains, or shifting snow or breaking his back on the bins he was raising Cain at the kerbside.
In summer he worked on the tar-sprayer and if the weather was good he would put some overtime in: you were up the road if you refused. It was hard graft and he would come home knackered each night. "If the working man could only get a week's money in hand we could have this system licked!", he was for ever telling his mates. With his way of going about it though, it was always the Bookies who were a week in hand and my mam who was licked by the system.
My mam would say: "You *are* a fool Harry! Giving it the Dogs after having worked hard for it all week!"
"Oh for Christ's sake! Don't start that up again. A packet of fags, a line on the Easy Six and two-bob on the Three Draws! I don't ask for much! I might as well be dead and out of it if I can't have a bob or two to spend how I like on a Friday night!". He would

slam the door so hard the room shook like an earthquake as he stamped upstairs to bed to sulk.

One week though, he'd been lucky. His three, seven, twenty-one system of doubling up his bet had won him a fiver at Belle Vue dogs. It was the first he had ever owned and the first I'd ever seen. I can still remember the curly, copper-plate writing promising to pay the bearer. It could hardly have got more attention had it been a personally signed photograph from Joe Stalin. Flanked by two brass candlesticks it stood for nearly a week propped in front of the clock on the mantelpiece before he gave it back to Belle Vue and deferred the Revolution indefinitely.

The following Friday was a real bad one. My dad had been so quick off the mark to regain that fiver my mam had missed him at the Town's Yard.

"We'll never have anything with him dragging us down all the time", she said, chucking her coat on a chair. "It's big-hearted Harry out there but he won't lift a finger for his own family. It's us that's going to the dogs".

My mam sat at the table staring fixedly into the teacup that was clasped in her hands, tears rolling down her drained, pale face. It was raining outside too, so I crept under the table, out of the way, with a couple of spoons, to play at boats with my marbles.

Mary Greenhalgh, our teenage milk girl, in her bother's brown overcoat and wellies, tapped on the door with a penny.

"Here, take the jug and get two pints", my mam said to me in a whisper. "Tell her I'll see her tomorrow". She was keeping the few bob she earned cleaning to pay off the grocery bill this week.

I did as I was told and took the tall white jug.

"Has your Jack got any Guinea pigs to sell?", I asked, as I followed her up the single step into the small cab of the milk-float.

"Yes, I think he has. I'll ask him and let you know".

"How much are they?"

"They're usually one-and-six but the tortoiseshell ones are dearer".

The float rocked with the added weight and the wheels moved a little: the shafts reared up on either side of the startled horse.

"Whoa! Bessie, Whoa!" Mary shouted, in a quiet voice.

THE DOGS OF WAR

The milk slopped in the churn and the chained lid clanked against the side. Mary gripped the rim of the churn-lid, twisted and removed it. The tightly fitting lid made a sucking noise as it came free of the churn. She picked up the long, copper, hook-handled milk-measure and her arm disappeared into the churn as far as her shoulder.
I stopped on the path on the way back to sniff inside the jug and took a long drink of the warm, creamy milk that smelt of cows and hay.
"You've been drinking that milk, you little devil, haven't you!? Just you wait 'till your father comes home!.
I wiped the creamy ring from round my mouth on the sleeve of my jersey and denied having touched it.
"You're a bare-face liar" my mam said. "I don't know what's going to become of you. You'll end up in the Reformatory you will!
Just at that moment Mr. Hunter, the window cleaner, who looked like a stickleback with his raw, red face and watery blue eyes, poked his head and shoulders in at the back door and saved me. He was in such a hurry to get round the estate he didn't stop to hear why he would have to wait until next week for his money.
"See you next week then, Mrs. Wild", he shouted, from halfway down the path.
The man from the Prudential attempted to get his dues from *my* money box with the aid of a kitchen knife. It was one of those Black Sambo heads with a crooked arm that fed pennies into the mouth from an upturned hand which someone had given my dad. With much poking and shaking and encouragement from my mam he managed to prize out two buttons and a penny. The penny rolled under the big mahogany dresser with the mottled mirror, which served as a sideboard, and went into permanent hiding.
"You'll have to leave it and I'll see you again Mr. Hardman", my mam said, pushing me out of the way to let him get up off the floor.
I stood by the side of the dresser looking at the new wireless set my dad had got for laying some turf. The old set, a big black beehive, had developed a loud, steady hum. The high pitched

FRIDAY NIGHT CALLERS

warble and whine when you turned the tuning knob had given way to a permanent crackle of gunfire and the set had been given to the rag and bone man in return for a couple of donkey stones. The "new" one, a worse for wear walnut box with no back, a dirty, brown, woven cloth front with a circular speaker imprint on it, had only two knobs and gave off the smell of warm dust which choked you when you put your nose near it. I could see two rows of valves and, reflected in the mirror on the dresser, the dull red glow of a wriggling wire and the bright white light of another.
"Don't stand there gawping all night", my mam said, "See who that is at the door".
It was the rent-man. He looked disappointed as he put his little black book back into the leather money-bag dangling from his shoulder and said to my mam: "It's six weeks now you know, Mrs. Wild. I'll have to report you this time".
"No, don't do that!", she said, "I'll come down to the Town Hall on Monday and pay off five shillings".
I knew what that would mean---another row. My mam would take my dad's suit---the one that my grandma had bought him to get married in---down to Broughton to that shop with the three brass balls over the door and I would have to fag along with her.
"Alright then", the rent-man said, "But I'm not supposed to let it go this long".

"If that's Michaelson at the door tell him I'm out", my mam said when the inevitable knock on the front door came. I knew it would be and so did she by the way she grabbed for her coat. Michaelson, and the doctor's man with the ginger moustache, bowler hat, and rolled umbrella, and the School Board man, were the only ones who came to the front door, all the rest went round the back.
"Orr. Why do I always have to go!", I began to say, but all the same I came out from under the table when I saw her feet moving towards the pantry for the carpet beater.
"Go to that door and tell him I'm out", she said, in a low voice from the back of her throat that I knew would bring a walloping for the least sign of defiance.
The coconut matting that covered the two square yards of cold,

THE DOGS OF WAR

concrete floor under the table where I played to keep out of my father's way had left a criss-cross pattern of pain on my knees and I rubbed at them with the palms of my hands as I grasshoppered my way to the door.

Michaelson knocked again, flicking the loose hoop of metal on the door-knocker against the letter-box to make a clattering rat-a-tat-tat echo down the empty hallway. He always made an effort to get round to our house early on a Friday evening, though not strictly for orthodox reasons.

As I half-opened the door from the kitchen to the hallway the letter-box lid quietly closed on a pair of plain, chocolate brown eyes. Michaelson had seen my mam through the gap, shrugging her shabby black coat on, ready to slip out through the back door.

"My mam said she's out", I said, but he had already pushed past and was breezing into the kitchen with a falsely cheerful: "Hello Mrs. Wild".

"Oh it's you is it? You nearly missed me. I was just on my way out. I'll have to leave it 'till next week", she said, as she steered Michaelson into the front room.

"Just you wait! I know you, you did that on purpose", she said through her teeth.

I pressed myself against the sideboard, shielding my ear with my elbow.

Michaelson emerged from the front room, replaced his black homburg hat and buttoned his loose gabardine. He took out a white linen handkerchief, draped it round his large, hooked nose and blew into it.

"All right then Mrs. Wild. What size does he take?", he said.

I could see the pores on his oily, olive skin as he bent down to draw a line round my shoe on the newspaper my mother had placed under my foot. He had thin, purple lips and a tongue like a Chow and his breath stank of fish. I held my head to one side.

"Stop wriggling about!" my mam said.

As Michaelson closed the door behind him I got a winger round the ear.

"Now look what you've done! I've had to get you a pair of shoes because I couldn't pay anything off that bill. How I'll ever pay for

FRIDAY NIGHT CALLERS

them God only knows!"
"Did the gas-man come this morning?", she asked, hopefully.
"Oh yes. I forgot to tell you, there's eight-pence behind the wireless", I said.
"Is that all? It's usually about one and threepence. Are you sure that's all he left? Come here and look me in the face!"
The gas-man had been that morning and emptied the meter that was in the cupboard next to the sink. It smelt of damp gas and donkey stones. I watched him pull out the long, tin box full of pennies and empty it on to the table. He spread the pennies with the palm of his hand and flicked them, one at a time, with the second finger of his right hand, off the edge of the table into the cup of his left hand. Piles of twelve accumulated in a row on the table. The last pile had only ten in it.
"Here, give these to your mother when she comes home", he said.
"Look me in the face", she said again. "If you're telling me lies I'll give you what for. Where's the slip?"
"It blew off the mantelpiece into the fire", I said, uneasily.
"I'll give you such a tanning if you're not telling me the truth", she said, raising her arm.
I ducked out of the way and scampered back under the table.
"Come out from under that table", she screamed.
"No. I'll come out if you don't hit me", I shouted back, defiantly.
I waited a few seconds then said, "I want my tea".
"You get no tea until you come from under that table and say you're sorry!"

When I eventually came out she thrust the eight-pence at me so violently I ran right round the table in fright.
My mam never had enough money but she tried her best to make ends meet. Unfortunately she didn't have much idea how to make the money last nor how to cook cheap meals. My grandma said she was a bad manager. She was always telling my mam to buy some bones from the butchers and make some soup or to get some mince and a few carrots and make Cornish pasties like she'd shown her. My mam tried her best but it was never good enough for my grandma. She was very good at cooking chips and chops and egg and bacon but when she had some money she preferred

to send me down to Roberts's for a tin of fruit or an Ellis's meat pie.

She said: "Run down to Lawson's and get three of chips and a fish with salt and vinegar on and take our Arthur with you. You can eat them on the way home, the pair of you".
When we got back home Miss Hicks, the clothing club lady, was sitting at the table with my mam.
"I suppose *you* want a cup of tea as well do you?", my mam said to me, reaching for the battered, aluminium teapot.
"Get yourself a cup from the sink".
The pots were piled in the green enamelled bowl in the sink ready for the washing-up that never got done. I chose the least chipped cup, swished a drop of water round the inside with my finger and swilled it under the tap. The milk-jug stood on the bare table-top, a blue bag of sugar by its side. I heaped in three teaspoonfuls.
"You'll get worms putting all that sugar in", said Miss Hicks.
"They're all sweet toothed, my lot", my mam said. "They take after Harry".
I finished my cup of tea and lay down on the flattened peg-rug my grandma had made out of a sack and some old coloured-clothes that she had cut into strips. I stared into the fire and let my eyes go glassy.
It was dark and cosy near the fire. The washing hung low from the six blackened bamboo poles that spanned the ceiling. I could catch the drips in my mouth. In the recess to one side stood the big, iron-framed mangle with the loose handle and the large three-spoked wheel with the creaking cogs for turning the badly worn wooden rollers. My mam would sometimes let me feed the washing through---long snakes of sheet and tight twists of shirt---but my dad used to shout at her and say:
"You'll have his fingers through there one of these days. You won't be told". Over the table an unshaded one-hundred watt bulb hung from a loose fitting directly out of the lath-and-plaster ceiling. The bulb was flecked with fly stains and the ceiling round was burnt brown.
I liked looking into the fire. You could see the knobbly faces of hob-goblins and sometimes volcanoes of tar bubbled out from the

FRIDAY NIGHT CALLERS

mountains of black rock or jets of vapour gasped and hissed like steam-engines as the blue-green gas-pockets squealed and whistled. I used to prod them with the end of the poker and they would crumble, disappointingly to dust.

My mam and Miss Hicks were well away: three cups of tea and there was no stopping them. I heard that Johnny Grocock had left his Misses---"her that used to be Lily Heys"---and gone to lodge with Nellie Greathead. "Her husband works on the Railway, a little fellow with a long head, you'd know him if I pointed him out to you". Mrs. Tickle was expecting another and poor Mrs. Sinclair had died. "How that woman suffered!" Not before time---or rather just before time---Betty Redford, from down the Grange, was getting married. "You should see the size of that girl! It's a disgrace! It was a litany repeated each week with different names but with the same "Eees!, Ahs!, Ohs! and Ha! Ha! Ha! Well would you believe it!" responses that inevitably ended with: "Do you mind if I pop upstairs before I go Mrs. Wild?", from Miss Hicks.

I felt embarrassed about Miss Hicks using our lavatory. There was never any paper and I always had to shout down for some.

I used to think Miss Hicks knew the Queen because she had the same kind of perm and earrings and a pearl necklace adorning her expansive chest but my mam said she was a business lady during the day and collected clothing club money for Mr. Jacobs to help pay the college fees for her son who was very clever and going to be an accountant.

When she reappeared the shine had left Miss Hick's nose and on her mouth had alighted a bright red butterfly.

You don't mind if I leave it until next week do you Miss Hicks?, my mam said as Miss Hicks rummaged about in her capacious bag for her book.

"Don't worry Mrs. Wild, if it's a bad week. I'll book you down for half-a-crown anyway and book down just half-a crown for someone who gives me five shillings. I can put it right in my book next week, but don't forget to remind me." And with that she left.

My mam thought Miss Hicks was "a real good sort", "a real lady", "not a bit stuck up". She always had a cup of tea and a chat.

THE DOGS OF WAR

"I'll take you to Mr. Jacob's warehouse in Cheetham Hill and get you a blue gabardine to go with your shoes when I get the bill down a bit", my mam said to me. "Our Arthur can have your old one: his is halfway up his back already.

My dad had lost. You could tell by the way he wiped his feet, deliberately and for too long, on the mat inside the kitchen door and his rueful look and the embarrassed way he lowered his eyes when my mam said, hedging her own bets: "Well? How've you gone on?"
"How d'yer think I've gone on!", he said.
My mam's face went as white as the washing on the rack.
I quickly made for under the table, again, pulling our Arthur with me.
"Now don't start", he said, throwing a crumpled maroon note on to the table. "There's ten bob there and if the weather's fine tomorrow I'll get some gardening in. I've a couple that want doing down Sedgely Park".
My mam was not listening though. The storm of tears and anger she'd been brewing all evening bubbled and burst and drowned out the sound.
"Just you wait", she growled, through her clenched teeth. "I'll show you! I'll tell that lot down there at the Yard what you're really like! You and your principles, you make me sick! How can you look me in the face and give me ten shillings to feed five of us on!"
She picked up the note and flung it at him.
"What kind of a wage is that?!", she screamed.
Rapidly the invective built up, the language becoming increasingly strong as the exchange got more and more heated and violent. "Greedy devil" gave way to "selfish sod" and "selfish sod" to "filthy skunk". "Filthy skunk" to "bloody bitch" and "bloody bitch" to "lousy bugger". "Bugger" to cup, cup to saucer, saucers to frying pan. Fists were flailing and lips were spitting curses as round and round the large, gateleg table of the little room they chased each other, frothing with fury. Chairs fell over and a whole possession of pots went flying to the floor as the table-cloth got dragged into the uproar. Next door were knocking

on the wall with a shoe. The racket ended abruptly with a backhanded black eye for my mam.

"Don't think you can come near me tonight! my mam screamed at the top of her voice to the quivering door as my dad escaped into the hall.

"You're mad!", he shouted. "Mad! Mad!, Bloody mad!", all the way up the stairs.

"You'll come home one of these days and find me gone!", she shouted back.

As she rooted us out from under the table she added, more quietly: "If it wasn't for you two and our Ernie I'd have been gone long ago. Get up stairs to bed the pair of you. You can have a wash in the morning. And if I hear one squeak out of you I'll be up there and---". We needed no second telling.

It was still raining in the morning. My mam went out early to light fires at the houses where she cleaned. It was Yom Kippur, or Yummie Kipper as our Ernie called it. He was always messing about with words was our Ern. My dad stayed in bed so we had to be quiet.

I peeped round the bedroom door and saw him stretched out, the white sheet pulled up over his face and tucked tight under the back of his head: his feet overhung the bottom of the bed. A gloomy half-light filtered through the many holes in the stretch of dark, red curtain that hung from the garden cane my mam had fixed up when the wire broke. We'd been playing at bouncing on the bed, the three of us. Our Ernie, the daft nit, had grabbed the curtain to save himself when he had unexpectedly bounced off. He blamed it on me---and after I had tried to help him get out of it by saying it was our Arthur. So my mam leathered the three of us. The air in the room was stale and I could smell my dad's socks. The chamber pot was only just under the bed. It was nearly half-full of liquid the colour of strong, brown tea. I started to wretch when I looked at it, as if my stomach was trying to leap out of my mouth. My dad snored under the sheet and rolled over.

The rain was incessant that morning and so was the row we made until at last, unable to lie in bed any longer, my dad rumbled down the stairs from above and came crashing into the kitchen.

THE DOGS OF WAR

"How many more times do I have to tell you!" he roared, feigning blows this way and that with the back of his hand as we scattered like rabbits. He swept me up in his grip and plonked me hard down on the draining board next to our Arthur and, grabbing our Ernie by the shoulders bounced him up to the ceiling like a pile driver before thrashing him down to the floor in a crying, crumpled heap.

It was always our Ernie who got it: a thin, contentious, bone of a boy with an excess of wits and a wilful way. Our Ernie was four years older than me and the butt of all my father's frustrations. He was the focus of endless rows throughout the tortured length of a miserable childhood. Always breaking his glasses, spending his dinner money on toffees, staying in the cinema to see the picture a second time round, coming home late, and running away from home to stay at my grandma's. His head was always in a book: he just didn't match up to what my dad believed a boy should be.

"Leave him alone Harry, you'll kill him!" my mother would scream, throwing herself between them. They were still at it when our Ernie was twenty-five years old. My dad couldn't stand him taking so long in the bathroom or singing opera in Italian at the top of his voice or fiddling with wireless for foreign language programmes.

My dad stood in the kitchen, hands thrust deep in his overall pockets, looking out through the cracked pane of the sash window (the one our Ernie had broken) at the steady rain which was drenching the small, square back garden. The side wall of the house end-on, with its patchwork of red and brown, common clay bricks, would have obliterated the sunlight had there been any. Beyond the palings Mr. Proudfoot came out for a shovel-full of coal, got drenched, and quickly went in again.

"He's got a damned good job at the Asylum has old Proudfoot. Must be on at least a fiver a week and here's me grafting away all week and not two halfpennies to rub together!", my dad said, before going into the front room to grub in the grate for a dimp.

The front room had a thin threadbare carpet square and a short-legged straight-backed armchair with a sagging seat and the springs hanging out through the bottom. My grandmother's couch

FRIDAY NIGHT CALLERS

was against the wall. I heard my father talking to himself, rehearsing his political arguments. He was quietly shouting the odds about someone called Sir Bernard Docker and what ought to be done to the likes of Tallulah Bankhead: strutting backwards and forwards he was adjusting his face in the oval mirror above the fireplace.

On Sunday the weather cleared and my dad went gardening. I was glad because when he came home he put five bob on the mantelpiece for my mam to pay some off the rent arrears. Good! I thought, I'll be able to play out on Monday instead of having to go to Broughton with my mam and my dad's suit. My mam went round to see her friend, Flo Tate, and came back with five Woodbines for my dad and they started talking to each other again.
By the time Friday tea-time came round again I'd managed to gather four-pence together by taking back jam jars and running a few errands for Mrs. France, next door. There was that penny under the sideboard but it still wouldn't be enough for a guinea pig.

I was sitting on the floor by the fire wondering whether I dare ask my mam to ask Mary Greenhalgh to ask their Jack to let me pay for a guinea pig at a penny a week when there was a knock at the front door.
"Oh my God!", my mam said. "That will be Michaelson already and I've not been down for Harry's money. He will have brought your shoes. Go and tell him I'm out and he can call back later.
At the door stood a small man in a smart suit and a sharp, unfamiliar face, currant brown eyes and a long, narrow, bald head with a bulge at the front.
"Tell your mother it's Mr. Jacobs", he said.
My mam had been listening at the hall door.
"Come in Mr. Jacobs", she said. "Is Miss Hicks ill or something?"
I stood with my ear to the front room door and listened to what was going on. Miss Hicks was no longer working for Mr. Jacobs, she'd been sacked. He had discovered that she had been fiddling her books by entering less than people had paid and then switching and swapping amounts of money about to avoid being

found out. The police had been called in and she had admitted it. She said Mr. Jacobs didn't pay her enough and she had borrowed the money until she was straight to help keep her son at college. Neither he nor she knew exactly who had paid what, Mr. Jacobs said. "She's got the books in a hopeless muddle!"
I knew my mam owed about seven pounds because she had told my dad it was only four and there had been a row about it. Anyway, she told Mr. Jacobs that she had nearly paid up for what she'd had and that as a matter of fact she had been paying off a bit extra because she wanted to get one of the boys a gabardine Mack.
"It must be around, er, let me think, er, about ten shillings I think it is that I owe", I heard her say.
I thought: "I bet she didn't look Mr. Jacobs in the eye when she said that. I suppose my mam's a bit too old though to go to the Reformatory".
Mr. Jacobs said: "We'll leave matters this week then Mrs. Wild. I'll call with a new book next week. You can bring him down to the warehouse in Cheetham Hill next Saturday morning".
My mother said "All right, a week on Saturday will be fine".
"Right you are then, Mrs. Wild. Good night. See you next Saturday" he said, as she saw him out.

My dad came home in a hurry and in a bad temper. I could tell by the way the heels of his boots rang on the path and the pace of his walk.
"Where the Hell did you get to for God's sake!?" he said, as he gave my mam two new looking pound notes. "I'll miss the first race if I'm not quick!"
He shifted the pots roughly on to the draining board and had a hurried wash, splashing the water about like a budgie and making a noise with his throat before spitting in to the sink.
"Oh Harry! Do you have to make that noise", my mam said.
My dad's overalls fell in a heap on the floor. He pulled on some clean ones hopping round the kitchen on one foot in his hurry to be off. The cup of tea my mam made him was too hot to drink and half of it went down the sink when he held it under the cold water tap.

FRIDAY NIGHT CALLERS

Michaelson came late. My mam thought he wasn't coming at all. Under his arm he had an oblong parcel tied up with string. He undid it on the table and tore off the thin, crackling brown paper to reveal a box with a Timpson's label on the end.
"Oh good!", I said, "Can I have the box to make a fort?"
"You can if they fit you", Michaelson said.
They were a bit slack and the left one hurt the side of my foot but I said they felt all right. I was made to walk, slipping this way and that, across the carpet in the front room.
"It's better to have them a little bit on the big side", Michaelson said as he deducted five shillings from the card and put his initials in the end column. "They'll give him room to grow".
I asked my mam could I keep them on.
"No! You can save them for Sundays", she said.
The other Friday night callers came and went, lucky or unlucky according to my mam's assessment of how much money she had or would have, and how much she would have to pay off the bills at the butchers, grocers, greengrocers, etc., to keep the credit going for another week.
Mary, the milk girl was late. I sat on the rug by the fire wondering if Joe Smithy, the greengrocer, would give me a wooden box to keep a guinea pig in and where I could get some wire-netting from. My mam was sitting at the table, as usual both hands clasped round her cup of tea, waiting for my dad to come home from the dogs. She was in one of her trances.
"Mam", I said. "Will Miss Hicks go to prison?"..
My mam slowly came back to life.
"Were you listening at that door, you little monkey!"
She paused for a second and then said: "Don't you dare say anything about that to your father!"
"No", I said, "I won't. . . if you'll give me one-and-a-penny for a guinea pig".
There was a knock at the door with a penny.

DIGGING FOR GOLD

I was running with my arms outstretched behind me, fanning the tail of my coat, pretending to be a bird. I turned the corner of the path and ran slap-bang into the coal-house door. The large black lump that sprang up on my forehead got a smear of butter but little in the way of sympathy, and fuelled yet another row between my mam and dad.

My mam had been asking my dad to put some boards across the front of the coal-house for weeks but he never got round to it and if five bags were delivered two of them spilled onto the path and the door wouldn't shut.

"Aw mam!", I said after I had stopped yelling. "The coal's been and I wanted to ask Mr. Hammersley had he any birds to sell. I ran all the way home from school!"

"You're not having a bloody bird so be told! It's bad enough having to look after you three, never mind blessed budgies", my mam said.

I had been pestering for a bird all week. In fact I was so desperate to have one I had tried to trap a starling, the day before, with the help of our Ernie. We had succeeded only in killing a sparrow. My mam would have murdered our Ernie if she'd known. We had rigged up a trap. Our Ernie nailed a big, loose, square of cloth my dad used for decorating to the frame of an old chair seat, tied a long length of string to a piece of firewood, and propped it under the wooden frame. Then scattered breadcrumbs underneath and hid me behind the kitchen door whilst he stood on a chair and looked out of the kitchen window to see if a bird had gone underneath.

At first the birds just took the bread from round about and flew up to Proudfoot's gutter with it but eventually a sparrow ventured underneath. Our Ernie bared his green-looking teeth and mouthed "Now!" Unfortunately the frame came down chop across the sparrow's neck and killed it. When I picked it up it was soft and still warm in my hand but its head was limp and lolled over my

DIGGING FOR GOLD

finger.

"You daft nit!", I said, "Why did you tell me to pull the string before it was underneath?"

"Don't call me a daft nit! It was you. You weren't quick enough!", he said, squinting at me through the shattered glass of his round tin-rimmed specs. "It was on its way out!"

He took the limp bird from me.

"We'll have to bury it before my mam sees it", I said. "No, we'll give it to Mrs. France's moggy". And before I could say "Don't!" he had thrown the dead bird over the fence in front of next door's lucky black cat.

On Friday night before Mr. Hammersley came for his money I tried a different tack with my mam. "Did you have a bird when you were a little girl?", I asked. After some pestering she admitted that she used to have a budgie when she was a child.

"What colour was it?", I asked.

"It looked just like a pale blue hyacinth, she said.

"Well why can't I have one then?", I said.

"Because you won't look after it. It was me that had to clean out that poor rabbit the pair of you let starve to death. Anyway you haven't got a cage so you can't have a budgie!"

"I thought you said Mrs Matz had one in her garage", I said, sulkily.

"Yes, but she's not going to give it you for nothing is she?", my mam countered.

There was a solid knock at the back door.

"Come in!", my mam shouted without getting up from the table. Mr. Hammersley appeared in his shiny, peaked coal-man's cap, his face black and his back hunched under the weight of a leather harness. A large pouch, fastened by a worn brass stud, hung from his belt.

That a grown-up could have such a black face fascinated me, and I stared at it intently, but what was more striking was his wet, red mouth and white, exaggerated eyes. I watched a thick finger and thumb feed a few pennies change out of a black paw into the cup of my mam's hand.

"How much does a budgie cost?", I asked, as he turned to leave.

"Oh! a lot of money", he said.

THE DOGS OF WAR

"Sixpence?".
"Oh! much more than that. One-and-six at least, for a young one", he said.
"See! I told you!", I said, turning to my mam. "They *are* only one-and-six.
"Well you're still not having one", she said.
"Aw, go on mam. It's my birthday on Sunday and you said ages ago I could have one for my birthday".

I had been pestering my mam to let me have a bird ever since Jeffrey Reynolds had been given one for Christmas, and I knew that if I didn't get one for my birthday there was no hope of ever getting one. "I'll get three-pence off Auntie Polly if she comes on Wednesday and my grandma is bound to give me sixpence for my birthday", I said.
I continued to pester long after Mr. Hammersley had gone until finally she got angry and gave me a slap across the ear, saying: "Now I've had enough of you for one night".
I went into the corner by the door to sulk. After a while I turned my head and said, "I know, if I ask my dad to let me go gardening with him tomorrow instead of our Ernie, he might give me a shilling. If I get a shilling towards it can I have one?"
Quite unexpectedly she relented.
"Oh! all right, all right, I'm sick of your mithering, but I don't know where the money's coming from! You'll have to think of something"
I was off like a whippet before she changed her mind. Instead of taking the path I cut across my dad's garden. I'd be in for a hiding if he recognised my footprints. I squeezed through the gap in the fence where a wooden railing was missing and ran through the rain as fast as my pumps would carry me up the hill to Mr. Hammersley's house.
The Hammersley's lived in the second block of houses up the Grange, the ones with green gates. It was easy for me to find because most of the gates were missing but Mr. Hammersley being a coal-man, they still had theirs.
I'd heard old Proudfoot telling my dad Mr. Hammersley had been fined a fiver for delivering short weight to the shops on the main

road. My mam said they had bugs and the house needed stoving. When I got my breath back I made my way down the gloomy entry. I heard the echo of my feet as I flip-flopped out of the darkness and knocked on the back door.

"Don't come in yet!", a voice shouted. "We've got the birds out!"

Ronald Hammersley, a white-faced youth with livid, red acne opened the door about a foot and I squeezed in sideways. Having disentangled myself from the net curtains that were hanging loosely from the door lintel I stood apprehensively in the kitchen on the mat by the door, back against the wall.

The Hammersley's kitchen was the same cramped size and layout as the one we lived in, with the same familiar black-leaded fireplace, and a sink and a draining board under the sash window and a gas stove by the side of it but the room was strikingly different. Along the wall where our sideboard stood was a battered settee and just above it, making it impossible for all but the smallest person to sit upright, and stretching the length of the wall from the hall door to the built-in cupboard next to the fireplace, was a triple deck of shelves on which stood row upon row of small home-made birdcages, each with a small, square, sprung door. Each cage contained a solitary bird. The top shelf was double and in some places triple-stacked so that some of the cages were almost touching the ceiling. Most of the birds were canaries; yellow or yellow with brown and black wing markings. Random splashes of colour located an occasional blue, green or white budgerigar standing impressively on its perch like a high-court judge. I stood gaping at them in amazement then tried to follow the flight of three loose budgies round and round the room. The mantelpiece was full of small, silver cups and other trophies; effigies of silver birds standing on round, black plinths. Two inscribed silver trays were propped behind the trophies and in the centre was a large silver cup with ornately curved handles. A photograph of Mr. Hammersly holding a birdcage in one hand and the large cup in the other was leaning against the centrepiece.

A much larger wooden cage was fixed to the wall above the fireplace and supported by two iron brackets. The crowd of birds it housed was a mixture of varieties and colours. Wild birds---mainly greenfinches and chaffinches and the odd linnet. They were constantly on the move, fluttering and hopping from perch to perch on the tree branch that was fitted from corner to corner of the cage or clinging to the bars or scuffing about for seeds in the litter layer on the floor.

A large black box with a leather carrying strap attached stood in the corner of the room near the sink and above it on a bracket jutting out from the wall was a brilliantly plumed blue and yellow parrot with a chain dangling from its scaly leg. The big bird kept up a constant throaty grumble as it wriggled the scaly living worms of its four-clawed feet sideways along its perch or looped the loop under its bar and splashed water from its pot as it did so. Occasionally it would utter a loud "Hello!" and "Who's a pretty boy then?"

Mr. Hammersley was sitting at the table eating his tea, the *Evening Chronicle* propped against a square, tea caddy displaying a picture of the king and queen. I could hardly recognise him with his face washed. A plain front-stud hung from his collarless flannel shirt and his dirty grey waistcoat was unbuttoned. His shirt sleeves were tightly rolled almost to his shoulders and his large blue-veined biceps bulged out from under them. I noticed that one of his hairy forearms bore a faintly green and red snake wound round a staff and that the other arm had on it a blue anchor with the name of a ship underneath. The back of his chair held the sleeveless leather jacket with the shiny, brass studs, that he had been wearing when he called at our house for the coal money. His raised fork held a small boiled potato which he offered to the budgie perched on his shoulder. As the budgie went to peck it he laughed and popped the potato quickly into his already over-full mouth.

"Come round here and let me have a look at you", he said through a mouthful of food.

I took a couple of tentative steps towards him. "My mam said I can have a bird and will you tell me how to look after it".

The smell of the stew Mr. Hammersley was eating mingled with the dusty smell of birdseed and the sweet sickly smell of bird-droppings and bugs that pervaded the room was too much for my young nostrils. The sneeze that I unsuccessfully attempted to stifle in the crook or my arm frightened the birds and there was a startled fluttering, a ringing of claws against cage bars, and a noisy beating of wings. The commotion sent a shower of seeds and husks down into the room. The dust made me sneeze again but I was able to trap it this time on the sleeve of my jersey.

"Well that's one thing you mustn't do. You mustn't make a sudden noise or you'll frighten them", he said.

Mrs. Hammersley was a thick-set little woman in a long, brown coat tied round the middle with hairy, white string and clad in coarse, brown, Lisle stockings and soft carpet slippers with heels overhanging the downtrodden backs. She tried to rise from the settee but fell back at the first attempt. She was wearing a navy-blue beret pulled down over her forehead to just above her eyebrows and half covering her ears. A fringe of mousey grey hair poked out at the sides of the beret and at the back a couple of curlers showed. A flicker of alarm crossed her bleak face at the dust and commotion and her wide-set bulging eyes, normally vacant of expression, came to life a little. She attempted once more to rise from the scuffed, leather-covered settee, saying as she did so, "What kind of a bird did your mother say you could have?"

The casters were missing from one side of the settee and I saw it wobble as she rose. Lumpy springs poked through in places and where she had been sitting there was a long, right-angle rip in the dusty, brown fabric.

"It was a budgie wasn't it?", she said.

I looked up at the cages and saw a pale blue budgie just like a hyacinth. But Jeffrey Reynolds' budgie was blue and I didn't want mine to be the same as his.

"No. My mam said I'd be better with a canary or something like that".

The brightly coloured budgies were inquisitively cocking their heads and chunnering at being disturbed, and the canaries were hopping from perch to perch. My eye was drawn to a brilliant bird in the cage over the mantelpiece that was making a pleasant liquid twittering from the topmost twig of the fitted branch. It had a vivid red, white, and black head, and a fawn front dusted here and there, brown and green. Its wings were black with a yellow flash across them. I noticed its tail had a line of white dots down it.

"I think my mam would like me to have that one", I said pointing to the bird.
"Which? That green one?, said Mrs. Hammersley.
"No. The one with red on its head", I said.
"Oh! you mean the Goldfinch!"
"That one with yellow on its wing", I said.
"Have you got a cage for it?", asked Mr. Hammersley.
"No", I said, "But a lady my mam does cleaning for is going to give her one on Monday".
"It's one-and-sixpence, that one, you know", said Mr. Hammersley. "Has your mother given you that much?"
"No", I said, "I haven't got any money with me. I've got to wait until my birthday, on Sunday, but I thought I'd come and make sure they weren't all sold".

I sat down to my tea later that evening wondering how I could get my dad to let me go gardening with him. I must ask him before he went out and that wouldn't be easy because my dad usually said he had "to see a man about a dog" on a Friday night and if he came home from work first he was always in a rush.
I heard the urgency in the heavy bootsteps on the path and my stomach sank because I knew he'd be going out straight away.
He had his coat off before he'd got through the door.
"Where's my tea then? Come on, get cracking, I'm going to miss the first race if I don't catch that bus", he said, as he disappeared upstairs to the lavatory.
"He can't get rid of it quick enough can he?" I heard my mam say, half to herself, as she put my dad's tea on the table. "Can't get rid of it quick enough!"
When he came down my dad was wearing his other coat over his overall and his face was cleaner. He pulled out an opened pay packet from the pocket of the bib in his overall and threw it onto the table. "There you are", he said.
My mam tipped two pound notes and a few coins onto the tablecloth. Her face paled. "You'll have to give me more than this Harry!", she said.
"Now don't start. You've got a bloody sight more than I've got", he said.

DIGGING FOR GOLD

"Yes, but there's our Ern's glasses to be paid for", she countered. "And I'm three weeks behind with the milk. For god's sake don't go and give it the Dogs again".

My dad raised his eyes to the ceiling and said, "Come on give us my bloody tea and let me get to hell out of it. I work bloody hard for my money and I'll spend it how I bloody well like!"

The row gathered momentum. Our Ernie's glasses, me running into the coal-house door, the milk bill, the rent, the groceries, my dad's smoking and tipping his ash all over the floor, throwing his money away on the 'pools, him never letting her see his wages slip. The list was endless and continued until my dad slammed the door behind him. I didn't get a chance to say anything about going gardening.

When his footsteps had disappeared a silence fell on the house.

"If it wasn't for you kids", my mam said, "I'd sling my hook. I would. I'd sling my bloody hook!"

I heard my dad come back early so I knew he had lost. My mam was out so I went downstairs in my pyjamas for a drink of water. My dad was sitting in his chair by the ash-grey fire with his hands clasped behind his head and his fingers dovetailed together staring at the mantelpiece. I stood on tiptoe and reached over the sink to turn the tap on. Over my shoulder I said in a quiet voice, "Are you going gardening tomorrow?"

"Aye, I suppose I'll have to ", he said, wearily.

"Can I go with you instead of our Ernie?"

"No, you're too young. It's better if that fool goes with me".

"Aw, go on dad", I said, "I want to get some money to buy a bird with. Our Ernie hasn't shovelled the coal in properly and he's broken his glasses again!"

"No", he said, you can come when you're a bit older.

It looked as if it was going to be more difficult than I had thought. As it turned out our Ernie was going with my grandma and auntie Pollie to see my dad's cousin at Bacup so my dad said I could go if it looked like being a fine day.

As luck would have it the weather was sunny on Saturday and my dad was up and out early. He had backed his barrow from under the corrugated iron lean-to and loaded it up with his tools. The barrow stood waiting for us, crouched on the path like a feeding insect, the long two pointed handles of the mower feeling the fresh morning air. My dad had folded a couple of sacks and flopped them on top of the blades of the mower for me to sit on. My mam had made bacon butties for us to eat before we went. Thick chunks of doughy shop bread and fatty fried bacon and an extra fried bread for me.

My dad stood with a tin mug of strong, sweet, milkless tea in his hand in front of the mirror over the mantelpiece watching himself eat. He took big bites from his butty and a great gulp of scalding tea and slopped it mushily round the inside of his mouth.

"Do you have to make that noise, Harry", my mam said, irritably.

"Come on m'laddo", he said, "we'd best be off".

He knotted his once white, silk scarf round his collarless neck, pulled on his peaked, cloth cap and with me following close behind stepped outside into the sunshine.

"Looks too bright to last", he said, glancing up at a flawless sky.

My mam followed us to the door.

"Harry!", she said. "Harry! I'll have to pay five bob off the groceries you know, and there's that one's glasses that need mending". Our Ernie was always 'that one' to my mam and dad when he wasn't there. "So don't think you're going out again tonight!"

"Oh! for god's sake don't start that up again", my dad said.

"Send him to Whittakers for ten Woodbines. I'll give you the money when I get back".

Two rough hands gripped me under the armpits and swung me on to my perch on the barrow, facing him.

"If I work hard dad, will you give me a shilling to buy a bird with for my birthday", I said.

"Now sit still and hold tight", was all he said in reply.

I watched the muscles harden at the base of his big thumbs and the sinews of his neck stretch taut as he gripped the worn wooden shaft handles. The wheelbarrow rumbled down the hollow flagged path and bumped down the curb by the gate onto the road. I curled my lips inwards round my teeth and squeezed them tight to stop them tingling as the squealing wheel ground against the

DIGGING FOR GOLD

gritty chippings.

It was two miles or more to Sedgley Park where the gardens were and my dad kept to the path where he could. By the time we reached the main road the regular click of the wheel over the flags, like a train, was lulling me to sleep. I could see the inside of the Hammersley's house as I dozed. Blue, green, and yellow birds appeared and disappeared and a miniature goldfinch imprinted itself on the back of my eyelid but the smooth-gliding train turned into a jolting, bone-rattling barrow again as it juddered over the sets of Bury Old Road and startled the birds away.

Most of the gardens my dad did belonged to houses of fairly rich businessmen. They were mainly the Jewish people my mam did cleaning for and we made our way in that direction. My dad kept to the road with his barrow to avoid people on the path. It was Saturday and there were many shoppers about in the non-Jewish quarter of Heaton Park. The crowd thinned but welled again as we neared the Jewish Synagogue. We overtook increasing numbers of men in suits and blue Melton overcoats and Homburg hats and small groups of boys with brightly coloured skull-caps miraculously clinging to the backs of their heads. Some of the men were carrying prayer-books and some were wearing embroidered silk scarves draped round their necks. The men walked together in conversation or slowly alone.

As we turned off Singleton Road into a tree-lined street my dad stopped, lowered the barrow to the ground. "By god!, it's warm!", he said.

My dad didn't have many gardens to do and most of the people he worked for didn't want them done regularly. They would let it get in a mess and my dad would have to work hard putting it right again and they didn't want to pay when he'd done it.

"Eight bob!?", they would say, "You've only been here four hours!"

My dad would argue but they said the rate was one-and sixpence and hour and they would seldom pay more.

"I'd like to see you do a garden in that state in four bloody hours!", he would say, angrily.

We stopped at one of the regulars and I was able to stretch my legs and rub some blood back into my numbed bottom.

THE DOGS OF WAR

My dad had a knack for gardening. "Watch me", he would say, "and you'll never be short of a bob or two". The blades of his mower were well set and sharp and would purr like a cat as they flicked the clippings into the grass-box for me to run and empty whilst he trimmed the edges with the long handled shears. He would square-up old lawns with stakes and string and rock his half-moon deftly back and forth along the line. If the string got snagged he would twang it with his finger and thumb. Where he'd hoed the borders looked as though the soil had been sieved.

My dad didn't knock to see if his regulars wanted their gardens doing, he just made a start. I stood watching him digging and picked up the weeds and stones he threw onto the lawn. I had a matchbox in my pocket with cotton-wool in it in case he turned up a chrysalis but I didn't see one. There were plenty of worms though. I watched one tie itself in a painful knot when my dad sliced it in two. It had a thick white band round it just beyond the cut and a mixture of liquid soil and blood oozed out from the severed ends.

His spade moved on down the border and I followed picking up weeds and stones, dropping them into the grass-box. A flicker of something red caught the corner of my eye.

"Dad!", I shouted, "There's a Goldfinch!".

"No, it's a Robin", he said hardly bothering to look up.

The Robin stood on the fence nearby with the end of the severed worm dangling from its sharp little beak, eyeing me sideways with its round brown eye.

"Aw!", I said, "I thought it was a Goldfinch!"

By lunch-time we had tidied up a couple of gardens but neither of the occupants were in and we didn't even have the chance of a cup of tea. My dad had been hoping they would be back before we left to do Mrs. Matz's garden, where my mam worked, so he could collect his two half-crowns, but they didn't appear.

"Blast it!", he said, "I'll have to come back".

My dad knew Mrs. Matz and when we got there he knocked on the door and asked her to make us a brew. I had to wait on the back door-step, holding the blue enamel billycan, until the kettle boiled. There was a heap of tea and sugar loose in the bottom and I wondered if I could swing the can full circle without it falling

out but she asked me to give it to her before I had a chance to try it. When she handed me back the billy-can she gave me a glass of fizzy lemonade. I drank it too quickly and the gas came down my nose and made my eyes water.
"Thank you very much", I said.
"Ask your father does he want some milk"
My dad didn't but when I returned she handed me a small, white porcelain plate with a wavy edge on which was a cucumber sandwich made from thin sliced bread and cut diagonally into four.
"I thought your father might be hungry", she said, "so I've made him a sandwich". She gave me a biscuit.
The plate looked even more delicate in my dad's big, hard-fingered hand and I heard him tut when he peeled the bread back and saw what was inside.
"Here", he said, "You have this".
I took a bite from one of the sandwiches but I didn't like cucumber so when my dad wasn't looking I threw it over the hedge and just ate the bread and butter.
The ground was hard to dig and overgrown and I heard my dad swearing at the weeds as I was gathering up the hedge clippings and stuffing them into a sack. The sky was becoming overcast and my dad kept glancing up at it as he worked saying, "I hope that blessed rain holds off 'till we've finished".
When he got to an easy bit I said, "Dad. Dad, will you ask Mrs. Matz has she got a birdcage she doesn't want in her garage?"
"Oh! you'll have to get your mother to ask her", he said.
"Aw, go on dad", I kept pleading, but all I could get out of him was, "We'll see, later".
My dad was finishing off down the bottom end of the garden and I was collecting the tools together when I heard the front door slam shut. I went round the side of the house and saw Mrs. Matz in high-heel shoes and a coat with a large, fluffy fur collar that almost hid her head. Mr. Matz was wearing a stiff trilby hat and he closed the front gate behind him. I went over to the garage door and tried to peer in through the join but I couldn't see anything.
"They've gone out", I said to my dad.

"They've what! "They'd better bloodywell not have!", he said, hurrying across the lawn and wiping his hands down the sides of his overall as he did so.
A second later he reappeared.
"Which way did they go?", he said, but I didn't know.
"Well that's the bloody limit!" he said, throwing his cap on the ground.

He left me standing by the loaded barrow whilst he went off to see if he could get his money from the two gardens we had done that morning, saying as he left: "If they come back while I'm gone don't let them go off again. Tell them I'll be back in five minutes". They didn't come back and I was cold by the time my dad returned. I could tell he was angry by the pace of his walk and the way the heels of his boots bit into the path and the way he rolled when he walked and held his arms curved.
"Half a bloody crown for a flaming day's hard graft!", he said as he approached.
"I don't suppose they've come back , have they?"
"No", I said. "Were the others in?"
"Only one", he said. "The Kersners have gone away for a week. The bugger of it is they won't believe it's been done when they get back!"

I walked at the side of the barrow most of the way home because my dad said I was getting too heavy to be carried. I could tell he was still angry by the way he looked and I knew there would be a row when we got back.
My dad usually cleaned his mower when he got home from gardening but this time he wheeled the barrow straight under the lean-to without bothering.
"Don't come in here with those boots on", my mam shouted as soon as I put my hand on the latch.
When my dad came in the first thing he said was, "Did he get me those fags?"
"Oh! my god! I forgot to ask him", my mam said, putting her hand over her open mouth.
"I don't bloody know. Here, run down to Whittaker's and get me

DIGGING FOR GOLD

ten Woodbines, before they close", my dad said.

"Aw!, why do I have to go!?", I said. "I'm tired!"

He handed me the half-crown he had been paid and I saw my mam's eyes follow it to my trouser pocket.

"Well, if I go can I have a shilling from the change to buy a bird with?", I said, as I pulled on my wellington.

"We'll see when you get back", my dad said.

"How much did you get paid then?", my mam asked my dad as I was closing the door.

"Nowt!", he said. "I didn't get paid".

"You're a bloody liar!" my mam said.

"Well ask him then, when he gets back. He'll tell you. I got half-a-crown!"

I could hear the row getting louder as I got further away from the house but by the time I got back all was quiet. There was a broken plate in the hearth and some potatoes on the grate and the remains of a chop burning on the fire. My mam was sitting on a chair, at the table, white faced, and holding her head between her hands.

"How much did he get paid?", she said, aggressively.

"They were all out", I said, "We only got half-a-crown".

My mam said nothing.

"Where's my dad?", I asked.

"In the front room, where do you think!"

"Aw, I wanted to know if I could have a shilling from the change for a bird", I said, stamping my foot.

"You're not having a bloody bird and be told", she said.

My dad would probably be in the front room until Monday or Tuesday, sleeping under his big overcoat and not bothering to undress, shave or wash. He would come out at night like an animal. You could hear him prowling about downstairs. He would raid the pantry, eating everything my mam had not managed to hide. If there was no bread in the old wash boiler, our "bread bin" he would eat a whole pot of jam with a spoon and drink all the milk straight out of the milk jug. If he was feeling particularly peeved he would take the valves out of the wireless set that stood on the old mahogany dresser in the kitchen and hide them so that we would have nothing to do in the evenings. My mam would miss her repeats of Tommy Handley and we'd not be able to listen to "Toy Town" or "Appointment with Fear". My dad would usually be speaking again by the end of the week but it went on for six weeks once, and us without the wireless too. "You have to laugh at the silly bugger", my mam would say when he eventually got fed up with the discomfort and went upstairs to bed.

After some argument I put the cigarettes and change on the mantelpiece and ate my tea. When I'd finished I went to the mantelpiece and took the shilling.

"Where do you think you're going with that!?", my mam said, getting up.

"To buy a bird", I said.

"You're not!", she said, "You'll have to wait 'till next week".

"I want one now!", I said, grabbing my coat and dashing into the hall.

I slammed the front door hard and hid behind the coats on the hallstand waiting to see if she would come after me. She didn't so I opened the door again and crept out, quietly.

Mr. Hammersley wouldn't let me have a bird for a shilling.

"And besides", he said, "You've no cage for it. You'll have to save up some more pennies. I'll keep one for you", he said, as he let me out.

I kicked the Hammersley's gate hard several times until one of the pieces of wood fell out of the centre panel. Ronald Hammersley was looking out of the window and saw me doing it.

When I got home I stood outside kicking the coal-house door until my mam came out.

"What are you doing that for!?", she said, grabbing me by the arm and pulling me inside.

When Friday came round my mam gave me sixpence and my dad gave me nine-pence. With the shilling I'd got from gardening and the three-pence each my grandma and my aunty Polly had given me for my birthday I had more than enough for a bird but by that time I'd gone off birds. If I could get another three-pence from somewhere I was going to get an orange box from the greengrocers and in the morning buy myself a golden agouti guinea-pig.

FEEDING THE GUINEA PIGS

If you deprive a guinea pig of food it won't half whistle: if you let a couple of dozen go hungry they sound like an aviary. I thought a flock of starlings had landed on our house that Saturday night.
"Oh my godfathers! Just listen to that row!", my mam said as we turned the corner into out street. She broke into a run that nearly jerked my arm out of my jacket.
"You're getting rid of those damned things. I've had enough of them! You'll have the whole street complaining and we'll get evicted if we're reported again".
The guinea pigs had been quiet enough when we left early that morning. I'd asked our Ernie to feed them later in the day. As a matter of fact I'd given him threepence to do it but he'd obviously not bothered: the rotten sod! It was his way of getting his own back. My mam had stopped him from going with us on the Railwayman's outing to Blackpool, (she'd been given some unsold tickets), because he'd set fire to the chimney with a pile of old newspapers my dad had been saving since before the war. Some of them were about Spain and one had a picture of the unemployed worker's march to London my dad had been on. The soot had blackened Mrs. Booth's washing, next door but two, and she'd threatened to tell the rent man we had been burning soot off the chimney. My mam had to agree to re-wash two of her sheets to keep her quiet. My dad went mad when he found out about the papers. It was me that split. Our Ernie locked himself in the lavatory and my dad almost kicked the door in but Ernie wouldn't come out. My dad had gone off to work threatening to kill him when he came home.

From down the path I could hear teeth tugging at the bars and claws rattling along the wires. In the half-dark the shed seemed to be swelling and shrinking visibly as it pulsed with fear-filling energy from the guinea pig's undulating whistles.
The shed was an Andersen shelter my dad had dug out of the garden when the war ended. He paid the council a pound for it

and re-erected it in the corner of the back garden, laid a crazy paving path and put a concrete floor in with some cement that fell off a wagon. But because my dad was a perfectionist, and never finished anything he started, I had to fit a rickety makeshift door I made out of pieces of wood kicked out of the panels of people's garden gates one dark night. The shed now housed nearly thirty guinea pigs. I was breeding them to sell to Metcalf, the greengrocer, who resold them to hospitals for research. He once told me that guinea pigs had human blood in their veins but our Ernie said it was more likely that Metcalf had a guinea pig's brain in his head. I bet our Ernie ten marbles and lost. A man in the St. John's Ambulance Brigade said it was pretty close to human blood so I made our Ernie accept clay ones instead of glass.

The guinea pigs snatched the cauliflower leaves out of my hand and made their ritual run round their cages before settling into their favourite corners to munch the leaves and gnaw at the stalks. The last to be fed was frenzied and I got a vicious nip. I had to wrap my hanky round it but the blood oozed through. I kept my hand in my pocket when I went in so that my mam wouldn't know I'd been bitten.

There was no sign of our Ernie in the house and no one in the street had seen him. My mam sent me to the brick croft to look for him but he wasn't there. "I'll bet the little devil's gone to the pictures and stayed in to see it through a second time round", my mam said.

Our Ernie was dead nuts on the pictures and would have gone every night if he'd had the money. He used to sneak in through the side door and hide in the lavatory when it was two separate houses. If we had to go before the second house finished he walked up the aisle backwards. He was always falling over or bumping into the ice cream lady.

My dad came home from the Dogs looking irritable. He was in a bad temper because he'd lost and had no money to buy fags. My mam said she wasn't giving him any and that if he had stayed at home and looked after our Ernie like a proper father he wouldn't need to borrow. That started it.

FEEDING THE GUINEA PIGS

"The bugger's not still out is he?", my dad shouted.
There was a right row. Pots were broken, pans were thrown. Our Ernie was in for some dead serious trouble when he came home.
My dad chucked my mam's coat at her and said that she could get up off her fat backside and go and look for him and that if he wasn't home within an hour of the pictures finishing she had better tell the police. And with that he slammed the door and went into the front room to sleep on the couch. We were in for another two weeks of moping silence and night prowling. He would take the valves out of the wireless again, drink all the milk and eat the jam up with a spoon.
During the rumpus I pinched a box of matches off the draining board next to the gas stove, slipped them into my trouser pocket and went back to the shelter to get out of the way.
I opened the rickety door of the shelter as quietly as I could. There was a scuttle of claws from the cages and a chorus of squeaks. Oats and sawdust rattled through the netting and showered on to the floor. A saucer thumped against a wooden partition and wobbled to rest. I pulled the door to behind me, put the hook in the eye and stood still, tasting the thick, black dark, listening to the noises settling down. The sweet, green smell of cauliflower leaves mixed with the charred smell of swede from last night's lantern and behind it the faint whiff of mouse pee. I would have to set the traps before I went to bed or, better still, on Saturday morning move the cages out and try to find the nests.
I pictured the balls of hay and the thick flakes of newspaper and imagined my finger poking amongst them to reveal the slow moving mass of blind, pink piglets opening and closing their delicate hands and twisting their semi-transparent bodies in slow motion, occasionally blowing bubbles. Our Ernie would flush them down the lavatory or give them to next door's cat.
I struck a match and lit a candle. The pearl of light wavered, warmed the wax and the flamed more brightly, casting long shadows. I lit another candle from the first and then a third letting the warm wax run over my fingers and drip on to my thumb. I peeled it off to look at the print. The ruby eye of an Abyssinian White glowed like an incense burner in the corner of a cage.
One of the big male tortoiseshells I kept for breeding purposes

THE DOGS OF WAR

poked his rounded snout from out of the hole in the sleeping compartment and, leaning his splayed hind legs to the ground, raised his head high, and slowly emerged into the run. As he did so he set up a murmur in the back of his throat not unlike a cat purring or a pigeon cooing and began a slow, deliberate mating stalk. The sow cowered in a corner her head low down between her two front feet.

I eased myself on to one of the apple boxes I had pinched from the back of the greengrocer's shop. The sharp edge cut into the bare flesh of my thighs and I felt the splinters but I took no notice as I watched the strange ritual, fascinated, hardly daring to breath. The scene excited but frightened me: I had never seen them mate.

The noise rattled on like a stick rickering a distant railing as round and round the cage he stalked, jerkily on the toes of his stiff little legs, his rear end held up and his usually bright eye glazed over. The sow moved out into the open but she would not let him mount. He nosed her in the side. Each time he lowered his head she kicked out from behind and scudded away, half turned, repelling him. I had to put my hands under my legs to stop the box cutting me. The noise distracted him and he began to nibble an oat. The sow dropped a hard, dry pellet and paused to scratch her ear with a back leg. I sat for an age waiting for the ritual to begin again but he was in no hurry.

The corrugated ribbing of the shelter was rusted in parts and reminded me of the sands at Blackpool. Our Ernie had missed a treat. I remembered the hard, damp grit between my toes and a painful pressure on the sole my foot, the numbing sting of cold sea water round my ankles. The Punch and Judy show appeared and disappeared, vivid images of donkey rides, jangling bells, those slow twitching ears, the bristly feel of fur under my fingers, postcards of big bottomed ladies, hard, pink rock that stuck to your teeth, all flickered through my mind like a peep show.

A sudden gust of wind came under the door and blew the candle flame like a blow-lamp. I pressed a sack against the gap and resumed my watch. The galvanised metal gleamed grey and white in the candle light, geometric crystals patterned it like frost on my bedroom window in winter. My shadow loomed large among the feathery fronds as again one of the candles faltered and flared: the guinea pigs sat still.

To pass the time I made silhouette shadows on the walls with my hands like my dad had shown me, weaving and bending my fingers to make a pageant of forms. Butterflies and badgers, snakes and bears, rabbits and beetles, painted a fresco round the cave wall in my mind. I heard the death's head hawk moth squeak, saw the pigeon we would trap later in the week and muttered pagan prayers to keep away the ghosts. The tortoiseshell guinea pig stood still, its eye alert, one foot raised from off the ground. Suddenly it started, turned, skidded on the wood shavings and disappeared into the sleeping compartment closely followed by its mate.

I opened the door to see what had frightened him: it was our Ernie.

"You rotten sod", I said, "Why didn't you feed my guinea pigs for me? Anyway, you'll get killed if you go in", I said, and I told him about the row and my dad sleeping in the front room and that my mam was going to the police to get them to look for him if he was not home when the pictures came out.

Our Ernie decided it was best to hide in the shed for the night.

"If you split on us again", he said, "I'll kill one of your guinea pigs".

I didn't say anything: you could never risk it with our Ernie.

Ernie pulled out from the wall the big bank of cages and jammed two small sacks of hay behind them to lie on. Some mice scampered away but there were no nests.

"All I need now is some food. I can sneak into the house tomorrow when they're at work and get back into the shed before they come home", he said, settling himself down on the sacks with his head poking out from the end. He looked like a coconut wearing glasses.

"I know", I said, "Why don't we go climbing over gardens. You could get some carrots from Hibberts and I could get a couple of cabbages from old Proudfoot's garden to feed my guinea pigs tomorrow.

It was tar black in the shadow of the back garden where the two loose palings were. We had knocked them off Proudfoot's fence ages ago and fixed them back on again to hang on two small nails so that no one would know. They were easily removed and we squeezed through the gap and on to the path on all fours, tiptoed round the back of the house and across the patch of grass with its square of light from the kitchen window. I looked back to see where our Ernie had got to. The nutter was looking through the keyhole of Proudfoot's back door. It only needed them to come out for a shovelful of coal.

"Psst!", I said, "You'll get us caught!"

Some of the gardens still had patches of grass, clumps of Dahlias, Michaelmas Daisies and trellis's of roses and sweet peas, but most were more like allotments---hangovers from the "Dig for Victory" campaign. Quite a lot had hen runs which could snarl you up if you weren't careful and there were one or two with peeling, soot-blackened pigeon coops, once bright grey and white. A good half of the houses had dogs, some of which slept in kennels outside the back doors. Jeff Reynold's dad had three greyhounds in a rickety pen in the garden. He raced them at Belle Vue. You had to know the neighbours as well as your geography to go climbing over gardens round our way. Our Ernie knew them like I knew the back of my mam's carpet beater.

We brushed our way bent-backed through Proudfoot's black-currant bushes, the strong, sharp smell of the leaves overpowering with its pungency.

"I bet there are Magpie caterpillars on these", I whispered.

My feet sank into the soft earth of the onion bed with its long rows of bulging domes, rising almost clear of the ground. The tops had already been broken: most had been knotted but one or two lay loose and bedraggled on the earth. There were three rows of cabbages just beyond. There was a beauty the size of a football, and solid too. I could smell the leaves and feel the drops of water on the surface and I heard it squeak as I pressed it with both my hands. But our Ernie said it was best to take the three end ones so that Proudfoot wouldn't notice.

"It's like laughing with a tooth out if you take the middle one", he said, "No one knows if you've had one out at the back".

We pulled up the end three, trampled the earth flat and dropped them over the garden that backed on to Proudfoot's to collect on the way home.

FEEDING THE GUINEA PIGS

Our Ernie, being a bit gangling, could make an attempt at the scissors over the railings separating the gardens but I was four years younger. By the time I had struggled over into Hibbert's he was already pulling carrots: gripping the ferny tops and tugging them clean out of the ground. I stumbled across the furrows of potatoes hearing the stalks snap as I trod across the hummocks.
"Do you want any potatoes?", I asked him.
"Yeah, we might as well have a few spuds", he said.

I scratched the earth away like a rabbit and delved my hands into the cool soil, feeling for the smooth, soft stones and tucking them, one by one, inside my shirt. A shaft of light suddenly cut across the garden and caught me full in the face as Mrs. Hibbert came out of the kitchen for coal. My neck hair bristled and a prickle of fear contracted my scalp. Fortunately she didn't so much as glance down the garden.
"Come on, we'd better beat it", our Ernie said.
He was up and over the railings before I could move. There was a dull crunch and a splintering and squeaking of glass that set my teeth on edge as our Ernie's shoe went through a cold-frame. He swore worse than my dad did when he once knocked an iron pan of soup off the kitchen fire all over his foot.
"Don't stand on that . . . " I heard Ernie say, as I took a run at what looked like a mound of earth backed up against the railings, intending to jump clean over the fence. But it was too late, my front foot sank with a sucking squelch through the crust of a pile of manure and straw. A steamy stench enveloped me as my other foot followed.
"Oh blast!", I shouted, "Why didn't you tell me!"
Our Ernie was killing himself laughing as I tried to clean up my steaming legs with grass and cabbage leaves. The stink was terrible.
"My mam will kill me when I get in", I said, attacking him with both fists.
A bedroom light came on in one of the upstairs rooms of the house next door and a woman in her underwear walked over to draw the curtain.
"Hey, did you see that!", our Ernie said.

THE DOGS OF WAR

Hindley's chickens clucked and squawked and scuffled as we passed the hen house and a growling dog ran to the end of its chain, but no one came out.

"I bet you couldn't hit that back door with a spud", our Ernie said, but I was in no mood to try. I couldn't think what I was going to say when I got in. The smell of my legs was a constant reminder of the trouble to come and I could feel the dampness inside my shoes as we made our way back to collect the cabbages.

Our Ernie found a large ball of thick, hairy, green string near a heap of bean canes.

"We'll have this", he said, "It'll come in handy".

A piece of railing snapped off with a splitting crack as I launched myself from the top of the fence and we had to lie low for a minute or two until a dog stopped barking. Ernie snapped off some sticks of rhubarb and ate a piece raw.

"Have some of this", he said, "It puts iron in your blood rhubarb does. It'll make you as strong as a steam engine".

We collected the cabbages and dropped them over the fence before us, dribbling them over the lawns as we made our way through the back gardens of the Approach. Our Ernie put his foot in a pile of soft soot. I heard the quiet, air cushioned puff of it just before a stifling cloud of the stuff reached my nostrils.

"You clumsy sod", I said, trying to breathe out twice through my mouth. "Let's make a run for it down Murphy's entry".

We tucked the cabbages under our arms like a couple of cup winners and with our shirts stuffed full of carrots and spuds made a run for it. When we were half-way down the tunnel our Ernie put his finger in the hollow of his mouth and made a noise like a tribe of Indians.

"Quick, round the Circle", he shouted, "I don't want my mam to see me".

I could hear Mrs. Murphy shouting after us: "I know who it is. Out at this time of night! Don't think I didn't recognise you. Just wait till I see your mothers!".

We did a quick lap of the Circle, knocking on the odd door as we went and came back to the Approach from the opposite side. It was all quiet in the street.

"Hold this cabbage", Ernie said, handing me his prize.

He tiptoed down Murphy's path and went up to the front door. Carefully, he lifted the door knocker and tied the end of the string to it. Then he went across the entry to Petit's. Measuring the string he frayed it on the edge of the brickwork until it parted and tied it to Petit's knocker. There was just enough slack for one door to open but not two. He gripped the loop of string in the middle and gave it a quick couple of jerks, knocking on both doors at once and ran across the road.
"Quick! Into Tickle's garden", he said.
We crouched behind the hedge, watching. Mrs. Murphy opened the front door and was almost trapped in two when it slammed shut as Mr. Petit opened his door. Each time the one opened their door the other slammed it to. We were splitting ourselves laughing as we made a run for it down the street and into our own garden. Our Ernie went to the shed. I took him some bread and a jug of water and locked him up for the night.
My mam was still out looking for him which was lucky for me because I was able to stand in the sink and clean the worst of the muck off my legs before she got back.
"What's that horrible smell?", she said, almost before she was inside the house. "And just look at your face: you look as though you've been up the chimney!".
I got a couple of slaps round the ear as she took my shoes and socks, one at a time between her finger and thumb, and flung them into the coal-house.
"You can clean those up in the morning!", she said. "Now get up stairs to bed".
"I don't suppose you've seen anything of that one, have you?", she said as I was going.
"No", I said, "I haven't".
My dad had locked the front room door. I heard her knocking on it and saying: "Harry . . . Harry . . . That one's not come home yet. You'll have to go up to Overdale and see if he's gone to your mother's".
It must have been the knocking on the front door that woke me up in the early hours of the morning. I could hear unfamiliar voices in the kitchen so I crept out of bed and sat halfway down the stairs, in my pyjamas, listening to what was going on. I heard my

THE DOGS OF WAR

dad say : "Yes, fourteen. He'll be fifteen in January but he looks more like a twelve year old. I'll strangle the bugger when I get hold of him. Yes, fair hair, with a fringe, and school glasses, round and silver with one lens cracked across the centre and a bad squint in his left eye". Sergeant Hewitt, the bobby from up the Grange was asking the questions. As he left I heard him say: "We'll keep an eye open for him. He might turn up at school tomorrow. We'll check with the headmaster".

I felt quite scared, knowing our Ernie was in the shed, so I hid under the blankets pretending to be asleep.

My mam and dad didn't go to work the following day. My mam went into Heaton Park looking for Ernie and my dad stayed at home, locked in the front room. I sneaked half a loaf and some milk out to the shed for Ernie and Ernie decided to risk sneaking into the house to go to the lavatory. He swiped five bob from the money my mam had hidden in a drawer upstairs to pay off the rent. He said he was going to go to Blackpool when the heat was off to try to get a job in an amusement arcade. The police couldn't find him. They came round two or three times during the day to see if he'd come back home.

I was coming back from the shed with a milk bottle when my mam caught me.

"What are you doing with that?", she asked.

I said that one of my guinea pigs was sick and I'd been giving it a drop of milk. She didn't believe me and went down to the shed and looked in.

"Are you sure you don't know where he is?", she said.

Fortunately our Ernie had heard her coming and managed to hide behind the cages, but it was a close thing.

That evening my mam noticed that the bread had gone and she immediately went upstairs to check the rent money.

"Right, now, where is he?, she said. "That money was there this morning: you must have seen him".

I denied it, of course, but it was no use. She locked the door and grabbed the carpet beater from out of the pantry.

"I'll beat the living daylights out of you if you don't tell me where he is!", she said, as I tried to dodge round the table.

I don't know whether it was good luck or bad luck but at that moment Sergeant Hewitt arrived to check once more whether or not Ernie had returned.

"I'm glad you've come", my mam said, "Perhaps you'll be able to get it out of him".

Sergeant Hewitt said it was a very serious offence to withhold information from the police. My mam again threatened to get rid of my guinea pigs. In desperation, and to give myself time to think, I said: "I think he's hiding in the old wardrobe in the boxroom upstairs".

My mam unlocked the hall door and they both tramped upstairs. Quickly I nipped out of the back door and down to the shed to tell Ernie to make a run for it.

"Quick!, I'll have to tell them", I shouted, as I dashed into the shed, but there was no response. I looked behind the cages and saw the vacant sacks and the half-eaten loaf.

When I got back to the kitchen there was Ernie, all soot and straw and cobwebs, and tears streaming from under his cracked glasses.

"You wait", he said, "Why did you have to tell them where I was!"

"But I . . . I thought you were still in the shed", I said.

About two weeks later I was in the shed, feeding my guinea pigs crushed oats and tea leaves. I was feeling good as I had just sold six young ones to Metcalf for research. Squeaks and whistles of anticipation came from the cages. I fed the golden agouties, the Dutch, and the Abyssinian whites and was about to feed the tortoiseshells when I noticed that the big male was not in the run. I scratched on the mesh with my finger but he didn't come. When I opened the sleeping compartment there he was, dead, on the floor, with a tight noose of hairy green string wound round his neck

GETTING MY OWN BACK

Whip and tops had suddenly disappeared from the school playground: the marble season had begun. Nobody organised this, it just seemed to happen. It was like magic. One day everyone was playing whip and top and the next day there wasn't one to be seen anywhere. Everyone was dangling a bag of marbles from the strings of a draw-bag or displaying a sagging bulge of marbles in the pocket of their trouser leg.
I was mad keen on marbles me. I pretended I'd dropped my dinner money down a grid on the way to school and bought ten marbles with some of it from old mother Crossley's toy shop. I won two more playing "follows up" on the way home from school. In "follows up" you played as you walked along. One of you would throw a marble on the ground ahead and the other would throw to try to hit it. I was good at throwing and hitting and a dab-hand at flirting with my thumb on the second go.
In the school yard we played "ringy" but kids were always kicking the marbles, pretending they weren't looking where they were going, just to start a fight or get the chance to nick a marble when they pretended to help you find the ones they had kicked. To play "ringy" you each had to put some marbles in a chalk ring, draw a line some distance away and throw a marble in turn to try to knock some out. Any marbles you knocked out you kept. Afterwards you took turns to flirt your marble with your thumb to try to knock out more. You could use your turn if you wanted to to flirt at someone else's marble and knock it away from the ring. With enough spin on it you could keep your own marble close to the ring and knock someone else's off into the distance.
I was usually good at "ringy" but Billy Benson, the Bookie's son, was using a big dobber and I ended up losing all I had, including two pink American ones I usually never risked playing with. When I said he'd cheated, using a dobber, he said: "Hard luck, you should have said that before we started!" If he'd been on his own I'd have had a fight with him but he had Victor Maffia and his brother with him so I just said: "I'll get you tomorrow

GETTING MY OWN BACK

Benson!"

"You and whose army!" he shouted, as I walked away.

I wept with rage on the way home. When you lost the lot to someone they were supposed to give you one back so you had a chance the next day but Benson, the mean bugger, hadn't given me one. I missed the weight of the marbles in my trouser pocket and the comforting sound as they grated against my leg when I walked. I couldn't wait to get even with Benson. "I'll get some marbles somehow", I said, out aloud. I'll show the mean sod!

My mam shouted at me for losing my dinner money. "D'you think bloody money grows on trees! Where am I going to get another one-and-ninepence from! Just you wait 'till your father comes home!"

She wouldn't let me play out so I emptied the drawers in the sideboard and rummaged through my grandma's button box trying to find some marbles. "Make sure you put all that stuff back!", my mam kept shouting at me. I finally found two long-lost bottlewashers: one under the oilcloth in a corner under the sink and another in the cupboard under the draining board. It had rolled behind the gas meter. Two were enough. I'd get my own back. I'd make that bugger Benson play "holey" tomorrow. "Holey" was my favourite game. I just couldn't wait for morning to come.

My mam worked at Woodthorpe making school dinners. She had to leave the house shortly after six o'clock in the morning to be there for six-thirty. My dad, who had been drafted along with most of the other council labourers into the Rescue Service, was on days and left at seven-thirty. Mrs. Jones from next-door-but-one came in and gave us a shout at about eight o'clock. We used to shout back "yes we're up" and bang our boots on the floor. Then we'd go back to bed. Occasionally we overslept and stayed off school the whole day: we were scared of going late. You got the cane if you were late twice in one week. We would still be in bed when my mam came home at three-thirty in the afternoon. Our Ernie always got the blame, and a good hiding if my dad found out.

We were already up when Mrs Jones arrived on Friday morning. Our Ernie tried to make us some toast but the fire wasn't red and

THE DOGS OF WAR

it wouldn't toast so we put lots of dripping on the bread. I wanted to be off to school right away but when the *Keep Fit* programme came on the wireless our Ernie made me and our Arthur do physical jerks. "Forward, side, together, back, side, together". He made us jump up and down to a plinky-plonk tune from a tinny sounding piano. Our Ernie was older than us and went to "the big school". Because Keith Dickenson had been run over by a lorry the week before our Ernie was supposed to see us across the main road. I kept saying: "Aw, come on Ernie, lets go to school now!" "In a minute. Stop mithering!" He was deliberately trying to make us late.

After the news, telling us that one of our planes was missing from a raid on the marshalling yards at Bremen, Dr. Charles Hill, the radio doctor, came on: "Don't let young Johnny drink the cat's milk: it won't do him the slightest bit of good", he said, in his rich fruity voice. Our Ernie imitated him and made us laugh: "And if dad wants to go down to the local for a pint of Guinness mum, well you just let him: it won't do him the slightest bit of harm", he would echo. I kept asking our Ernie to help with the pots but he just kept fooling about and making more mess. "Aw Ernie, I won't be able to have a game of marbles if we don't go now!", I said, but he didn't take any notice.

Freddie Grisewood on *The Kitchen Front* tried to explain how to make a four-course meal for eight people out of three ounces of dried egg and a quarter of spam, the war-time rations, or something equally ridiculous. Our Ernie put substitute ingredients into a pan on the gas stove, saying in a Freddie Grisewood voice: "Half a bottle of blue-black ink, two heaped spoonfuls of earth, a handful of dandelion leaves and three worms". He added a dead mouse and fluff and hair from my mam's comb and stirred it into a gritty, stinking stew which he threatened to make us eat when it boiled. "Eye of newt and sole of boot. Leg of frog and hair of dog". He was an avid reader, our Ernie. He knew all the right words and he deliberately misquoted, cackling demonically: "Stir the pot brother, stir the pot!" He added a cupful of water and when it boiled threw the lot on the fire which at last had reddened. There was a frightening bang which made our Archie jump a foot in the air as a piece of stony coal exploded in a shower of shale and sparks on to my grandma's peg rug. An angry, fizzing hiss belched out a huge billow of steam and sooty smoke from the grate as the water boiled and bubbled on the coals. It plumed into a cloud and was trapped by my mam's wet washing hanging from the bamboo rack suspended from the ceiling above. "My mam'll kill you for that" I said, as Ernie grabbed his comics and disappeared through the back door.

By the time we'd cleaned up the mess in the hearth our Archie and me were late for school. My row was already marching in when we got there but I managed to tag on the end. As we passed Standard four's row I whispered to Billy Benson: "I'll play you at marbles after school". "Ringy", he said. "No, holey", I risked shouting over my shoulder. As I passed the headmaster, at the door, he said: "Report to my desk after prayers, you".

"Another stroke of the cane this afternoon", I thought.

"Holey" was played in Whitaker lane. Whitaker lane ran away from the main Bury Old Road and alongside the school wall down a gradual slope towards the Congregational Hall where we had our school dinners. It was unadopted and unmetalled. Generations of marble players had dug small, two-and-a-half-inch diameter holes about three or four inches deep in the hard-packed earth near to the wall: they looked like rat holes.

Billy Benson was crouched down on his haunches, his cupped hand, containing six marbles, stretched out before him. He was practising keeping his marbles in a group and getting them in the hole first time.

"What you playing then?", he said.

"A oner", I said.

"A oner! A oner!", he laughed. "I'm not playing a oner!"

It was possible in "holey" to play a oner, twoer, or even a tenner, as many as you could hold in one hand. "I've only got two", I said.

"Alright then, a twoer. We'll play in this hole", he said, pointing to the one he had been practising at.

"No, we'll play in that one on the other side of the lane, then it will be fair".

"Oh go on then!", he said.

In "holey" the idea was to cup your marbles in your hand and

throw them into the hole from a line scraped out on the earth a few feet away. You could have as many as three or four players and you tossed up to see who would throw first. Benson tried to use his two-headed penny. I knew he would. Everyone knew he had one. His uncle had made it for him and he had not been able to resist boasting about it.
"Come off it Benson! We'll use my "Honolulu" penny".
"Ay lets have a look at it!" he said, snatching it out of my hand.
For some reason the Royal Mint had made two versions of Victorian pennies, with Britannia's trident in different positions. A "Honolulu" penny was one on which Britannia's trident was resting in her crotch rather than on her thigh. Boys at our school called that region of a girl's body "a loo loo". A "Honolulu" penny was a pun on this.
Benson won the toss and threw first. He got both marbles in but despite my hand being sore from the afternoon's caning, so did I, so I collected all four.
"You jammy sod!", he said.
I put one marble in my pocket as insurance and said: "I'll play you a threeer".
I threw but only got one in. Benson threw and got two in.

If you failed to get all the marbles in the hole at the first throw you took it in turns to try to knock the remaining allies into the hole with the middle joint of your index finger until you missed one. The other player then took his turn to try to knock them in. The winner was the one to knock the last allie in to the hole. You had to knock the allies in crisply with your finger, first time, without steering or following the marble towards the hole otherwise you would be accused of "nurring" or "slurring" and be made to forfeit your go. There were endless disputes and requests to "take it again" and there was always an audience taking sides. It usually ended with someone shouting "grab your dibs!" Predatory bystanders would dive after the allies in a free-for-all. Endless fights and permanent feuds resulted.
Even though Benson had got two in I knocked the last one in so I collected all six. Benson tried to say I'd nurred it but everyone around agreed I hadn't.

Several more games were played and though I lost a couple I ended up with twenty marbles, including my two pink American ones and my lucky bottlewashers.
"I'll have to go now", I said, sensing that my winning streak could not go on for ever.
"Scared of losing?", Benson jeered.
"No, I'm not", I said.
"Yes you are". "No I'm not".
"One last game then?"
"Yeah, one last game", all those around said.
I didn't want to look "chicken" so I said, "OK then, but this is definitely my last game".
"I'll play you a twentyer", Benson said.
"Don't be crazy. You can't hold twenty in your hand!"
"We'll make the hole bigger, move the line nearer and use two hands", he said.
I had no answer to this so I just said: "No, I've got to go now".
"Go on play him". "Yeah, don't be a spoil-sport play him!"
Despite the hollow feeling in the pit of my stomach, with everyone saying I was scared to play I had no choice but to reluctantly agree. I was sure that if Benson lost Victor Maffia or his brother would shout: "Grab your dibs!"
The hole was so large and we were so near it all you had to do was to pour the marbles in from above. I was first and all mine, except one, went into the hole with a glassy clatter. Benson poured his on top and briskly knocked in my stray allie. There was a brief gasp and then a great cheer went up. He'd won! I couldn't believe it. I must have been crazy to agree to the game! I'd lost the lot.
Benson's eyes were shining and his face was flushed as he pounced on the hole, laughing hysterically. His grasping hands scooped the marbles out and poured them into his bulging allie bag like a miser handling gold. I just stood there, pale, staring at the hole, with this sinking feeling in the pit of my stomach.
With other kids there Benson had to give me one marble back but he refused to play another game.
"No. You said you had to go after this game", he said.
"I'll play you on Monday then", I said, biting back the tears as the

crowd of watchers, still discussing the game, moved off down the lane.

"I might do. We'll see", Benson shouted back, without turning round.

When I got to school on Monday I went to find Benson but he hadn't come. His mother had sent a note through Victor Maffia to the Headmaster saying he had a cold and would be off for a few days. I was sick with disappointment. I desperately wanted to win my marbles back!

"Why did he have to be ill!" I said, stamping my foot. "By the time he comes back the marbles season will be over!" I could play someone else, I supposed, but it wouldn't be the same. It had to be Benson. I wanted, desperately wanted, needed, desperately needed to get my own back. "Why did the bugger have to be ill!", I shouted.

LOOKING FORWARD TO FRIDAY

It was better to to misbehave on a Friday than a Monday at our junior school: that way you didn't have to wait for the cane. If you behaved badly on a Monday or any other day of the week you had to wait until Friday afternoon. At the start of lessons on Friday afternoon wrongdoers from the various classes would line up in front of the Headmaster's desk. Their crimes would be read out and the number of strokes announced. It was the doubtful good fortune of Standard four to witness these canings.

I was not due for the cane that Friday so on the Thursday night I was looking forward to school. We had sums on Friday morning and I was good at sums. I always finished the fractions first and I liked doing problems. I was not one of those "chancers" who put their hand up in mental arithmetic tests when they didn't know the answer. In the afternoon we had private reading. You could choose a story book out of a big box kept locked in the tall double-doored cupboard near the blackboard. I was reading *Babies of the Wild* in which fox cubs survived a thumb-biting few days in the lair on their own whilst their mother, the vixen, gnawed through her back-leg to escape from a gin-trap. Leverets were carried by the scruff of the neck out of the path of a whirring combine-harvester by an exhausted mother hare, chased for hours by a hunter's dog. I could hardly wait to know what would happen to the pine martens trapped in that hollow tree about to be chopped down.

On Friday morning we were up early but our Ernie, who was older than us, made us do physical exercises when the *Keep Fit* programme came on the wireless. Our Archie and me were late for school and I missed the chance of a game of marbles. We had to stand in the cloakroom porch with Elsie Bain--she lived nearby but she was always late--until prayers were over. It was raining and the coats piled on the pegs smelt sweaty and damp. The windows were steamed up except for one which had been recently broken. Someone had been sick on the floor. Mr. Askew, the caretaker, came in and put some brown peaty stuff on it. It smelt overpoweringly of that sweet earthy disinfectant which stays up your nose all day, and in your mind for the rest of your life.

We got told off by the headmaster for being late and when I tried to make an excuse about having a long way to come he said: "Well I live in Bury and if I can get here on time so can you!" I said to our Archie: "When we get home you must tell my mam our Ernie got us into trouble".

I got three sums wrong in Mechanical arithmetic and I couldn't do one of the Problems. When I took my book out to be marked Mrs Mitchell said: "Well! I am surprised!" and she called me a donkey! I didn't put my hand up at all when we had mental arithmetic.

Dinner time seemed ages away so I went up to the front and said, like we had been told to do: "Please Miss may I leave the room?" "You must wait until Carol Bell comes back" Mrs Mitchell said, in an irritated voice.

When the bell finally went for dinner-time we wiped our pens on our cloths and the ink monitors collected them. They counted them carefully and put the inkwells on a tray whilst we put our sum-books on the shelves under our desk-tops. Because there was too much noise, and Michael Hamberger had banged his desk lid down, the pens had to be handed back and we had the collection again. "Quietly this time!" By the time we had filed out and lined up in the yard for dismissal we had lost nearly ten minutes of dinner-time.

It was smelly fish and white cabbage for dinner that Friday so I didn't eat it and the rhubarb pie was sour. Spud Ellis, Brian Naylor and me pretended to go to the lavatory. When we got outside we pooled our money to get three-pennyworth of chips from Newtown Street chip-shop. We played "follows up" on the way there. I lost two of my best marbles to Spud Ellis. The chip-shop was an end terraced house which abutted on to the main road. The owner had put a door and a window at the end to face onto the road so as to attract more trade. Next to it was a red-brick building with a tall, pointed roof. "Wesleyan Church" was embossed on the door lintel. Next to the church were two shops attached to the Parkside Hotel and beyond that a new block of

LOOKING FORWARD TO FRIDAY

two-story flats. Our school was some two-hundred yards beyond the flats.

The first shop past the church was an Upholsterers owned by Mr. Horrocks, a man who knew my dad. The shop windows either side of the door had the bottom half painted brown for some reason so you couldn't see in. The windows were never cleaned and were coated with a thick layer of dust thrown up by the passing traffic.

Naylor, or Nay Nay as we called him, was the first to finish his chips. He used his greasy forefinger to trace over some faintly discernable letters on the Upholster's windows. The word FUCK appeared in large capital letters across one of the windows and OFF across the other. Just at that moment Mr. Askew, the school caretaker, rode by on his bike. Spud Ellis and me pretended we were not with Naylor. When Mr. Askew had gone I said: "You've done it now Nay Nay! Askew will tell Old Pa Hume and we'll be in trouble!" "I didn't do it! Those words were already there!" Naylor almost screamed.

Most of the kids in our class didn't like Mr. Askew. He had an uncanny knack of appearing from nowhere whenever you were up to some mischief. I quite liked him though. He gave me marbles from down the playground grid and a threepenny-bit for shovelling the coke through the manhole into the cellar on Tuesdays after school.

There would have been no need to worry about Mr. Askew though had we known that Mr. Horrocks was sitting in his van, watching us from across the road. He was a devout Methodist and a lay preacher at the Weslyan church. "Caught them at last!", he said, out aloud to himself. "I'll be up at that school this afternoon!"

Mr. Hume, the headmaster, took us for silent reading on Friday afternoons. It gave him the opportunity to do the register and other clerical work. I didn't like him because he never taught us anything and he had his favourites. He used to put his arm around the prettier girls and give them a cuddle. With us boys he put on an angry expression.

Mr. Hume was of middle height, chubby and in his late fifties. He had a short, thick neck, a square, fleshy face and small, piggy

THE DOGS OF WAR

eyes enlarged by thick, brown, horn-rimmed glasses. They were slack and he used his middle finger to push them up his nose. He had bushy, ginger eyebrows and short-cropped grey hair on a balding head. Ginger hairs sprouted from the backs of his freckled hands and from around his wrists. He wore a brown or a grey suit on alternate days and a dark grey one when the school inspectors came. His tie had a tiny tight knot. The bottom button of his waistcoat was always undone. A gold watch-chain hung like a skipping rope across his bulging stomach. He was constantly fumbling in his fob-pocket, palming his watch, and checking the time, even though there was a large clock clicking away on the side wall of the classroom.

Mr. Hume kept his cane prominently on view, resting across the pegs that held the blackboard on its easel. At the least noise he would look up, uncannily always at the culprit, and his face would inflate and redden. If he was very angry his face took on a purplish hue. If he went out and came back in to a noise he would rush through the door with his legs bent at the knees like Groucho Marx, grab his cane and run up the aisles between the rows of desks swishing it from side to side, roaring and spitting: "How many times do I have to tell you to keep quiet when I am out of the room!" He would then pick on someone, generally a slow-witted, scruffy boy with yellowish "candlesticks" running from his nose, called Barry Dunston, or his brother, Peter, who had been kept down a year. He would thrust his face to within an inch of Dunston's face and pummel him in the chest with his fist before dragging him by the ear, or hair, out to the front to cane him. Dunston used to turn his head away when he held his hand out and, like we all did, try to hold his hand slack with his thumb lower than his index finger. It was murder if you got hit on the thumb joint, like it was if you pulled your hand away and the cane caught you across your finger joints. You never pulled your hand away! If you pulled your hand away Old Hume would get even angrier, grab hold of your wrist, swipe you across the legs and give you an extra whack on the hand.

Old Pa Hume was in a very bad mood this Friday. There had only been three boys to cane and when he had announced what they had done to deserve the cane it didn't seem fair to me that they should all of them get three on each hand. They had been swinging on the cloakroom bars before school and one of them had put his foot through the window. The other two hadn't really done anything. We were all very quiet.

When the caning was over and the three of them had gone back to their classroom Mr Hume walked up the aisles looking angrily from side to side. He saw a marble on my desk and he picked it up and put it in his pocket! I had only put it in the pen-groove to look at it!

I had just got back to my desk with *Babies of the Wild* when Mr. Askew ushered in Mr. Horrocks. I kept my head down but I couldn't read for trying to hear what was being said. After what seemed hours Mr. Hume walked down the aisle, stopped at my desk and got hold of my ear between his finger and thumb:

"Come with me you!" he said, menacingly. "I want the names of those other two".

I stood in front of the class looking sullenly down at my feet.

"Well?", he said, pushing me in the chest with his fist.

"I don't know them! I was just walking past on my way back to school".

"Don't tell me lies or you'll get such a thrashing!" he said, picking up his cane.

I could feel the tears coming up as I tried to get my breath to say something. Despite gasping out that I didn't know what the words meant and that I didn't know the other two because they weren't from our school he gave me three strokes of the cane on my left hand.

I tucked the hand between my legs and stamped my feet and snivelled audibly.

"Now will you tell me!" he said, his face going purple.

"I don't know who they were", I sobbed.

Mr. Horrocks was asked if he could identify the others but he could only be sure about me. He thought Naylor was one of them but he couldn't say for certain. Naylor denied it saying he had gone home at dinner time.

Mr. Askew excused himself saying he had to get back to the boiler-room.

Mr Hume turned around to face the class and he glared at each boy in turn. In a very quiet voice he said: "This is your very last chance to own up. If I find out later it was one of you you'll be in very, very, serious trouble!"

He turned back to me and shouted angrily. "And this is your last chance too. I'll give you until Monday to think about it. Hold your other hand out!"

He gave me three more strokes of the cane on my right hand. I nearly bit through my lip. Tears were running down my face as I went back to my place, both hands tucked tightly under my armpits.

There wasn't a murmur from anyone all afternoon. There was no noise either as we filed out at four o'clock to put our books in the cupboard.

Old Hume wasn't watching the cupboard. I pretended to put my book in the box but instead I wedged it under my armpit, inside my coat.

When we were outside Naylor and spud Ellis each gave me some marbles for not splitting on them. As they handed them over my arm slackened and the book fell on the floor at my feet. I looked round furtively and saw a head poking up just above the cellar steps. It looked like Mr. Askew. But when I looked again it was Old Pa Hume, watching us through the railings.

MOVING ON

My mam wanted to swap our little terrace pebble-dashed council house for a semi with a brick-built scullery. There was one on the front of the road that had been bombed and rebuilt. She had even asked the rent man: but we three wouldn't let her swap. It was sixteen houses away round the corner and for Archie, Ernie and me to move out of the street we had been brought up in seemed like emigrating to another country. We wouldn't know anybody round there we protested and besides, "they're all snobby". "And what about my dad's garden!", our Ernie added. "And the bonfire", said Archie. Left to us kids in Polefield Approach even Manchester would never have been discovered let alone America.

So when Twissy opposite told us they were moving to St. Margaret's it was like announcing his premature death. Twissy's dad was too old for the regular fire service and they were disbanding the A.F.S. He was leaving early to be the verger at St. Margaret's church and they were moving into the house that went with the job. My dad said they were moving on in the world. The house was only four-hundred yards from Polefield Approach but it might have been four-hundred miles as far as we were concerned. We'd never see Twissy again and he'd miss the bonfire. The street had not been the same since Cliff Jones got drowned and Eric Tickle started work: it would be empty without Twissy. I remember saying to our Ernie: "Aw 'eck, I wish the war hadn't ended".

The Twiss's couldn't afford Pickford's new van, or even Barlow's old one, so Clarke, the carrier from Heaton Park had been booked to do the moving. His flat farm cart, piled high with scratched second-hand wardrobes, scarred tables, straight-back chairs and rickety brass-knobbed beds stood in the street below our bedroom window. Mrs. Twiss was scuttling out with bags and cases stuffed with clothes and bedding and screaming at their Sheila for dropping the pillows on the pavement.

The shaggy skewbald pony jangled the dull brass fittings on its harness as it tossed its nosebag to get at the last of the oats. Every few minutes it blew down its nostrils to make a noise with its lips like one of those old motor boats on Heaton Park lake. The pony held its tail high and on the road behind a pile of highly polished droppings accumulated to cluster glistening and steaming in the cold morning air. You could smell them in your imagination: my dad's roses were in for a treat. He'd be out later on with his bucket and shovel.

A rime of early frost had both blackened and whitened the privet leaves and a light fog muffled the grunts and gasps escaping from Mr. Twiss as he struggled to load the cart before people were out and about. As the cart disappeared into the thinning fog we caught a last glimpse of Twissy flopped like a limp rag Guy Fawkes into his dad's battered old armchair high up on the back of the cart. Legs dangled about in space above the tailboard and long baggy trousers hung down where a pair of feet should have been. His scruffy black Mac, torn at the back, was half open. The belt was so tight it nearly cut him in two. His mam had wound a bright-red woolly scarf round his neck. "You'll be the death of me, I'll swear you will", she said. A cold, bleached face peered back at her, like a sad clown's, through the face-hole in the blue Balaclava. His dad's trilby, jammed on his head, pushed his ears out like a couple of bright red poppies. We could still see his image long after the sound of the cart wheels crunching the chippings had disappeared.

Twissy, though only thirteen, was a gifted artist: that is to say he could draw and paint nude women better than anyone else in our street. He even painted one on my best blue tie. It seemed, from what we could gather from his breathless, panic stricken gabbling, that he had been given a room of his own at the new house and having nothing better to do had produced half a dozen drawings of nude women. They were copies from his dad's Tit-Bits and some Naturist magazines left by the previous verger in the loft, the entrance to which was in Twissy's bedroom. He had used his imagination for the sexual parts and had even introduced some extra-rude bits here and there. We younger kids were agog as he described his inventions. Having produced the drawings he'd got a hard on and now that he could no longer spy on their Sheila as

she got undressed, and play with himself under the bedclothes, he had used the nudes to excite himself. Just as he was going to hide the drawings in the loft his mother had burst into the bedroom---she was always doing that---and caught him. She was mortified. She was well aware he was up to something--she'd tried to catch him before---but this! This was filthy, unbelievably filthy! "You wicked little sinner. You'll burn in hell you will". Sobbing, she sank down onto the bed. "Just you wait till your father comes home".
But wait was just what Twissy was not going to do. He grabbed his coat and Balaclava and made a run for it.
"Bloody 'ell Twissy, yer dad'll kill yer", our Ernie said. He was like that our Ernie.
"What are you going to do?", asked Archie.
Twissy said he would have to hide until he thought of something. We decided to put him in our air raid shelter until somewhere better came up.
The Andersen still had bunks in it, though we had broken off some of the cross-boards to mend the rabbit hutch and others had split, but the bottom bunk was still useable. "You're a bloody lucky sod, Twissy. We were going to use these bunks for the bonfire", said Ernie. Archie said we'd be able to get the sleeping bag my grandma had made out of an eiderdown and that peg rug must be somewhere under the stairs. The hedgehog might be a bit of a nuisance at night though. "Hey, Gypsies' roast hedgehogs: you'll be all right for something to eat", Ernie said.
Prickles had escaped from his box and somehow got behind the galvanised wall of the shelter. You could hear him scraping the corrugated metal when he moved. It set your teeth on edge and made you dance your feet. Yes, food would be a bit difficult, the shops had shut, but we could get a few bottles of cider from the off-licence. Candles we had: pinched from the ironmongers ready for bonfire night.
The curved metal roof sweated when it rained and water dripped from the bolts. Puddles formed in places on the floor but apart from that it was a perfect hiding place. Twissy wasn't so sure. Next morning he was ready to surrender.
Their Sheila had been round to ask if we had seen anything of

him. She told us his dad was going to murder him. The police were searching the park for his body and they were thinking of dragging the lake. His mother had been given a sedative by Doctor Woodhead. Twissy went as white as a pet rabbit when he heard all this but we talked him out of surrender. Charlie Twiss was not one to spare his fireman's belt and our Ernie said the return of Twissy was all he wanted to start his new job as a grave digger.

That night we raided the bonfire on Sandy Mount estate. Sandy Mount was near to Heaton Park: their gang always had lots of wood. Twissy was scared of being seen but he came with us. We waited at a distance until the guards had been called in for bed and then crept silently along the railings at the edge of the croft. There was no moon. A chilly damp fog concealed us. A quick sprint across no man's land and we were each gripping the trunk of a sapling or grasping for a wooden box. "Now!", shouted Ernie, and we each pulled and yanked and ran.

A roar went up from within the bonfire and a gang of four Sandymounties struggled out from under the wood where they had been settling down for the night to sleep, on guard. They pelted us with stones as we ran, dragging the wood after us. Some we had to let go to snarl up the chase but it was still a worthwhile haul we got away with.

"Christ! my bloody head's bleeding", said Ernie when we reached the safety of the Approach.

"Too bad", I said.

"Do you think they recognised me?", said Twissy.

"Did they bloody heck", said Ernie. "And stop whining".

Twissy was going to pieces: he wouldn't stop snivelling. He was not used to being neglected like we were and he missed his mother despite the way she continually nagged him. He hadn't washed for three days and he was constantly shaking: his face twitched on its own.

"We'll have to do something quick or he'll give himself up and spoil everything", said Ernie. Ernie liked the excitement, the secret life and the intrigue. Most of all he liked being interviewed by the police. He looked so daft, our Ernie did, with his ginger fringe and freckles and his squint and those steel-rimed glasses

with the sticking plaster across one lens. Nobody thought he had the brains to tell lies but he could run rings round the coppers. He had even seen a reporter from *The Guide* and been offered half a crown: "For any information you come across Mr. Wild". He showed us a piece of paper with a phone number on it.
"What are you going to do about Twissy?", Archie asked.
"I don't bloody know", said Ernie.
But later Twissy said he would be all right if he could get somewhere warm to stay until he got enough money to go to Blackpool to look for a job. Even half a crown to buy some Woodbines would be a start he said, looking at Ernie. But Ernie made no response.
The following night, though it interfered with collecting bonfire wood, we decided to help Twissy get a warmer bed by breaking into the empty house on the front of the road---the one my mam wanted us to have---sooner or later the police would search the air raid shelters and we'd all be in trouble. Ernie took the chopper from our coal shed and I had the Commando knife I'd swapped for my stuffed magpie. "We could break into a bloody bank with these buggers", Ernie said, but the woman next door came out with a torch and a dog. We fled down the front path and out on to the main road just as people were coming home from the pictures. "Bloody 'eck, I've been seen. I'll have to hide somewhere else", said Twissy. "Well make sure it's somewhere warm" our Ernie shouted as we left him. That night I had a bad dream about Twissy.

It was Charlie Twiss's last night in the A.F.S. On Monday he started his new job. He had misgivings about them laying him off from the regular fire service but he would not, on balance, be sorry to go. The new job was not entirely to his liking but he didn't think it would get him down and at least he'd be able to see more of the kids. He would miss his mates though. A bottle party had been laid on at the Station and they were keeping their fingers crossed that they would not be called out. They would have to go easy on the booze until the end of the shift but they would be able to let go when the relief crew came on at one.

THE DOGS OF WAR

It should have been quite a jolly occasion and Charlie was doing his best to keep his end up in the snooker knock-out competition, but to tell the truth he was worried sick about that lad of his. "Where the devil could he be?", he thought, as he took another long pull on his pint. The police said they'd had two reported sightings but nothing definite. "If only Bella had turned a blind eye to those drawings".

"For Christ sake, come on Charlie! Charlie! We've lost nearly two minutes already. Can't you hear the bloody siren going!", the Chief Officer shouted as he disappeared down the pole-hole to the engine.

Charlie was off like a damp banger. To tell the truth he was feeling slightly drunk. "Where to?", he said, struggling into his jacket as the engine rounded the corner out of the station.

"Polefield. Bonfire's been set alight. Usual bloody thing I suppose. Buggers can't wait till tomorrow".

The bonfire was big and blazing fiercely. It was well over ten feet high and made largely of timbers pinched from the railway sidings. You could hear the crackle of dry wood and the hiss and sizzle of damp saplings from more than twenty yards away. The roar of the draught and the smell of burning wood smoke filled the streets beyond Polefield Circle. Smoke from the garden rubbish thickened the fog and burning embers showered over the rooftops. Near the fire was a can of petrol and there must have been a store of fireworks inside the bonfire. Bangers were exploding and rip-raps leaping erratically from the flames. Roman candles spouted red and green balls into the air. The fire, glaring ever more fiercely, was reflected back from forty or so windows. Strange figures seemed to be shimmering and dancing about on the far side of it, in the flames; a purifying pagan rite.

Old mother Heys had seen four small forms leaping about, whooping and laughing and running off in the direction of Sandy Mount. By the time she had hobbled across the gardens to raise Mrs. Tickle they had gone and it was like daylight in the gardens. The heat was unbelievable. The Guy Fawkes on the top was well alight, she said, and there were flames round the trilby hat. The red scarf was alight and the white face had disappeared as the figure folded and fell. She thought she heard screeches, she said. And those were surely real screams coming from inside the fire. A figure had struggled from the flames, she was sure, and had flown off over the gardens. Mrs. Tickle said it must have been one of her chickens caught roosting in the den the boys had made inside the bonfire. She sent their Eric to phone the fire brigade from the call box in Polefield Gardens when the trellising caught alight but it was too late to save it.

Our Archie was running frantically round and round the fire screaming hysterically that Ernie and Twissy were sleeping in the bonfire to guard it but as usual nobody took any notice of him. He kept dashing at the fire attempting to pull the logs away and only gave up when his hair got singed almost to his scalp.

The fire engine bell woke up the whole neighbourhood. There must have been over a hundred people crowding down the entries to the back gardens by the time the first hose had been coupled and attached to the street hydrant. Those of my dad's dahlias not keeled over by the frost got snapped off and someone tramped all over his rose beds. He was livid.

The water gushed powerfully and almost took the two firemen gripping the nozzle with it. The jet slewed round drenching Mrs. Jones and a dozen other women before arcing into the air and focusing on the fire. There was a sizzling his of steam and in less than ten seconds the fire was out. Darkness was everywhere and all went momentarily quiet. Only luminous grey smoke was visible: swirling first, then slowly rising in a curling column from the black heap of wood.

"Bring the hurricane lamps", shouted the fire officer. What's that about someone being in there guarding it? Stand away will you!".

The firemen began removing the charred logs and the heavy half-burnt sleepers from the fire.

"Are you sure it wasn't a Guy Fawkes?", asked the fire officer.

"No. It was definitely moving", said Mrs. Palmer. "I saw it move".

"Oh my god! You're right! Move away there will you! Keep those kids back! Where's the police? Sergeant Hewitt! Over Here! Phone an ambulance will you!".

Charlie Twiss lifted the partly burnt remains of a half-grown youth in his arms. He knew those remnants of Balaclava and he didn't need to look at what remained of the face.

"Christ all mighty", he sobbed. "It'll kill his mother".

I saw our Ernie heading for the phone box. His hair was singed away and he had no eyelashes. His face was as black as a fire back except for two white rivers and his tongue looked extraordinarily red. His trousers were burnt down one side and his leg was blistered.

"My mam will kill you when she sees you", I said.

"Aw sod off. Don't you know Twissy was in the bonfire?", he snapped at me.

"Jesus Christ!, he wasn't was he! Didn't he get out with you!?. Bloody hell! What happened?".

I listened from outside the phone box as Ernie spoke to the reporter.

"Yes, that's right, a fire. A bonfire . . . In the back gardens at Polefield. Twissy didn't manage to get out. Yes. Twissy's dead. Yes. Dead. All right, Yes. From the beginning. Yes, O.K. We'd gone back to our shelter. . . Shelter, Yes, our air raid shelter. To drink some Woodpecker's. . . Yes, cider, four bottles. Yes, that's right Twissy was drunk. He could hardly walk. Yes, he'd drunk a lot more than me. We took two sacks of hay that was supposed to be for the guinea pigs, a bundle of old newspapers and a shoe box with my fireworks in it. Yes. O.K. I'll speak more slowly. We had made a wigwam under the bonfire with two gates we'd pinched from up Polefield Grange. Hey!, don't say we pinched them will you! No. It was made of railway sleepers and things. The biggest we'd ever had. Bigger than V.E. night. We had to borrow Mrs. Tickle's ladder to put the Guy Fawkes on . . . No. No. My mam didn't know. No. She didn't know we were going to sleep out to guard it. I had to creep down stairs when they'd gone to bed. Twissy was already there. He'd scattered the hay under the gates and made pillows out of the papers. . . No he was asleep. He just grumbled at me when I tried to wake him. Yes, that's right, drunk. I must have gone off to sleep too because I woke up and thought I could hear it raining. Yes, O.K., more slowly. I could hear something swishing on to the bonfire. Then I smelt petrol and there was a whoosh and the whole bloody bonfire seemed to go up at once. . . Frightened? I'll say I was frightened. I was bloody shitting myself. Hey don't say shitting. Yes. I shouted out and struggled out from under the wood. . . Yes, from under the wood. It was all blazing. I kept shouting "Twissy!", "Twissy!" I thought at first he'd got out at the other side . . . Of course I tried to get back to help him but it was too bloody hot! My trouser leg was on fire . . . Yes. It must have had petrol on it. Twissy was screaming and, and the gate slipped and a sleeper fell on him I think . . . 'Course I was scared. You'd have been scared too, wouldn't you! I couldn't put my trousers out . . . No I jumped over the fence into Banister's. . . Yes. Afterwards I thought I'd better phone the fire brigade. I ran to the phone box and I met Eric Tickle coming back. He said he'd already phoned. . . Yes. Yes. Will I get that half crown you promised? I said will I get that half crown?---Get out Archie will yer---Aw bloody heck, he's rung off".

The funeral had been delayed for nearly three weeks. There had been police enquiries and an autopsy to be gone through. Death by misadventure they said it was. Sergeant Hewitt had cleared his throat rather ominously before reading Ernie's account from his notebook and Twissy's dad had told how he found the body. The kids from Sandy Mount got a right ticking off by the Coroner and he asked for his remarks to be widely reported. He said it was "a saga of moral turpitude" whatever that might mean. "Unaccountable delays in the fire brigade reaching the scene of the fire . . . Under age drinking . . . Railway property desecrated . . . Children living in a state of complete neglect: matters for the proper authorities to look into and to take whatever action was appropriate". He told our Ernie he was a very lucky lad to be alive and Ernie said. "I know my lud". My mam gave him a right pummelling when she got him outside. "Showing me up like that", she said. By the time she'd done with him the reporter had gone. Our Ernie was fuming, again. He'd not only lost the chance of getting his half crown but also the five Woodbines and matches he'd promised himself.

The day of the burial the fog had cleared and the smell of smoke had long gone from the streets. There had again been a keen frost

THE DOGS OF WAR

in the night and the last of the dahlias had gone from the rest of the gardens. The sky was a pale blue and completely cloudless. It was bitterly cold. The Chestnut trees around St. Margaret's cemetery had lost most of their leaves and the sun glowed through the crisscross of black branches like an orange fireball making the last of the leaves look like luminescent candles. The leaves on the path were no longer crisp and the pall bearers had to tread carefully. I noticed Twissy's dad had a black patch sewn on his sleeve. An Armistice Day poppy was still in the buttonhole of his jacket. His eyes looked red-rimmed and sore. The faces of the mourners were starkly white beneath their black hats and veils. Twissy's mam was as white as a ghost: she looked the image of Twissy. She was sobbing and shrunk. My mam had to help her along.

A mound of dark earth, salted with frost, stood on the far side of the grave. The family were at the front and the remainder of the mourners were scattered between the tombstones at the back with their heads bowed. Our Ernie was fidgeting about. Just as the vicar was saying: ". . . He cometh up and is cut down like a flower; he fleeth as it were like a shadow . . . ", a magpie flew by. Ernie whispered to me in a voice people could hear on the other side: "The vicar looks just like a magpie". He was right, he did. My mam said to Ernie, threateningly, through her teeth: "Just you wait till I get you home. I'll magpie you!"

The coffin had been lowered, " . . . earth to earth, ashes to ashes, dust to dust, sure and certain . . . " had been said and Twissy's sister, who was quite openly crying, had thrown a white flower and a handful of earth into the hole when Ernie, who had at last got his half crown from the reluctant reporter at the cemetery gate, and had been flicking it up in the air behind my mam's back, missed and dropped it. It bounced off the toe of his boot and jumped straight in to the grave with Twissy: you could hear it clunk on the coffin lid.

Our Ernie went back to the graveyard the following day to take two rose bushes my dad said would do well in a cemetery. He'd refused to take the bag of horse manure. He was hoping to recover his half crown and praying they'd not yet filled in the grave. As he walked away from the Approach it struck him that with Twissy gone there wasn't a lot, apart from my dad's garden, to stop us moving to the front of the road. His spirits dropped even further as he picked his way through the tombstones. He saw the side view of a man shovel the last of the earth into the hole, straighten up, mop his face with his handkerchief, and lean on his spade to gaze at the mass of still fresh flowers and wreaths heaped nearby.

"I don't suppose you found a half crown did you?", said Ernie.

"Perhaps if we had got there a couple of minutes sooner", said Charlie, to himself, bitterly . . . "If only I hadn't put those "Tit-Bits" in the loft . . . If only Bella hadn't been so damned prudish. . . If only . . ."

"I don't suppose you found a half crown did you?", said Ernie again, more loudly but less hopefully.

Mr. Twiss started. "Oh it's you is it!"

"I don't suppose . . . ", Ernie began again. But then he faltered. "My dad's sent these roses for the grave", he said.

Mr. Twiss took the rose bushes from Ernie and said: "That was a very generous gesture of yours yesterday, Ernie. I've asked the reporter from *The Guide* to mention, in the account of the funeral, that Ernest Wild threw his last half crown into the grave for his friend".

Oh! er . . . yes".

There was a two minutes silence, then Ernie turned to go. As he did so he said:

"Generous. Yes. Generous. Even I hadn't realised I could be so generous. Maybe he'll buy some Woodbines with it".

THE YEAR OF THE BUTTERFLIES

Mr. Hilton, an amateur entomologist whom Twissy's dad knew, recruited Twissy and me to collect caterpillars for him off some poplar trees growing in old mother Mitchell's garden. He wanted fifty poplar grey larvae for a survey that was being done on colour variation in the urban moth. He knew there were plenty of caterpillars on the trees but Mrs. Mitchell, who lived down the Grange, alone, with her several cats was peculiar. She'd seen him but had not answered the door when he'd knocked. He didn't wish to upset Mrs. Mitchell or to be seen loitering in the lane which gave access to the back gardens of the houses in the Grange, so he asked us to get the caterpillars for him. We were more than willing.

Mr. Hilton was a familiar figure on Polefield estate. He was in his mid thirties and unmarried. He lived with his mother, a widow, in a better type of council house off Poppythorn lane, across the road from Polefield. A slightly built man of medium height, he had a hollow chest and walked with a noticeable round-shouldered stoop. He had a good looking, thin, pale face with hollow cheeks and unusually red high spots. He was always well turned out, in a casual sort of way. His small, thick moustache matched the colour of his dark brown trilby hat. The bottle-green Harris tweed jacket he invariably wore had leather patches on the elbows and contrasted with his newer, grey flannel trousers. Mr. Hilton was a consumptive. Prior to the war he'd been in and out of sanatoria and had never been fit enough to work. To get fresh air and fill his time he had developed an interest in natural history. He started collecting butterflies and moths and joined the Amateur Entomological Society. He'd bought a dog to keep him company on his collecting expeditions. People admired the animal's trim condition and before long he found he could make a few shillings giving the neighbour's dogs a haircut or clipping their claws. Mr. Hilton used the money he earned to buy butterfly nets, setting boards, relaxing tins, pill boxes, killing bottles and display cabinets and soon built up an impressive collection of

THE YEAR OF THE BUTTERFLIES

Lepidoptera.
During the war, along with other invalids and the disabled Mr. Hilton had been directed into civilian war work; in his case as a controller with the A.F.S. which was how he came to know Twissy's dad. He passed Twissy's house two or three times each day on his way to call on his lady friend, Miss Margaret Eyres, one of two middle aged spinster sisters who lived with their tall, skeletally thin father down the Grange. Often, when we were helping Twissey's dad in his vegetable garden Mr. Hilton would stop and pass the time of day. More likely than not he would produce a round, black pill box, with a glass top, from his pocket and show us a moth he had caught or a caterpillar he had found. We were fascinated by the different shapes and colours and wanted to know their names. It amazed us to learn that caterpillars were called larvae and pupated and became chrysalides and that some even spun a cocoon. After Mr. Hilton had gone Twissy's mam would come out and tell us not to breathe in his breath or let him cough on us.

Mrs. Mitchell's back garden was a wilderness, overgrown with thickets of raspberry canes, tall grass, Golden Rod and Rosebay Willow Herb. When we arrived, clutching two large biscuit tins to put the caterpillars in, we were surprised to hear old mother Mitchell calling to her cats: she seldom left the house. We could see her small, dumpy form struggling through the wands of Golden Rod back towards the house. We walked on to the end of "the backs". By the time we returned she had gone indoors.
The branches overhanging the lane were too high to reach so we climbed the fence into the garden. I looked back and saw our Arthur had followed us. "Can I come in as well", he said. Archie, as we called him, was two years younger than me and I had to look after him while my mam was at work. He followed me everywhere. We didn't mind having him with us some of the time but it could be irksome, and more so now we were into our teens. "Oh all right then", I said "but you'll have to be quiet".
Twissy was the first to find a caterpillar. It must have been an inch long, grey and hairy. It clutched the edge of half eaten leaf with its claspers, its mandibles chomping away. We watched it

for quite a time before popping it into the tin with its leaf. We soon found more and in a short time we had twenty or so and before long fifty. As we climbed the fence to leave, old mother Mitchell came out and shouted that she would get the police on to us.

Collecting the poplar greys fired our enthusiasm: we too were going to be entomologists. The thrill of searching and finding a caterpillar was more exciting than anything we had ever known. Twissy and me decided to go to Half Acre the following day, collecting for ourselves. Archie wanted to come too but we managed to "lose" him.

Polefield estate had been built on the grounds of Polefield Hall. You only had to walk round the Circle and down Polefield Grove to be out in open farmland. Beyond Stafford's farm the countryside was unbroken as far as Unsworth and Simister. It was a paradise of lanes and hedgerows for bird-nesting expeditions and there were many ponds where we could catch sticklebacks, newts and frogs. Some old houses off Cuckoo lane, towards Besses o'th Barn, had been demolished before the war and not rebuilt. The site was full of rubble and had been colonised by Foxglove, Ragwort, Thistle and Willow Herb. It was known locally as Half Acre. We'd often played at soldiers there, during the war, among the ruins. At the bottom of Half Acre there was a high wooden fence behind which was a line of mature black-poplar trees. It was to these that we made our way.
The branches of the Poplars hung low over the fence and there were convenient mounds of rubble which made some of the higher branches accessible. The lower leaves were young, green and heart-shaped and looked appetizing. We began systematically turning them over but failed to find any caterpillars. It was only when we turned our attention to the older leaves on the higher branches that we found a few Poplar Greys. There were not as many as on Mrs. Mitchell's trees and I was feeling a bit disappointed when suddenly Twissy let out a shout. On the leaf he was holding was a large, fat, green caterpillar about three inches long with a sharp looking horn above a pair of claspers at

THE YEAR OF THE BUTTERFLIES

its rear end. We danced with excitement: we'd never seen anything like it. Along the segments of it's body were tiny red dots. It had three pairs of legs just below its head and four pairs of fat legs in the middle in addition to the claspers at the back. We tried to pick it off the leaf to look at it more closely but it refused to let go. We searched for more but there were none. "It might be a rare one", said Twissy. On the way home we stopped to look on the leaves of a Poplar tree in someone's garden. I found what looked like three little brown pearls on the underside of a leaf. Twissy thought they might be eggs so we took them home with us.

The following day I was working in the bakehouse at Roberts's. Twissy went to Prestwich library to get a book out on butterflies and moths and then went collecting again. Our Arthur went with him. When I saw Twissy that evening he told me the caterpillar we'd found was a Poplar Hawk and that the three eggs on the leaf were Puss Moth. He and our Archie had found a wonderful looking purple caterpillar with lumps on its back which he said was a Pebble Prominent.

In no time Twissy became an expert in identifying caterpillars and surprisingly our Arthur was quite good too. Twissy's dad made him a glass fronted box to keep them in. We would sit in Twissy's bedroom for hours checking out butterflies in Newman's book of British *Lepidoptera* or watching the caterpillars feed. The Puss Moth eggs hatched and grew into spectacular larvae: chunky green beasts with enormous heads fitted with a red mask and huge black eyes. They wore a brown, triangular saddle and had white circles on the sides of their segments. Most spectacular of all were their long, forked tails, armed with orange whips, which they lashed in the air if alarmed. They looked like Chinese lanterns. Before they pupated they each made a rock hard cocoon which they attached to the side of the box. We broke one open, at the soft end they leave to help the moth get out, and found a large wriggling chrysalis inside.

Mr. Hilton showed Twissy how to set butterflies and moths. We bought cork and flat wood from a shop in The Old Shambles, in Manchester, and made setting boards. Twissy's dad had access to Carbon Tetra Chloride used by the fire brigade. He brought some home and we made a killing bottle. It was not as good as the Cyanide Mr. Hilton used. Sometimes a moth or butterfly would revive on the setting board and we would have to soak a piece of cotton wool and put it to its nose. When setting a butterfly you had to do one wing at a time making sure you got the setting needle in a vein near the thorax to move it. It could be tricky getting the forewings at the right angle so the underwings could be seen. You could easily make a hole or damage the scales and lose the colour. We used strips of thin perspex to hold down the wings. Twissy was much better at it than me.

Before long Twissy had acquired a show case and a small collection of his own butterflies and moths. He painted the word *Lepidoptera* on the lid. Archie and me caught Silver and Golden Y's on my dad's night scented Stocks and we helped Twissy collect a whole series of Magpie moth variants off his dad's blackcurrant bushes. Soon kids in the neighbourhood were bringing us finds: Buff Ermine moths, Red or Yellow Underwings, Garden Tigers and Ghost moths. Twissy's cousin found an enormous moth with a skull and cross bones on its head, on a croft in New Moston, the other side of Heaton Park from where we lived. We took it to Mr. Hilton who told us it was a Death's Head Hawk moth, the only British moth which made an audible sound, a squeak. "It's very rare to find one of these in the north of England. Well done lads!", Mr. Hilton said. He announced the find in the *Manchester Guardian*. We felt very important.

Twissy's mam made us a couple of butterfly nets out of some old gauze curtains. We spent days chasing Ringlets and Meadow Browns, Coppers and Skippers and the occasional Fritillary, through the fields of Buttercups opposite Overdale Hall where my Grandma Wild had a flat. The Meadow Browns made us laugh. They chased each other frantically, flying low over the field, then spiralled up into the sunlight, twisting like barley sugar sticks. We often caught them, two at once sometimes, joined together, mating.

The grounds of Overdale Hall had long been neglected. Many of the trees were gnarled and Rhododendrons had grown leggy. Most of the specimen shrubs were lost in banks of brambles. A line of pear trees grew at the edge of what had once been a lawn

THE YEAR OF THE BUTTERFLIES

and in the broad overgrown bed in front of the trees grew a magnificent Buddleia. You could smell the sickly, sweet scent yards away. The tapering florets hung down like purple nightcaps. We used to push our way through the head-high grass, ferns, angelica and rosebay taking care not to be seen from the flats and combine butterfly collecting with stealing pears. The pears were hard but the Buddleia was teeming with Tortoiseshell butterflies, Red Admirals and Peacocks, with their large, colourful, eye markings glided about in the drowsy heat or rested on the flowers, wings spread, drunk on nectar. We didn't need a net. You could easily catch them in a jam jar. Afterwards we would visit my grandma for a drink of water.

At night-time, in front of the fire in our kitchen, making toast, I would go into a trance and day dream about our expeditions to Overdale: A gang of giggling boys squirming like worms over dead ground to steal unripe pears that would crack your teeth. Creeping through the long, seed-shedding grass. Weaving through clumps of Rosebay Willow Herb, brambles clutching my coat. Ropes of purple Buddleia. Flickering Peacocks. Smart Red Admirals, black velvet, scarlet and white, Tortoiseshells, a Painted Lady. A rap on a window. A panicky scramble. Creek of an aged shoe, bulging with bunions. The dull rubber thud of a ferrule, slow across the floorboards. A round stump of finger (chewed by a dog when a girl) pointing down a stick to a twisted leg. The smell of pee on the seat where she sat. Hair, singed ginger at the ends by a hot curling-iron. Her parting: a silver path through a dark wood. The dismal fire of old rhododendron twigs. Smoke spiriting up a chimney a yard-and-a-half wide. A bamboo table: a white gas mantle. Strong black tea, brewed in the cup and strained through the teeth. A dam of leaves silting her mouth up. Pthuth. She would spit the tea-leaves back into the fine, white, bone-china cup she cherished and tell you your fortune, if you were lucky.

And lucky we were. The summer of 1947 was exceptionally hot and ideal for butterflies. Many Continental species seldom seen in England became commonplace in the South and helped by the exceptionally warm winds blowing North found their way to Lancashire. Painted Ladies were frequently sighted and even a

THE DOGS OF WAR

Camberwell Beauty was reported somewhere in the North East. Mr. Hilton told us to look out for Clouded Yellows as they were present in large numbers this year and we might never see them again. Some had been sighted in Cheshire and they could be in the district already. They liked Lucerne and if we came across a field of it in our ramblings we were to let him know. He described the plant as being like a large, straggling clover with a big purple head. He said farmers use it as cattle feed and it puts nitrogen back into the soil. Twissy and me looked up Clouded Yellow, *Colias croceus*. It had orange-gold wings with brown edging on the upper side of both its fore and under wings and a brown spot on the yellow area of the forewing. The underside of the wings each had small dots on them and a line of visible dots or circles tracing the line of the dark brown edging of the upper side. We could have painted you one we spent so much time poring over the illustration.

We toured the farm lanes on our bikes braving the cart ruts and pot holes, looking out for Lucerne, and at the same time keeping our eyes open for bird's nests. Ducking low to avoid the whipping hawthorn branches. Stopping when we came across an Elderberry bush in the hedgerow to search for the Song Thrush's nest it almost certainly contained. But it was too late in the summer: the mud inside was crumbling, the eggs all hatched and the fledglings flown but the lovely green smell of the Elderberry tree stayed with you for hours afterward.

We had given up hope of finding a field of Lucerne and had turned for home when we encountered Mr. Hilton walking his dog. He took a couple of large pill-boxes from the gas-mask bag he used as a haversack and showed us two Clouded Yellow butterflies he had captured in a field of Lucerne near the Simister entrance to Heaton Park. He warned us that the farmer would not be pleased if we trampled his Lucerne and advised us to keep to the edge of the field. It was too late to go now: the sun was going down and the butterflies would be resting.

Next day was fine, the sun shining brightly in an almost cloudless sky. Twissy and me armed ourselves with jam jars and our home-made butterfly nets. We gave our Arthur a couple of bottles of Tizer to carry and set off in a state of great anticipation. The road to Simister ran alongside Heaton Park reservoir. We knew it well from the fruitless forays over the railings to find seagulls eggs. There were plenty of gulls but never any nests. A lane off Heywood road followed the reservoir round and after a quarter of a mile or so met up with the wall of Heaton Park. We had no difficulty finding the field of Lucerne just beyond the entrance to the Golly ponds. We'd been there many times before the war. People used to sail model boats on the ponds but the park had been taken over by the R.A.F. for the duration; they were covered with bull rushes now and only Coots and Moorhens were able to sail on them.

We crept through the Hawthorn hedge and looked out over a large field of Lucerne. The plants seemed limp and bedraggled despite the glistening dew on those where the sun had just drawn back the shadow of the hedge. One or two Cabbage Whites could be seen flying erratically hither and thither but no Clouded Yellows. We skirted the field, keeping close to the hedge to avoid being seen from the farm house in the fold of a hill three fields or so away towards the distantly visible village of Simister. Then we saw them. Not one or two but what seemed like hundreds. There were probably only a couple of dozen but they flew fast and low, crisscrossing. We stood amazed: overawed by the sight of them. We chased them all over the field regardless of Mr. Hilton's advice, sweeping them down with the net and trampling the Lucerne in our excitement. We caught nine but two escaped as we tried to get them from under the net and into a jam jar without damaging them. We were all set to catch more when a gun went off in the direction of the farm house and we saw a man running across the fields towards us. Quickly we gathered our nets and jars and dashed through the hedge and ran up the lane to the safety of the park.

We were too scared to go back the following day but a few days later our courage returned and we made another visit to the field but the weather had changed. A thunder storm was coming on and there was not even a Cabbage White to be seen. Twissy set the specimens and we took them to show Mr. Hilton. His specimens looked somewhat bedraggled, with patches of scales missing, whereas ours looked perfect. "By god!", he said, "These are absolutely magnificent! And so professionally set. I've not seen a better range of Clouded Yellows than these, anywhere. Well done lads. Well done!".

As we were leaving Mr. Hilton showed us an article in the A.E.S. Bulletin. It said that the Fylde coast was an excellent place to see the Six Spot Burnet and the Common Blue in addition to Fritillaries and a wide range of more common butterflies and moths. There was an article on the Goat moth which said that: "At Freshfield, near Southport, half way down the lane from the railway station to the beach, is a gate which is closed once a year to preserve the road's private status. Just beyond the gate is a rotting tree stump in which there are Goat Moth larvae. In the pine woods, on the left, a colony of red squirrels might be seen". Mr. Hilton said he was going to Freshfield the following day with a fellow naturalist to have a look at the stump and to catch some Common Blues. "If we get a good haul I'll let you have a one or two Blues", he said.

Twissy was nearly two years older than me and a natural leader so it was as much a surprise to me as it was to him when later in the week it was me that suggested we should go to Freshfields to get some Goat Moth larvae.
"If we set off early we could be there and back by dinner time", I said.
"Don't be daft, it's over thirty miles from Prestwich. Mr. Hilton didn't say they'd still be there. Anyway, my mam wouldn't let me go".
"We could say we were going to Prestwich Clough for a picnic or something. My mam'll leave some corned beef for my dinner tomorrow, she always does on a Wednesday. I could make it into some sandwiches".
"No, it's too far".
It was not like Twissy to raise objections and I wondered if it was because I had made the suggestion. But the idea of going to Freshfields became irresistible the more he thought about it.
"We'll go, but I've no money!", he said.
"I've got some left from my tips. We can use that. We don't need

much. We can buy a platform ticket and say we're collecting train numbers".

I felt a bit mean leaving Archie on his own all day but it would be too risky with three of us.

We had no difficulty with the platform tickets at Manchester and at Southport there were crowds of people. The ticket collector had no time to look at the tickets we gave him. To be on the safe side, though, we bought two returns to Freshfield so we could switch to the Manchester platform without going through the barrier on the way back.

A wooden sign told us it was Freshfield. It stood in a colourful, neatly tended garden with dazzling whitewashed stones for edging. The name of the station was repeated on the clapboard facia of the cabin-like station shelter. There was no sign of the sea and no one to take our tickets. We walked down the ramped path and stood indecisively at the open gateway. Instead of the lane we had expected we were on a proper road with kerbs and pavements. There were houses and bungalows with parched lawns and hydrangeas of varying shades of pink and blue but no pine woods.

A lady in a twin set with pleated skirt and a pile of blue-grey hair under a silken headscarf was walking an angry looking white Scottie dog which growled and barked repeatedly when it saw us. It pulled at its lead and she bent down and picked it up and held it trapped and growling under her arm: "Jocky, she said, "don't be such a silly dog". She took in Twissy's bulging haversack, the butterfly net and the blue Rescue Service valise of my dad's I had on my back. "Are you going fishing?", she asked. When we told her we were Entomologists going to catch butterflies she widened her eyes and said: "Well, you should be lucky, there are lots of them on the dunes at the edge of pine woods. It's quite a way but don't lose heart, you'll come to the sea shore, eventually".

As we walked we saw large numbers of hairy caterpillar crossing the road, on their pupation march. They looked like Tigers, Buff or White Ermines. We couldn't be sure and we argued about which were which. We collected some of the bigger ones taking care not to touch the hairs with our fingers.

THE DOGS OF WAR

The houses ceased and the bungalows became more numerous. Soon the metalled road was just a few sunken kerb stones with a gravel path and only the occasional bungalow and then no bungalows at all. The pines crowded in on either side, shading one half of the lane and leaving the other in bright sunlight. There were Tortoiseshells about and one or two Blues but they kept too far ahead for us to catch them.
The lane became an earthen track dusted with soft brown pine needles in the middle and piled inches deep with them at the edges. The air was hot and resinous; the hum of insects almost scary. We still couldn't see the sea and there was no sign of the gate. We imagined we saw red squirrels in the woods but they were nothing more interesting than rabbits. It was further than it looked to the small, white opening between the trees at the end of the tapering road.

We almost missed the stump. The gateposts were concealed by grass and weeds and entwining blackberry bushes and the gate itself was a simple pole lying half hidden in the grass at the edge of the pines. The stump was in fact a large, dead, rotting tree. It was the smell that attracted us as we were about to pass it. It certainly reeked of something and we were more than prepared to believe it was goat. The outer part of the trunk was solid enough but the inner core of the trunk was spongy and rotten. We couldn't see any caterpillars but there were plenty of holes. Twissy hacked off a large lump which half filled the valise, confident there would be caterpillars inside. After we'd done it we realised it would have been better to have got it on the way back.
By the time we got to the dunes we were hot and sweaty and quite weary. Most of the lemonade we'd brought with us had been drunk. We wanted to wash our hands to get rid of the smell of goats but the sea was too far out. We stood on the top of a high dune looking West, the sun high above us. The distant sea shimmered in the heat and it was impossible to tell where the sand ended and the sea began. To the right the beach disappeared towards Southport and to the left stretched down towards Formby. We'd never seen so much sand. We lay on the wiry grass in a hollow between two dunes and held our sandwiches in the

THE YEAR OF THE BUTTERFLIES

grease proof bread wrapping we'd brought them in.

There were small ponds and marshy stretches between the pine woods and the dunes and many flowers and succulent plants we'd never seen before. On the Ragwort were lots of Six-spot Burnets with glossy black bodies which looked more like beatles than *Lepidoptera*. Their long black feelers were slightly clubbed and more like butterflies than moths. There were so many we picked off only the perfect specimens. Their black wings shone with a greenish metallic sheen and six red dots stood out boldly on each forewing, matching the blood red under-wings. We found some where the spots had coalesced: they might be rare specimens, with a bit of luck. We'd got more than just a lump of wood to show Mr. Hilton.

We kept alive most of what we caught but we had too many and had to kill some. We poured Carbon Tet. on a pad of cotton wool and put it in the collecting jar to quieten the catch before transferring it to the bigger killing bottle. We would need to relax them later.

We caught a brilliant yellow Brimstone butterfly, several Small Coppers and about a dozen Blues and by that time we'd had enough of collecting. The tide was coming in and we managed to walk almost to the sea but the ribbed sand was hard on our feet. There were lots of knotted worm casts but not much else: one or two fish egg-sacks and a couple of razor shells and a cracked rubber football was all we found.

When we got back to the dune where we had left our things a man was standing near them. He seemed quite friendly. He asked what we were doing and we showed him some of the butterflies. As we were leaving he touched my leg: it was more like stroking really. I didn't quite know what he was doing. I shrieked,"Get off will you", and we ran off towards the lane as fast as our jam jars and haversacks would allow us. The man stood where he was, watching us go.

We set the Six Spot Burnets and took them round to Mr. Hilton's along with the piece of rotten tree stump. We knocked, twice, and as we waited for him to come we heard him coughing in the hallway. He opened the door a little, shook his head, and from behind the handkerchief he was holding to his mouth, said: "Not

THE DOGS OF WAR

now boys. Some other time", and closed the door.

As the summer nights shortened towards autumn the Rosebay Willow Herb lost its lustre and turned to seed. We went back to Half Acre to search for Elephant Hawk moth caterpillars. We'd read they rested low down the stems of the Willow Herb at night and the early part of the day but in the afternoon climbed the stalks to feed. The caterpillars were easily spotted. They were exceptionally long, four or five inches, quite fat and brown like the heads of bulrushes. They had extended front segments which they waved to and fro when searching for food. Twissy said they looked like elephants reaching out for buns. Our Archie found the first one. It quite scared us. It contracted its head and its trunk into its abdomen making its two large eyespots swell in a menacing way when I touched its velvet back. It was only because we'd read that caterpillars were harmless, though some hairy ones could make you itch, that we had the courage to pick them up. We collected six, though we could have taken more, and housed them in a box in Twissy's bedroom, feeding them large quantities of Rosebay leaves. After a week or so they stopped feeding, marched round the cage for hours, then burrowed into the earth on the floor of the cage and pupated. We would have to wait till next Spring for them to hatch. By the look of the pictures we'd seen of the beautiful pink moths it would be a worthwhile wait. Mr. Hilton would be very impressed.

An early frost killed off the Dahlias and many of the other plants drooped, blackened, withered and died. The butterflies and moths disappeared from the gardens and the crisp autumn weather turned wet. We were in for a bad winter, everyone said. We heard from Twissy's dad that Mr. Hilton had been to the sanatorium again but was coming home soon. He must be getting better we thought. We saw him once, through Twissy's window, struggling down the Grange in the rain, to visit Miss Eyers; clutching his coat collars together against the wind with one hand and holding his trilby on with the other. We heard later he'd had a relapse and was critically ill. We wanted to go to see him but Twissy's mam said we were not to. A week later Twissy's dad told us he was dead.

THE YEAR OF THE BUTTERFLIES

Twissy and me kept up a bit of an interest in butterflies and moths and we can still put most of our friends to rights on matters entomological. But by the following summer Twissy was nearly sixteen and we were more interested in girls than *Lepidoptera*. It was Archie who nurtured an enthusiasm for natural history and in due course surprised us all by getting a place at University to study Botany and Zoology. I must ask him about those Six Spot Burnets when I next see him.

SELECTIVE EDUCATION

Soon after I went up into Standard four Mr. Hume, the Headmaster, who taught our class sums and who took us for silent reading on a Friday afternoon, gave me a note to take home to my mam asking her to come to school to see him. I thought I was going to get into trouble so I didn't give it her. I burnt it on the fire whilst she was at the chip shop getting fish and chips for our tea.
A few days later Mr. Hume asked me had I given her the note and I said I had.
"Well ask her to let me know when she's coming to see me", he said.
That was easier said than done. I hardly saw my mam during the week. After school I worked at a Grocer's and Confectioner's either in the bakehouse or taking out 'orders'. By the time I had scraped the cake tins, made up and taken out the 'orders', cleaned out the window-bottoms and helped mop the shop floor it was more often than not after half-past six when I got away. My mam was usually out when I got home: round at her friend Flo Tate's gossiping or at the pictures with our Ernie. Thursdays she went to the first-house pictures at Heaton Park cinema and stayed on for Variety night. Instead of second-house pictures they had a *Compere* and local people did turns, playing the accordion, singing, tap-dancing or telling jokes. By the time I got in from playing hide-and-seek or black-rabbit or climbing-over-gardens she would have come home and gone to bed. She had to be up early in the morning for work.
When I got home my mam was out. She had gone to help prepare the food for a Bar mitzvah at Mrs Matz's where she did cleaning on a Sunday morning. She had left some money on the mantelpiece for chips for my tea. After playing out I listened to Tommy Hanley's *Itma* and afterwards to Valentine Dyall in *Appointment with Fear* on the wireless (this is your story-teller, The Man in Black, huh huh huh uaaarr!). Then I had my wash. I was too frightened to go to bed immediately.
I used to wash before going to bed so that I wouldn't have to wash

in the morning. We always washed at the kitchen sink even when it was cluttered up with the day's unwashed pots. That night I had put the towel over the oven door near the fire to dry. It must have been too near because whilst I was doing my knees I smelt burning. The towel had caught fire and flames were leaping up towards the washing hanging from the rack above the hearth. I panicked, grabbed the flaming towel, screwed it into a ball and plunged it into the water in the sink. I was shaking with fright. A few weeks before, two children had burnt to death in a house fire on Polefield Hall Road and I had been having nightmares about it since. I could smell my singed hair as I put my shoes on and took the remains of the towel to the top of the garden and buried it. I left the door open to get rid of the smell. Later, after I had finished my wash, I noticed that the burnt cloth had scorched my fingers brown. They looked as though they were stained with nicotine like my father's were. "Oh bloody hell!" I said, "My mam'll think I've been smoking!"

It was eleven o'clock when I went to bed. I must have been asleep when she came home, and I nearly missed her the following morning.

My mam worked at Woodthorpe, a large converted mansion, where they made school dinners. They were distributed in containers to the various schools in and around Prestwich, including ours. She left for work shortly after six o'clock in the morning and got home at about three-thirty in the afternoon.

I heard her get up and go downstairs and I shouted:

"Mr. Hume wants to see you".

"Have you been getting into trouble again!", she shouted back up the stairs.

"No. He just wants to see you", I said.

"You must have been. Why else would he want to see me! Did he give you a note?"

"No. He just said he wanted to see you!"

"Well how can I see him, I'm working. They'll stop my money if I have time off!"

There was a few seconds silence then my mam shouted up in an irritable voice:

"Oh tell him I'll come to-morrow morning. I'll try and get half an

THE DOGS OF WAR

hour off work, but if you've been in trouble it'll be the carpet beater this time, I warn you now!", she said as she slammed the front door.

I couldn't settle to do my sums the following morning, knowing my mam was coming to see Pop Hume. I pretended not to know who it was when she appeared at his desk but I could feel myself going red.

My mam and Mr. Hume talked in whispers, so I couldn't hear what they were saying. After a few minutes Mr. Hume called me out. All the other kids stared at me as I walked to the front. Mr. Hume glowered at them "Now get on with your work!", he said, as he conducted me and my mam into the infant's cloakroom. He let go of my arm and looked at me intently.

"I've just been telling your mother you are one of the best scholars in the class, even though you don't always behave yourself. You and the others in the top set will have to start doing homework. The ten of you will have to stay behind after school on Tuesdays and Thursdays for half an hour's extra work. You'll all have to do homework at the weekend as well if you are to get through to the grammar school but your mother says she doesn't think you'll do it. Will you? Don't you want to go to Stand Grammar School?"

I remained silent, looking down at my feet. When I was in the second of the two infants classes I had been energetic and disruptive, fidgety and always talking. I was as often standing behind the coat-stand in disgrace as sitting in my place. But I was first with my hand up to answer questions and I could read well. I always got a star for my work. I remember one particular morning, even though I hadn't done anything mischievous, Miss Mather sent me to Mr. Hume. Instead of telling me off he said: "I'm going to put you up into Standard one to see how you get on". So I was a year ahead of my age group but when I got to the end of the year in Standard three I had to stay down to let the others of my age catch up. All my friends were in Standard four. I hated having to do the same work all over again. Mrs Mitchell moved me about the class to help the others and sent me on errands. By the time I was in Standard four I had begun to dislike school. Most of the boys from our estate I was friends with had

SELECTIVE EDUCATION

moved on to Hey's Boys' Secondary Modern School where they played football. I was desperate to join them. There was only Joe Gooch and Jeff Reynolds left from the council estate all the others were 'stuck up' kids from the Heys estate or sissies from around St. Margaret's.
"Well? Have you lost your tongue?"
"I want to go to Hey's Road", I said. "All my friends go there. I want to play football with them".
My mam looked at Mr. Hume and said: "He's football mad. He won't do homework. I just can't keep him in at night. As soon as he's had his tea he's off out. I don't see him 'till it gets dark. I wish you would tell him Mr. Hume. He's out 'till all hours!".
"Is that right?", said Mr. Hume.
"Well, I work at Roberts's after school and on Saturday morning taking out 'orders'. I have to play out sometime", I said, in a sulky voice.
"You will have to do homework if you want to go to Stand Grammar School you know. A lot depends on my recommendation. I won't be able to recommend you if you don't do homework".
I could see myself never being able to play out so I said, emphatically: "I don't want to go to Stand. My dad said I'd end up a pen pusher if I went there".
Mr. Hume stood staring at me, his lips pursed, his head shaking from side to side.
My dad was in the Rescue Service. He had no trade but was proud of the fact that he worked with his hands. He despised non-manual work. He was an 'upside-downer' who revered the working class. Before being drafted into the Rescue Service at the start of the war he worked as a general labourer on any kind of job that came up: mending the road, emptying dustbins, dock work, gardening, anything. For most of the 1930's he'd been unemployed. He had been active in the *Communist Party* and *The Unemployed Workers Movement* and got himself black-listed. It had been impossible for him to get a regular job. He didn't want us to suffer a similar fate but he didn't actively do very much about it.
All through childhood my dad kept telling us: "Get a good

THE DOGS OF WAR

education and you'll get a good job. What he meant by a good job was an apprenticeship in one of the skilled trades such as joinery, printing or engineering. "You'll be alright if you get a trade", he used to say, but he wasn't seriously interested in our education. I remember, later, he wouldn't even sign the form for me to do the thirteen-plus for the technical school because he'd had a row with my mam the week before and wasn't speaking to any of us. So much for his interest in our education!

And he despaired of our Ernie ever getting a job. Our Ernie was four years older than me and six years older than our Arthur. He was a cack-handed, thin, weedy boy, with a bad squint and glasses and his head always in a book; not by any means your ideal candidate for manual labour.

My dad used to say: "He'll never work, that one." (Our Ernie was always referred to by my dad as 'that one', even when he was present). "I don't know what'll become of him. He'll never work. There might be a chance for the other two".

"My dad doesn't want me to be a pen pusher", I said again.
Mr. Hume again shook his head.
"Well, it's up to you Mrs. Wild. Let me know on Monday what you decide".
I definitely didn't want to do homework and I didn't want to give up working for Roberts: I had got used to the money and so had my mam. She left it for me to decide.
On Monday I went up to Mr. Hume's desk before lessons began and said: "My mam doesn't want me to do homework".
After that Mr. Hume moved me out of the right-hand row where the top set sat and put me next to Michael Hamberger to help him with his sums. I sometimes had to sit next to Carol Bell and Ruth Mangel to help them with their reading: I didn't like sitting next to girls. When Mr. Hume wanted messages taken to other schools he sent me with them. I liked going with notes to Hey's Road. I used to watch them playing football. On the way back I would watch workmen digging up the road or gaze into toy-shop windows. It used to feel strange though, being out of school with no other children about: everywhere looked bigger and quieter. I used to wonder what the people in the street were doing and why they

were not at work. Perhaps they wondered what I was doing and why I wasn't at school. Anyway I was glad I wasn't.

At first I thought I'd been smart to get out of doing homework, I used to scoff at the others having to do it but underneath I was uneasy and secretly envious that they could take their school books home whilst the rest of us couldn't. It made them seem special somehow, more serious, more grown up.

Spud Ellis and Ronnie Cheetham had been bought shiny leather satchels for Christmas and soon all of them in the top set had satchels, even if only canvas ones. Some of the other kids had them too but it seemed to me a bit ridiculous having a satchel just to bring your lunch in so I didn't have one.

I still came near the top in the class tests but I was lower down than before and Mr. Hume paid less attention to me and didn't give me the same work as the top set. I had been off school looking after our Arthur who had mumps so that my mam could go to work and I'd missed doing fractions. When I asked Mr. Hume why you had to invert and multiply to divide he wouldn't explain it. He just snapped at me: "Don't ask stupid questions, just get on and do it". I didn't like Pa Hume and I wanted to get even with him.

On the next class test instead of coming in the top three as I usually did I came sixth. I could feel my cheeks burning as he paused and looked at me as he read out the names. I didn't like it that Shirley Wright and Kathleen Cable, girls, had come higher than me. The following day on the way home from school I asked my friend, Naylor, to show me his homework book. After that I regularly borrowed his books in exchange for helping him. Unfortunately his dad got killed in the 'D-day' landings and he left our school to go to a boarding school run by the Freemasons. I borrowed Fred Batty's books after that but his father too had been drowned early in the war in the Navy and his mother got help to move him to Bury Grammar Preparatory School as a fee payer so that he could automatically transfer to the senior school through the entrance exam rather than have to pass the eleven plus.

I missed a lot of lessons having to go messages and having to accompany Mr. Benson, the School Board man, round the streets to help to identify truants or to knock on the regularly absent

THE DOGS OF WAR

Peter and Barry Dunstan's door whilst Mr. Benson hid behind a wall after they had failed to answer his knocking earlier. Despite all this by the time the Eleven-Plus examination came round I was again in the top three in the class tests. I still wanted to go to Hey's Road but I didn't want to be seen as a dunce and I wanted to get even with Old Pa Hume for taking me out of the top set and sitting me next to Michael Hamberger and those girls. I wanted to pass the selection exam even though I didn't want to go to the Grammar School.

I missed out on the practice papers on the three Tuesday evenings before the Eleven-Plus and as the top set weren't allowed to keep the papers there was no way of finding out what the tests were really like. One of the girls told me that there were all sorts of puzzles with circles, squares and triangles that you had to fit together, or identify the odd one out, and lists of letters where you had to complete the sequence but it all seemed a stupid waste of time to me.

We sat the Eleven-Plus at Hey's Road School along with kids from The National, St. Margaret's and Park View. Not everyone from the British school was allowed to sit the exam and Pa Hume was cross with me for changing my mind and saying I wanted to sit. It was only after some grumbling that he agreed to put my name down.

The Assembly Hall where we took the test was enormous and was also used as a gym. There was a full-size stage at one end and the floor was marked out for Badminton Courts. There were wall-bars around the walls and wooden vaulting horses and benches stacked at the back of the Hall. I remember I was so excited at being at Hey's Road I couldn't concentrate on the tests at first and I just sat there looking round for ages after the others had begun. After I had done the Composition, the Comprehension and the Precis I did the sums but when I came to the puzzles I didn't know properly what I was supposed to do and by the time I had got the hang of them the bell went for us to stop and I had only done half of them. When I got outside I realised that I really wanted to pass and go to Stand: I didn't want to be lumped in with Michael Hamberger and Carol Bell and all the other dunces.

Just before we broke up for the summer holidays Mr. Hume

called me out of class and took me into the infant's cloakroom. He told me that much to his surprise, in view of my not having done homework, I had done very well in the Eleven-Plus. I was borderline, he said, on one part of the test and he had been asked to make a recommendation about borderline cases.

"Do you still like football?", he asked, and I told him I did. "Do you still work at that grocer's?" Again I said yes. He looked at me for a long time and said: "I don't think you would be happy at Stand".

"I think I might be", I said. "I was top in the last class test".

"Well I warned you that you had to do homework didn't I. You make it very difficult for me. There's another borderline case and he did the homework. There aren't places for both of you. I'm surprised you've done as well as you have without homework. You put me in a quandary, do you know that?"

I looked down at my feet. I didn't like him and I didn't want to tell him I'd been doing homework on my own.

"On balance I think you had better go to Hey's Road. You won't have homework there and you'll be able to play football. It's a pity. Off you go".

When the official letters were sent out and the results published of the eight of us remaining from the original top set seven had passed. I was the only one who failed to get selected. I was not at all happy to go to Hey's Road and I didn't get on the football team either!

HEY'S ROAD SCHOOL

Most of the teachers at Hey's Boy's Secondary Modern School were male, young, enthusiastic, and recently demobilised from the army, navy or air-force. They were good teachers, on the whole, and friendly towards us, but there were exceptions. The Headmaster, George Storey, a disciplinarian in his sixties, had been in charge of Prestwich police force throughout the war: he was anything but friendly. Neither was Old Slingsby, nor Mr. Fielding, our form teacher, he wasn't friendly either. The women teachers were pleasant enough and one or two were---how shall I put it---interesting, let us say.

As the men came back from the war in 1946 most of the older women-teachers were retired but some women teachers were kept on: Mrs. Whip, Maths; Mrs. Dawson, History; Mrs Dean, Transition, and young Mrs. Webb, P.E. Mrs. Webb was the wife of the Gardening teacher, Jack Webb, a war-time survivor who, shortly after returning, tragically pierced his foot with a fork whilst demonstrating to us the danger of its misuse. The wound got gangrene and Jack had to have his foot off; then part of his leg; then another part, and another, and when he ran out of leg, he died. Mrs Webb recovered from the shock but surprisingly she never remarried.

The Woodwork teacher, Mr. Slingsby, an old man near to retirement, managed to cling onto his job. He had taught my dad Manual, as he called it, at Hope Park school when my dad was a boy and Hope Park a mixed-sex school. He was a sadist, Slingsby. He would cane you with a hammer handle for the most trivial reason. Each year he managed to make at least one new boy faint from shock. He would approach a boy mis-using a cutting tool, such as a saw, a plane, or a chisel, and produce a match-box from his pocket saying: "The last boy that used a saw like that had a nasty accident. Let me show you". The match box had the back edge missing so that as he cupped it in his hand and opened it Mr. Slingsby could insert his thumb into the box so that it reposed on a nest of red ink-soaked cotton-wool which he had placed inside. Being his own real thumb it was a very convincing severed one. Michael Hillier turned green, fell flat on his back and cracked his head open on the parquet floor.

Mr. Fielding, the Geography teacher, a serious, scholarly man with little sense of humour, was our 1A form master. I think he had been in "bomb-disposal" during the war but perhaps it was a schoolboy rumour. Anyway, he had a very short fuse. I remember one summer's day the sun was shining direct and dazzling onto the row of classroom windows that looked out across the distracting approach-road to the school. The room grew hotter and hotter as the morning wore on and eventually Mr. Fielding realised that it was the heat and not his boring lesson which had caused half the class to nod off to sleep. He asked me to open the bottom vents and then the top sky-lights using the window-pole which was propped in the corner next to the wall-mounted blackboard at the front of the class. I was pleased to be asked: we were all new boys and it made me feel noticed: made me feel important. I took the long pole in both hands, hooked it in turn into the eye of the catch on each of the six windows lowering them noiselessly into the open position. I went quietly to the front of the class and placed the tall pole back in the corner and returned to my seat.

Mr. Fielding was standing to one side of his desk, facing the class, with his thighs pressed hard against one of the desks in the front row explaining the mysteries of river courses. How on alluvial plains rivers eroded their own banks and occasionally made "that interesting natural phenomenon the ox-bow lake" when, entirely of its own volition, the propped pole started to slide along the wall in the direction of Mr. Fielding.

I stared at the pole in a fixation of bemused horror as it moved in slow motion along the wall. When it was immediately behind Mr. Fielding, as if by magic, or some malign magnetism, the pole changed direction, hovered for a moment and then fell and struck Mr. Fielding on the right temple with a loud thwack, then thudded to the floor. There was a second's stunned silence before a loud cheer roared out from the class and a chorus of feet started stamping. Mr. Fielding flinched, sagged slightly, then reeled round the room clutching the large, blue-black egg growing alarmingly on the side of his head before staggering out to the

THE DOGS OF WAR

wash-room to splash it with cold water.

When Mr. Fielding returned the class was still bubbling with laughter and guffaws and the hubbub of re-tellings for those who had been dozing off. "Very funny Wild! You did that on purpose didn't you!"

I intended to simply say "no I didn't" but instead what came out was hysterical, uncontrollable laughter as my mind did a re-run of the event. There was clearly some deep-seated psychological relief being expressed here, that the injury was not serious, mixed with a shock reaction to the event and the slapstick comedy of it, derived, in all probability, from reading too many comics and watching Laurel and Hardy films at the pictures on a Saturday morning but these derivatives escaped the insight of Mr. Fielding. All he could see was an unrepentant buffoon who had caused him humiliating pain and a not inconsiderable injury. His hand came suddenly from somewhere behind his back in a broad arc and gave me a mighty whack across the ear. "Stand outside the room until you're ready to apologise!", he shouted at me.

I stood, helpless, against the corridor wall, shaking with hysterical mirth as I re-lived the scene of the levitating pole, propelled by the prankster poltergeist, which had clearly long been planning to get Mr. Fielding for some arcane reason known only to itself and had spied its chance through me. The more I laughed: the more I laughed. I just couldn't control myself. The laughter rang out louder and louder, amplified by the favourable acoustics of the narrow, glass-sided, tin-roofed corridor. When the classroom door opened, and Mr. Fielding came thundering out, I was bent double, eyes streaming, both hands over my mouth in an attempt to stifle the noise: "Right Wild down to the Headmaster's study. We'll see if he can give you something to laugh about. Tell him what you've done and tell him I want you caned!"

I didn't knock on the Headmaster's door, I simply stood in an imaginary line outside, hoping that he was not in but too fearful to knock and find out. He had a terrifying reputation as a caner, George Storey, and I knew from the junior school how painful caning could be. I was still intermittently chuckling as I stood there but in a much more controlled way. I was desperately hoping I would be able to keep from laughing out aloud when I had to explain why I was there when the door opened and Mr. Storey came out. "Can I ask you what you find so amusing", he said, with a furrowed frown on his face. I told him what had happened in the classroom and protested that I had not placed the pole in an intentionally precarious position and that I didn't know why I couldn't stop laughing about it.

Mr. Storey had been watching me intently throughout my account whereas I hardly looked at him, for fear of laughing, so I couldn't read him properly. I had never seen him close up and was surprised what a thin, grey, lined, smoker's face he had and how hollow his cheeks were. He looked ill, though his eyes were clear and alert enough, and brilliant blue: like Adolf Hitler's, I thought. His facial expression seemed quite kind but it hadn't changed throughout my account, nor did it when I tried to stifle yet another bout of laughter. Surely he too could see the funny side of it!

When he said: "Come into my room", I thought I was simply going to get a telling off.

I followed him into the warm, cosy, carpeted study and stood at the side of his desk. "I'm surprised at you, Wild", he said. "I had a very good report of you from Mr. Hume. Hold out your hand".

I thought at this point I was going to get one stroke of the cane at most but he gave me three on my left hand, the swine, and he hurt me very badly.

I was quietly crying when I left the room and I was still crying when I got back to the classroom. I didn't go in. I just turned round and went home.

Mrs. Dawson took us for history. She was an attractive looking fair-haired woman in her early thirties with a pleasant open face, intelligent blue eyes, good teeth and a winning smile. Her body was voluptuously ample and emanated vitality. She had a broad mobile bottom, strong thighs and a full, round, equally mobile bosom which she kept disappointingly covered in a high-buttoned blouse or, very occasionally, wobbling about, bra-less, under a lightly stretched jumper. Along with the young Mrs. Webb, a taller, thinner, less desirable woman, but a woman with some sex appeal non the less, she provided a focus for our rapidly awakening, albeit prurient, sexual, teenage fantasies. There was

THE DOGS OF WAR

endless speculation about whether Mrs. Dawson would or would not do it with a schoolboy, unlike Mrs Webb about whom we had no doubt. Mrs. Webb took the first-years for P.E. and often came into the showers to supervise what was going on. Her frequent peeps round the wall at the naked boys were anything but coy and she had even been known to give some of the bigger boys a helpful rub down with a towel if they looked like being late for the next lesson. This dubious interest in our welfare was more than enough evidence for us to label her a rampant nymphomaniac who probably doubled as a prostitute in the evening after school. The general opinion was she was definitely up for it. Eric Tickle confirmed it.

Prior to Jack Webb returning from the war, Eric Tickle, a fourth year boy who lived in the same street as I did, used to go to Mrs. Webb's house on a Saturday morning to help her do her garden. Eric Tickle's tales of how, after gardening for an hour or so she would invite him into the house held us all lustfully envious and slaveringly spellbound. After gardening Mrs. Webb would feed him tea and cakes whilst she went upstairs to have a bath after which she would shout him to come up to dry her. He would describe how he rubbed her hot, damp body through the double bath-towel whilst she put her arms around his neck and kissed him. Or she would suggest that he too might like to take a bath--- Eric varied the story a little with each telling. He would describe how she came into the bathroom in her dressing gown to help him get dried. How she would rub, caressingly, between his thighs and comment on what a big boy he had grown into. Her dressing gown, which was, inevitably, sensuously silky, had slipped open whilst this was happening and his hand had been gently placed on her pulsating breast. He never finished the story. "Go on. Go on Eric!" we would urge, "What happened next?". "What happened next?". "What happened next I leave entirely to your imagination", he would say, " but I emerged from the house two hours later a very happy Eric". It was all a figment of the priapic Eric's wishful-imagination but even the most sceptical of us couldn't help thinking, as we sat on the lavatory or whilst exploring the naked body of Mrs Webb for ourselves in our beds that night, that it might after all actually be true. Anyway, whether it was true or not, she always did it for us.

John Harvey and me sat on the front row immediately in front of Mrs. Dawson's desk which was on a slightly raised dias. Our double-desk was flush against it but a little lower. John was much taller than me and precociously mature for a twelve-year-old. He had more pubic hair than anyone else in our class. He also had the deepest voice and the biggest dick in the class, an object which he was constantly displaying beneath the desk, even in daylight. When the room was darkened for an Epidiascope slide show boys sitting in adjacent desks would be invited to feel its size or he would blatantly masturbate it. He wasn't the only one. I'm sure Mrs. Dawson knew what we were up to but she unblushingly ignored what was going on.

Mrs. Dawson used to sit at her desk marking books whilst the class were copying notes from the board or reading text books. She sat with her legs about a foot apart and with her skirt, which was normally well below her knees, rucked up above them. You would have had to have grovelled under her desk to know this and that is precisely what John Harvey was constantly doing. He would give us daily reports as to what kind and colour of knickers Mrs Dawson was wearing and whether her suspenders were black or white. "What are you doing down there Harvey?", Mrs. Dawson would ask if she noticed his disappearance. "Looking for my pencil Miss", Harvey would say, innocently. "You are always dropping it on the floor. If you drop it once more today you'll get detention!"

Occasionally I would drop my own pencil and if she didn't look up after a decent interval I too would quietly slip down underneath the desk to have a look up that dark, inviting passage beneath Mrs Dawson's skirt and marvel at those erotically exciting suspender-stockinged legs. It was a breathtakingly exotic experience and quite addictive. I could understand how Harvey had become obsessive about it.

One day Harvey joined me under the desk to help find a pen which I hadn't dropped. "Watch this", he whispered. To my horror Harvey crept forward, his hand held out in front of him, stiff, straight and upright. He inserted it, without touching, between

THE DOGS OF WAR

Mrs. Dawson's thighs. I was absolutely petrified as his hand went gradually further and further up Mrs Dawson's skirt. Past the stocking tops it went, past the area of pale white flesh with the black suspenders, and on and on to stop within an inch of Mrs. Dawson's crotch before being withdrawn slowly back again. My head was almost exploding when I surfaced.

In the playground afterwards Harvey bet me a shilling I couldn't do what he had done. It was three weeks before I plucked up the courage but I won that shilling.

A TALE IN THE STING

As I drifted back to consciousness I thought I heard my mother's voice in conversation outside the tent. Surely they hadn't sent for my mam. I glanced down at the throbbing arms which lay before me on the blanket through the slits where my eyes used to be. To my astonishment my arms were completely blue. I manoeuvred to try to pull off the sheet to look down at my naked body. I could feel my back, hard on the ground, through the thin straw palliasse and I winced with pain. My body was totally blue too. Then I realised what it must be. "Oh God!" I groaned to myself. "I look like a bloody ancient Briton, daubed with blue wode!"

My body was hot and throbbing, my head was swollen and sore but the worst pains were in the palms of my hands. My hands were so swollen and stiff I could hardly move my fingers. My legs felt hot and swollen too. I imagined the skin bursting open like fried sausage: the pain was excruciating.

A voice I recognised as Mr. Ferguson's, our deputy head's, said: "He's going to be alright Mrs. Wild but it wouldn't be advisable to take him home with you on the bus. We must at least wait until the swelling goes down". "Bloody dead right I thought". The idea of jolting up and down on a bus in this state put me in a panic until I realised the total impossibility of it.

"The doctor said it would take two or three days at least for the swelling to go down. He's given him some tablets and left us a lotion; though we'd already painted him with dolly blue. There's not a lot else we can do. The doctor took most of the stings out last night but we'll have another look at his head and his hands when he wakes up".

There was very little light in the tent. I was lying on my straw palliasse with my feet towards the centre pole. The other palliasses were neatly folded, with boxed blankets, interleaved with sheets, placed squarely on top. They were arranged in the usual circle around the tent's perimeter in front of the brailings. The ground-sheets had been left covering the floor and the brailings had been left rolled down. Derek Baguley's billy-can with water in it was standing beside my bed. "I hope they don't expect me to drink out of that", I thought. I'd been rotten to

THE DOGS OF WAR

Baguley and I now wished I hadn't.

Baguley was the smallest boy in our tent. He was underdeveloped, timid, effete and vulnerable. Teasing Baguley gave us all a common interest and in a funny kind of way bound us together. It even made Baguley part of the group and he seemed happy enough to accept his role as the butt of our cruel humour. It was the price of belonging that we made him pay. Not only did the others take the piss out of him they tried to put it back into him. Baguley was a good sleeper: he went to sleep the moment his head touched the kit-bag he used as a pillow. Unbeknown to Baguley we used his billy-can to pee in during the night to save us the walk to the latrines which were all of twenty-yards from the tent. With something to pee into you could do it in the tent and just lift up the brailing and pour it onto the grass outside. Nobody told Baguley so he never washed the billy-can before filling it with tea from the urn when he went for breakfast in the morning. "What are you all laughing about?" he would ask. "What's so funny?"

I heard the door flap being unlaced. It opened and Mr. Ferguson came in accompanied by my mam. "Oh my god!", she said. "What have they done to you!" I managed a feeble: "I'm O.K." but that was all.

My mam gave me some toffees and a bottle of pop and said I was to come home as soon as I felt able to travel. To avoid an argument I agreed but I had no intention of going home early. If I got better enough to go I would be better enough to stay but that kind of logic would be lost on my mam so I didn't say anything. I'd been looking forward to the school camp for months and there was no chance I was going to miss it now that I was here. We'd only been here three days, there were thirteen left to go.

We'd been preparing for the school camp for weeks. Practising erecting and striking the school bell-tents on the sports field and later putting up the large, hired marquee; cleaning the stoves; polishing the brass-handled cooking pans and dixies; disinfecting milk churns to store our water in; studying maps of the area of Chatburn and Clitheroe; and having lessons on flowers, trees, insects, and the wildlife of the English countryside.

Along with half a dozen other boys I had been chosen for the

A TALE IN THE STING

advance party. We had travelled with the tents and other equipment in a truck a day before the others so as to have the tents pitched and the camp set up before they arrived. I was looking forward to staying on an extra day to take the tents down when the others had gone. Everyone was envious of us. "Two extra days! You lucky jossers!", they kept saying.

When my mam finally went I lay on my bed feeling ill and miserable. "Everything happens to me!", I thought to myself.

"If only Billy Whipp hadn't put his foot through that wasps' nest!"

"Why did it have to be me that got stung!"

"Some use having two extra days if you have to spend them in bed".

The previous day had been ideal for our incursion over the border into Yorkshire: a clear blue sky except for a few powder-puff clouds round the rim of the hills to the north-west; a high, warm sun and just the faint trace of a breeze to keep at bay the more torrid temperatures we'd been having since we arrived: ideal for walking. I was very excited: I'd never been to Yorkshire and I didn't know what to expect.

We ate an early breakfast of cornflakes and fresh, creamy milk from the farm followed by crispy bacon, two eggs, fried tomatoes and fried bread which the duty fatigue tent got up early to cook for us. After we had eaten we cut our own cheese or corned-beef sandwiches and packed them into our haversacks along with a tomato and some fruit. Then we set off for the unknown.

Len Layton, the fourth-year prefect in charge of our tent---a lanky, blonde, blue-eyed, youth with a good-looking face that would have got him into propaganda films in Adolf Hitler's Third Reich---was to lead us through the fields, woods and dales to Gridlington: a fair distance over the Yorkshire border from the valley in which Chatburn lay. We were in a happy mood, laughing at Frank Drabble ribbing Baguley about how like piss the tea tasted in a morning. The narrow path was dead straight and went first through a field of sheep-grazed grass, then through a field with a herd of young, black and white Friesian bullocks which clustered together and followed us, inquisitively, as far as the fence. Later, the cattle-fields gave way to tall meadow grass.

We walked in single file, one behind the other, like African explorers. I trailed my hand in the grass noting the masses of buttercups and meadow-sweet and the occasional red poppy, flowers we had been told to look out for. The grass was cool to touch but the fields, overall, had a soft, warm, yellow cast which began to dazzle me as the sun grew warmer and the breeze declined. It was one of those days you remember from childhood, later, when you look back: the hum of insects and the low drone bees busily at work amongst the red and white clover; the rickering stridulation of the grasshopper you can never find in the long grass; the cloud of midges in your path which you squeeze your mouth shut against so as not to swallow and then have to breathe out down your nose to run through; the frightening, angry cloud of big brown flies which rise in a swarm as you pass the unexpectedly fresh cow-pat on the path.

Small Blue butterflies, Small Coppers and the occasional Skipper flitted about on the path ahead and there were dozens of Ringlets and Meadow Browns chasing each other a few feet above the meadow. Occasionally we crept up close to look at a Tortoiseshell or a Red Admiral butterfly feeding on a drying cow-pat. The colours were so freshly painted, so vividly blue, so white and red, and the blacks and browns so like thick velvet you wanted to stroke them. I collected butterflies and moths so I knew the names of them, just like I could recognise the eggs when we went bird-nesting. Everyone used to ask me: "What's that one Wildy? Eh Wildy, what's that one?" I couldn't believe that other people didn't know the names.

The fields gave way to woods, mainly oak trees with rough, deeply grooved bark which felt hard and sharp on your palm when you touched it. The acorns had not yet fully formed so we couldn't pick them. Some of the leaves had mottled brown growths like freckles on their undersides. I jumped up and grabbed a branch with a bunch of oak-apples on it. Two of them were rock-hard with a hole like a bead but the other was a pale, creamy-pink, soft and slightly spongy. I cut it open with my penknife and found a small wriggling grub inside. Mr. Ferguson told me later that it must have been the larvae of the gall wasp. I didn't know that.

The trees had plenty of leaves on so the woods were shady but the sun filtered through in parts and there were open spaces with lots of small shrubs, bracken and brambles and the occasional moss covered log with clusters of old, grubby looking bracket fungus on their damp, crumbling undersides. Again there were lots of butterflies and I saw a Speckled Wood in one of the clearings.

We ate our lunch in a clearing on the edge of a wood in sight of a large, still, sunlit pond, almost a small lake, with tall reeds round the fringe and in parts reaching almost to the centre. Occasional solitary bull-rushes stood proud of the other reeds, their velvet, dark-chocolate brown heads poised in the air like bell-ropes. Numerous small electric-blue dragonflies skimmed the surface of the water near the open edge of the pond. I went over to have a closer look at them. The surface of the pond supported a great many pond-skaters, gliding about on their spread-eagled legs. There were lots of water-beetles too in the pond and one or two water-boatmen. They oared themselves down towards the muddy bottom as I bent to look more closely at the pond-skaters. I thought too that I saw a crested newt disappear deep down amongst the roots of the reeds but I could have been mistaken. A large, brown, predatory dragonfly patrolled back and forth across the pond and part-way into the wood.

On the far side of the water there was a sedge-filled swamp in which one or two Herefords were squelching about whilst higher up, in the drier part of the meadow, more cows were lying down chewing their cud, twitching their ears and blinking to disturb the annoying flies attempting to settle on their eyelids.

The sun was high and hot and despite the heat there was still a faint hum of insects but they didn't detract from the stillness of the scene nor from the quietness that fell when the echo of our voices came and went across the water. I was reluctant to leave the pond, it was so interesting.

When we set off on our walk again I was the last in line. We skirted the edge of the pond to following a narrow, damp, and in parts muddy path back towards the woods. We hadn't gone far when there was a sudden clamour ahead and then loud shouts and everyone started to run. My mind was still at the pond behind me and I didn't know what was happening so I was a little late in starting to run after them. Suddenly I became aware of a loud,

THE DOGS OF WAR

angry, buzzing and whining and I was shrouded in a cloud of ferociously angry wasps. Someone's foot had slipped off the path and punctured a wasps' nest which was buried just below the surface of the ground near the side of an old, rotting log. Instead of running forward after the others I hesitated and then turned back but I was too late. By the time I had turned they were all around me. I shouted frantically to the others for help and flung my arms about to beat off the rapidly increasing numbers of wasps. In my panic I forgot to run and within a second or so the wasps were swarming all over me. They landed in my hair and stung my hands as I tried beat them away. I screamed and cried out with pain each time one of their sharp, burning, red-hot needles pierced my skin. I remember looking down and seeing my bare legs clad in what looked like thick, black and yellow football-socks, there were so many wasps clustered onto them. I began running back towards the pond brushing the wasps from my legs as I did so and crushing the bodies of the wasps in my hands as I pulled them out of my hair and off my face. I was in a state of hysterical terror by the time I got back to the pond.

I could hear loud hoots of laughter coming from the others. Attacked by wasps. Very funny. But Len Layton, who had been in the lead, and Baguley, of all people, heard my frantic screaming, realised the seriousness of what had happened and skirted back through the woods to help me. They grabbed me just as I was plunging through the reeds into the pond. Between them Len and Baguley helped me pull the crushed and writhing wasps out of my hair and to get them out of my clothes. There were twenty-one stings on my head and face alone, they told me later. There were numerous stings on my chest and lower body where the wasps had got down the front of my shirt. My shirt had come out of my shorts leaving an exposed area of flesh on my side. It was red and swelling rapidly. My legs were covered with stings. I was shaking with shock, terrified and hysterical. I sobbed and cried and winced with pain as they carried me back to camp on a makeshift stretcher made by two boys who were in the scouts.

Mr. Ferguson took out some of the more obvious stings and bathed me in dolly-blue whilst one of the other teachers went to the village to 'phone for a doctor. He took his time in coming and then Urrmed and Arrhed as to whether or not he should send for an ambulance to take me to hospital but after getting some tablets down me and giving me an injection he decided to leave matters there and see how I looked in the morning. "Give him plenty of warm sweet tea to drink and keep an eye on his temperature", he said, as he left.

I was put to bed and covered with a sheet. The others were given strict instructions not to disturb me. That was a joke. I was in agony: burning and throbbing everywhere. My eyes had glued themselves shut but I couldn't sleep. On the backs of my burning eyelids I could see magnified wasps twitching their antennae and bracing their legs to thrust their curving, black and yellow abdomens round and down to jab me with their needle stings. I lay as still as I could the whole night long listening to their terrifying angry whine. And I wished I was dead.

In the morning I was, in fact, still alive, and there was a bonus I now realise. My experience with the wasps, painful though it was, has made me remember the good bits about that day out in Yorkshire just as vividly as the bad ones. I'm still terrified of wasps though. But then, who isn't.

A MUSICAL INTERLUDE

Most of us used to treat Music as a bit of a joke which was a pity because the Music teacher, Mr. Edgar Lumsden, was an enthusiast and our attitude must have driven him to despair. He was a tall, painfully thin, narrow-shouldered man of about twenty-three with a shock of black, curly hair, prematurely streaked with grey. What was distinctive about him though was the extraordinary Adam's apple which ran up and down the front of his neck like the mouse up the clock in the nursery rhyme. We used to compete with each other to chime in its movements with a recitation of Hickory Dickory Dock.

Mr. Lumsden was highly strung, volatile, and much given to shrieking and the demonstrative gesture. If we sang out of tune or got the timing wrong he would throw his head back, screw up his eyes and open his mouth extremely wide to form an elliptical "O" and wail "No! No! No!, whilst stamping his foot and violently flapping his hands from the ends of his upraised arms. Had he started us off on songs with catchy tunes like the ones we had learnt at the junior school such as "Bobby Shafto's gone to sea", or "What shall we do with a drunken sailor", or even songs like "Cherry Ripe" and "Sweet Lass of Richmond Hill", songs we knew and could sing, he may have stood a chance but they weren't in the curriculum. "Saw a youth a morning rose" was not what kids with flagged back yards were into and "Who is Sylvia, What is she?" evoked a variety of bawdy answers from the swains who would rather commend her to lend her grace to the streets behind Piccadilly Gardens than to anything even remotely refined. Most of his teaching-life Mr. Lumsden lived in deep despair because despite his enthusiasm most of us didn't like his kind of music, or wouldn't admit to anyone that we did, and he couldn't inspire us to change our attitude towards it. Part of the problem was that those who were learning the piano privately were so far ahead of the rest of us that we felt excluded and only those who could afford instruments got a chance to learn how to play one. Most of Mr. Lumsden's attention was given to the musically able: the rest of us had to content ourselves with singing, and singing gave us all sorts of scope for tom-foolery. The problem was compounded by Mr. Lumsden's inability to keep discipline. He struggled to do so but because he had to play the piano whilst the forty of us sang he could not detect who were the trouble-makers. Even when he let us sing one of the songs we knew, he couldn't win. But what infuriated him most was the fact that we had alternative words for all the old songs and that we sang them blatantly despite their obscenity. "Men of Harlech" was perhaps our favourite:

*"You're the guy who fucked my daughter,
Filled her belly with spunk and water,
Now she's got a baby daughter,
Coming through the rye".*

Had Mr. Lumsden somehow been able to engage our enthusiastic gusto for songs with a good tune and real-life lyrics we could have won the Welsh Eisteddfod for him, but "Who is Sylvia!". "Who is Sylvia!". I ask you!
And despite his efforts at Christmas time to get us to sing the right words to "Hark the Herald Angels Sing" the next lines for most of us were always:

*"Beecham's pills are just the thing.
Oh so gentle, Oh so mild!
Two for mother, one for child.
If you want to go to heaven,
Take two three four five six seven.
If you want to go to hell
Take the bleeding box as well".*

One day Edgar Lumsden kept me back amongst a dozen or so other boys: candidates for the school choir. I can say with certainty that nobody on that day longed for the wings of a dove more than I did but unfortunately Ernest Lough, the celebrated boy soprano, must have been using them at the time and God, about whom I had serious doubts even then, but to whom I none the less fervently prayed for deliverance, missed yet another opportunity to convince me of his existence. I would have given anything, even my best conker, to have been able to fly far away, far away out of the window and on to the football field where I should have been, and would have been, but for a tolerable rendering of "The Trout" by an invisible small boy standing behind me in the music lesson that morning. To my astonishment, after the class Mr. Lumsden asked me to come to an audition for the choir at one-thirty. Despite protests that I was down to play football and couldn't sing a note he said: "I'll be the judge of that. One-thirty this afternoon".

At one-thirty those of us who had been earmarked for the choir flocked in from the playing-field and clustered round the music-room door. Edgar Lumsden, or Elgar Lumsden as we called him for reasons unknown to most of us, said he would listen to us one at a time: "to separate the sheep from the goats" was how he put it. Unfortunately, because my name began with a "W", I was almost the last to be heard so I had to listen to all the other boys, bleating away, for most of the afternoon.

When at last it came to my turn Mr. Lumsden stood close beside me, his head cocked upwards to one side, his large Adam's apple quivering in his throat and his big, round eyes fixed high on the music-room ceiling as I attempted to emulate the famous Master Lough. I got as far as: "far away, far away would I. . ." when he interrupted me.

"Yes, that will do. Coat!"

"Goat!" I shouted back at him in shock and disbelief, imagining hours of agony on stage rehearsing for school concerts or up there on show during morning assembly to be sniggered at as a sissy.

Mr. Lumsden looked at me impatiently.

"Coat!, I said, not goat! Get your coat and go and join the others".

Greatly relieved, I followed the flock of rejects down the corridor and out through the door into the fresh air. It was too late for a game of football but at least I wasn't in the choir, and that was certainly something to sing about.

RADCLIFFE TECH.

"Hey! You two! Out!"
I thought we'd been rumbled but it wasn't "Sunday Service" shouting---that's Mr. Len Service, our P.T. teacher---it was Toothill, the Baths' Superintendant. I could see "Two'til-four" leaning on his squeegee, pointing to the last of the stragglers from our morning swimming class dawdling near the exit door.
Nobby Rushton and me were wagging off school dinner hoping for an extra swim. We were hiding in the stalls on the side of the pool in the municipal baths next door to the Tech. we attended, naked as the honest truth, shivering from head to foot.
The cubicles were designed to let you look out on the pool and I was standing on the seat, leaning forward with my arms dangling over the door, looking across at Nobby. My chattering chin was resting on the door-top edge, taking a well-earned break from its morning labours. (For the last time Wild, will you for God's sake be quiet!). We were waiting for "Two'til-four" to finish squeegeeing the showers and go back to his office for his pie and peas or some cheese and onions as it turned out.
Toothill was taking his time despite the well-practised way he was wielding the squeegee. He was a man in his early forties, lean, active, medium build, with disproportionately long, stringy arms. He was inappropriately dressed in a brown herringbone suit (He must have been to a meeting, Rushton said.) with his trousers tucked into a pair of out-size white wellingtons. I could see his bald head bobbing up and down behind the shower wall; you couldn't miss it.
Toothill had alopecia and was entirely hairless. The tightly stretched skin on his skull was semi-translucent grey and showed the sutures and the skull bone-structure giving the illusion you were looking at something Hamlet's grave digger had dug up. His face was equally skull-like and made worse by the boneless saddleback nose and the small, pointed, bad teeth of the congenital syphilitic. His loosely hinged lower jaw protruded beyond his upper jaw. Toothill really was quite cadaverously unattractive.

THE DOGS OF WAR

He glanced in my direction but I knew he couldn't see me. His thick-rimmed, bottle-end glasses magnified his eyes enormously but they didn't much help him see. How he managed to locate people in the baths was a mystery but somehow he never failed to point his finger at even the quietest or least unruly swimmer and say: "Hey you! Out! You've been in long enough!"

I looked across at Rushton again and Nobby's pale equine face with its long, soft nose and earnest brown eyes stared back at me from over his cubicle door. The pale blue pool was as still as float glass and the dark blue lane-lines straight as the tram tracks on Bury Road. Now that our class had gone for dinner there was no one in any of the other cubicles and no one changing behind the wrought iron railings on the balcony above. There was no noise except for the amplified echo of a couple of chirruping sparrows trespassing on a beam under the high skylight roof.

"I bet Rushton's still got his cossie on", I said to myself.

As Toothill disappeared through the swing doors at the bottom end of the baths Rushton nodded his head and both doors swung back with a bang as we each took a header into the pool. We crossed in the middle and with one easy movement hauled ourselves on to the side and into the opposite cubicle. I shook the water off me and rubbed my face on Rushton's towel.

"You cheating bastard Rushton", I shouted across the pool.

We had dared each other to dive in naked but Rushton, the rat, had kept his trunks on.

"Right! You can pay for a table at the Grot", I shouted.

"Let's do it again; I'll do it this time", he shouted back.

But before we had time to repeat the performance the swing doors opened again. A draft of cold air wafted the smell of chlorine under the cubicle door as a woman and a boy I recognised came in. It was the boy with no arms. Last year, for a dare, he had climbed the pylon on the railway line beyond the tunnel at the end of Water street. There was a livid electric flash and an almighty crack like a splitting tree. The boy's arms just fizzled away and he dropped to the ground like a dead bird. He'd been lucky to stay alive, they said. I thought he was unlucky not to be dead. I remember seeing the ambulance and the fire brigade on my way back to school and I can still smell the ozone and taste the cordite smell of burnt electric cable which hung about in the foggy air.

I put my swimming trunks on again and did a few frantic lengths of the pool whilst it was still empty before going to join Rushton under the hot shower. The chlorine had made my eyes sore and the skin on my fingers was crimped and bloodless. We stood in the shower watching the boy and the woman in the shallow end of the pool. The boy swam like a seal, flipping his feet and holding his chin out of the water, occasionally rolling on to his back for relief whilst the woman stood by, watching him. We had tried this technique ourselves once but found it impossible to stay above water.

After a while the boy and the woman got out of the pool on the far side by way of the steps. They went quickly through the ladies' showers and into a cubicle to get changed. Rushton and me were still fooling about in the mens' showers when they came out, dressed. They had to walk past us to leave the baths and as they did so I noticed that the woman's glossy black hair was still wet and uncombed.

"Now you go straight back to school. I want to dry my hair and have a bite with Mr. Toothill before I go down to the market for some vegetables", she said, as she went past.

"Cor did you see the tits on her! Like a pair of prize bloody onions!" Rushton said, when the woman was out of earshot.

"No I missed 'em."

"Big as bloody Jane Russell's!"

I pictured for a minute the breasts of the half-breed woman we had seen in a film called *The Outlaw* at the Odeon cinema the night before.

"What time is it Rushers", I asked.

"It must be nearly half-past", he said.

"Are you going back this afternoon or shall we go for a game of snooker?"

I didn't need persuading when he said: "Naar, it's Maths this afternoon. Let's go to the Grot for a game".

After the warmth of the showers the cold winter air that met us in the entrance hall made me catch my breath. I needed a pee.

"Wait for us here Rushers", I said, as I went down the corridor to the toilets.

The lights were out so I had to walk slowly, feeling my way with my hands.

As I was passing the side room where they kept the water polo equipment I heard a low moaning noise. I stopped and listened. There it was again!

Quietly I opened the door and saw the woman from the pool sitting high-up on a table, her arms outstretched, bracing her hands on the table-top. Her head was thrown back and her glossy black hair hung down, loosely. Her eyes were closed and her mouth was wide open. Her white silk blouse was open too and off her shoulders. Mr. Toothill's squeegee rested in a corner; his bottle-end glasses were lying on the table-top, staring at me. The blank back of "Two'til-four"'s brown herringbone suit was towards me and his small, balled skull was nuzzled down between the woman's two prize onion-shaped breasts. The pair were too engrossed to hear me, or so I thought. I pulled the door quietly too and tiptoed back down the corridor.

"Bloody hell Rushers!", I said, "You'll never guess what I've seen!"

As Rushton crept down the corridor the door to the polo room opened and Toothill's cadaverous head appeared below the lintel and shouted:

"Hey! You two! Out!".

As we went down the steps to the street I said to Rushton: "If I'd been that woman he'd have had to have shouted: 'Hey! You two! Out!' a bloody sight louder than that to get me to show him me prize onions".

"Dead bloody right!", said Rushton.

It was quite dark and foggy outside the Baths. Even though it was only a little after two o'clock the street lights were on. The dull yellow light from the gas mantels reflected off the wet, metallic-looking flagstones. The lamps made the pavement glisten but gave very little cheer to the dingy street. The row of terraced houses opposite the baths showed in dim outline through the clinging drizzle. The smoke from the chimneys, trapped by the cold fog, hung in a dark cloud above the rooftops. The atmosphere, as usual, smelt sooty from the smoke. There was the added smell of dye in the air. It came from the dye-works behind the houses and mingled with the equally pungent smell of hops and malt from the brewery at the end of the street.

"It makes you want to be back at Heys Road, doesn't it!" Rushton said.

"Yeah! At least there we had a new school and playing fields".

"And proper teachers".

" Yeah. Radcliffe's a lousy school in a lousy place. I wish I'd never passed", I said.

Along with the others from our school we had both failed the eleven plus. In the case of Rushton and me and the others from Heys Road it was not that we lacked brains but because in our local authority area there were places at the Grammar School for only eleven per cent of school population. In other areas of the country the percentage of the school population at Grammar School was well over thirty percent. You could, of course, go to Stand or Bury Grammar School if your parents were rich enough to pay but ours were most definitely not so we ended up at Heys Boys' Secondary Modern school.

But Heys Road was not the end of the road as far as our Secondary education was concerned. Six of us had, to our misfortune as it turned out, passed the examination at age thirteen and been selected for a technical education at Radcliffe Technical College under the Government's post war policy of tripartite education. Gold, copper and brass my dad called it. Mr. Storey, the Headmaster, called us to his office. We had missed half of the mid morning break by the time we were ushered in by the Deputy Head. We stood in a row in front of Mr. Storey's desk. After a minute or so he he looked up from the document he was reading and said:

"I'm very pleased to tell you that you have passed to go to Radcliffe Technical College".

He said our selection was based on Government policy which was based on the Norwood Report, 1943. "I'll read out to you what it says":

"The educational system has thrown up three rough groupings of children with different types of mind: pupils interested in learning for its own sake, who can grasp an argument or follow a piece of connected reasoning; pupils whose interests and abilities lie markedly in the field of applied science or applied art---that's you boys, you fall into this second category---and pupils who deal more easily with concrete things than with ideas---and that's us at Hey's Road", though he didn't sound too convinced.

We fidgeted: we wanted to get out into the playground before the bell went. Boringly he read on: "For these three groups of pupils three types of secondary school are needed---grammar, technical and modern schools". At last he stopped reading, looked at us over the frame of his glasses and said: "You have brought great credit on the school. Well done!"

Mr. Fielding, our form teacher at Heys Road was far from convinced he'd got blocks of concrete to deal with. He was very upset when he heard that we had passed to go to the Tech. and tried hard to dissuade me and the others from taking up places. He clearly didn't accept what Mr. Norwood said and quite plainly didn't want to go along with the Government's policy. I remember when we got back from seeing Mr. Storey he said:

"Why do you want to go to Radcliffe Tech? I've heard very bad reports about it and you're doing very well here. You might even be able to stay on and do School Certificate if you remain here. We were hoping to start a small class in a couple of year's time but that won't happen if we lose all our best pupils. You six going going from the one class will have a terrible effect on the ones remaining and it will be awfully demoralising for the teaching staff!".

We didn't really understand what he was on about. At the time I remember feeling quite proud to have passed. It seemed like success and made up a bit for the increasing sense of shame I felt as I got older for having failed the eleven plus. After all, I had been near the top at the Junior School and I knew I was as good as some of those who had passed. I had no idea what to expect at Radcliffe but I was very keen to go to the Tech.

After coming out of the Baths we would normally have turned left, away from the school, and made a detour across the railway line to get round to the Billiards Hall which was in the cellar under Radcliffe Market but because it was foggy we turned right. We kept close beside the low wall, topped with tall iron railings, which fronted both the Baths and Tech. buildings. The Tech. and the Baths were joined and had been built together from bright red Accrington brick in the latter part of the nineteenth century but to look at them now you would have thought the bricks had been black. The buildings had identical entrance doors and other similar external features and the same thick, solid, ornamented, interior green half-tiled walls in the corridors. To stop you mistaking one for the other the relief inscription on the arched facade over the door said Municipal Baths for the one and Mechanics Institute for the other.

All the lights were on in the Tech. Building and I could imagine the lessons going on inside but the windows were high up enough for us not to be seen. Neither of us looked round when we heard footsteps hurrying to catch us up. I thought it was Mr. Toothill so there was no point in running; he knew both Rushton and me from our regular visits to the Baths. A voice I recognised, not Two'til four's but that of Mr. Warburton, our Metalwork teacher, said, "And where do you think you two are going".

He was all grey gaberdine, glasses and trilby, Warburton, with his slight frame and his thin bony face with its thick horn-rimmed specs. He was the youngest teacher on the staff by far and though he must have been at least twenty-six he was smaller, and looked younger, than some of the boys in the year above ours. Rushton tried to make out that we were going to catch a train before they stopped running but "Warblefly" said: "It's up to the school to decide when it's foggy enough to cancel classes and not you!", and he frogmarched us up the steps and through the main door into the Tech.

As we were being marched down the corridor we were unlucky enough to meet "Taffy" Howell, the college principal. He concerned himself mainly with day release and evening classes and left the more onerous running of the junior Tech. to "Dicky" Vose, his deputy, who desperately wanted the Principal's job. Howell was sixty-five and due to retire at the end of term. He was reputed to have been both a coal miner and a professional wrestler and by the look of him you could believe both. He was short,

THE DOGS OF WAR

squat and swarthy and built like a bow-legged bulldog and just about as brutal. He was reputed to pull boys towards him by inserting his fingers up their nostrils. When they were close enough he would hold the fingers of his hand out stiff and give his victims an excruciating jab in the ribs.

"Well done Warburton! It is Warburton isn't it?" he said, in reply to Warburton's unnecessary: "Just caught these two sloping off, Mr Howell".

Half way down the main corridor Warbuton stopped, opened a door and bundled us, without explanation, into a classroom where "Dicky" Vose was just finishing explaining, on behalf of someone called Pythagoras, that the square on the hypotenuse of a right angled triangle is equal to the sum of the squares on the other two sides. I could not see how this piece of information could possibly have a bearing on my future life but it must have struck me at the time as important in its own right as I promptly committed it to memory.

We tried to squeeze between two rows of desks to our places. "Dicky" Vose looked cross.

"Stand over there by the door, I'll speak to you when I've finished", he said.

We did as we were told without our usual back-chat. We quite liked "Dicky" Vose. He and Mrs. Cherry, were the only proper teachers on the staff. We called him "Dicky" because on Fridays, his day to take Assembly, instead of his usual plain tie he invariably wore a large, brightly coloured, spotted, bow-tie. He was somewhat foppishly middle class: posh voice, good manners, handsome Tyrone Power-type face, straight, black, brylcreamed hair brushed flat back from his forehead, tweed suit, handkerchief in top pocket and a second one protruding from his cuff and University Educated as were Mr. Harrison (Science), Mrs. Cherry (English and Economic History) and Mr. Moss (Economic Geography). "Dicky" Vose emanated refinement, unlike the remaining five members of staff who were just ordinary blokes. They had been recruited from local industry. Some of them had been in the army and, having technical qualifications, had been promoted to the rank of Sergeant Instructor. They had relished the power and status their rank had given them. Someone said Jim

Settle had been an Officer (in the Mental Corps, Rushton said). They had found it difficult to adjust to shop floor engineering work with its low status and minuscule prospect of promotion. Waiting for dead men's shoes, they realised, would long leave them barefoot. Close supervision, poor pay, long hours and no pension unless they were lucky enough to be taken on "the staff" in an office job was a bleak prospect. They had been attracted to teaching in a Technical college by the nine o'clock start, twenty-four hours class contact time, long holidays and relatively better pay at a time when the average industrial worker was on forty-six to forty-eight hours, including Saturday morning and compulsory overtime two or three nights a week. They could put up with jibes that teachers were not men among boys but mere boys among men.

There was Walton, who taught us bricklaying and woodwork; Warburton, metalwork (turning, fitting, drilling, and blacksmith's work) and Mr. Settle and Mr. Service who both taught Engineering drawing and P.T. and had M.I.E.Mech.E. qualifycations as well. Nobody knew what qualification Mr. Jolly had. Whatever it was it certainly didn't help him teach Maths. To teach in a Tech. it was not necessary to have a degree or even a teaching qualification; a City and Guilds Final Certificate or other technical qualification would do. It let in all sorts of untrained "teachers" who might have been just about suitable for instructing older apprentices in repetitive skills but none of these so called teachers should have been let loose on bright thirteen and fourteen year olds like us. We never did any interesting subjects like Biology or Shakespeare and there were no Music lessons, and not even Gardening. We were going to start French at Heys Road but they didn't do that at the Radcliffe Tech. It was all Woodwork, Metalwork and Engineering Drawing. I used to like Science at Heys Road but in the first year at the Tech. this was reduced to just chemistry with Harrison. There was never enough equipment and it took half the lesson to get the Balances right. We were supposed to work in groups but it always ended up with one or two who were good at it doing all the interesting bits. The rest of us just had to watch and then write it up. Apparatus; Hypothesis; Procedure; Conclusion. Most of never really

THE DOGS OF WAR

understood the point of what we were doing so we just messed about.

The bell went, Vose's lesson ended and everybody began to troop out. Rushton and me didn't want a telling off so while "Dicky" Vose was talking to a couple of boys, Rushton and me joined the exodus and went along to Mr. Jolly's room for the second half of our once a week Double Maths.

Mr. Jolly, the Maths teacher, was laughably misnamed. He might have been Jolly once upon a time but I suspect the name was ironic when it was originally given to his ancestors. He'd been a morose, gloomy man when we first had him but recently had become severely depressed as a result of his fifty year-old wife's early death from cancer. He had withdrawn into an almost catatonic state. It took a great effort for him to get out of his chair and write on the blackboard the page number of the Maths book we each had to pick up from the pile on his desk as we walked in.

Having written the page on the board he would sit behind his desk in his black suit, white shirt and black tie, with his elbows on the table and his jaw cupped in both hands, fingers in his ears, and stare directly ahead. He was totally impervious to the hubbub of noise that gradually built up as boys openly talked, read comics, played noughts and crosses or shove-halfpenny on the desk top. There were one or two: Manning, Warren and Tonge, who had an aptitude for Maths and liked doing sums; they got on with the work, despite the racket. The rest of us just messed about.

"Hey, Nobby", I said, "Have us a game of shove-halfpenny".

"How much?", he said.

"Threepence a game".

"Go on then", he said.

There were well-worn goals and side lines carved on most of the desk tops. Everyone played shove-halfpenny during the dinner break but as me and Rushton mostly missed dinners and went out to the Baths or the Grot or mooched about the shops in Radcliffe we played in Jolly's Maths class. He took not the slightest notice. He didn't even look when the halfpenny flew onto the floor. I had lost ninepence by the time the Maths period was coming to an end.

"Jolly well serves you right!", Rushton quipped.
"Lend us your book, Warren", I said.
"Sod off", he replied.
"Go on Warren: threepence", said Rushton.
"O.K. but don't put your grubby fingers all over it".

Rushton passed over one of my lost threepenny bits.
Several others wanted to borrow the book and once it was out of his hands Warren had little choice but to let them. By the time the book got to me there was little of the lesson-time left and the bell went before I had finished copying the work. Warren grabbed the book back.
We milled out past Jolly's desk placing our Maths books in one pile, the Log Tables in another and our exercise books in a third pile. I knew they would not be marked by next week so I could finish copying the answers then. Jolly marked the books every three or four weeks but only with a tick or a cross: he never corrected or checked the workings-out. Since his wife died he had stopped doing specimen answers on the board. It was a nuisance if you didn't know where you had gone wrong. He never set any homework, but then, none of the other teachers did. We thought ourselves lucky. Had we stayed at Heys Road we would have had homework every night and weekends as well.
As we were leaving the building "Dicky" Vose stopped us and said, in his posh voice:
"Come to my room before classes in the morning. I would like an explanation for your absence from my class this afternoon".

On the train on the way home to Prestwich Rushton and me discussed what story we should tell "Dicky" Vose in the morning. Rushton with his excessive imagination and propensity to exaggerate almost everything he said was for telling Mr. Vose that we had found the body of the boy with no arms floating on the floor of the Baths and had tried to revive him.
"We'll say we had to stay there so the police could take statements in case he was dead when he reached hospital".
"Don't be bloody daft Rushers! They'd be wanting to give us a medal. It would be better to just say we stayed on at the baths

THE DOGS OF WAR

after the swimming lesson and say something like you swallowed some water and the chlorine made you feel sick. I'll say I was going home with you in case you were ill again".

In the end we decided simply to say we were going home because it was foggy. Rushton was to claim he didn't want to be late for his paper round and I was to tell Vose I took out orders for a Grocer and Confectioner and that the last time it was foggy the trains stopped and so did the buses. We'd say we had to walk three miles to Whitefied to catch a bus and that it was half past six before we got home, which was true. He'd believe us: everyone knew that Radcliffe was built in a hollow with the Irwell running through the centre. It was renowned for its thick pea-soupers. There were so many houses and factories belching out smoke that in the winter it was almost too grey to see even when it wasn't foggy. The worst he could do would be to tell us it was up to him to decide whether we went home early or not.

In the event we didn't need an excuse: "Dicky" Vose was off sick. We had been outside his room nearly quarter of an hour before Mrs. Entwistle, the Secretary noticed us and told us that Mr. Vose was off, sick, and would "not be in today". What she did not tell us, because no one knew it at the time was that "Dicky" Vose would not be in again, ever.

Three months later "Dicky" Vose hanged himself. Heslop, a boy in our class whose parents were well-off and lived in the same street as the Voses, off Stand Lane in the posh district of Whitefield, told us the news. No one believed him until all 200 or so boys attending the Junior Tech. were told to assemble in the Gym, which doubled as an Assembly Hall, for an important announcement by the new Principal, another Mr. Walton, just to confuse everybody.

Walton simply told us that Mr. Vose had died, unexpectedly, after a short illness. Everyone was very quiet and after a short speech by Mr. Harrison saying how much the school owed him and how much he would be missed we went back to our classrooms. Heslop told us the whole story the following Monday.

It seems Vose's wife had been "carrying on" with her next door neighbour's husband: she was supposed to be the woman's best friend. Last year Vose got to know about it and put his foot down, or so he thought.

"Anyway, she left him six months ago", Heslop said.

A woman who cleans for the Minister at Stand Unitarian Chapel told Heslop's mother that "Dicky" Vose went round to the Vicarage sobbing and crying and told the Minister he couldn't live without his wife. The Minister tried to get Mrs. Vose to go back to him but she refused and told him she wanted a divorce.

"Dicky" Vose didn't want the scandal and it all coincided with him being told he hadn't got the job of Principal at the Tech., "It brought on a nervous breakdown".

When it became clear that his wife had gone for good "Dicky" Vose had gone off sick, become reclusive and, more recently, Heslop said, had began to neglect his appearance. It seems he ventured out of his house seldom and then only at night to take his pet dog for a walk. Before his death he had not been seen for some time and the neighbours had become worried about him. They got no answer when they knocked. At first they thought he'd gone away or been admitted to hospital but they got more and more worried when they heard the dog barking. It wouldn't stop barking, day and night, and eventually the police had been called. They broke into the house through the French windows and had found "Dicky" Vose's body in an upstairs bedroom. He had hanged himself by the cord of his dressing gown from a hook behind the bedroom door.

We were twenty-minutes late for Woodwork and Chippy Walton was not pleased. I could tell we were in for trouble by the expression on his bleak, grey face which failed to respond when I told him we had been to see Mr. Vose. He stared straight at me and said, in a restrained low voice, almost without moving his lips: "You're lying boy. I happen to know Mr. Vose is off sick today".

"Yes, he is, but we didn't know that until Mrs Entwistle told us. We'd stood outside his room twenty minutes before she told us. You can ask her, Sir. She'll tell you!".

Like many small men Chippy Walton compensated for his lack of stature by cultivating a contrived presence and by exercising all the power his position gave him. He was as dapper a little man in his way as Dr. Gobels; smart suited and notable for the tiny tight knots in his ties but his steely, psychopathic, staring eyes could make a snake blink.

When he did speak he said:

"Well, as you're so late you'll have to sharpen your own chisels. You can use an oil stone; I've switched off the grinding machine and I'm not putting it on again for latecomers!".

This news was a disaster for me. It would take ages and I could never get a good edge with an oil stone. All the stones were old and had a groove in the centre which meant you could never hold the edge flat nor at the right angle. I would probably not finish my bookcase.

I had enjoyed making my bookcase and I was looking forward to taking it home. The sides and "V" shaped base were held together by dovetail joints but the cross struts fitted into the sides by means of mortice and tenons. I had spent a lot of time on the joints and done them quite well. Chippy Walton even said so. I had been allowed to glue them and leave the work in a portable vice the previous week.

When I went to the storeroom to collect my work there was only one bookcase left on the shelf. It didn't look like mine but it had my name label on it. When I took the vice off and stood it on the bench it didn't rest squarely but rocked about. I knew some sod had swopped it: the joints didn't look anywhere near as perfect as I remembered them. I finished the ornamental bevelled edges on the back and sides and then tried to file the feet level but that only made the wobble worse so I had to leave them as they were.

"That's a shoddy job if ever I saw one. You can't have more than five out of ten for that" Walton said, when I took it to him for marking.

"Someone's swopped it. This isn't mine. Mine was perfect last week!", I protested.

When I asked him could I go round to find out who'd taken mine he said:

"No, it's too late. You should have been here on time!".

He could see I was near to tears but he wouldn't give me more than five out of ten and you had to get at least seven before you could take your work home. I was bitterly disappointed and to make life worse he wouldn't let me start on my stool until next week. I had to spend what was left of the woodwork period doing bricklaying.

Bricklaying was not all it was cracked up to be. We never actually got to handle a brick or mix cement let alone lay one but we knew a brick measured three by four-and-a-half by nine inches and weighed nine pounds and that mortar needed three spades of sand to two of cement to make.

"And a couple of Paddy's": Rushton shouted out. He got three whacks on the hand from a piece of one by one for that.

I had to draw to scale an isometric projection of a brick showing the dimensions and diagrammatic examples of Common English Bond, Old English Garden Bond, Flemish Bond and indicate the Headers, Stretchers, King Closers and Queen Closers. I was glad when the period ended despite the fact that after dinner it was metalwork, which I detested.

Between a Radcliffe Tech. school dinner and no dinner there was very little in the way of competition. Throw in an extra swim or two or a game of snooker and the school dinner had very little chance. Given the options who would choose those lousy, blackened spuds, that stinking cabbage and the tongue of an old rubber boot? But money was short and the dinner was just about edible on a Thursday so Rushton and me had decided to stay. We planned to miss pudding, sneak out without Moss seeing us and run down to the Grot. for a quick game of snooker. We would just about have time. I met up with Rushton in the corridor and together we managed to jostle our way to the top of the cellar steps.

The school dining facilities were in the cellar of the building and comprised an inadequately small room in which had been installed six trestle tables each capable of seating just about twelve boys. Even with the two sittings not everyone could be accommodated but quite a number of local boys went home to dinner and quite a number of the others failed to turn up. If you didn't get a place at the first sitting which was the most popular of the two you had to wait for the second sitting. As a consequence there was always a rush to get there and a queue to get in.

When Mr. Moss, the Geography teacher, opened the dining room

THE DOGS OF WAR

door the crush on the cellar steps collapsed and everybody tumbled down the steps on top of each other, like a pile of rolling stones. Moss was frantically shouting, "Get back! Get back, the lot of you!" but he had no option but to let those at the front in so as to relieve the pressure from behind. Some wag who knew his Tennyson was shouting: "And those at the back cried forward and those at the front cried back!"

The room was low and airless and the smell of cabbage, accumulated over the years, was all-pervasive. The green, painted walls seemed to sweat cabbage from their pores. The liquid linoleum floor covering was the colour of cabbage and always tacky so that your shoes stuck and pulled a little making you aware of it when you walked. There were no windows in the dining room and the yellow-looking electric light bulbs were unshaded.

In the dining room the queue thinned out and snaked its way in and out of the small, side kitchen where a bench held a couple of dixies, one containing mashed potatoes and the other carrots, and two trays: one containing circular cuts off a roll of fatty-looking meat, with bits of string attached, and the other a mess of slimy-looking boiled onions.

We took our food to our tables and sat down on the long, low, narrow, rickety, backless benches. Inevitably someone would rock back before the meal was over and half a dozen of us would end up on the floor. The table monitors came round with glasses of water which we were forbidden to touch until after the toast. Which crazy teacher had thought up making us participate in a toast before we could eat I do not know but he must have had a perversely masochistic sense of humour and an intense hatred of his colleagues. The toast produced a daily ritual response which did absolutely nothing for the monarchy but provided plenty of mirth for the boys, intense irritation and humiliation for the member of staff on duty, and cold food for everyone.

The duty teacher, Mr. Moss in this case, was required to say, after first having struggled long and hard to achieve silence: "I propose a toast. A loyal toast to The King, the Duke of Lancaster". We, the boys, were required to respond: "The King, The Duke of Lancaster", then, drink a gulp of water and begin to eat. What happened each day, however, with perfect, unsolicited accord, was that every boy missed off the last word of the toast. So, round one was: "The King, the Duke of". Round two: "The King, the Duke". Round three: "The King, the", and so on until absolute silence. The sequence was of course accompanied by threats, exasperation, or resigned weariness on the part of the duty staff member. Meanwhile the dinners were getting colder and colder.

Depending on the popularity of the member of staff or their vulnerability to being "wound up" the ritual might go on through up to three complete sequences. In the case of Mr. Moss it invariably went to three. Mr. Moss was Jewish and there was a lot of anti-semitism about despite the defeat of Nazi Germany and the horror pictures of Auschwitz and Belsen with which we were all familiar. The Israeli Jews were engaged in a fight for an independent State and were fighting not only Arabs but the British as well. British troops were being killed and the St. David's hotel had been blown up with the loss of many British lives. As soon as Mr. Moss turned his back there were shouts of "Up the Arabs". The Stern Gang got a favourable mention as did Irgun Zaiume Levi. Rushton got caught for an "Up the Arabs" and received a resounding slap across the head which signalled our capitulation in the next round.

Whilst Mr. Moss was pushing the pudding queue into line me and Rushton slipped out of the dining hall.

The same dark, foggy, day as yesterday met us outside school, save that sod's law had just kicked in to turn the drizzle to rain. Had there been anyone daft enough to take bets Rushton and me could have made a fortune out of weather forecasting. Neither of us had raincoats though; we had ridden to Radcliffe on our bikes. There was no option but to get wet; we would have looked ridiculous in bright, yellow, oilskin capes. We would have to run as fast as we could to The Grot., seeking whatever shelter we could find for a reviving breather, en route.

We made it as far as the tobacconist's on Dumer's lane and stood under the awning, hands on knees, heaving and gasping for breath. I was so puffed I could taste what seemed like blood in my mouth. When he'd recovered, Rushton went into the shop and bought two Woodbines and a box of matches. He offered me a

THE DOGS OF WAR

cig. even though he knew I was about the only one in our class who didn't smoke. I was tempted to take it but the image of my dad, rowing with my mam for forgetting to buy his cigs. and rampaging round the house or grubbing about in the grate, desperate for even a dimp, made me shake my head.

A huge waggon piled high with bales of raw cotton and pulled by two pairs of steaming, shire horses, with frothy mouths, trundled by. I almost ran into the spare horse as we dodged behind the waggon and slipped and slithered across the wet cobbled sets that surfaced the main road. The sharp, acrid smell of the hot, glossy horse droppings and the stench of fresh horse piss rising from the road made my nose twitch and left an indelible taste in my mind's memory. I can still see the spare horse's moustache dripping slimy saliva and the brightly coloured rosette attached to its head-halter. Its flanks are steaming and its tail is plaited into a short rope-like pigtail.

We took a short cut through a factory yard and turned into a narrow street between two continuous rows of mid nineteenth century terraced houses. They all looked alike, despite the odd donkey-stoned step. You wondered how the owners found the right one, even when it wasn't foggy. We had to jump the puddles on the uneven pavement, where the rainwater lodged, and watch out for dog dirt and the numerous oysters of greenish looking phlegm that bronchitic old men had coughed up.

When we reached Radcliffe New Road we turned left down the hill towards the Bus Station. We ran as far a Woolworth's and ducked into the doorway. There were several other people in there, sheltering from the rain, and although they were all grown-ups me and Rushton were a good half-a-head taller than most of them. That was one of the things that struck you in Radcliffe; all the people were small and either as thin as whippets or as waddlingly fat as frogs or the toby jug on the window-sill we had just passed. Almost all were grotesque or deformed in some way. Many of the older women had goitres which girdled their throats like small pneumatic tire-innertubes. Most of old men had bowed legs. The fat ones rocked from side to side as they walked. The thin ones looked as though they had piles. Some people had both-legs and knees bent at a forty-five degree angle from their feet;

twisted by Rickets so far to the right they made their owners look "Z" shaped. You never saw a normal looking person in Radcliffe. They all seemed to have some deformity or looked physically odd for some reason. Head too large, too small, too long, too domed, bulging eyes, bottle-end glasses, bad teeth, one arm, three fingers, no legs, all sorts of peculiarities. They were quite unlike the people in Prestwich where Rushton and I lived.

I had just finished telling Rushton about coming to Radcliffe with our Ernie towards the end of the war, a couple of years previously, to see where the V2 Doodlebug had landed on the Co-op shop in the road at the side of Woolworth's when the door to Woollies store opened and Roy Greathead and another lad from our school were roughly pushed out onto the pavement by a man and a woman shop assistant.

"Don't let me ever catch you in here again!" the man shouted after them as they made off.

They would not be pleased we had seen them being thrown out of Woollies. Nicking things from Woollies was probably Radcliffe Tech's most popular school sport but none the less shaming for those who got caught. It never led to a prosecution but it might be reported to the school and it could query the pitch for everyone else. It could even lead to a ban on boys from the Tech. going in there like it had done for those from Radcliffe Secondary Modern School.

Rushton looked at me and said, "They probably told 'em they were from The Secondary Mod. If we play our cards right they might even give us something to keep quiet about it".

"No chance", I said.

The rain eased a little and the doorway emptied. Rushton pinched the end off the cig. he had half-smoked and put the dimp in his top pocket.

"Come on he said. I'll race you to the Grot."

The Grot was a low, though large, cellar under the indoor market adjacent the bus depot. The Grot was short for grotto, not grotty, a word in vogue much later but one that would have been entirely appropriate had it been around at the time. It housed a dozen Lupton's snooker tables and a corner bar which attracted a regular clientele of seedy looking local layabouts and a lunchtime influx of potentially truant schoolboys aspiring to be the next Joe Davis. The licensing laws were not strictly enforced down there and some of the bigger, older looking boys would purchase halves of bitter for the rest of us though you had to be discreet about drinking it and disown the glass if challenged by the occasional copper who popped in for a chat and a free drink with the barman. It was quite dark in the cellar and the air was blue with smoke but once your eyes adjusted and the shadowy forms came into focus everything was quite visible. The large, wide, oblong light shades, low over the tables, produced pools of light which reflected the brilliant colours of the balls. Triangular splashes of red, wonderful blues, pastel pink, shiny brown and green and vivid yellow contrasted with the black and the beautiful white spot-ball. It was magical. Luckily there was one table free in the far corner. Rushton promptly booked it for half an hour.

The thin, rat-faced, bespectacled barman wore a green eyeshade, held in place by a thick elastic riband round his head. The arms of his large, white, green-striped shirt were shortened by two tight elasticated arm bands round his biceps. He looked like someone out of an American gangster movie. He tilled the nine-pence fee and handed us two cues from the rack together with a cube of blue-green billiard chalk and a triangular frame.

"You'll find your balls in your pockets", he said, with a straight face.

The green baize cloth had been freshly brushed, the nap looked new and the cushions well sprung. The ball I tried them with rebounded off all four sides without losing speed: we'd got a good table. I set up the yellow, brown, green, in the balk semi-circle, blue in the centre, pink at the apex of the triangle and the black at the back of the pack of reds while Rushton was chalking the tips of the cues and setting up the score-board. We tossed a coin and Rushton spotted off.

The reds were potted quite quickly but the score remained fairly even and by the time we got onto the colours there was very little in it. Rushton potted blue and pink and with four difference in the score everything turned on the black which rested against the cush at the bottom end of the table. White was near the blue spot. Most of the games on the other tables had finished by this time

and our end game attracted quite a crowd of boys from the Tech. Six-penny bets were being placed on who would win. Rushton took the Rest and leaning low across the table jabbed at the white with his cue. The black came hard off the cush and rocketed down the table into the right-hand corner pocket. A gasp, followed by a loud cheer, came from the crowd of boys but was immediately hushed. The white, which had spiralled along the cushion, had come almost to rest on the rim of the bottom left-hand pocket. It teetered as if undecided what to do, tossed a coin, so to speak, and then disappeared inside. I'd won! There were shouts of "Oh no!" and "jammy sod", but Rushton had no option but to pay up. He wanted to have another game to recoup the table fee but there wasn't time. We could not miss another afternoon class. We didn't know that "Dicky" Vose would not be in the following day.
"I'll get my own back tomorrow". Rushton said.
I took back the cues, chalk and frame and retrieved the shilling deposit.
"Come on Rushers, we'd better get a move on. I don't want to be late for metalwork. Not after Warburton caught us yesterday". I said.
It was a struggle pushing our way through the crowded market hall. The trestle stalls were close together and the aisles were jammed with people buying mainly fruit and vegetables or wet fish which wasn't rationed. There were a number of second hand clothes stalls and quite a few stalls selling crockery or cheap jewellery. A man in a belted, trench-style mac, asked us did we want to buy a watch.
We had almost made it to the open outer-edge of the bus depot. side of the market when Rushton grabbed my arm and said:
"Hey, there's that woman!"
"What woman?", I said.
"You know, the one in the Baths!".
Sure enough, she looked remarkably like the same woman. She was waiting at the number six bus stop. The woman was dressed in a smart blue two-piece costume with a large matching blue handbag in her hand. She had on a pair of blue high-heeled shoes and a blue pill-box hat with a veil. She was linking the arm of a spivvy looking man with a pencil moustache and wearing a heavy

looking camel-coloured coat and a dark brown wide-brimmed trilby hat. The man was looking at his flashy, gold wrist watch and you could see he had a gold ring on his finger.

The man detatched himself from the woman's arm and walked with a stiff-legged limp over to ask something of the bus-inspector. It was obvious the man had an artificial leg.

"She must go in for cripples", Rushton said.

Heslop, who had joined us asked what we were looking at. When I pointed out the woman he said:

"I know her. It's "Dicky" Vose's wife".

We just made it back to the Tech. in time to join the stragglers going into the workshop for Warblefly's metalwork class. Rushton and me were moving off lathes and on to forge work. I was quite looking forward to doing forge work despite an initial disappointment. For some silly reason I'd thought it would be about learning to shoe horses, which captured my imagination despite the daunting prospect of coping with a live beast, but factory forge-work was what we were going to do and that was, as far as I could gather, all about making brackets and pokers. Still, the poker would come in handy at home and Blacksmith's work had to be better than bench work and lathe turning.

We had spent the first four weeks of metalwork on bench-work and the second four on lathe-turning. In bench-work we had to make a set-square. This involved first learning to file metal, in particular the edges of two rectangular pieces of metal. Once we had got them to the correct length, and square, we had to drill them and rivet them together to make the finished set-square. It was difficult to keep the file level and I had to keep re-doing mine to get rid of the rounded edges. When I finally got it right I had to french chalk the two pieces, scribe a fixed point on each piece so that they aligned, punch a small hole for the location of a drill-bit and drill the holes on a large lethal-looking drilling machine. Greenhalgh the boy before me in the queue for the drill lent too far towards the drill. His hair got caught and it almost scalped him. His hair was completely sheered off at the front of his head and a flap of skin had lifted off. There was blood all over the machine. Greenhalgh was rushed to Bury General Hospital to have the flap stitched down. When he came back to school he told us they had shaved off the rest of his hair. His head was swathed in white bandages, like a turban. After the accident we were not allowed to use the drill until it had been fitted with a guard so Warblefly drilled my set-square for me.

It was quite easy putting in the rivets but if you didn't hammer them in hard enough, or flat enough, you ended up with either a wobbly set-square or one that wasn't at the right angle or one with both faults. Mine had both.

I'd been glad to get on to Lathe work but only for a few minutes. Lathe work was supposed to sort out those who were suitable to be a Turner in an engineering works. It was the last thing on earth, I quickly realised, that I wanted to be. In the class we had to insert a cylinder of metal into chuck, secure it, set a tool at a right-angle to the protruding bit of metal and watch it endlessly traversing and cutting the metal. Occasionally you had to stop the lathe and measure the diameter with a micrometer until the cylinder was the prescribed size. Watching paint dry or concrete set would have been exciting by comparison. True, the gleaming spirals of lathe-turnings looked attractive as they curled off the cylinder of metal but the smell of the coolant, a milky-white oily liquid you poured in a constant stream onto the metal from a hand held oil-can to stop the cutting blade overheating and sheering the cutting tool, made me feel sick. You can see how after four boring weeks of lathe turning Blacksmith's work seemed an enjoyable prospect.

Mr. Warburton switched on the electric furnace and showed me how to use the hand bellows to blow up the coke to the right temperature. He gave us each a stiff leather apron to wear, a pair of tongs for the hot metal and a long, solid, square length of metal. The idea was to make a poker by forming a circular loop on one end of the length of metal and a point on the other. A number of twists, like a barley-sugar stick were to be made in the middle to provide ornamentation for the poker. It was all very much easier said than done. If the metal wasn't hot enough to start with, or you took too long working on it, you got nowhere hammering it and it wouldn't twist in the vice if it went cold on you. It took me four weeks of hot, fume-choked toil to make that poker but I must say I was quite pleased with it when it was finished. I got seven out of ten for it. I nearly left it on the train when I was taking it home but I did eventually get to poke my mam's fire with it.

The last session on a Thursday afternoon alternated between Geography with Mr. Moss, or Amos we called him, and English with a dash of Social and Economic History with Mrs. Cherry(ripe). Amos was a mug and jug teacher whereas Cherry-ripe was a talk and chalk, question-answer, write a summary in your own words, type. Whereas Amos strolled up and down the aisles between the desks, his tight, fat fists gripping the coat lapels of his seedy looking grey suit, dictating notes to us off the top of his head, Mrs. Cherry sat on the front desk with her feet on the seat, her skirt stretched tight across her thighs and her knees very close together and talked to us.

Amos was in his mid forties. A bald headed, short, fat, paunchy man with olive skin and a seven o'clock shadow. He had an unmistakeably Jewish nose with the nostrils curled under and liquid looking dark brown eyes. He had no idea how to control a class. Dictating notes was his way of coping with the chaos which would have ensued had he stopped pontificating and we had stopped writing. Anyone who asked him to repeat something or said: "Hey Sir, you're going too fast" was immediately given a cuff across the head and told to leave a space and copy it from someone else. "In your own time boy". To give him his due though he had a remarkable knowledge of the import and export of British coal, steel, iron, cotton and ship-building tonnage, knowledge in which, unfortunately, none of us was the slightest bit interested; not least because much of it related to pre-war Britain and was ridiculously out of date. Occasionally he gave us a Roneoed map of the world and, having displayed a large version of it on the blackboard, on which he had identified some of the major ports of the empire, he got us to put dotted lines for the shipping routes between them. He always filled the forty-five minutes of the lesson so there was time only for the briefest question as we trooped out of the room and you never got a straight answer. He was always too glib or supercilious. I remember someone once asking him, in all seriousness the difference between history and geography since what Amos taught us seemed eminently historical to us, and he just came out with the old kid's comic cliché: "history's about chaps and geography's about maps". "Off you go!", he said.

Whereas Amos was a boring teacher, Cherryripe, despite her appearance, was an interesting and entertaining one. She was a fawn coloured woman of forty. She invariably wore a fawn two-piece costume, had a pale fawn coloured face and fawn coloured hair which was short and shingled at the back making her look somewhat mannish. Her hair at the front was done in a series of loose rolls one behind the other like those serried golden waves rolling onto the coast you see in those badly-painted seascapes on sale in sea-side gift shops. Her oval-shaped glasses had rather heavy dark-brown frames, with ears, which gave her a somewhat mephistophelean look. They had a long corded string attached to stop her losing them. She would talk to us about the effect of the three-field system of cyclical crop rotation and its impact on food production and the sustainable population and show us pictures of Jethro Tull's seed drill. She would tell us about Crompton's mule, Hargreaves' Spinning Jenny or Arkwright's loom and how they revolutionised cotton cloth production and she read us exciting accounts about the Luddites and machine breaking. It was much more interesting than boring old Amos's yards of cloth and calico or tons of coal and steel. Later she would go to the blackboard and ask us to recall the main points of what she had said. We would then write an account of what she had told us in our books in our own words.

Roy Chandler put up his hand and said:

"Please Miss can I use my ball-point pen?"

"You know the rule about pens. Either use the one provided and an ink-well or a fountain pen with blue-black ink", Mrs. Cherry said.

After the lesson, when the others had gone, Chandler, Rushton and me stayed behind to get Mrs. Cherry to tell us more about the Luddites. The discussion broadened and Mrs. Cherry asked us how we were getting on at the school generally. I remember we complained that it was boring and that we only had Social and Economic History every other week. Chandler said:

"There's too much metalwork and woodwork and engineering drawing. We'd rather do proper lessons like they do at Stand Grammar school".
This prompted Mrs. Cherry to say:
"Yes. You three would have been far better off at the grammar school; you have the ability and the interest. I can't think why you weren't selected to go there at eleven".
I remember feeling quite bucked up by this remark.
Before we went Mrs. Cherry asked Chandler to show her the pen he had referred to. She had not previously seen a ball-point pen though she had heard about them. We hadn't even heard about them. Chandler's uncle had been to America to see his daughter who had married an American G.I. soldier and had brought the pen back as a present for Chandler. Mrs. Cherry tried out the pen and Chandler let Rushton and me try it out too. Rushton and me were impressed and envious but Mrs. Cherry said the writing was characterless and he'd better stick to using his fountain pen.

Engineering drawing took up the whole of Friday morning. There was no special engineering drawing studio so we had to use one of the labs. The stools were hard and the benches flat. Some of the "T" squares had chips out of them which ruined the straight lines we drew with our carefully sharpened chisel-edged pencils. Quite a number of the drawing boards were pitted and there was usually a scramble to get a good one. Jim Settle, the Engineering Drawing teacher, had a magnificent, free standing, proper drawing board; large and wide and set at an adjustable angle. It had a weighted easy-glide set-square with a see-through vertical. He had very little interest in teaching us anything. He was one of those authoritarians who liked to give you the impression that you had a choice in matters but in fact you had none. It was like dealing with Henry Ford or the Maffia: "You either do it or you do it". His two most famous phrases were: "You will do that, won't you?" and "You won't do that, will you?"
The instructions were already on the blackboard when we went into the room. Jim Settle was ensconced behind his drawing board industriously drawing. A casting had been drawn on the blackboard in front elevation and plan view. The instructions

were to draw a side elevation and an isometric projection.

There was a good deal of noise as stools were shuffled about and "T" squares collected. Boards were banged down on desks and scuffles broke out as boys tried to swop worn ones for newer looking ones whilst the original claimant was rummaging in his satchel underneath the bench.

Jim Settle's angry red face appeared above his drawing board.

"Quiet!", he barked, glaring round the room.

The noise subsided immediately and he returned his attention to his drawing. Presumably he was engrossed in something he was originating or some free-lance work he was being paid for. After half an hour or so he left off what he was doing and strolled round the room administering criticism. We each kept a wary eye on him. Suddenly, for no apparent reason, his face turned puce. He ran between the benches, grabbed the nearest "T" square and whacked Greenhalgh, who had presumably been talking or pulling faces, across the back with it, catching the back of his head. He pulled Greenhalgh off his stool and, putting his spitting, spluttering face close to Greenhalgh's, began pummelling him in the chest with his fists. It was utterly disproportionate and quite terrifying to the rest of the class who had not observed what had brought on this tornado of violence. He ought to have been locked up. We were convinced he was mad. Unfortunately for us "Sunday Service" was off so we had him for P.T. that Friday afternoon.

Settle's voice echoed round the high-roofed gym.

"Right! You've got two minutes to get changed. The last one, and anyone else not out in the gym by quarter-past, does fifty press-ups!".

I slipped the knot of my tie and looped it over my head ready for putting on again. I couldn't get the buttons of my shirt sleeve cuffs undone so I just bit them off and put the buttons in the breast pocket; my mam could sew them back on. To save time I left my underpants on and wore my shorts over them hoping they wouldn't show. Nobody spoke whilst changing; everybody was frantically tearing off clothes and stuffing arms and legs into vests and shorts whilst watching the wall-clock second hand jerking inexorably round the clock-face. We all knew that Settle meant

what he said. Fifty press-ups! The bastard!
I was not the last and I beat the clock by a good five seconds. Greenhalgh was still half-dressed and resignedly seemed in no hurry to get into his P.T. kit. We had the Vaulting Horse, the Box, the Benches, inverted for balance-walking, and the Beam, with its dangling ropes, out by the time Greenhalgh emerged.
Settle blew hard on his whistle and we all stood stock still.
"Come here Greenhalgh!", he shouted. "What do you think you are playing at!".
Greenhalgh slouched across the gym towards where Settle was standing.
Settle, who was dressed in baggy blue shorts and a white vest which contrasted with his scarlet face, was holding a large, heavy medicine-ball close to his chest in both hands. When Greenhalgh got near Settle suddenly propelled the ball hard at Greenhalgh's face, shouting as he did so: "Don't try and make a fool out of me, Greenhalgh!
Greenhalgh turned his head just before the moment of impact and the ball hit the side of his head and knocked him to the ground.
"Can't catch either, can you Greenhalgh!", screamed the infuriated Settle. "Get over in that corner and do press-ups until I tell you to stop!"
You could here the anger in Settle's whistle as it screamed like a steam engine to signal us to begin circuit training.
Five times round the gym clockwise, five times anti-clockwise, up the wall-bars, down the wall-bars. Balance-walking along the inverted form, posing on one foot whilst bending down to pick up an imaginary handkerchief, vaulting over the Horse, side jumping over the Box, walking round the gym on your heels, squat haunch-crouch-crab-walking, all these I could do quite well despite Settle finding fault but when it came to climbing the ropes I was about as agile as an elephant trying to climb up the side of a gasometer. Some boys, closer to the monkey than me on the evolutionary scale, could shin up the ropes with effortless ease. They would grasp the rope high up, one hand above the other and spring lightly off the ground, trapping the rope with their prehensile feet. Defying Newton they were touching the gym roof before I had even got off the ground. Despite not being fat I

somehow hadn't the strength in my arms to haul myself off the floor. The rope was slippery, like a snake, and seemed to have a life of its own. The more I tried to grip it with my feet the more it slipped and wriggled away from me and I was left dangling like a disabled spider about a foot above the floorboards. Fortunately Settle had gone across to Greenhalgh and was busy bullying him into completing the fifty press-ups so I was able to drop off the rope in a heap and move on to leap-frogging.
Greenhalgh was made to stand against the wall-bars whilst we played five-a-side football.
"I said stand Greenhalgh, not lean!" Settle shouted periodically.
It was always Greenhalgh that Settle picked on. It was odd really because Greenhalgh was by far the biggest in the class, and quite bright. He'd had his teenage growth spurt early and at nearly six feet he was by far the tallest of us and quite broad-shouldered too. He was a good three inches taller than Settle. I suppose by picking on Greenhalgh Settle was hoping to tell the rest of us something.
When the games had finished and the equipment had been stowed away Settle lined us up and said: "You've got three minutes to get dressed and line up here again. Wait! Wait! From when I blow the whistle".
There were no showers so it was just a matter of getting changed and lining up again to be dismissed.
The whistle shrilled out and we made a mad scramble for the changing room. Greenhalgh, I noticed, just walked and didn't alter his pace when Settle shouted: "Get a move on Greenhalgh!"
Dressed and in line we fidgeted, waiting to be dismissed.
"You are none of you going until Greenhalgh is here", Settle shouted, looking at his watch.
The minutes ticked by. Still no Greenhalgh. Settle was visibly reddening with rage, his face expanding like a radish. He too wanted to go home.
Greenhalgh casually strolled out of the changing room and walked towards his line.
"Come here Greenhalgh!", Settle barked. "Come here!"
Greenhalgh, his face pale and his teeth clenched, changed course and walked towards Settle.

THE DOGS OF WAR

When Greenhalgh was within striking distance Settle raised his hand and whacked it hard across the side of Greenhalgh's head. Greenhalgh cringed, recovered, clenched his teeth again and put up his fists.
"Oh. you want to box do you!", Settle screamed. And dropping his arms to his sides and dancing on his feet he said, "Come on then, hit me. See if you can hit me!"
Greenhalgh hesitated, then lunged forward and jabbed at Settle's face with a straight left. Settle took a step back. His right hand shot out and gripped Greenhalgh's wrist taking his arm high above his head. It looked like a quick victory for Settle. Still holding Greenhalgh's arm Settle raised his own left hand as if to slap Greenhalgh across the head but Greenhalgh was moving forward and Settle was on his back foot. From somewhere close to the floor Greenhalgh's right arm swung up in a perfect arc Settle would have praised on a drawing-board and with all Greehalgh's strength and momentum behind it his fist belted Settle in the solar plexus.
Settle's mouth gaped open but no sound came out. His body folded in the middle as he let go of Greenhalgh's wrist and fell to the floor with a thud. "Like a big, slack sack of shit", Rushton said afterwards.
Greenhalgh raised his foot to kick Settle, thought better of it, paused for a second to look at the now writhing body, turned, blew on his knuckles like in the films, squared his shoulders and without saying anything or looking at anybody walked casually out of the gym.
Nobody moved. Nobody spoke. We were absolutely dumbfounded. But you should have heard the racket when we got out of that gym.
We were too late, the train was already moving when we reached the top of the steps. A porter stood between us and it with a large fob watch cupped in his left hand and a flag in his right, flagging the train away. The guard's head stuck out through the door-window of the last carriage. There was no chance of jumping on.
Chandler and me flung ourselves flat on our backs on the long bench seat that ran the length of the open, barn-like railway station.

Rushton was gasping for breath. "Bloody heck. We'll have to wait another hour!".

I looked sideways and saw him bent double with his hands on his thighs, sucking in great gulps of air, his back heaving up and down.

We had run a good quarter of a mile, all the way from the Grot in the town centre, along Dumer's lane and up the steep approach road to the station with its huge advertising hoardings urging us to use Brylcream or drink Camp coffee. We had seen the train and heard its squeaking wheels braking in the station. Ignoring the ticket collector's protesting shouts we had flashed our contracts in his face, taken the steep steps in three-at-a-time leaps that would have done credit to a deer, only to watch the train disappear without us.

As I lay there recovering my breath, looking up at the soot-blackened roof and listening to the station noises, I suddenly had a vivid flash-back. I could never go on to Radcliffe station without this happening.

I was flat on my back again, my head hanging over the edge of the platform with the electric rails only three feet below me. Stanley Tonge was astride my chest pressing the air out of my lungs. His knees were on each of my biceps and his hands gripped my wrists. I was trapped. The only way I could get him off me was to heave my legs up and propel him over my head but that would throw him onto the electric line and I couldn't do that.

"Every time you blink I'm going to smash your face", he said. And he did.

Each time I blinked his right hand released my left wrist and he thumped me hard in the face. I could taste the blood from my nose in my mouth and I was worried that he'd loosened my teeth.

It was clear that Stanley Tonge didn't like me and I certainly didn't like him. Ordinarily we kept out of each other's way but when you are in the same class that is not easy to do. Rushton and me were always making jokes and talking in class whereas Stanley Tonge just wanted to get on with his work. He was right really but nobody liked swots and he was also mean and a bully. He would never give anyone a piece of his toast or save anyone

THE DOGS OF WAR

his apple core. Because he was big, nearly as big as Greenhalgh, he was always picking a fight. There was hardly a day went by when he wasn't waiting to get someone or other after school. Some boys stayed off school if he was out to get them and Alan Stott left because of him.

I had banged his arm in class when he was doing Engineering Drawing and his pencil had skidded across his drawing board spoiling the drawing. Despite saying it was an accident and I was sorry he'd said:

"Right Wild you've been asking for it for a long time. I'll get you after school".

I had lagged behind after school hoping he would have got an earlier train but he had waited for me on the station and jumped on me from behind. Before I could shake him off he had me on the ground with my head over the platform. There were plenty of other boys from our school about, some supposed to be my friends but no one came to help me. Everyone was scared of Stanley Tonge.

"I'm going to hold you here 'till the train comes", he said.

I was terrified and despite myself I was crying and sobbing. He was perfectly capable of doing that. The weight on my arms became excruciatingly painful as he rolled his knees into my arm muscles. I remember wishing I was that boy with no arms we had seen at the baths.

I could hear the train coming. Voices were shouting, "Get off him Tonge", "Let him up, the trains coming!". I think it was the porter who finally pulled him off and dragged me out of the way of the train.

I started shaking. "What's the matter? Are you alright?" Rushton said.

"Yeah. I'm cold. I was just shivering to get warm", I said.

It was our last day at Radcliffe and I was not sorry to be leaving. We had skipped school dinner for the last time and gone for a swim. After final Assembly we had been let out early and we'd just managed to get a game of snooker before the Grot closed. It didn't seem like two years since I had stepped off the train from Prestwich onto the platform opposite that on which I was now sitting. I could still remember the feeling of pride, excitement and elation I had felt. It was a far cry from what I was feeling now. I was excited at the prospect of starting work but I was very apprehensive as to what I could do and I'd no idea what I wanted to do either. Fielding had been right. Radcliffe was a lousy school and we probably would have been a lot better off staying at Hey's Road. I couldn't believe I was fifteen already and about to start looking for a job.

The train rumbled into the station and noisily squealed to a stop. We got into the carriage immediately opposite to where we had been sitting. There was one other person in the coach and, too late, we saw he was wearing a clerical collar. Chandler slammed the door shut and the vicar looked up from the book he was reading with an annoyed look on his face. We spread ourselves out, flopped onto the bench seats and put our feet on the seat opposite and began ribbing each other. Rushton took out a packet of Woodbines. He was just about to light up when the clerical gentleman said:

"This is a non-smoking carriage young man. And do you mind taking your feet off the seats".

Chandler and me complied but Rushton left his feet where they were. He let the match he had struck ignite his cigarette, took a long drag and then dimped it out on the floor. The vicar's head remained bent towards his book but it was easy to tell he wasn't any longer reading it.

Rushton lowered his voice. "Did I ever tell you that story about a vicar", he said to Chandler.

Chandler reddened and glanced towards the corner where the vicar was sitting. He said nothing and the vicar pretended not to hear.

Rushton continued in a low voice but one which the vicar could not fail to hear.

"Well there was this vicar and he went to this house to collect the donation envelope and the man who answered the door was wearing only a night-shirt. When he had put the envelop into his black cloth-bag he said to the man. I don't wish to appear inquisitive but do you mind if I ask why you are wearing a night-shirt so early in the evening".

Chandler was fidgeting uncomfortably and looking more and more embarrassed as the story unfolded. His face could have competed with Jim Settle's. The vicar remained head bent into his book.
"Well, this chap said they were having a party and it was part of the game to wear a night-shirt. All the women are in one room and all the men in another. The men all have night-shirts on and they have to walk upside down on their hands into the women's room and the women have to guess who it is. Well, this vicar said to the man. Do you mind if I join in and the man said: No you can't. Your name's been mentioned three times already!"
Chandler glanced furtively at the vicar and tried to keep his face straight but when I burst out laughing he too exploded into laughter.
"It's a good un that, innit," Rushton said as we tumbled out of the carriage at Bess's o'th Barn station and rolled about the platform creased with mirth.
"Aye, did you see the look on that vicar's face", Rushton shouted.
When the train had gone and we'd recovered a little we went down the platform to the slot machine to get a bar of Nestle's chocolate each and sat in the waiting room eating it.
"What are you going to do for a job?", Chandler asked me.
"I don't know", I said. I've got to see the Youth Employment in Prestwich on Tuesday. My dad said Printing's a good job. I wrote to the Evening Chronicle but I didn't get a reply".
Most of the boys in our class who lived in Radcliffe were going into small engineering firms as apprentice Turners or Fitters. They would have to go to night school two or three nights week to get City and Guilds qualifications. One or two lucky ones had got into Mather and Platts or Simon Carves where they had apprentice schemes with day release classes leading to National, Higher National and M.I.E.Mech.E. qualifications. Johnny Warren had got a job at Agecroft Power Station and Stanley Tonge was going to be a Draughtsman. Much to everyone's surprise Greenhalgh was staying on at the Tech as a Lab. Technician. He would have not got the job had Jim Settle not left at Christmas to go back into industry.
Rushton said he was going to work in the insurance office where

his mother had a cleaning job.

"I'm going to work in my dad's butcher's shop. He wants me to take over the business when he retires", Chandler said.

"Are you going to open your leaving certificate?", Rushton said to me.

"'Course I bloody am. If it's no good I'll throw it away before I get home. They don't even know we get them".

"I'm going to open mine then", he said. "Are you going to open yours Channers?"

"No, my dad would kill me".

Not everyone got a leaving certificate, some just got a slip of paper with their results on it. Those who had done well enough to qualify for a leaving certificate were called up onto the stage in Assembly and handed a large, brown, sealed envelope. Johnny Warren had been handed a book as a prize along with his. I felt sorry for those who didn't get a certificate. Even though it wasn't a proper nationally recognised School Certificate from a proper examining board like they got at the Grammar school it might help in getting a job.

Rushton took the foolscap envelope out of his satchel and tried to carefully prise the flap up with his penknife but it was securely stuck.

"I know, why don't you wet it: it will come open easily then. You can say you dropped it in a puddle.

"Good idea", said Rushton, and he took the envelope off to the Gents.

Rushton already had the certificate in his hand on his return. The red printing saying, "Radcliffe Secondary Technical School Leaving Certificate" had smudged a little with the excess of water Rushton had used. On the back of the certificate was a list of subjects and a legend indicating "A" for Distinction, "B" Credit, "C" Satisfactory.

Rushton had been given a "B" minus for each of the subjects: Practical Mathematics; Mechanical Drawing; Workshop Practice; Elementary Science; English (including Geography and Industrial History) and an "A" for Physical Training.

I tore open the flap of my envelope without bothering to make it look accidental. I had three "A" minuses, a "B" plus for Practical

THE DOGS OF WAR

Mathematics and a "B" for Elementary Science.

Chandler couldn't resist opening his and despite taking care with it he would be in trouble when he got home. He had a mixture of "A's" and "B's" but a glaring "C" for Practical Mathematics.

"My dad won't be too pleased with that "C"", Chandler said.

"Bloody Hell, my mam'll kill me!", Rushton said.

"Yeah, you can see why they put it in a *fools*cap envelope", I said.

"Very funny, I don't think", said Rushton.

I wasn't too pleased with my "B" for Elementary Science though given the effort I had put in I suppose I was lucky to get a "B".

Rushton had suddenly gone very quiet. After a minute or so his face brightened up.

"Have you got that pen of yours on you Channers?", he said.

Chandler said that he had.

"Well lend it to us will you?"

Chandler unclipped the pen from his inside pocket and handed it over.

Rushton took the pen and tried it on the back of his envelope. He spread the Certificate out on the seat beside him and with a series of deftly executed down strokes converted all his "B" minuses into "B" pluses.

"There you are", he said. "That looks a lot better, doesn't it. My mam'll be pleased with that".

As we walked down the steep pathway from the station I thought: I'm going to miss old Channers and Rushton, especially Rushton's jokes. And all that nipping out of school and into the Baths for a quick swim. And life certainly won't be the same without a run down to Radcliffe for a game of snooker in the Grot. Still, it's got to get better. Even if I end up in some boring old factory job at least I'll have some money and I won't have to listen to that stupid loyal toast or eat another of those bloody awful, lousy, school dinners.

I peeled off to go home. Chandler and Rushton went a different way from me. As they disappeared into the mist I shouted after them: Hey! You Two! Out!

A MISCARRIAGE OF JUSTICE

Prologue

When my mother died, our Ernie, who never married, stayed on at our council house in Polefield Approach. I keep the garden tidy for him now that I have retired. He never asked me to: I suppose I do it for my mother really. Anyway, it gives me something to do and I like to have a chat with the neighbours. There aren't many of the originals left these days: a couple of Rogans, a Currie, Robert Leech, and a few Tickles here and there. I can see resemblances though in some of the passers by, especially the children. I'm often stopped in my tracks by a small boy who looks for all the world like Eric Tickle or a little girl who can't be anyone other than Pollie Dodd's great granddaughter she looks so like the young Beryl I knew fifty-five years ago. And Margery Tickle who I mistake for her mother. She looks just like Mrs. Tickle used to look. White hair, a walking stick, the same lame leg. It's a good job longevity is not a characteristic of dogs, there were plenty about in the old days and I'd hate to think one would have grown up to look like old mother Johnson or Mrs. Dickenson. Freddie Murray was around until last year but he had a stroke. He recovered, except for a limp arm and a stutter, sold up and went to live near his son in the South of England. Mrs. Cheesborough says he hates it. Polefield's like that. Margaret Vickers was over from Belgium last year photographing Polefield Grange. She married a Belgian but she keeps coming back. But most from the old days are dead and buried now: Mrs. France, Mrs. Jones, Mrs. Booth, Mrs. Heys, Lily, Mrs. Twiss, Annie Batty, Mrs. Price, the old gossips, Mrs. Dickenson, Johnson and Hall. Their husbands died before them, mainly from pie and chips, Woodbines and beer and most of their children too: boys I used to play with: Keith Dickenson, Clifford Jones, Jimmy Atkins, John Ellison, all dead before they grew up, let alone grown old. Each time I do his garden our Ernie adds another to the memorial scroll for me. "Do you remember Eric Piesy, he's dead, and Dennis Thompson, he's dead. The images these names conjure up: it's

like going to the pictures.
Last week I was down on my knees behind the privet hedge clearing up the grass clippings from the gutters of the lawn like my dad used to do. Our Ernie was watching me work, and as usual, rabbiting on about this and that when he said, "Oh, I didn't tell you did I. You're not going to believe this". I didn't let on that I didn't believe any of his "romances" as my mother used to call his inventive lies. "Johnnie Grocock's died".

"I'm surprised it took him so long", I said. "He must have been getting on for eighty at least". I realised as I said it that if anyone on Polefield estate was going to live beyond their three score years and ten it would be Johnnie Grocock. He'd always been a road-walker and a keep fit fanatic. I remembered our Ernie telling me that Johnnie had run, or perhaps walked, in every Manchester marathon since it began and he'd be no chicken whenever that was. He'd been quite a memorable character too and not just because of his name, and you can imagine what we as kids used to make of that, especially when coupled with the name Nellie Greathead. Most of the names of people on our estate had made me laugh as a child. I used to lie in bed thinking about them. We had our share of ordinary names like Smith and Jones, Webster and Wynn and some a bit funny such as Garlick, Rimmer, Hares and Pye, Twiss and Longmire, France and Tighe. But Nora Sidebottom, Dorothy Proudfoot, Bertie Rook, Freddie Batty, Carol Bell and Alan Badcock used to make me laugh out loud. The best of all though were Johnnie Grocock and Nellie Greathead. I used to do a perm with them like my dad did with the football pool numbers: Nellie Greatcock, Johnnie Grohead, Nellie Headgro, Johnnie Grogreat, Nellie Cockhead, Johnnie Headgro, Nellie Headcock, Johnnie Hedgerow. . . .

Our Ernie interrupted my reverie, saying, "But that's only the half of it. Guess how much he left in his will?".

"I've no idea", I said. "I'm surprised he had enough to leave to justify a will. Who would want an old wheel-barrow, a cap and a pair of old trainers! Even your tatty trousers and coat are better than his old tramp's outfit".

"Eight-hundred and eighty-eight thousand pounds!"

"Come off it Ernie! You're having me on! It can't possibly be that much!"

"No. It's true. It was in the Guide this week. He's left it all to his daughter, Margaret, and some "in trust" for her children".

Ernie went on to tell me that when Johnnie Grocock had to leave Ward and Goldstone, where he worked as an electrician, he'd been given a lump sum of redundancy money. He bought some shares in an Electronics Company which went up almost immediately and it got him interested in the Stock Market. He invested his gains in Amstrad at a time when they were starting to do well and was lucky enough to sell before Alan Sugar's empire started to unravel. He stuck with Computer Companies and made a killing with the ups and downs of Dixon's and er, uhm. . . I.B.M. I think it was.

"He was very knowledgeable. He used to bring me the *Financial Times* when he'd finished with it on a Saturday and pick my brains as to what was a good buy", Our Ernie said.

"Does that mean you've made a pile also?"

"No. I have a few shares now but I never had the money to buy any like Johnnie Grocock did", Ernie said.

Later in the day as I was going to the Chip-shop, for a Jumbo Cod and French fries as they now call fish and chips, I met Margery Tickle, as I have never ceased to call her. Well, Margery Gilmore doesn't seem quite right somehow.

"What's this I hear about Johnnie Grocock leaving you a pile of money in his Will Marge.", I said.

"Oh yes! Wonders will never cease! Fancy him having all that money though. He didn't seem to have two ha'pennies to rub together!"

"Our Ernie told me it was eight-hundred and eighty-eight thousand pounds. That can't be right can it? It can't possibly be that much!"

It is you know. He left the lot to their Margaret and her children. Mind you from what I hear it's all tied up in Trusts so that she can't just spend it. She'd be through it in no time she would. I can't understand him leaving it to her though. She never had anything to do with him after Lily died. Even at Christmas she wouldn't have him round. He told me that last Christmas he was

so lonely he went out and bought a cat. I said he could come round to us for Christmas dinner but he never came. He used to bring me wood for the fire each week on that old wheelbarrow of his. I'm bloody cross with him. They were offcuts that he got from somewhere down Heaton Park but he would never tell me where they came from. I miss them now he's gone".
"Did he ever marry Nellie Greathead?", I asked.
"Oh that's another story. Ask me next time I see you. I must get down to the Chemist now before they close".
"Well at least tell me what Johnnie Grocock died of", I said.
"Cancer. He was in a lot of pain at the end. He had a lump on his arm for a long time. The doctor said it was nothing to worry about but he got a swelling under his arm: the lymphs they said it was. They took the lump off and I think he had some surgery under his arm. I know he said he couldn't lift his arm properly to shave. It's sad really. But fancy him having all that money! He might just as well have not had it for all the good it did him".
When I got home that evening I couldn't stop thinking about Johnnie Grocock. What a character. What a sad character!
A couple of months ago our Arthur and his wife Bronwen called at my place on their way back from their holidays in Scotland. We started to talk about old times, as you do, and I happened to mention that Johnnie Grocock had died. Arthur and I swapped a few reminiscences about life on Polefield Approach and Bronwen said what amazing names and what interesting characters. "Why don't you write it down", she said. So I did. . . .
.

When Mr. Shakespeare wrote "The lady doth protest too much, methinks" he must have had Nellie Greathead in mind. Before her stunningly brazen announcement appeared in the local paper only people living on Polefield estate knew about "her and her goings on" but after her bombshell in the *Prestwich and Whitefield Guide* everyone in the district knew. The whole of Prestwich was buzzing with rumour. Old mother Johnson whom my dad called "the eyes and ears of the world" and Mrs. Dickenson, "the *Daily Mirror* on legs", took up permanent residence on the pavement near the shops, going at it fifty to the dozen with every passer by. Our Ernie said Adolph Hitler couldn't have made a bigger impression if he'd dropped a bomb on Polefield Approach or appeared in person in his underpants.

My mam couldn't wait for me to get back from Whittaker's with the *Guide*.

"Here let me have a look" she said, snatching it out of my auntie Pollie's hand.

"I don't know what all the fuss is about. Here, let me read it!", my grandma said, snatching it in turn off my mother.

My grandma propped her walking stick against the corner of the fireplace and sat herself down on the one good chair we owned in front of the fire and rummaged in her voluminous, home-made handbag for her glasses.

"Oh let me read it Annie, you'll be all day: your glasses are upstairs in the bathroom".

"Well don't stand there gawping you gormless thing, go and get them for me", she said to me.

Grandma Wild perched the glasses on the end of her nose and started to read the announcement in the *Guide* silently to herself, mouthing the words as she did so.

"Read it out! Read it out!" my auntie Pollie and my mother chorused together as they jostled each other, straining to look over my grandma's shoulder.

My grandma stumbled over the heading: "LEGAL ANNOUNCEMENT" which was in big black bold capitals but recovered herself and began to read, slowly, and in an exaggeratedly dramatic voice, following the words with her short, round, deformed, nailess index finger:

> "I Nellie Greathead of 3, Polefield Gardens hereby give notice that from this date onward legal proceedings will be taken against any person or persons making slanderous assertions or publishing libelous material impugning the character and good name of the aforementioned Nellie Greathead. Signed, Nellie Greathead".

"Eee, well I never!" exclaimed auntie Pollie. "What does that mean, impruning".

THE DOGS OF WAR

"It means cutting the privet hedges" our Ernie said.

Even though he didn't like our Ernie, or his jokes, my dad grinned as he clipped him round the ear.

My mam said: "Don't be such a fool. You shouldn't be in here, you two. Get off out, we want to talk".

As we went out of the door I heard my dad say: "She must be crackers. Absolutely crackers! Or perhaps she's a lot cleverer than any of you think. Putting that in the paper is like publishing the Banns. She could be doing it purposely to let everybody know, or to get one over on Lily Heys, but its more likely she wants to prevent poor old Johnnie Greathead from getting a divorce and kicking her out of the house".

My dad knew more about Nellie Greathead than he was prepared to let on. I remember one night, during the early part of the war, after we had changed the clock to double summer time and it was still light long after ten o'clock, my dad had finished doing the garden and was leaning over the front gate fishing for compliments on his handiwork and itching to get on his political soap box. Now that Russia had been attacked by Adolph Hitler he couldn't wait to tell anyone who would listen how clever Joe Stalin had been to make a non-aggression pact with the Nazis: you'd have thought he was being paid for it.

"Old Joe knew what he was doing", he would say, winking his eye and nodding his head to the left as he bashed the ears of passers by.

He claimed he had known all along that Stalin was no friend of Hitler and that by grabbing part of Finland he'd gained time to build a defence line to save the Revolution whilst letting the Capitalists fight it out amongst themselves. Had he known about these efforts on behalf of the Party Harry Pollitt would have been so proud of my dad he'd have recommended him for a Lenin prize.

My dad had lit another Woodbine: I knew he wouldn't be going in just yet. I made myself scarce behind the privet hedge so I wouldn't be sent in to bed. I peeped up the road and saw Roy Greathead's dad walking down Polefield Approach. He worked on the Railway at Salford goods depot., on nights. He was a peculiar looking little man who could well have walked straight out of a crowd scene in a Lowry painting. He came from Salford and was about four feet eight tall and quite skinny looking. I think he was the son of one of those under-size soldiers who got wiped out in a single night on the Somme in the first world war, the Salford Bantams I believe they were called. His body was the right size for a normal small person but his shoulders sloped upwards to his neck at a sixty degree angle as if they were trying to make him look taller, which they did. What made Johnnie Greathead such a short arse though, as we kids called him, was his extraordinarily short legs which seemed to lack thigh bones altogether. They were also slightly bowed which brought his rather bulbous bottom ridiculously close to the ground. You could see how his forebears came to be called Greathead. His rather long face was topped by what midwives call a sugarloaf head. He had quite long, highly lacquered, black hair which was combed straight back from his domed forehead, without a parting, and shiny like a patent leather shoe. He had on his usual long, greyish, dirty, beltless, gabardine raincoat. It slipped down his shoulders and made the sleeves too long. His gas mask bag was hanging from his right shoulder by the padding and flapped against his side as he walked. Under the other shoulder was tucked a tin with sandwiches in it. All in all, I remember, he looked like one of those little clowns at Belle Vue circus. You know, the ones who, when they are walking after the tall one who pretends he doesn't know they are there, keep behind him even when he turns round; or the ones who, when they walk round the ring, can sit down and immediately bob up again to continue walking without missing a step because their bottoms are so close to the ground; that's just what Mr. Greathead looked like. You expected him to repeatedly sit down and bob up again as he walked along Polefield Approach.

Mr. Greathead must have been early because as he approached my dad, he said, in a voice which startled me by its high pitch: "Hello Harry. Have you got a minute. I've been wanting to talk to you".

"Do you want a fag?", my dad said, holding out a packet with one Woodbine in it towards Johnnie Greathead's dangling hand.

"No thanks: I've got my pipe here", Mr. Greathead said,

THE DOGS OF WAR

thrusting his hand under his mac lapel to produce from his jacket top-pocket a highly polished pipe which gleamed like a horse chestnut. I remember it well: you do when you're a child.

I watched him take a pouch from his raincoat pocket and after sucking wetly and repeatedly up the stem of the pipe to make a little bubbling sound, he charged the pipe with tobacco, rubbing the shreds between his finger and thumb whilst feeding it into the bowl, tamping it down with his index finger, like a bird pecking bread. After using what seemed like half a box of matches and sucking his cheeks in and out like a talented trumpeter he finally produced a huge cloud of smoke through which he said, in answer to my dad's enquiry as to what was the matter.

"It's that bugger Johnnie Grocock. I just don't know what to do about him!".

"Why, what's he been up to?", my dad said.

"I don't want this all over the estate Harry. You won't mention it will you. Not even to your Missus".

"No of course I won't", my dad said.

You know he's been on leave for well over a week now. He's waiting for his ship to be repaired, I think, but he's being a bit cagey about it. Says he's not supposed to say what the problem is or when he's due back. It's all that "careless talk costs lives" business. I know he said the boat he was on had an anti magnetic mine device fitted last year so it was probably an air attack, or perhaps a torpedo, that did the damage. He took up with Mrs Heys's daughter last time he was home. You know, Mrs Heys, the widow who lives round the corner on Polefield Circle. Her husband got killed right at the end of the last war and left her with two kids and another one on the way. Well, he persuaded Mrs Heys to let him stay at her place rather than keep traipsing back and forth to Heaton Park. Crafty move. Mrs Heys moved out of the Box Room and let him sleep in there whilst she slept on the sofa downstairs. Albert and Leonard,the sons, slept in the biggest bedroom and Lily was on her own in the small one. Well it was asking for trouble wasn't it! A twenty-one year old sailor and a twenty-six year old woman in a double bed in the next room".

"Too bloody true it was! What the Hell did she think was going to happen!", my dad said.
Well, it apparently did. She's six months gone and despite the loose dresses its beginning to show".
"Well, now you mention it, I thought she was leaning back and walking a bit flat footed the last time I saw her", my dad said, but Mr. Greathead interrupted.
"When Lily told her mother she hadn't seen anything for two months Mrs. Heys went through the roof and said she must write to that Johnnie Grocock and tell him they would have to get married, and bloody quick too. She didn't want the neighbours gossiping. Said she was not having her good name dragged through the gutter by a smart arse like him. Of course he says he never got the letter. Between you and me Harry, I don't think Johnnie Grocock really believes it's his. Anyway Mrs. Heys won't let him stay at the house 'till he marries Lily".
"Well, you can see her point, can't you", my dad said.
"Well", Mr. Greathead continued: "You know how he gets up at six every morning, puts on his shorts and singlet and goes road-walking round Heaton Park wall. He's a right one for keep fit. Five miles! It must be five miles at the very least. I don't know how the hell he does it!"
"Yes, I know he's a walker. I've seen him coming back. I used to do the same myself, years ago but he's a pro, that one, you can tell. Holds his head up high to breathe; tucks his elbows close in; fists clenched, punching his way forward from the chest. Moving his shoulders to give himself impetus. You can tell he's a pro. You watch the way he rolls on the balls of his feet. Always keeps one foot on the ground so he won't be disqualified. Little round bum mincing along. Perfect technique for a road-walker and the right build too. Tallish, long legs, no excess weight, just enough for stamina, a perfect athlete".
My dad was clearly impressed by Johnnie Grocock, if not to say envious.
"Aye, er, yes, well," said Mr. Greathead, "about a week ago, he was just passing as I got off the bus at Heywood Road. He'd finished the serious walking so he waited for me whilst I got a paper from Whittaker's". Mr. Greathead paused for a second:

"Now you will keep all this under your hat won't you Harry".
"Aye, I might be a talker but I'm not one for gossiping", my dad said.
Johnnie Greathead continued. "He told me Lily was expecting a baby and he had to get out of the Heys' house as soon as possible. He said he supposed he would marry Lily but he would need to get permission from the Captain of his ship. Mrs Heys didn't believe permission was necessary under the circumstances and wanted him out of the house "till he does the right thing by our Lily". He asked had I a spare room he could rent until he went back off leave. Said he was expecting a telegram any day now. Well, you know me Harry, I like to help people out if I can, so I said he could have the spare bedroom. Me and the wife sleep in the big bedroom and our Roy sleeps in the Box-room so we have a room going spare. When I told Nellie she was not keen on the idea but when I told her he had a ration voucher and a living allowance and that she could keep the extra money she got more enthusiastic. I told her she would have to make him a bit of breakfast but he would have his evening meals at the Heys's with Lily. With me working nights, I said, she would feel safer if the siren went".
"I was an absolute fool Harry. An absolute fool! Especially after him telling me about Lily Heys".
"Why what's happened?", my dad said.
"What's happened! He's knocking-off my Missus, that's what's happened!"
"Bloody Hell! Oh that's not on Johnnie! Are you sure?"
"Of course I'm sure! Well no, I'm not sure but all the signs are there. I can even smell his hair oil in the bed, and I can tell by the way they keep looking at each other. She can't leave him alone. It's that bloody sailor's uniform. She's like a bitch on heat. Ignores me. Talking to him all the time, touching his arm, laughing and giggling like a bloody schoolgirl. It's sickening. She's even got our Roy calling him uncle Johnnie."
"That doesn't prove anything. He could have just gone in and lain on the bed for some reason when she was out", my dad said.
"No, it's not just that. She always used to come to bed before I went to work but she doesn't want to do that now he's there. Says

she feels embarrassed with someone else in the house downstairs. I tell you, Harry, there's been nothing doing for me since the day after he arrived. I know Nellie, she's not one of your 'once a week while the kids are at Sunday school' women. She wants her bit of pleasure every night. None of your 'Not tonight I've got a headache'. I don't know what I'm going to do about it, Harry. Its driving me crackers thinking about it. I can't stop wondering what they're up to while I'm at work. My inside's shaking the whole time!".
"Well if you're that sure bump him one and tell him to go!", my dad said.
"It's all right for you Harry, you're over six feet tall. I'm only four feet eight inches!"
"Well you'll either have to tell him to go, or put up with it. Why don't you confront her with it?"
"Where would that get me? She'd only deny it".
"Well then, if you're not prepared to do anything about it you'll have to grin and bear it. She's not the only one round here going off the rails you know. You should be thankful it's not one of the airmen from Heaton Park that she's taken a fancy to. They're here for three months and some are on the permanent staff. There's two or three billeted in every street. Hetty tells me some right tales about what's going on while their husbands are away in the army. May Adams, on the corner, just down from you, she's had a child. Her husband's been a P.O.W. nearly eighteen months. It's been adopted by the vicar and his Missus at St. Margaret's. She tried to tell Hetty that she didn't know how it had happened. Said she hadn't slept with anybody, can you believe! I told Hetty to tell her the last time that happened three wise men came from the East and I haven't seen many of those about on Polefield estate. Reg Pye's wife has gone off as well. She's gone after that airman she had billeted on her. It's going on all over the place, Johnnie. There are even jokes about it. 'Knock on the front door and then run like hell round the back'".
"Well it's not a joke I can tell you Harry, and anyway I'm here. It's going on while I'm here, in the bloody house!"
"Aye, well, I suppose that does make a bit of difference. Anyway, he won't be here much longer. There is a bloody war

on. They're not going to let him sit at home enjoying himself with Gerry on the doorstep. They'll be needing all the sailors they can get now they've started sending convoys to Russia. You'll see, she'll forget about him when he goes back".
"She won't you know. It's gone too far this has. I know Nellie. When she wants something she damned well gets it!".
"Well why don't you let the women sort it out then: they're good at that sort of thing. Have a word with Mrs. Heys. If she gets wind of what's going on she'll have him back there double quick".
"Oh no she won't you know! I've already told her. Far from making things better, it's made matters a bloody sight worse. She says if that's really what he's up to he's not going to marry their Lily if she has anything to do with it".
"Over my bloody dead body!", she said.
"She even said if she were younger she would have kept it dark about Lily and pretended the child was hers. Lots of mothers down in Salford used to do that you know, tag one on, but she's too old, Mrs. Heys. She must be sixty if she's a day. She must have gone and told Lily what I'd said. It's made Lily ill. She's taken to her bed. Been there since Tuesday. Went to bed, won't eat, won't speak to anybody, just weeps and sleeps. It's a right bloody mess I can tell you Harry. Anyway, I'll have to go now or I'll miss that 73 bus and I'll be late for work. I'll come and see you a bit earlier tomorrow night if you don't mind Harry. It's been a big help just talking to someone about it. Don't mention it to anyone now, will you, whatever you do", he said, as he hurried off.
My dad had finished his cigarette but he took one last drag at the dimp: it was too small to save. It nearly burnt his lips as he tried to remove it between the pincer of his index finger and his thumb. He dropped the remains of the cigarette on the path and rubbed it in with the ball of his boot. I remember thinking that my mam would be glad Johnnie Greathead had refused that last Woodbine. My dad would have a cigarette to smoke in the morning. He wouldn't be rummaging about in the empty grate in the front room for a dimp, spoiling for a row, whilst she was making his sandwiches or try to get her to rouse our Ernie out of

bed to go and catch Mr. Jones, next door but one, before he went to work, to borrow a couple of fags. As he turned to go indoors my dad saw me hiding behind the hedge.
"What the bloody hell are you doing there. I thought I told you to go in half an hour ago!"
"I did. But I came out again just now to see if my mam was coming home", I lied.
My mother was working late, helping Mrs Matz, the Jewish lady she did cleaning for in Sedgely Park, get the house ready for her son's bar mitzvah.
"How long have you been there?"
"I've only just come out!" I said, sulkily.
Fortunately my dad's attention was distracted by the Post Office telegraph man puffing up the Approach on his bike. My dad went to the gate and craned over it to see where he was going, saying as he did so:
"I'll bet he'll be going to Johnnie Greathead's".
I went down to the gate and saw the bike turn into the Circle. He was going to Lily Heys' house.
The following evening about nine o'clock there was a knock at the front door. My mam told our Ernie to go and see who it was.
"It's that Mr. Greatinghead from up Polefield Gardens", our Ernie said, as he came back into the kitchen.
"I've come to have a word with Harry, Mrs. Wild", Mr. Greathead shouted down the hallway.
"Don't stand there at the door. Come on in, Johnnie", my mam shouted back. "Harry's not in yet. He's down at the Town's Yard getting the Rescue bus ready for tomorrow but he should be here any minute now. They're sending the "Rescue" to Great Budworth, in Cheshire, for more training. They've built a mock bombed street there for them to learn to tunnel under houses. Sit yourself down. How's Nellie? I haven't seen her for ages. Would you like a cup of tea: I've just made one. How's your Roy? He's still only small isn't he. I was only comparing him with our Boris the other day. Still, it's nothing to worry about because you're both small aren't you. I wish my three would slow down a bit: they take after Harry. We'll not be able to fit in here if they keep growing like they are doing: we'll need a bigger place. I'd

love one of those houses on the front of the road with a separate scullery. Mrs. Price told me you've got a lodger: that sailor that's walking out with Lily Heys, isn't it? Are you still working down in Salford?

My mam never stopped talking. Mr. Greathead couldn't get a word in. He'd still not managed a reply when a few minutes later I heard the steel heel of my dad's boots ringing on the path. The latch on the back door clicked up and my dad came in. He didn't look too pleased to see Johnnie Greathead sitting there by the fire but his expression changed for the better when Mr. Greathead got up and offered him a cigarette, saying: "I won't keep you a minute Harry".

"I thought you smoked a pipe", my dad said.

"I do but I have a few Woodbines by me in case I run out of baccy".

My dad and Mr. Greathead went out leaving my mam with her string of unanswered questions.

I wanted to go outside to listen to what my dad and Mr. Greathead were talking about but when I pleaded with my mam she wouldn't let me go out.

"Aw go on mam," I said, "Just until our Ernie comes home from the pictures".

"No! It's an early night for you two. Go on. Get up those stairs, the pair of you", she said emphatically, herding our Arthur and me into the hall. "Your father will be tired after working late. He won't want you two around while he's having his supper".

"Orr, go on mam. It's only nine o'clock. It's still light and I can't get to sleep when it's light".

"No. You can stay down until I've given our Arthur's knees a good scrubbing, I've never seen such filthy knees, I'll have to stand him in the bath. You must come up when I call you".

When my dad came in he took off his beret and threw it onto the sideboard. He draped his blue battledress top round the back of a chair, rolled his sleeves up above his bulging, blue veined biceps, and tucked the attached collar of his shirt inside out under his shirt to expose his red neck and white chest. He then went to the sink, which was piled with pots as usual, for a wash. He was snorting and spitting and clearing his throat with a terrible noise as my mam came into the kitchen.

"Oh not over the pots Harry", she shouted. But it was too late. My dad turned round with his eyes screwed shut.

"Oh don't you start. Where's the towel?", he said, groping around with his hands held out like a blind man.

My mam passed him a threadbare towel off the oven door and took a brown dish from the oven containing the remains of a meat and potato pie my grandma had made, earlier, for our dinner. She put the dish on the table in my dad's place. "You can eat it out of the dish, Harry: it will keep it warm", she said. "Now you get off up to bed and let your father have his supper in peace. You can have a wash in the morning".

I didn't move so she made a rush for the pantry door where she kept the carpet beater. She never hit us with it: the threat was enough. I made a dash for the door and ran up the stairs. When I got to the top I turned to go down again but thought better of it. I went to the bedroom and put my pyjamas on. Then I crept quietly down the stairs again and pressed my ear against the kitchen door, listening to the grown ups talking, like I did most nights.

"What did Johnnie Greathead want", my mam said.

"Oh nothing. He's having a bit of trouble at work and wanted some advice".

"What kind of advice?",

"Oh nothing. It's all over now. It's not worth talking about".

A few days later I met Eric Tickle on the way to school. His mother had been friendly with Mrs. Heys for many years. Mrs. Hey's, though not a qualified midwife had helped deliver all Mrs. Tickle's children, and most of the other children on Polefield estate. If someone died it was always Mrs. Hey's who was sent for to wash and lay out the body. She also took in laundry. The Tickle's small, square back garden, along with the others in their block backed on to the side of Mrs Heys' neglected, long back garden. Mrs. Tickle had had a makeshift gate put in the fence and Mrs Heys let the Tickle's chickens roam there. (the Tickle's kept a dozen or so chickens and quite a few people on the estate were rationed with Mrs. Tickle for eggs). Mrs. Tickle was always popping across for a natter on some pretext or another. Between them, Mrs. Hey's and Mrs. Tickle knew everything about every-one on the Estate and being such good friends they were constantly up-dating what they knew. If anyone knew what had been going on between Nellie Greathead and Johnnie Grocock it would be Mrs. Tickle and anything Mrs. Tickle got to know Eric knew about sooner or later because almost everyone on the estate called in at the Tickle's for a gossip or to pick up eggs and Eric Tickle didn't miss much.

"What's been going on between Mrs. Greathead and that sailor Lily Heys is going out with", I said.

"How do you know about that? It's supposed to be a top secret. Mrs. Heys doesn't want anyone talking about their Lily".

"I overheard Mr. Greathead saying something to my dad the other night".

Eric said, "Johnnie Grocock's gone back to sea now, but he's got a right lump on his forehead where Lily Heys hit him with her shoe".

"Blimey! What happened then?"

"I'm not supposed to talk about it. My mam said she'd kill me if I repeated a word of what Mrs Heys said".

"Aw, go on Eric. I'm your best friend", I said."

"Well don't tell anyone, will you. Mrs. Heys came to our house last night to see my mam. They went into the front room to talk but I could hear every word of it from the kitchen. She said a telegram marked 'Urgent: War Office Business' had come the other night for Johnnie Grocock telling him to report back to his ship no later than 18.00 hours the following day".

"I know. I saw the telegram man go there."

"Because it was urgent Mrs. Heys decided to take it round to Greathead's where Johnnie Grocock was staying. She thought it might give her a chance to see if there was anything in what Johnnie Greathead had told her. There was no answer when she knocked so she went round the back to see if there was anybody in the kitchen and she saw the bedroom light on. She went round the front and kept on knocking and eventually Nellie Greathead came to the door. She only opened the door a couple of inches but Mrs. Heys said the coat she had thrown on fell open and she could see Mrs Greathead had nothing on underneath. When Mrs. Heys asked if Johnnie was in Mrs. Greathead said: "No, he's gone to work". Mrs. Heys told her she meant Johnnie Grocock and Mrs. Greathead went bright red and said he had gone out doing his road- walking. When Mrs Heys told her there was an urgent telegram for him and that he must come round and collect it as soon as he got back Mrs Greathead started sobbing, saying: "Oh no, no, he can't have to go back so soon!"

"Unbeknown to Mrs. Heys, Lily had heard the telegram come and had got out of bed, dressed, dabbed a bit of powder on her face and a smear of lipstick and followed her mother to Greathead's. Mrs Heys said she didn't know Lily was standing behind her and the door was not open enough for Mrs. Greathead to see her either. Hearing Nellie Greathead sobbing was too much for Lily: she ran at the door with both hands outstretched, knocked Mrs Greathead to one side and ran up the stairs shouting Johnnie, Johnnie, where are you! She was just in time to see the naked Grocock, still with a French Letter dangling off the front of him, disappear into the bathroom carrying his clothes and shoes in a hastily assembled bundle. Lily shouted: Johnnie! Johnnie! and hammered on the door.

Just a minute. Just a minute Mrs. Heys heard him shouting, I'm just having a Jimmy Riddle. He tried to pretend he had come into the house through the back door and, being desperate to have a pee, had gone straight up to the toilet whilst Nellie was answering the front door. Lily shouted: you're a barefaced liar. I saw you go in there just this second. When he emerged from the bathroom fully clothed, in his uniform, and grinning like a rabbit it was too much for her. She shouted into his face: "If you'd been out walking you'd have had your bloody walking things on".

Mrs. Heys said Lily bent her leg back behind her from the knee, ripped her high heel shoe off with her right hand and whacked him on the forehead with it.

Johnnie tried to dodge, twisted and fell arse over tit down the stairs with a tremendous clatter and lay splayed like a slain animal on the hall floor.

Mrs Heys said Lily shouted: Oh my god! Oh my god what have

THE DOGS OF WAR

I done! What have I done to him! Nellie Greathead screamed and rushed over to raise Johnnie's head, cradling and hugging it and echoing Lily's: Oh my god! Oh my god what has she done to him! Mrs Heys scuttled into the kitchen for a bowl of cold water and a flannel and dashed some water on to Johnnie's face to bring him round. Johnnie began moaning and eventually opened his eyes. He asked where he was and what had happened to him.

Mrs Heys said she thought he was pretending to be unconscious, and to not know what had happened, to get himself out of trouble. Anyway when it was clear he was alright it ended up with Lily and Mrs Greathead weeping and hugging each other. Mrs. Hey's said she couldn't believe it.

While all this had been going on young Roy had woken up and come halfway down the stairs to see what all the row was about. When Mrs. Greathead saw him she shouted to him: Tell them Roy, tell them, I was in bed with you when that knocking came wasn't I. Yes, he said, yes, I remember, you were reading a story to me and I fell asleep.

Mrs Heys said she helped Johnnie pack his things up and despite Nellie Greathead pleading that he was too dazed to walk the distance she made him go to her house with Lily so that she could see him off in the morning. 'Seeing as how you haven't been able to see him off tonight' she had said to Lily.

It was Nellie Greathead's turn to take to her bed. Mrs. Price who lived next door to the Greathead's, and not one to miss the opportunity to boost her self importance by passing on a bit of gossip, happened to be coming back from the shops at the same time as my mother on Saturday morning. My mam caught up with her and said: "Come in for a cup of tea and tell me what's happening with Mrs. Greathead". Word had already got round to my mam that there had been rumpus the night before Johnnie Grocock went back off leave.

Mrs Price settled herself down at the table. I was in the corner pretending to be reading my comic. I could tell they were all set for a bit of scandal-mongering by the way they put their heads together and lowered their voices. Mrs. Price had first hand knowledge of what was happening because both Nellie and Johnnie Greathead had confided in her. Johnnie Greathead had told her Nellie wasn't well and had asked her to pop in occasionally and see that she was alright. He was worried about her but he couldn't afford to be off work as he didn't get paid when he was off. He had told her that when he got home one morning he was surprised to find that Johnnie Grocock wasn't there. He'd asked Nellie where he was and she had broken down, weeping, saying he had had to go back and that she loved him and couldn't live without him. "Life's so unfair", she'd said. "There's Lily Heys carrying his child when it's me he really loves!" She was distraught and irrational, talking of going to Portsmouth to be with him, "Though what good that would have done with him out in the North Sea, beats me", Johnnie Greathead said. Mrs. Price said Johnnie Greathead had told Nellie not to be so bloody daft. "It's what comes of reading too many of those bloody books she gets from the library". He'd tried to reason with her. Told her he was a good husband. Always worked hard so she wouldn't have to go out to work. That he didn't go out boozing, like some men. Didn't gamble. Saved his money. Didn't even do the football pools. Took her to the pictures on his night off every week. The longer the list grew the more harm he had done himself. Instead of reminding her what a model husband he was she had screamed that what he was saying only confirmed for her what she already knew. That he was a jealous, mean-minded, tight-fisted, boring, unromantic, nonentity and that she didn't know how she could have been such a fool as to marry someone like him when there were Johnnie Grococks about. She had run up the stairs to the bedroom, slammed the door and wept inconsolably into her pillow for an hour or more. She had stayed in bed for days, saying she was too ill to get out. The only time she got up was to go down the Approach to meet the postman to see if there was a letter from Johnnie Grocock.

"I tried to reason with her myself, Hetty, but she wouldn't listen", Mrs. Price said to my mam.

"I said to her: You're a married woman Nellie. You've got Roy.

You're ten years older than he his. He's engaged to Lily Heys. She having his baby. What do you think you are playing at love". It just washed over her. D'you know what she said. She said: "Lily Heys doesn't love him like I love him. No one could love him like I love him. Lily Heys! She's nothing, nothing to him. He told me he doesn't love her. How could he love her. She's stupid, fat, ugly. She's nothing compared to me. She's trapped him by telling him she's pregnant. She's not pregnant. She's telling him that so that he'll marry her. It's her mother whose put her up to it. He doesn't love her. He's told me so. He told me that even if he has to marry Lily Heys he'll still belong to me".

"I couldn't believe it Hetty. It was like she was reading it from a book. She said: "When he's with me I can smell the sea in his hair and feel the swell of the ocean in my bosom. The freedom, the freedom of the sea! You have no idea Mrs. Price what he does for me. He's wonderful! Wonderful! What does Johnnie Greathead do for me? Keeps me cooped up, washing, ironing, cutting up his bloody sandwiches, cleaning his house, over and over and over again and waiting, waiting, waiting, and for what? One night a week at the flaming pictures. Well Johnnie Grocock's made me realise there's more to life than that. I want him and I'm going to have him and no bloody Lily Heys is going to stop me. Kid or no kid. I'll kill her before I'll let her have him!".

"I think she's going off her rocker Mrs. Wild".

"Oh she'll get over it, we all do", my mam said.

Early the following Saturday morning I was at the side of the house cleaning my bike before going to do messages for Mr. Roberts, Grocer and Confectioner. I stood up to stretch my legs and as I did so I saw Mrs. Heys and Lily going down Polefield Approach towards Bury Old Road. Mrs. Heys was, as usual, wearing her carpet slippers and was dressed in her usual old, loose, brown coat with her matching pudding basin felt hat resting on her ears. Her round shoulders, stooped posture and shuffling walk made her look much older than her sixty or so years. Lily, on the other hand looked much younger than her twenty-six years. As a rule she was a solid, stodgy, badly dressed woman but she looked much less so today. She was all dolled up in a tight-fitting, light blue two-piece costume which would have been alright except for the skirt which was too tight and must have been nearly two inches above her knees. Her stomach bulged at the front and tightened the skirt so that it accentuated even more her big bulging bottom at the back, the lobes of which wobbled like two, shelled, hard-boiled eggs each time she took a step forward. Her high-heel shoes, with their glossy, black ankle straps were inappropriate for a woman with her type of thick, white, stockingless, legs and made her wobble when she walked. What was surprising, though, was that she was wearing a large wide-brimmed hat with a half-veil shading her eyes and nose. It was like one of those that film stars wear in the pictures. The case she was carrying looked heavy and she was obviously struggling with it. Fortunately Mr. Rook, who lives next door to the Tickles, overtook them and offered to carry the case to the bus stop for her.

As the three of them turned the corner I saw Mrs. Greathead hurrying down the Approach. She stood on the corner of the shops and watched Lily go to the bus stop. She stayed there to watch Lily and Mr. Rook get on the number seventy-three to Manchester. Mrs Heys waved to Lily and turned to walk back home. Mrs. Greathead dodged back round the corner and began to walk quickly down the Approach towards home but she stopped, suddenly, and turned back towards the shops. She and Mrs Heys passed each other on the pavement as I passed them on my bike. Nellie Greathead said something to Mrs. Heys which I couldn't quite hear but I did hear Mrs. Heys's reply: "It's none of your business but yes, she is going to Portsmouth: to get married to her fiancee, Johnnie Grocock. At a Registry Office, thanks to you, but neither you nor anyone else is going to stop her. She'll be back Thursday and she'll be Mrs. Grocock, a respectable married woman, which is more than I can say for you! Mrs. Greathead was crying when she turned to run off up the Approach.

When Lily returned from Portsmouth she was wearing a thick gold ring on the third finger of her left hand and a smile on her

THE DOGS OF WAR

face. "Like the cat that got the cream", Mrs. Tickle said to my mam. Three months later she gave birth to a daughter. Johnnie Grocock remained at sea. He did not put in an appearance on Polefield estate until the end of the war but it was rumoured that he wrote regularly to Nellie and very occasionally to his wife. Mrs Greathead remained brazenly at her gate and every day went down the street to meet the postman.

Johnnie Grocock was not the only serviceman whose return from the forces was awaited with both eager anticipation and some trepidation by a woman on Polefield estate, though not all for the same reason. Mrs. Holland didn't know if she could cope with her husband's scarred face with its missing eye and his arm cut off at the elbow. Mrs. Helliwell, no longer in love with her husband, blanched at the prospect of her legless man's homecoming from the military hospital. There were some women whose men were not coming back at all and to see those who did was a distressingly painful reminder of those they had lost. Mrs. Tickle was bitterly upset and tearful again over the death of her son, Willie, when his friend, paratrooper Fred Jackson, who had been captured at Arnhem in that badly managed bridge fiasco, returned. With each returning soldier Mrs. Tickle relived the anguish, biting her fist and shaking as she did on seeing the telegraph boy prop his bike outside her house and walk briskly down the path to hand her that dreadful, impersonal telegram saying: "I regret to inform you of the death of your son Lance Corporal William Tickle, R.A.M.C., killed in action on. . ..". It was no consolation to learn later, in a letter from his C.O., that he had been blown to pieces along with two others of his squad by a hand grenade "whilst gallantly leading a stretcher party", to pick up a wounded officer, through the rubble of what had once been a picturesque late medieval Normandy village.

Mrs Batty's husband, Petty Officer Charles Frederick Batty, had been drowned at sea somewhere off the coast of Singapore. There were others on the Estate who were soon to wish their husbands had never returned. Peggy France, our next door neighbour, could be heard plainly through the kitchen wall

rowing with her husband, an ex-unemployed joiner who had been glamorously transformed into Flight Sergeant Alec France, the navigator of a Lancaster bomber, and who, three weeks after his demob date, had at long last managed to find his way home. Rummaging through his kit Peggy had found a bundle of letters from a string of women stretching back to the beginning of the war. "So this is what I've been waiting for all these years", she screamed through her tears.
"Who the bloody hell told you to touch my kit bag anyway, you meddling bitch", he shouted back.
Bitch, bugger, bastard, fucking whore, were just a few of the new words their four year old son Ian was able to add to his lexicon that night. He probably already knew the word cow but had never previously associated it with his mother. He screamed for them to stop for all his lungs were worth but with no result. Pots and pans began flying. Hair was being torn out and eyes blackened. "You'll have to go round Harry, they'll kill one another", my mam said. My grandma took off her shoe and banged, loudly on the wall. There was a sudden silence. A few minutes later next door's front door banged shut. My mam ran to the front room and came back to say that Peggy France had left with the child in her arms. "She must be going round to her mother's".
As my mam said this an excessively loud burst of music came from next door's gramophone. It was the tune of Chopin's dead march, slowly, and dramatically, grinding out, with some comedian singing:
"Last night I dreamt I was bloomin' well dead, as I went to the funeral I bloomin' well said: Look at my grandma, bloomin' old hay bag. Oh ain't it grand to be bloomin' well dead!".
It was the first of many performances of that record we heard through the wall in the coming weeks. I still know the verses to this day.
But it wasn't just the France's who were having trouble adjusting; there were whispers and reports from all over the estate of rows, leavings, threatened and actual divorces. And many a returning soldier bit his lip, so to speak, as he looked anxiously, and in vain, at the child he had never seen to try to

find some trace of himself in the tiny creature, with its mother's skirt tightly clenched in its fist, the thumb of the other hand in its mouth, peeping shyly at him from behind her welcoming back.

Johnnie Grocock's homecoming was awaited eagerly by not just one woman but the two women in his life. There were others too on Polefield estate who remembered his dramatic departure and were anticipating his return with, to say the least, considerable, if not equal interest. Among them my own mother, grandma, and auntie Pollie, who all loved a bit of scandal. They were not to be disappointed.
When Johnnie did eventually come marching home he made an impressive spectacle. It was the middle of a fine, dry, Saturday morning and there were many shoppers about to see him alight from the 73 bus. He stood out, prominently, being in uniform. He swung his kit bag deftly on to his shoulder and neatly avoided dislodging his round, white-topped, sailor's hat. His bell-bottom trousers flapped in the light breeze and his highly polished shoes caught the sun as he stepped out towards the Approach, leaving in his wake the admiration of the women shoppers and a ripple of animated conversation. I could see him through Roberts's shop window. I remember his tight-fitting navy-blue jersey and the well-laundered, white, back-bib collar of his shirt with the blue lines edging it and the loosely knotted Nelson's ribbon at the front. What impressed me most though were the knife sharp, transverse creases across the legs of his trousers and how tightly the trousers fitted over his bottom. Instead of the mincing walk and thrusting shoulders of the road-walker I remembered, he now rolled his shoulders from side to side and moved with a matelot's rolling gait. His face, though still quite long, had filled out a little and his tan radiated like sunshine and accentuated the whiteness of his teeth. He still had a slight look of the rabbit about the mouth because his top front-teeth were slightly prominent, and slightly crossed, but the irregularity made him seem more characterful somehow.
Though not many people knew Johnnie to speak to, as he had not been brought up on the estate, nearly everyone who passed him must have guessed who he was. There were many more

women than my mam watching from behind the curtains to see whether he would turn in the Circle or carry on towards Polefield Gardens. He looked up towards the Gardens but he turned in to the Circle and went to Mrs Heys' house. There must have been nobody in because he left his kit bag on the step and went up the road to Nellie Greathead's house. My mam says he was there twenty minutes but Mrs. Johnson, who lives in the Gardens, says it was at least half an hour. What is not in dispute is that he went there and afterwards went to Mrs. Tickle's to wait for Lily and Mrs. Heys to return.

Mrs. Tickle told Johnnie she was not surprised Lily and her mother were out. "They'll be down at Princess Street cleaning the house".

Mrs. Tickle told my mam, later, that Johnnie seemed quite relieved when she told him Lily had been lucky enough to rent a little terraced house in Heaton Park near the bottom of Orange Hill Road, where the allotments are, in Princess Street, just round the corner from Randlesome Street.

Johnnie had said: "Well that's good news. It will save a lot of trouble if I'm living down there".

Now that Johnnie was back Mrs. Greathead, who seldom went out, other than to the shops, adopted a new routine. She was no longer to be seen in a morning leaning over the gate watching for the postman. Each afternoon she went down towards the shops but anyone watching, and there were quite a few people watching, would have seen that she was not going shopping. She was wearing make up and had on her better coat. Had they looked carefully, and there were more than one or two who did, they would have seen that the shopping bag she was carrying contained a lightweight blanket.

It was the school holidays and I was working at Roberts's full-time. As I sat on the small folding step ladders in the shop watching out for customers putting things into their bags without paying for them, in the interval between the shop door-bell ringing and Eddie Roberts making an appearance in the shop, I would often see Mrs. Greathead going past.

One afternoon I was taking an accumulator to the wireless shop at St. Margaret's when I saw Mrs. Greathead go through the park entrance into the area of the park which had been given up by the R.A.F. and opened again to the public. Johnnie Grocock was waiting for her. I saw him quite openly run up to her and hug and kiss her, after which they walked together into a small nearby wood beyond our school air raid shelters.

When Johnnie's demob leave expired and he was officially out of the Navy he got a job as an electrician, the trade he was apprent-iced to before he was conscripted into the Navy, at Ward and Goldstone's in Frederick Road, Salford, and Mrs. Greathead's afternoon shopping jaunts ceased. Johnnie took up road-waking again.

Though Johnnie made out to his workmates that he was happily married, as a reason for turning down their invitations to go to the pub or spend Friday night with them at the Palais in Manchester, this was certainly not the case. Marriage was a prison and he actively disliked Lily but having agreed to do the right thing he felt he had a duty to stand by her. Besides there was the child to whom he had quickly grown quite attached. Despite this consolation he spent his evenings desperately aching for Nellie, watching his life tick away with every movement of the clock and gloomily reflecting on his circumstances.

He realised only too well that whereas he and Nellie had a natural affinity he and Lily had a profound antipathy. Whereas he was early to bed and early to rise she lay in bed until the middle of the morning and never got up to see him off to work like other wives. If he wanted fresh sandwiches he had to make them himself otherwise put up with those Lily made the night before. He was by inclination a clean, tidy person, who liked his living quarters ship shape; Lily was a natural slattern who generated and multiplied squalor with every slap dash activity she performed. He seemed to spend all his time cleaning up after her. He couldn't for the life of him imagine what she did all day. His meals were never ready when he came home from work and were invariably from tins. He was fed up with corned beef, tinned beans and tinned tomatoes. He'd had enough of that tack in the Navy. True, there was rationing but what about vegetables? Lily didn't seem to have heard of them. She just looked at him blankly when he mentioned them. "Oh if you want that kind of thing you'll have to cook them yourself!" And it was him who had to go down to the chip shop two or three times a week for pie and chips. When he complained Lily would retaliate with: "You try looking after a bloody kid all day like I have to do and see how you like it!" He knew it was more often than not Lily's mother who looked after the child while Lily sat on her fat bottom in front of the fire with her skirt pulled up over he thighs getting her legs mottled with give away patterns.

Lily was seldom in when he came home from work and it was often a cold dark house he came home to. He would even have to clear out the ashes and make the fire. Lily would be still up at Polefield or when she wasn't his mother in law would be sitting in his chair, swilling tea and gossiping. They both seemed totally indifferent to the child's dirty dresses and untidy hair. They never cleaned the food from round its mouth or wiped its nose. There was always thick yellow snot, like two wax candles, which came and went from Margaret's nostrils as she wheezily breathed in and out. He couldn't stand the sight of it. If only Nellie had been the child's mother!

His thoughts constantly turned to Nellie Greathead: her spotlessly clean, neat, warm, comfortable kitchen and clean table cloths and the flowers and potted plants she kept around the house. What a contrast! Lily was gormless, dark, stodgy, graceless and had grown fat and flabby round the stomach since having the baby but Nellie, Nellie was so radiant, fair. Her hair. . . "rivalling the golden sunlight". . . well, slightly brownish actually. But with such smooth luminescent skin. And you wouldn't have known Nellie had had a child. She was small but trim, and her figure so shapely. She moved with the grace of a goddess, rhythmically emanating sexuality. Why in the name of all that's bright and beautiful did he ever think Lily attractive? But he knew the answer well before the thought was formed. Ships were being lost and sailors drowned. The Hood, The Ark Royal, The Barham all sunk. H.M.S. Dunedin, a ship his mates from training had been on, torpedoed. He had not wanted to die without having been with a woman. He was the only one in his ship's mess who had never had sex, or at least the only one who

THE DOGS OF WAR

admitted it. His mates had ribbed him saying he was letting the Navy's reputation down. They had given him a packet of Durex when he went on leave and said he must buy all of them a pint if he brought it back unopened. He couldn't believe his luck when Lily had suggested they left the dance early and he went home with her. She must have known her mother would be out. She was up the stairs and into bed as soon as she could get his pants off. "It'll be alright. You don't have to use one of those things at this time of the month", she had said. Like a fool he had believed her. Her mother was conveniently out each night for the remainder of his leave. Two months later he had got the letter. It was his mates' turn to buy him a pint. Nellie---pure, sweet, honest, Nellie---she would never have done that on him, never in a thousand years, he thought.

One night he was "miles away" and fingering the letter from Nellie in his coat pocket when he heard himself saying out aloud: "Why did she have to be married!"

Lily turned round from the sink and said: "What's that you said!" I was thinking about work. "I said I don't know why I have to be so harried!"

Nellie had written him a letter which fortunately Lily had not intercepted, suggesting that he leave Lily and go into digs until she could persuade Johnny Greathead to either leave or to let him come and lodge at her house. She said she could not just tell Johnnie Greathead to go since the rent book was in his name.

He wanted so much to be with Nellie but on his wage he knew he could not afford to go into digs. He could certainly not support Lily and his child and Nellie and her boy and pay for digs. And Johnnie Greathead would be unlikely to give Nellie anything if she told him to go. He would have to think of something else.

On Saturday afternoon, as usual, he headed for the park, as prearranged but having the child with him was an almost insurmountable difficulty for the intimacy they both craved. He feared that Nellie would become frustrated and do something silly if he didn't come up with something. "I've had an idea. I'm going to take up road-walking again", he said.

On Monday night about ten o'clock Johnnie went upstairs and

changed into his walking gear. As he walked towards the kitchen door Lily looked up from the magazine she was browsing through and seeing Johnnie she stood up and said: "And where do you think you're going at this time of night".
"I'm going road-walking. I thought I told you. I'm taking it up again".
"You're not going out at this time of night. You'll get yourself knocked down".
"Don't worry, Lily, I won't. I'm going round the park wall. I'll be about a couple of hours. You mustn't wait up for me. I'll sleep downstairs on the settee so as not to wake you up".
Before Lily could object any further he went out and set off up the street as fast as his road-walkers feet could carry him. Lily could not believe it. She sensed immediately that something was going on but she couldn't leave the child to go after him to find out. She stayed awake until well after twelve o'clock but must have dozed off in the chair. She awoke at about two-thirty, it was pitch dark, she was stone cold: the fire had gone out long ago. Her first thought was that Johnnie must have come home and, not wishing to disturb her, gone to bed, but when she went upstairs he was not there. The bed had not been slept in. She felt as though the bottom had not just dropped out of her stomach, it had dropped out of her whole world.
"I'll bet he's gone round to that bloody Nellie Greathead's", she said through her tears, and loud enough to wake her sleeping child.

Johnnie had not intended to stay the whole of the night with Nellie Greathead and it was lucky Nellie had the presence of mind to set her alarm clock. She wanted to be up early to change the sheets in case Johnnie Greathead should catch the early bus home. It was still dark outside and nobody saw the figure in road-walking gear slip out of Nellie Greathead's back door, skirt the house and having jumped a couple of fences emerge from a gateway a couple of doors down. He was back at his own home in good time to wash, change, make his sandwiches and be off to work at his usual time without anyone but the two women being any the wiser.

THE DOGS OF WAR

After Lily told her mother what had happened Mrs. Heys was shaking with anger. She said: "Don't worry. Albert and Leonard will soon sort him out. He's not going to get away with this if I've anything to do with it".

But Lily would not hear of her mother instigating anything, or even mentioning the matter to Johnnie. She didn't want to make matters worse and she did not want anyone to know about her husband's nocturnal jaunts. She would deal with it herself, she said. She did not realise this would be much easier said than done.

When Johnnie arrived home that evening the house was tidier than usual and a fire was struggling to burn in the grate. Lily had Johnnie's meal in front of him on the table almost before he had time to get his coat off and wash his hands. The two spam slices she had fried for him, though not exactly sizzling on the plate, were at least hot. The peas were out of a tin but there were freshly boiled carrots and potatoes to go with them.

"This looks very nice" Johnnie said, with undetected irony, as he sat down.

After he had finished his meal Lily, whose face he thought looked unnaturally pale, said, in a very controlled and unusually quiet voice: "Why didn't you come home last night?"

"I did come home", he said, his face breaking into that foolish rabbit-like grin she had seen that time outside Nellie Greathead's bathroom. "You'd gone to bed".

Lily lost control and shouted: "Oh no you didn't! I waited up until half-past two and you still hadn't come home, so don't tell me your lies!"

"Well I don't want a row. Believe what you like. It won't make any difference!"

Lily looked round for something to hit him with but there was nothing other than the empty dinner plate. She grabbed the plate and before he could dodge out of the way smashed it over his head with the full force of the fury that had been building up all day.

"Don't think you can tell me your damned lies and get away with it", she screamed. "You went round to that whore Nellie Greathead didn't you. You. You. You despicable piece of dog

dirt. Well bugger off to bloody Nellie Greathead if that's what you want. See if I care. But don't think you're coming near me again! You bloody pig!"
Johnnie was shocked, livid and shaking. "I'm not staying here to put up with this, I'm off", he said, as he headed for the door. Lily stood rigid, arms stiffly by her sides, fingers splayed and stretched, and in tears in the Kitchen and then rushed after him shouting "No! Johnnie! No! I didn't mean it! Johnnie! No! Johnnie! No Johnnie please! Please don't go!

A couple of hours and a couple of pints later he returned. Lily was not in the kitchen. He went up stairs and knelt at the side of the bed and said.
"Look Lily, we've got to get this sorted out".

Lily was far from happy with the terms laid down by Johnnie Grocock but she had to put up with them or he would leave her she knew full well. And there was no possibility of her supporting herself and the child. Her mother could look after Margaret but she herself wouldn't be able to get a job. Now the war was over all the jobs were for men. Single girls stood a better chance with shop work but they had to leave most jobs if they got married and she couldn't go out cleaning, she hated cleaning. She didn't know whether she loved Johnnie or not but she did know she didn't want the disgrace of being divorced or him just leaving her. Johnnie had made it clear that though he loved Nellie Greathead he wanted to do the right thing by her but probably that was just hedging his bets in case Johnnie Greathead got to know what was going on and put his foot down. But she knew deep down that but for little Margaret, Nellie Greathead or no Nellie Greathead, he would probably start some other affair which would put her marriage under threat. He was too restless: men like him, she now realised, never settled down, they were always looking for something different. They're never satisfied with what they'd got. Perhaps in Johnnie's case it was the novelty: he'd never had any other woman before he met her. Perhaps he felt he'd missed out on things. If she let him do what he wanted for a while perhaps he would get fed up with Nellie. He couldn't afford to leave. He could hardly keep one household going on his wage let alone two. With time it might all fizzle out. Whatever happened she did not want her mother to know what she had agreed to, at least not yet. There was no telling what she would do and Albert and Leonard had never liked Johnnie. All sailors were fairies to them: they would love an excuse to give him a going over. No, if she kept quiet about it no one need know.

So Johnnie Grocock kept walking. Three nights a week he slipped out of Lily's house in his road-walking gear and into Nellie's house; and three mornings a week he slipped out of Nellie's without the neighbours noticing and was back home in time for his own neighbours to see him leave for work at his usual time.

At first Nellie was happy with the arrangement which was more than can be said for Lily. She could now have Johnnie for whole nights and not feel guilty or threatened. The arrangement might have gone on indefinitely had not Nellie become jealous of the disproportionate amount of Johnnie's time Lily had managed to retain. "Why should she have you four nights and me only three", she nagged Johnnie, gently but incessantly.

Johnnie didn't let on but he liked to see her jealous. He had been impressed by his mates motto in the Navy: "treat 'em mean: keep 'em keen" and it boosted his ego to have Nellie want more of him. He would have liked to have reorganised the calendar on an eight day week basis and kept the best of both world's but that would have encroached on the weekend and been impracticable as Johnnie Greathead was on a regular night shift. But Nellie wanted all of him, not just an extra night. She did not want to be a mistress, the other woman. She knew full well from the novels she read what happened to mistresses and besides concealing things from Johnnie Greathead was becoming difficult. He had not said anything, yet, but he was clearly suspicious. She had heard him questioning the boy, asking had he seen anything of uncle Johnnie recently. She had been buying extra sweets for Roy and all the toys he wanted ever since he had wandered into the bedroom one night but it was only a matter of time before he let something slip or even started to blackmail her. She had already given way to a couple of tantrums and let him play out long after his usual bedtime. Yes, she was sure Johnnie Greathead knew something was going on. Perhaps she should not have kept on refusing his demands for sex. Her excuse about a prolapsed womb and the need for complete rest and abstinence for a prolonged period of time was not altogether convincing.

"Next time you go to the doctor's I'm coming with you", he had said, the last time they had discussed it.

He didn't need to: the inevitable happened quicker than she thought. Her husband must have got something out of Roy or been tipped off by some observant, insomniac neighbour she imagined, when she reflected on events later. What she did not know was that it was Mrs. Heys who had tipped the wink to her husband. When Mrs. Heys had paid something off her milk bill she had been told, not very cryptically, by the Co-op milkman that if she watched "a certain house in Polefield Gardens about 5.30 a.m. on a Tuesday, Wednesday and Saturday mornings she might, like one of those bears that go down in the woods today, be in for a big surprise."

In the event it was Nellie who got the big surprise. Johnnie Greathead came home early on Saturday morning and caught her and Johnnie Grocock in the kitchen standing far too close together. Had he been ten minutes earlier he would have caught them in bed and even closer together.

Nellie reddened and look flustered to see her husband standing in a state of shock on the door mat. She would have known exactly what to say had he started shouting and swearing but he didn't. He just stood there, still as a garden gnome, and started crying.

Johnnie Grocock was the first to recover. He looked Johnnie Greathead straight in the eye and said, rather too breezily, "Lily threw me out last night. We'd had a row over me going out walking and she locked me out and said I could bugger off back to the Navy. I couldn't think where to go so I came round here hoping you'd be in to see if I could have my old room back. Just temporary like, until she gets over it or I find somewhere more permanent. Nellie said you'd gone to work but she didn't think you'd mind, didn't you Nellie. I was just on my way back to

Princess Street to see if I can get some of my things. "You don't mind me having the room for a day or two, do you Johnnie?".
"Of course he doesn't", said Nellie.
Johnnie Greathead sank into his easy chair, sobbing.
"Now you get off. I'll talk to him. Bring your things round later on", Nellie said.
So that's how it was. Johnnie moved in with the Greathead's and reversed the road-walking routine, visiting Lily three nights a week and one day at weekend to see his daughter. The neighbours at Princess Street were none the wiser.

Lily hadn't made any friends at Princess Street and had little contact with her neighbours so keeping matters quiet at her end was easy enough. She simply said to the few who enquired that Johnny worked away a lot and when he was home he worked shifts: Polefield was a different matter. Keeping anything quiet on Polefield was as difficult as keeping butter on a hot knife.
Tongues had never been quiet but they started wagging at a different tempo when the two Johnnies started to go out together and "brazen hussy" became the most popular phrase on the estate. Nellie seemed oblivious. It was not that she wouldn't have cared had she known exactly what was being said behind her back: she would have cared as much as anybody and more than most but Nellie had a blind spot. She believed that so long as her husband was living with her she had respectability. People could think what they liked but they could not know, and, if she had anything to do with it, would never know what was going on behind her four walls. There were many on the estate who had lodgers. True, they were mostly elderly couples or elderly widowed women with a young male lodger but what was wrong with a younger woman with a husband having a lodger she would like to know. She ignored the fact that she knew only too well. Surprisingly, and unknown to her, Nellie had the support of Mrs. Heys.
Mrs. Heys knew there was no point in rebutting the obvious but she had been telling the few who were bold enough to ask her outright why Lily's husband was living with the Greathead's that Lily and Johnnie were going through a difficult time adjusting to

married life together. They were not the only ones having difficulties, which was true, and Lily thought it best if they had some time apart so that she could decide whether or not she could live with Johnnie. "It will be like a second courtship for them", Mrs. Heys said. It might have convinced Albert and Leonard, but even that is doubtful, but it didn't convince anyone else. But in deference to Mrs. Heys, who was herself a most prolific gossip, and in recognition of her usefullness at life's crisis points, the sound of whispering on Lily's score was piano rather than fortissimo.

One Saturday morning about three weeks after Johnnie Grocock moved in with the Greathead's I was, as usual, giving my bike its weekly wash by the side of the house. My dad was in the front garden clearing the trimmings from the gutters of the lawn which he had just mown when a voice called out from the gateway. I looked up and saw Mr. Greathead framed between the gate stumps which were about the same height as himself. I remember thinking what a coincidence as I had just been musing about Johnnie Greathead: it was as though my thoughts had conjoured him up. Things happen like that when you are cleaning your bike.

My dad groaned a little with stiffness as he stood up to have a chat. "You're out and about early", he said.

"Aye, I've had enough Harry, I'm leaving. I can't stand any more of it. I've got myself some digs down in Salford with a cousin of mine and her husband: just near the Railway Depot".

He told my dad that when Johnnie Grocock first moved in he thought things were going to be alright. Johnnie was friendly; they went out together. Johnnie introduced him to some of his mates and he'd even begun to enjoy the odd half of bitter. Johnnie had been installed in his old room and Nellie and himself had the big bedroom, though there was still nothing doing as far as 'you know what' was concerned. But last week, he said, all that had changed. He'd arrived home from work one morning to find the sleeping arrangements had been revised. "You mustn't go into the bedroom; Johnnie's still asleep", Nellie said in a cold and decisive voice.

"She'd had the bloody cheek to move our Roy into the small

room, Johnnie into the big bedroom with her and move my things into the Box-room. She said it was ridiculous for things to go on the way they had, she couldn't put up with all the pretence. "No one outside need know", she said. She didn't want gossip but if I didn't like the arrangement I would have to go and she would have to put up with it.
There was nothing I could do about it Harry. She's absolutely besotted with the bugger".
"You're a bloody fool Johnnie! You don't want to let them kick you out! You should have bumped him one like I told you to, years ago, and you wouldn't be having all this trouble".
"Aye , well, it's alright for you to say that Harry, your more his size. He's a big bugger and he's fifteen years younger than me. I'd stand no chance. Anyway, I wouldn't give her the satisfaction of seeing it. No, I've had enough. I'll bump into you at the Dogs sometime Harry, eh?" and with that parting remark he picked up the enormous suitcase he had with him and struggled off with it down the Approach towards the bus stop. Mr. Rook overtook him. I heard him say, " Here, let me help you with that Johnnie, you'll do yourself an injury".
As Johnnie Greathead and Mr. Rook turned the corner almost all the curtains on the Approach fluttered a farewell. A dozen doors opened and the noise of the scandal-mongering could have been mistaken for that of a flock of birds. Mrs. Heys was first among them, orchestrating the singers of the post dawn chorus.
All the following Sunday and for weeks afterwards tongues were flapping like the bells in St. Margaret's church tower and the more loudly they peeled the more resolved Mrs. Heys became to do something about matters but Lily was hopeful that Johnnie would come marching home a second time and implored her mother to wait and see how things turned out. "Things might be different for her after the "honeymoon " period like they were for me. He is still my husband and he is still coming to my house even though Johnnie Greathead's left home", she added quietly.
Mrs Heys found it difficult to believe that things would take a turn for the better but decided to leave matters as they were for the time being. Johnnie meanwhile continued his road-walking and despite the inconvenience of it continued to maintain Lily's

good name amongst her Princess Street neighbours by leaving for work from her house three mornings a week.

To help preserve her own self-image Nellie seldom went out during the hours of daylight and when she did she tried to keep her head held high despite being ignored by the neighbours with the singular exception of Mrs. Price whose hints and reports of what people were thinking made Nellie more and more distressed as she realised she had in fact lost all trace of respectability. There were even rumours that she was carrying Johnnie Grocock's child. Ironically she found that she was. Her embarrassment and distress at confirming what the gossips were saying was strong but didn't last long. Within a week it had given way first to acceptance and, much to Johnnie's surprise, elation.

Whether or not Nellie had planned it, or whether Johnnie Grocock had been forgetful of precautions in a moment of abandon, was the subject of endless speculation on the part of my mother and my grandma, to say nothing of everybody else. The gossip and rumour were confirmed when it became apparent that Nellie was putting on weight. "In a place where it just shouldn't be", our Ernie chimed in with the words of George Formby's popular song, and before long the backwardly inclined body, flat-footed walk and the bloom of pregnancy became unmistakeable. Either "Aunty Maggie's remedy" had not worked or Nellie had not bothered to take it.

Had there been a vote on it an overwhelming majority of the neighbourhood would have put up their hands for Johnnie Grocock being the father of Nellie's prospective child but a few romantics or one or two believers in divine justice would have voted for Johnnie Greathead. The more mathematically minded were in no doubt but as most of the people on the estate were not very good at sums there was scope for both points of view. Mrs. Heys was in no doubt as to who the father was. She felt ashamed, furious and vindictive by turns but overwhelmingly it was revenge that she wanted.

At Mrs. Hey's instigation the gossip turned to hostility and Nellie found herself shunned, even by people for whom, in the past, she had done favours. Some openly turned their backs on her or went inside when she passed, slamming their front doors behind them as they went. Albert and Leonard Heys were recruited to paint footprints leading from the direction of the Heys' house to Nellie's front door. A brush was left on the slab canopy above the front door. More controversially dog-dirt was put in an envelope and pushed through Nellie's letter-box.

The effect on Nellie was unexpectedly dramatic. Her stubborn disregard for public opinion shrank as her abdomen rose. She became nervous, edgy and more and more distressed. She had a show of blood and the baby threatened to miscarry. Johnnie panicked, took the day off work and called Dr. Jamieson who came immediately and ordered Nellie to remain in bed for at least a week.

After a day or so in bed Nellie felt better and when he came home from work one evening to Johnnie's surprise he found her at the table, writing. When he asked why she was out of bed and what she was doing she said she was feeling much better and that she was "not going to be intimidated by that lots' filthy tongues".

"I'll show those bloody, jealous, hypocrites! I could tell their husbands a thing or two about what they got up to during the war with those airmen from the park. I'll put a bloody stop to them talking about Nellie Greathead, I can tell you! I'll go and see a Solicitor, that's what I'll do! That'll put a stop to their wagging, bloody tongues.

Johnnie was alarmed by her agitated state and said: "No Nellie love, leave it. Don't take any notice. You'll only make matters worse and if you threaten people they'll talk all the more. They'll say there must be some truth in what they're saying otherwise you wouldn't be so upset and after all's said and done we are living together and you are having a baby. If you make threats you can't follow up you'll make yourself a laughing stock. Just leave it: they'll get tired after a while and find someone else to gossip about".

Despite the common sense of Johnnie's protest Nellie did consult a Solicitor and went down to the Guide Office the very next day and instructed them to put an item in the Legal Notice's column.

"I want the wording like this", she said, handing a piece of paper over the counter to the clerk. Nellie paid for the insertion and was about to leave when the clerk said: "Just let me read it out to you so that we don't get it wrong":

> I Nellie Greathead of 3, Polefield Gardens hereby give notice that from this date onwards legal proceedings will be taken against any person or persons making slanderous assertions or publishing libelous material impugning the character and good name of the aforementioned Nellie Greathead. Signed, Nellie Greathead.

Nellie felt utterly exhausted when she got back from the *Guide* office. Even with the support of the wall she barely managed to stagger to Mrs. Price's door before she felt a tremendous surge of pain in her abdomen. She screamed and collapsed into the hallway when Mrs. Price opened the door. "Run and fetch Mrs. Heys, quick, she's having a miscarriage!", Mrs. Price shouted to her husband.

Nellie never forgave Mrs. Price for sending for Mrs. Heys. She blamed Mrs. Heys for causing the miscarriage in the first place and to have her witness the event was the final indignity. The hatred was mutual. Mrs. Heys blamed Nellie for the destruction of Lily's marriage and to see the evidence of Johnnie Grocock's infidelity before her eyes was almost too much for her. Grudgingly she made Nellie comfortable and said to Mrs. Price. She'll survive: her kind always do. You must get Dr. Jamieson to have a look in; I don't want anything more to do with her. She's made her bed: she can lie in it.

When Nellie was strong enough to walk the distance she went down to the Council offices and got the rent book changed to her name. Shortly afterwards she asked could she exchange the council house in Polefield Gardens for one in Whitefield if she could find someone willing to swop. Three weeks later Nellie left Polefield for good.

Epilogue
The other day I was on my way again to our Ernie's house to do

THE DOGS OF WAR

the garden, taking with me what I had written about Johnnie Grocock and Nellie Greathead for him to read over before I sent it off to Arthur and Bronwen when I met Margery Tickle again; "off to the shops". It was no surprise. Everyone still seemed to live from hand to mouth on Polefield, just like my mother used to do. Most of the women spent half their lives traipsing up and down to the shops. With some you'd think they'd caught their garter on a shop-door handle. They're no sooner home than they're bouncing back for something else they've forgotten.

I said: "Hello Margery. Are you going to tell me? Did Johnnie Grocock ever marry Nellie Greathead?"

She stopped, lent on her stick and said: "No, he lived with her on and off, just as he always did. She had a miscarriage you know and moved out of the house and went to live up at Whitefield, I think it was. It's so long ago you forget. He never divorced Lily Heys. In fact he never really left her. He was always going back, staying a few days and then going back to Nellie's. Even when their Margaret got married he still went back but he never had any feeling for Lily, not really. I remember him coming round to our house when Nellie died. He sat at the table and cried his heart out but d'you know he never shed one tear over Lily. I remember, he brought some wood round on that old wheelbarrow of his and I made him a cup of tea. He sat down at the table chatting away like, as usual and he said: "Oh by the way, Lily died" and he just went on chatting about something else. When I asked him when she died he said, "Let me think now, it must have been last Wednesday", and that's all he ever said about it.

"That's incredible! Was he generous to them with his money?", I asked.

"Generous! Him generous! Nobody knew he had any money. They never had any money, either of them. Nellie always dressed better than Lily but that had nothing to do with money. I'm sure neither of them knew he had any money. In fact he didn't have any money. All he had were bits of paper. He always dressed in the same scruffy old coat and that baseball cap the wrong way round and those dirty white trainers. He was only one up on a tramp at the end and he used to be so clean and meticulous *when Nellie was alive. He used to make a few shillings from the wood, and he delivered the freebie newspaper on the Estate with that wheelbarrow of his. Twopence a copy they paid him. But that's all he had besides his pension. All that money. It wasn't real. He never saw a penny of it. He was too damned miserly, letting it make more for him, ever to spend any. He might just as well not have had it for all the good it did him. Eight-hundred and eighty-eight thousand pounds and never spent a penny of it. What can you say? What can you say!*